The Cosy Christmas Chocolate Shop

Caroline Roberts lives in the wonderful Northumberland countryside with her husband and credits the sandy beaches, castles and rolling hills around her as inspiration for her writing. She enjoys writing about relationships; stories of love, loss and family, which explore how beautiful and sometimes complex love can be. A slice of cake, glass of bubbly and a cup of tea would make her day – preferably served with friends! She believes in striving for your dreams, which led her to a publishing deal after many years of writing. *The Cosy Christmas Chocolate Shop* is her fifth novel.

If you'd like to find out more about Caroline, visit her on Twitter, Facebook and her blog – she'd love to hear from you!

🐦 @_caroroberts
f /CarolineRobertsAuthor
carolinerobertswriter.blogspot.co.uk

Also by Caroline Roberts

The Torn Up Marriage
The Cosy Teashop in the Castle
The Cosy Christmas Teashop
My Summer of Magic Moments

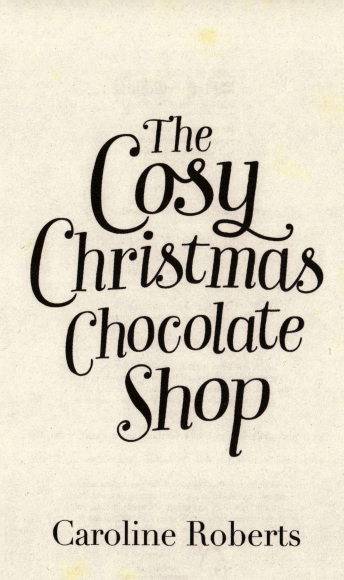

The Cosy Christmas Chocolate Shop

Caroline Roberts

Harper*Impulse*, an imprint of
HarperCollins*Publishers*
1 London Bridge Street
London SE1 9GF

www.harpercollins.co.uk

First published by HarperCollins*Publishers* 2017
3

A catalogue record for this book
is available from the British Library

ISBN: 978-0-00-823628-1

Set in Minion by Palimpsest Book Production Limited, Falkirk, Stirlingshire

Printed and bound in the UK by CPI Group (UK) Ltd, Croydon CR0 4YY

MIX
Paper from
responsible sources
FSC™ C007454

For Richard

'All you need is love.
But a little chocolate now and then doesn't hurt.'

Charles M. Schulz

Part One

1

Silver baubles, dangly stars, fairy lights and chocolates, hundreds of chocolates, filled the shop.

'Hi, how can I help?'

'I've been put in charge of the sweets for the children's Christmas stockings – any ideas?' The thirty-something gentleman smiled hopefully.

'Of course. We have reindeers, Santas, and angels in chocolate lollipops – great stocking fillers. There are figures of Father Christmas, too. Also, we have snowy stars in a pretty bag – little girls love those, I can vouch for my nieces – and packs of chocolate-dipped fudge.'

'Well, there's three kids to cater for, two boys and a girl, so can I have a selection? Oh, and I'd better get a nice box of chocolates for the wife.'

Emma pointed to the three sizes of gold boxes, positioned on the top of the truffle and ganache refrigerated display. 'Large, medium or small?'

With a queue listening in behind him, and thoughts

of fulfilling Christmas wishes on his mind, he went for the large.

'Any particular favourites for your wife?'

'Umm, she likes champagne truffles and caramels, I think, but a variety would be good.'

'Great, I'll pop a couple of champagne truffles in, and some caramels, with a lovely selection alongside that. Just give me a few moments and I'll get them all ready for you.' Emma set to work with boxes, bows and silver and gold ribbon, turning the gifts into works of art.

'Wow, that all looks great. Thank you. So, how much do I owe you?'

Emma tallied it up on the till. 'A total of fifteen pounds thirty, please.' She popped one of her Chocolate Shop by the Sea business cards into the package.

'Thanks.'

'You're welcome, and have a really lovely Christmas,' Emma smiled.

Four o'clock, Christmas Eve afternoon, the till was pinging, the shop door chiming, and still the queue of last-minute shoppers continued to grow. Emma, proud owner of this gorgeous little chocolate shop in the harbour village of Warkton-by-the-Sea, Northumberland, and her assistant, Holly, were buzzing about like Christmas elves. In fact, they looked very like elves, dressed as they were in their festive jumpers, Holly with a Christmas pudding across her chest and Emma a red-nosed reindeer. Emma was also sporting dangly red-bauble earrings. She wished she had put some lighter clothing on now, though, something like a T-shirt: it was bloody warm dashing around, the two of them cramped in the serving space behind the counter, dressed in winter woollens.

Holly was serving an elderly chap from the village.

'Hello, Stan. How's Hilda?' Emma asked him.

'Not too bad thanks, Emma. Getting over the cough she had last week. But I thought it best she stayed home today. I've just been getting a few last-minute groceries in – we were low on milk and teabags – and then I thought it might be nice to cheer her up with some of those lovely coffee creams you do.'

'Sounds a good idea. I'm sure she'll appreciate it.'

Holly passed him over a prettily tied cellophane bag with his chocolates in. 'There you go, Stan. I popped an extra one in for luck.'

Emma gave her assistant a mock-shocked look, and then smiled.

'Well, take care then, lassies, have a good Christmas.'

'You too, Stan – and give my best wishes to Hilda. Happy Christmas!'

Emma had a chance for a breather for a few seconds as Holly began to serve the last customer waiting. Her feet were throbbing, despite being in her comfiest trainers, and her fingers were aching from all the delicate tying of ribbons and making up of boxes and gift bags – as well as having been up from 6.00 a.m. making more batches of truffles and chocolate lollipops to see them through. She gazed past the window display of baubles and dangling snowflakes that reflected the twinkle of the fairy lights in the shop, and out to the street. It was dark already out there, these short December days, but from the glow of the street lights she could tell it was still dry and a touch of frost was glinting on the pavements. She might get a chance to take Alfie, her springer spaniel and best friend, out for a quick walk down to the harbour once they'd closed. He'd been cooped up upstairs all afternoon with them being so busy.

A figure dashed past the window and came in, clanging the door. It was Danny who worked as the bar supervisor in The Fisherman's Arms, the pub down the road.

'Afternoon, ladies. I need a box of chocolates for my girlfriend. Something fancy-looking.'

'Hi, Danny,' Emma greeted him.

'Which one's this, then?' Holly chipped in cheekily. To be fair, he'd had about six different girlfriends in the past six months.

'The lovely Helen – and less of your cheek, young lady,' he quipped back.

'Large box then, Danny? I'll giftwrap it for you, shall I?' Em didn't bother asking which flavours she liked as he probably didn't know her that well yet.

'Perfect. How's tricks, Holly?'

'Been busy, hasn't it, Em? Just a little lull for now.' With that, a family came in, seemingly a dad and his two kids, who started to browse the shelves. 'Oh, and there we go again,' Holly added.

'Yeah, I think we'll be having a busy night down at the Fisherman's too. Christmas Eve usually gets cracking. You coming down, girls?'

6

'No, quiet night in for me,' said Emma. She couldn't imagine being in a big noisy crowd, not tonight.

'What about you, Hols?'

'Nah, my mum and dad want me home tonight. Family day tomorrow and all that.'

'Ah well, see you around then. Maybe over New Year.' He paid, taking a box beautifully wrapped in star-patterned paper with a big pink ribbon around it from Holly.

'Maybe.' Em left her answer deliberately vague. 'Cheers, Danny. Oh, and there's a gift tag for you to fill in on that box,' she added as he turned to leave.

'I'll try and remember,' he grinned.

'Merry Christmas!' the girls chanted.

'And to you too!'

Five o'clock, their usual closing time, came and passed. There were still customers milling about in the shop and Emma didn't want to lose any business – she needed all the income she could get – so kept going. She offered Holly the chance to leave but her assistant said she'd stay and help until the last customer had gone, bless her. Holly was nearly seventeen, eager, bubbly, and friendly with the customers. Since she'd started a few weeks ago, on Saturdays and the odd day in the holidays as she was still in the Sixth Form at school, the young girl had proved to be a bit of a godsend. Emma had been managing on her own up until that point, trying to keep to a budget and do everything herself, but as her chocolates were becoming more popular, and the shop better known, it was hard to keep up with the

7

chocolate-making as well as serving behind the counter. It was lovely to have some company in the shop too.

The Christmas Eve queue continued. It was always a bit crazy, this last-minute Christmas Eve rush, as though no one was going to be able to buy chocolates ever again, or that the Christmas break would last a month. But she'd be open again in a few days' time! Oh well, she certainly wasn't going to complain; though it was tiring working all hours, Emma enjoyed the buzz and the build-up to Christmas, loved crafting the chocolates and thinking of new festive flavours to mix up with the traditional favourites, and she needed every last penny. It had been a bit of a poor year, profit-wise, even with the shop getting busier, as costs seemed to be going up all the time, and January was a desperately slow month, so December's takings were going to have to see her through until Valentine's Day at least.

It was twenty to six when the last customer, a woman in her twenties who was on holiday with friends, picked up her bag of festive goodies, thanked Holly and Emma very much, and wished them goodnight and a Merry Christmas.

'Have a great break and Merry Christmas!' Holly sang.

Emma followed the lady to the exit, thanked her, then popped her head out to check there was no one else on their way. The street was clear, and the winter chill swept in. She shut the door, turning its little wooden sign to 'Closed'. *Phew* – she rested her back against the door for a second.

'Well done, Hols. That was one busy shift. Thank you. I'd never have managed without you.'

She took the young girl's wages for the day out of the till and gave her an extra twenty-pound note.

'Oh, thank you so much!' Holly gave her boss a little hug.

'And hang on.' She dashed to the back kitchen to find her assistant's Christmas gift, some special bubble bath and matching body lotion, with a hand-picked box of Holly's favourite chocolates.

'Aw, Emma, thanks. I didn't expect anything as I've not been working here that long. I feel awful now as I haven't bought anything for you.'

'Hey, no worries. There's no need. It's a thank you for working so hard for me. You've settled in really well.'

'Thanks, Em, and honestly I am *soo* happy to be here. It's the best thing I ever did, leaving that horrible chip shop in Seahouses. I smelt of chip fat all day and my hair was always greasy. This is like working in heaven. Chocolate heaven. It's like my all-time ideal job.'

All was quiet. Holly had gone and Emma cashed up and just stood for a few moments taking in her little shop in all its twinkly, cosy Christmas glory: the two bay windows that looked out over the quaint village street of stone cottages, the wooden shelving stacked so prettily, the reassuring hum of the refrigerated counter, the rows of chocolates she had worked so hard to create . . . And to think, seven years ago she wouldn't have even known how to make a truffle or how to temper chocolate – hah, back then she'd have thought that meant getting mad with it, which in fact did happen very occasionally!

She loved her little chocolate shop, her business, her life here. It really had saved her, given her back a purpose in life, when things were at rock bottom.

Right, then, she shook herself from her thoughts; she mustn't dwell on that for there was one very eager spaniel upstairs no doubt desperate to get out.

Emma leaned on the stone harbour wall, watching the street lights catch on the water, the gentle waves lapping the sides of the boats that were moored up. It was a small harbour that had been used for centuries for fishing. There weren't as many boats now, she'd been told, but some still went out daily, weather permitting, for their catch of herring to take to the smokehouse to turn them into kippers, a local speciality, or maybe some cod, or crabs. From July to September they'd be out checking the lobster pots which were now stacked on the shoreline next to an old coble-style boat, along with colourful buoys and thick rope and nets.

A small group of people walked past; Alfie perked up to greet them and Emma smiled. They were heading up the small rise, seemingly to the pub. Soon afterwards its heavy wooden door opened as they went in and she could hear its noisy chatter spill out along with the beat of music as the light spilled across the pavement. She could sense its vibrancy: the log fires would be lit, the Christmas decorations up, and several of the villagers as well as holidaymakers would be gathered noisily. She loved the community feel there, but it was not for her tonight.

10

'Come on then, Alfie.' They headed the opposite way, past a row of cottages, and then down to the beach. It was dark, but there was enough moonlight to make her way through the dunes, to stand and hear the hush of the sea as it lapped against the shore. She wasn't afraid of the dark, she'd been there many an evening like this. She couldn't stop the memories, but that was fine. In a way, that was what she was here for. It didn't matter if she needed to cry, or write his name in the sand, or to scream at the seagulls that life was bloody unfair. Alfie just loved the freedom of the beach, where he could run his loopy circles and make leaps at seaweed sticks of kelp. But it was chilly; Emma could see her breath misting and she was glad of her thick woollen coat and her hat and gloves. She wouldn't stay too long; it had been a hard day and she was ready for an easy supper, would find herself some Christmas film on the TV to settle in front of and then an early night – she'd just let Alfie have five more minutes.

They wandered back towards the harbour, passing a couple, arm in arm, who nodded a friendly hello at them. She climbed the small hill, reaching the front of The Chocolate Shop, which was an end-of-row, sand-coloured stone cottage, converted many years ago into a shop. There were two bay windows with a wooden door in the middle. Emma stood staring at her little shop for a few seconds. She had left the fairy lights on, and with all the festive decorations it looked rather enchanting at night. ''Twas the night before Christmas . . . ' Her mind wandered back to the magical stories and that bubbling feeling of excitement of the Christmas Eves of her childhood, which seemed so far away right now.

Tomorrow was Christmas Day and she was heading over to her brother James's house to spend time with his family, as they'd kindly invited her for Christmas dinner. Of course it would be lovely to see her twin nieces opening their gifts, and enjoy the magic of the day with them. Chloe, her sister-in-law, was going to cook a traditional roast turkey meal with all the trimmings, and Emma's parents were coming across too. It would be great to catch up with them all, especially after having been so busy in the shop of late.

But it was always another year where someone was missing.

2

Boxing Day

Emma pulled her coat tight around her and snuggled into her red tartan scarf.

Waves crashed to shore in a white froth, an overnight wind having whipped them up, and sea-salt spray hit her face every now and then. It was refreshing, enlivening. She hadn't slept that well. She'd needed to get out, feel the wind in her hair, and the beach was calling her once again.

She was the only one on this whole stretch of the bay. Well, her and Alfie, who was pacing the sands beside her. Everyone else was probably still tucked up in bed, snoozing off their Christmas dinners and hangovers. Emma picked up a leathery strand of brown seaweed with a thick root that made a great stick, launching it into the air and away. Alfie leapt up animatedly and was off on the chase. It made her smile.

All the what-ifs, the might-have-beens and if-onlys were still there, *always* there, in her mind. But they didn't

13

change anything. A whole future wiped away. *Their* future. Seven years ago. And she missed him still, so very much . . .

Yes, she'd got on, made a life for herself. You didn't get much choice. She'd moved here to Warkton-by-the-Sea six years ago, to a whole new venture with the chocolate shop, and a massive change from her role as a teacher specialising in food technology at a secondary school on the outskirts of Durham city. When the big stuff happens, it shifts your axis, makes you think about what you really want out of your life. She had gone back to visit one of her favourite holiday haunts, spotted the cute, slightly derelict-looking stone cottage on the little main street with its For Rent sign, and never looked back. And so The Chocolate Shop by the Sea was born.

It had once been a toy shop, apparently, but had been closed down for several years, and was in need of a little TLC. Inside, it was small but quaint and very cosy, the original front room being the shop area. Her dad, a keen DIYer and her brother, James, had helped her to do it up.

She had living quarters upstairs for her and Alfie, using the kitchen downstairs as her chocolate creating zone. Life had got better. Time had softened the blow, if not healed it. She wasn't sure she wanted to heal, really; she certainly didn't want to forget. Why would she ever want to forget someone so special? Anyhow, her new life was fine, and she had made some lovely friends in the area.

A movement up in the dunes caught her eye. Someone in a dark jacket, a man; he seemed to be alone. He was up early. So, it was just the two of them on the beach now. She felt a little irked that someone else had invaded her space. Okay, so there was about a mile of beach here, she admitted to herself, and it was a public space.

She strolled on, playing with Alfie and relaunching the seaweed stick. The dog looked up, alert, ears pricked, as he saw the man too. Emma took a brief glance along the beach. Damn, the guy was heading her way, walking behind her at a reasonable pace. Why couldn't he have gone the other bloody way?

A sudden gust of wind blew up. As she bent low to pick up the stick for Alfie, it somehow peeled off her scarf, unravelling it and sending it twirling down the sands. She started to run after it, had nearly got to it, when another gust took it from her reach and away. The scarf then cartwheeled down the beach and she gave chase. She *really* liked that scarf; it was fine wool, cosy, she'd had it for years . . . Luke had given it to her on their first Christmas together. But as soon as she got anywhere near it, the damn wind whipped it up again and it would relaunch.

The man on the beach must have spotted her dilemma and started jogging towards the errant item. He diverted, made a quick dash, and soon had it trapped under his boot. He grinned across at Emma as he picked it up, shaking it a little to loosen the sand from it. She waited as he caught up with her. He was tall, and broad-shouldered under his coat with a friendly face, dark hair, and a nice smile.

'Thank you.'

'You're welcome. It's a bit blustery, isn't it?'

'Just a bit.' Her tone was ironic. 'So, you're out early too.'

'Yes.'

'We must be mad.' It wasn't yet 8.00 a.m. and had only just got light.

'Probably.' He smiled softly.

Or sad . . . or lonely, Emma mused.

They began to fall into pace beside each other.

Alfie then nudged in between then, wanting his share of the limelight.

'And who's this, then?' The guy rubbed the spaniel's head, making the dog's tail wag even more.

'Alfie. He's good company. Gets me out and about.' Oh great, she was sounding like she lived a hermetic, spinsterish existence with her dog. Actually, it wasn't so far from the truth. Well, she'd nearly been married, would've been if fate hadn't stuck its big bloody nose in.

'Right.'

'Are you local?' She hadn't seen him about before. She'd have remembered him for sure. Those big hazel-green eyes, fixed on her right now, wouldn't easily be forgotten. He had cropped dark-brown hair and a stubbly beard that kind of suited him. Nice, even, white teeth when he spoke. 'No, just staying for a few days in a holiday cottage along the road there.' *Nice* eyes.

'Ah, okay.'

'You?'

'Me?'

'Local?'

'Oh yeah, I live in the village. Been here about six years now.'

'You're lucky. It's a really scenic place. Bit wild here today, mind, but I kind of like that.'

She was trying to place his accent. A hint of the local North Eastern Geordie, but well spoken.

'Yeah, Winter's launched itself with a vengeance,' she replied. 'But I like that too, when the sea's all wild, and the clouds are inky-grey and stormy.'

Alfie went off to investigate some clumps of seaweed on the tideline. They were nearly back at the dunes below the village that she usually walked back through. 'I'm heading this way.'

'Me too – I've got the car parked there,' he clarified.

They smiled politely at each other, his smile reaching his intense dark eyes. If she wasn't mistaken there was a slight frisson between them. But she wasn't quite sure. She hadn't actually fancied anyone since Luke. Was that what this was? Did she fancy him? Oh, wow.

'Clearing your head this morning?' she asked.

'Yeah, you could say that.' He looked thoughtful, as if there was more to it than he wanted to divulge.

The spikey marram grass of the dunes began and Emma started to climb the sandy track. She was aware that he was close behind, coming to a level with her as the path widened when they approached the beach car park. She sneaked a sideways look. He was, in fact, rather gorgeous with a tall, athletic frame, as much as she could tell under his Barbour-style jacket and jeans. All too soon they were at the car park in the dunes and he was saying that it had been nice meeting her and that he had to go.

Weirdly, she realised that she didn't want that, as if there was already some connection between them. He stood and just looked at her for a few significant seconds and she guessed he might be feeling the same way too.

Then he stepped towards her, took her hand in his. His grasp was warm, smooth, gentle.

'Thank you,' he said. 'I think you've helped me make my decision.'

And then he moved closer again, looked right at her with those deep, dark green eyes, and leant in to kiss her delicately on the mouth. He smelt gorgeous, all cool-citrus aftershave, his body next to hers, warm and strong and real. She hadn't been this near to a man in a long, long while. It was a surprise, yet it felt so very natural. The kiss became passionate, his arms around her now. One of her hands reaching up to his neck, stroking his hairline, as she pressed her lips firmly against his, finding his open mouth, his tongue. Oh boy.

Then he stopped, stepped back, with a surprised smile, 'I'm sorry, I hope . . . '

'It's fine. It was nice.' She suddenly felt shy.

'Look, sorry, but I really do have to go. ' He started to move towards his vehicle, a jeep type, pausing as he got there. 'How can I find you?'

'The chocolate shop in the village. You'll find me there.'

'Okay. Right.' He processed the information, smiled at her, then ducked into the driver's seat.

'Your name . . . I don't even know your name,' Emma called. But the words were lost on the wind as he closed the vehicle's door.

She watched, stunned, as he waved from behind the windscreen, and then drove off.

3

So, what do you do after a rather handsome man has kissed you quite out-of-the-blue in a car park in the dunes? Well, you walk back, in a bit of a daze admittedly, wondering a) if that really did just happen and b) is he a nutter, possibly high on drugs, or a bit of a madman with an axe in his car boot? And then you head back home and go and make some chocolate bars.

Well, that's what you do if you run a chocolate shop. Emma wandered back along The Wynding, a narrow lane that led from the beach, past the small harbour, where the coble fishing boats were moored, along to the stone cottages of the main street and The Chocolate Shop by the Sea.

She passed the first window which had the Christmas display she had so carefully set out several weeks before. There was a small, real pine Christmas tree with red and gold baubles and matching coloured tinsel, with little sparkly white lights. A wicker basket of her best chocolate gifts took pride of place, filled with chocolate snowmen and Santas, all handcrafted, alcohol-infused truffles, candied orange slices dipped in dark chocolate, and more. She'd soon have to empty it and come up with a fresh idea for January, she realised. Why did that make her feel rather glum?

Emma headed past the shop front and in through the adjacent alleyway to the back of the row of cottages, to keep a very sandy, wet Alfie away from the main shop. She unlocked the door, went on in, and headed straight up the stairs, as the downstairs kitchen was for chocolatier use only, and was a pet-free zone for health and hygiene reasons. She gave Alfie a rub-down with his old towel once they reached the top landing and settled him in his dog basket in the tiny kitchen she had in her cottage flat. Then, she carefully washed her hands, popped her hair up in a ponytail, and headed down to the shop's kitchen to set about making a batch of chilli and lime dark-chocolate bars. She also made a batch of the latest flavour she'd created just before Christmas, ginger and cinnamon; perfect for a cold winter's day.

Christmas was the busiest time of The Chocolate Shop's year, and supplies were depleted. Naturally, the New Year period would be quieter. There would, of course, be that couple of weeks' lull, where chocolate was the enemy and gym memberships were eagerly signed up to. She'd spot more people jogging on the beach for a while – and then they'd realise that what they *really* wanted to do on a cold, grey January day was to cosy up on the sofa, by the fire, with a chocolate treat and a good book.

She had taken a few days off for Christmas and closed the shop, giving Holly the week off too. The young girl had been chatting about her plans to go socialising with her friends, no doubt sporting her new iPhone she *sooo* hoped her parents had got her for Christmas, and the new outfits and shoes her Saturday job money was going to buy – a trip with her girlfriends to the Metro Centre and the sales was lined up for today.

The day passed quickly and quietly for Emma, working away, radio on, crafting her chocolates. Her mind drifted to the strange incident on the beach whilst she rolled a truffle centre between her palms. She wondered if that guy might appear at the shop . . . might he be staying locally? And what decision was it that she'd helped him to make? She kept an ear out for a knock on the door, but no, no sign of him. She decided to put it down to experience and get on with her working day, crafting truffles, boxing others up, making the displays look good, making a list of supplies to order. There was always something to keep her busy, to keep her mind focussed. Her little chocolate shop and Alfie were more than enough in her life.

After all, that guy could be anyone. In fact, who on earth went and kissed a complete stranger in a car park?

4

New Year's Eve loomed on the horizon – not Emma's favourite night. She felt pressured to be out having a 'great' time, when all she really wanted to do was to stay at home, treat herself to a shot of Baileys in her hot chocolate, whilst watching a movie in her PJs and slippers, cuddled up with Alfie on the sofa. That way she could have an early night, so she didn't have to see midnight in and didn't have to think about facing another year alone.

Instead, she'd had her arm twisted by Bev, her closest friend, and Joanne, both from the village, so here she was in The Fisherman's Arms, having beer slopped down her back, party poppers thrust into her hands and any minute some strange guy's lips would be thrust on hers in an attempt at wishing her a Happy New Year! Her mind slipped to the man on the beach again – he kept popping up in her thoughts, uninvited. She wondered what he was doing for New Year? She'd rather it was The Kiss, as she'd named him to herself, lined up next to her;

that might not be too bad at all, rather than the portly middle-aged fisherman, reeking of a mix of lager and stale kippers, who seemed to be purposely edging into her zone. She downed a big gulp of white wine as Big Ben started to chime on the TV screen they had blaring out, and managed a swift side-cheek manoeuvre as the fisherman moved in for the inevitable kiss.

'Happy New Year, pet!' he slurred.

'Happy New Year,' she replied with a pasted-on smile.

Then Bev and her hubbie, Pete, found her, congratulating her with hugs and kisses.

'Have a good one, Em.' Bev hugged an arm around her.

'Hope so. You too, my lovely friend.'

Even though Bev was nearly ten years older than Emma, the age gap just didn't seem apparent. They had first met a few weeks after Emma had come to Warkton at a summer fete down by the harbour. Bev had said hello, then introduced her to several new faces in the village. Later they had chatted away, Bev intrigued by the opening of a chocolate shop in their village. She always joked that it was the talk of chocolate, not Emma herself, that first captured her attention and sealed their friendship.

Joanne and a few more acquaintances from the village moved to be beside her, pushing through the throng of revellers that were crammed in like sardines, with shouts of 'Yay! Happy New Year, darling!' whilst topping up Emma's glass with bubbly. Danny came out from behind the bar to make the most of kissing a whole bunch of ladies at once, giving Emma a warm, friendly peck on the cheek, then moving along the row. 'Happy New Year, gorgeous ladies.'

'Hey, Em, my fab-ul-ous boss. Happy New Year, hunnn!'

There was Holly, in a bright red dress, brown wavy hair bouncing around her shoulders, with a slight slur to her voice, tottering beside her in high heels. 'New shoes – aren't they brilliant?' She raised a leg, showing a bit too much thigh, which, judging by the grin on his face, Danny didn't seem to mind, and indeed, her new black stiletto killer-heels.

'Amazing – I don't think I could even walk in them,' Emma commented with a smile. 'Happy New Year to you too, Hols.'

'Have a good one, Em. Wonder what this year will bring? I'm looking for the man of my dreams . . . well, Tom will do.' She laughed giddily, full of hope, and expectation, which was just how it should be at sixteen and three-quarters.

'Well, I hope it's a special year for you, Holly.'

There were more hugs and introductions to Holly's group of young, vibrant friends.

New Year: a new chapter, a time for hopes and dreams, wishes and resolutions. Emma could only think about getting through tonight; tomorrow, a whole year, too much to take on. She still felt stuck. Yes, of course she'd find moments of happiness where she could; she had great friends, a wonderful family, and her very special chocolate shop, and for all of that she was thankful, but beneath it, her heart still felt sore.

Smile, chat, mingle some more, another round of drinks, one more glass of bubbly, and at last, just after 1.00 a.m., the chance for Emma to get back to her little cottage and her bed.

The next evening all was quiet in Emma's small living room. New Year's Eve had been survived and another New Year's Day was over – well, nearly. Phew, she'd made it through another festive season and she could chill out a bit now with a slower few weeks in the shop, but it never lasted. Who would want to live in a world without chocolate, for heaven's sake?!

Em snuggled up on the sofa, with Alfie content beside her.

For a second her mind flashed to the man on the beach on Boxing Day. Might he come back yet? Come and find her there in her little chocolate shop? A week had now passed since they'd met, but it was all a bit too bizarre. And, how would she feel if he really did? Wouldn't it seem a bit stalkerish? He might have that axe lurking in the back of his pick-up, or perhaps she'd just imagined he was handsome, and he'd walk in with a crooked nose, squinty eyes, and yellow-stained teeth. But the image she had fixed in her mind was far from that. Anyhow, strangers just didn't kiss you in a car park like that. Certainly not *like that*! Oh yes, it was all coming back vividly now. Boy, talk about making your toes tingle.

She smiled, remembering one of her Great-Aunt Emily's phrases which she'd chided her with when she was a teenager: 'Just because he makes your toes tingle, it doesn't mean he's right for you.'

Luke had made her toes tingle, mind you. Many times.

She sighed and stroked the soft fur of Alfie's head. Though he'd been asleep, his tail responded instantly, thwacking down happily on to the sofa cushion.

'We're okay, aren't we, Alfie?'

It was meant to be a statement, but it came out sounding like a question.

5

Though the shop was closed for another day over the New Year break, Emma was in the kitchen early making up a batch of whisky truffles. She liked to keep herself busy, would spend the time off preparing for the next few weeks, and warming whisky truffles were always a good seller through the winter months.

She melted the dark chocolate, then warmed the whisky just to the point where a little vapour was coming off it, next she'd whisk them together. The smell was rather delicious, even this early in the morning. She'd look forward to trying one with a cup of rich coffee later. The ganache mix she'd made had to refrigerate for at least four hours before it would be ready to roll into the circular centres, ready to dip in melted dark chocolate. Bliss.

There was a knock at the back door, footsteps, then a head popped round, all dark-brown curls and a cheery smile.

'Oh, hi, Holly. Good to see you.'

'Hey, Em. Happy New Year! I was just in the village fetching some milk and the papers for Mum. Thought I'd pop in and say hello.'

'Happy New Year. But we did see each other on New Year's Eve.'

'Ah yes, so we did – it's coming back to me now. I was slightly squiffy at that point. Soz. Anyway, I wanted to find out when you'll need me back in next.'

'Well, it's going to be pretty quiet for a few weeks . . .' She saw Holly's face drop. No doubt she'd spent all her recent wages on her New Year's Eve outfit. 'But you could maybe help out for a couple of hours each Saturday afternoon. It'll give me the chance to do some crafting. I'm sorry, Holly, I really do wish I could give you more hours, but January's just not a great time.' She'd be counting the pennies as it was. 'We'll be busier in Feb for Valentine's Day, though. I'll need you loads more then, and on the build-up to Easter, of course.'

'Okay. No worries.' The young girl smiled, though she still looked a little disappointed.

Emma felt awful; she so wished she could give her more work. Holly was a great help and lovely with the customers, chatty and friendly behind the counter. She was nice company for Emma too. But the business *really* wasn't making enough for her to keep paying for extra hours. As it was, she probably could have managed without Holly for the whole of January. She could craft the chocolates in the evenings – she had enough time on her hands – but she wanted to help the young girl and she'd really need her to stay on for when it got busier in the spring. Some other business might snap her up otherwise, and that would be such a shame, both for Emma and The Chocolate Shop.

'Making more supplies, I see.'

'Yes, dark choc whisky truffles.'

'Mmm, I love those.'

'Actually, I'll only be two more minutes making the mix for these. Do you fancy staying for a coffee?' Em realised the company would be great. She hadn't seen a soul yesterday.

They were soon settled on stools in Emma's kitchen with cups of coffee in front of them. The whisky truffles weren't quite ready, but she did have a few chocolate-orange ones left that she'd made just before the New Year.

'Aw, thanks, Em, this is so nice. I always used to love coming in here, even before I got the job. It's such a magical little shop. I used to stand there, browsing the shelves, choosing my favourites, or sometimes trying something new because you have such *gorgeous* flavours. And the smell . . . ' Holly smiled. 'All that cocoa scrumminess; just amazing.'

She'd spotted the sign that Emma had put in the shop window one day, saying a part-time assistant was required and had walked right in and introduced herself there and then, not wanting to miss the opportunity. The work was ideal for Holly, fitting in with school times, study, and exams, yet a welcome break from that too.

Emma had tried to make her feel welcome and they got on well despite the age gap. She took time to train her on how best to deal with the customers and let her watch and learn the chocolate-creating process, even asking for Holly's advice on new flavours and chatting about ideas. They'd come up with a cranberry and pistachio truffle in the run-up to Christmas which was a real hit with the customers. Holly's confidence had grown so much since starting here and it was lovely that the two of them got on so well. There was a big age difference, nearly twenty years, she found out, so Em felt a bit like a mum-figure and friend all rolled into one.

'So, looks like you had a good night on New Year's Eve?' Emma commented.

'Yeah, The Fisherman's Arms was buzzing, wasn't it? We were at a party before that, at my mate Laura's house.'

'Was Tom there?'

Tom had been Holly's crush for years and she'd spilled out all her romantic hopes and dreams to Emma. The pair had been school friends for years but, for Holly, something had changed at around sixteen. She felt they could be more than friends. As yet, Tom had been slow to catch up, or lately even notice her.

'Ye-es.' Her answer was noncommittal. '*He* was there, but *I* might as well have not been, for all the time he spent chatting and canoodling with bloody Kirsty Chase. Okay, so she is the best netball player in the school. And she's tall and leggy, with silky, long blonde hair. But she can be a bit dim, sometimes.'

'Ah, I see. Sorry, petal. Doesn't sound like it was your night.'

'Not really. But hey-ho . . . Did you have a nice night? I thought it might have been just you and Alfie and a night in before I saw you?' Holly looked at her in horror, though that didn't sound a bad option to Emma really.

'No, I do have some friends, you know,' Emma laughed.

'Oh, I didn't mean it like that!'

'I know. Well, I had an early supper with Bev and Pete, and then we met Joanne and a few others for drinks out in the village and then ended up in the Fisherman's like you lot, of course. It was nice.'

Fine, pleasant, amusing. It didn't make your toes curl.

'Yeah, it was a pretty good night. Didn't feel so hot the next day, mind.'

'Hah, no, I bet.'

'So, I'll come in next Saturday then. What time?'

'About one-ish.' Emma pulled a sorry face; frustrated that she couldn't give Holly more hours. 'Say one till three. We can sort out the window display if it's quiet, think of something bright to cheer January up a bit.'

'Oh yes, I'll have a think on it. I like being creative.'

'Fancy a chocolate-orange truffle, Hols? They're like a posh version of the Terry's.'

'Ooh, don't mind if I do.'

'We have to check for quality control, naturally,' Em grinned.

'Of course.'

One became three each, just to triple-check the product. They ended up with chocolate-smeared lips, grinning like loons.

'That definitely passes the taste test. Wow!' Holly was beaming.

Oh, yes. This was one of the best parts of the job – the chocolate tasting!

6

'January's doing my head in.'

'Hello, Bev,' Emma recognised the voice of her best friend. 'What's up?'

'It's just so dull and grey. Christmas is over and I have no money left, and no parties to look forward to.'

'Ah, and we're only a week in to it, too.'

'I know, and that's even more depressing.'

'We could have a girlie night in. Needn't cost more than a bottle of Prosecco.' In fact, she'd been given a bottle as a Christmas gift – even better.

'Now you're talking.'

'Yes, a movie night. I can get something up on Netflix. Funny or sad?'

'Not sure. I need some cheering up, I think, but then I do like a good sloppy romance that makes you get the tissues out.'

'Well, I'll have a think on it. I'll get some popcorn in too. We'll do it properly.' It sounded fun. They could chat and cosy up. It might just be what Emma needed too.

'You don't have any chocolate, do you?' She could hear the smile in Bev's tone.

'Nah, never keep it in.'

They both laughed.

'I've just about finished my Christmas supplies, Em. Well, to be honest, let's say *Pete* has just about finished *my* Christmas supplies. The gorgeous ones you gave us were gone within the day, the Heroes tin has a couple of mini Milky Ways left, and that's about it.'

'Do you want a goody bag to go down to the shop with, before the movie? A bit like a pick 'n' mix?'

'Oh my, you know me too well, Emma Carter. Can I really? That would be heaven. I get to raid a chocolate shop, drink Prosecco and watch some hunk in a movie, all in one night. That is *such* a plan. I feel cheerier already, just thinking about it. Thanks, Em.'

'You're welcome. That's what friends are for.'

She could spare a few chocolates from the shop; yes, funds would be a little tight for the next couple of months for sure, but right now she had her Christmas takings safely banked, and she could always steer her friend towards the last of the festive favourites. After all, no one would be looking to buy Rudolph chocolate lollipops or Santas for another year now.

'So, when shall we do it?' Bev asked.

'Are you free Friday?' That was two days away.

'Yep. I'm sure that'll be fine. As I say, I have no other plans.'

'Well then, let's make it a date.'

'Definitely. You're on.'

Friday morning, Emma set to work removing the shop's Christmas window display. Down came the tinsel, the baubles, and the little Christmas tree, which she decided to repot out at the back. She stood the last chocolate Father Christmas moulded figure on the counter, ready to discount, along with some of the Rudolph lollipops, some white-choc stars and Christmas pud truffles, but decided to leave the fairy lights that ran along the counter and shelves. They would give the place a little welcoming glow.

She had found some pretty yellow witch-hazel blossom flowering on a small tree in her back yard – a sign of spring to come – and put it in an old jam jar which she'd tied a green silk ribbon around and added snowdrops. As customers would be feeling the pinch from Christmas on their waistlines *and* their pockets, she started to make up mini packs of fudge and truffles to display along with the flowers. Ideal little pick-me-ups and gifts. There were still the occasional holidaymakers about at this time of year, including those hardy ramblers who persevered in all weathers, as well as couples taking shelter at the hotel at the top end of the street.

It had been a quiet day. She'd only seen two people in the shop all day, when a familiar face called in.

'Hi there! So, the Christmas decs are coming down.' It was Holly, looking a little morose.

'Yeah, I always hate this bit . . . but look, I'm putting

some bright yellow blossom out with snowdrops. What do you think? You can help me some more with ideas tomorrow.'

'That's really pretty. Do you want me to carry on bagging up the chocolates here? I've got a spare half hour. Well, it's either that or heading back to face my homework. And to be honest, I need a little break. I'm only just off the school bus.'

'That'd be great . . . thanks, Holly. How's school going?'

'It's okay. Busy, especially now it's Sixth Form and you just feel that pressure, you know, to get good A-level results next year. The grades are so important for uni or whatever I decide to do afterwards . . . agh, I don't even know what I want to do afterwards.'

'Just keep working hard, Holly, and you'll be fine – that's all you can do.' That was pretty much her mantra in life at the moment.

'Yeah. S'pose.'

Em thought back to when she was eighteen. She'd quite enjoyed school, but wasn't totally sure what she had wanted to do as a career either; teaching had seemed a sensible option, so she had gone off to uni in Durham, enjoyed student life, passed her degree, then taken a PGCE for a year and got herself a teaching post. She'd always loved cooking and specialised in food technology, but not all of her secondary students were that committed, and thought of it as a bit of a 'dossy' subject, which could be frustrating. It was fine, though; she got paid pretty well. And she had met Luke when he had started work at the same school a year after her. She probably would have stayed in that line of work had everything not veered off course spectacularly. But then . . . it really made you think that life was too short to be working away at something you didn't love.

She wondered for the umpteenth time how Luke would have felt about her becoming a chocolatier.

'You okay?'

'Ooh, yep, just in a little world of my own for a minute there. Cuppa?'

'Sounds good.'

'Tea okay? I feel quite thirsty.'

'Great.'

'I'll just pop the kettle on.'

She left Holly bagging up packs of truffles and fudge. The young girl was busy tying on ribbons in shades of bright pink, yellow and green, as Emma came back carrying two mugs. 'Here.'

'Thanks.'

'They look pretty.'

Holly was scraping scissors along the ribbons to make the ends curl.

'The colours will go really well with the blossom in the display. Give it a cheery feel. You really are a ray of sunshine here, Holly,' Emma added.

Just then the dinging chime of the door went. They both looked up. Holly was already positioned behind the counter, so Emma stood back as a blond-haired young man wandered in. He looked about twenty and she saw him glance at her assistant with a shy smile, before perusing the shelves.

'Can I help you?' Holly said, her face blushing pink, nearly matching the bright ribbon in her hand.

'Umm, well, I'm looking for a gift.'

'Okay, well, what kind of a gift? Birthday?'

'No, no, not a birthday, just a general thank you. More of an everyday gift, I suppose.'

'Okay . . . well, we can tailor-make gift boxes. You can choose any favourite flavours and then we can put in the number of chocolates you'd like.'

'Right, yes.'

'For a lady?'

'Yes.'

'Okay then. Well, there are truffles, ganaches, fruit flavours, alcohol, nuts – it's up to you, really. Have a look in the counter here.'

'Just a mixture would be great. I don't mind. I'll let you choose.'

Holly took a medium-sized gold-coloured gift box and a pair of tongs and started taking various chocolates from the counter display, placing them on to the scales. She stopped at eight, saying that would cost just less than five pounds, including the box and wrapping.

'That's fine. Can you pop a couple more on, then? Thanks.' He pulled out his wallet from his trouser pocket.

'Okay, so that'll be five pounds eighty altogether. And, if you just give me a second I'll wrap them properly for you . . . pink, red, or gold ribbon?'

'I don't mind. You choose.'

Emma saw him give Holly another smile.

'Pink then.' That was Holly's favourite colour. Bright,

bold and bubbly, just like she was. Holly did her magic with bows and curls, and popped the gift box into a crisp, white paper bag, tucking in one of their Chocolate Shop business cards.

There was a moment as Holly handed back his change when their eyes met. Holly seemed to go a shade pinker. Em had to smile, though she pretended to be busy with her window display again.

The young man left with a polite, 'Thank you'.

As the shop door closed with a ding, Emma said, 'Now *he* was a nice-looking lad.'

'Yes,' Holly answered, her tone a pitch higher than normal. She watched the young man walk past the window, gave him a brief, friendly smile, and went back to packing up the gift bags once more.

Emma grinned across at her. It might be a good thing that someone other than the apparently offhand Tom at school had taken her assistant's attention.

7

There was a knock at the back door of the cottage and Emma went to answer it and seeing who it was or, more exactly, *who* it was and *what* she was wearing, burst out laughing.

'I'm all set,' Bev grinned, making her way into Em's back kitchen.

'I can't believe you've actually walked around here like that.'

Bev lived a ten-minute walk away across the far side of the village.

'Yep, well, why not? I drew the line at coming across in my slippers, mind – they're in the bag, along with a bottle of Prosecco and some cheesy nibbles.' She offered up her carrier bag to Emma.

'You look like some crazy bag lady.'

'Well, thanks.'

Bev stood before her in a full-on zebra-print onesie.

'Right, well I suppose I'd better go and get mine on, then. Don't want to be outdone. There's two glasses ready there on the side so you get the Prosecco popped and poured. I'll just be one minute.'

'Can I still raid the chocolate shop like you promised?'

'Yes,' Emma shouted from halfway up the stairs. 'But wait until I get back.'

'Meanie.'

Em found her giraffe-print onesie on the chair in her bedroom, where she'd left it last night, and stripped off her jeans and jumper combo and pulled it on. She felt cosy straight away. Right, slippers on. So, she was ready for their 'big night in'.

She arrived back down in the kitchen.

'Can I fill my goodie bag now?' Bev's eyes lit up.

'Yes, go on then.' Emma led the way through the door from the back hallway to the shop, and switched on the lights.

'Yippee!' came a squeal from behind her.

'Bev, anyone would think you were four, not forty-odd.' But Emma was smiling as she spoke.

'I know, I know. I still can't quite get over the fact that my best friend actually has a chocolate shop. How did I get that lucky in life?!'

This evening, with it being especially dark outside, Em had to admit it did look rather like a chocolate version of Aladdin's cave, with neatly piled truffle and ganache gems, gold and silver foil boxes, trails of ribbons and coloured packaging.

'Here.' Emma passed her friend a cellophane bag. 'Go on, fill it. But, if you wouldn't mind, take a few of those Christmas pud truffles and snowy stars that are left on the counter; that'll help my stock situation. They've got to be eaten in the next week or so before they go out of date.'

'No worries. I'll gladly take them off your hands. What do you fancy, Em?'

To be honest, Emma had seen and handled so much chocolate in the past few weeks, she wasn't sure. But she was always partial to a soft-centred caramel.

'Just a couple of the chocolate salted caramels – those ones over there. That'll do me.'

They were soon settled upstairs with a glass of Prosecco in hand, the chocolate goodie bag nestled between them, and their slippered feet propped up on the coffee table.

They'd laughed their way through *Bridget Jones's Baby* and cried their way through *The Notebook* – a classic romantic film and novel that Emma always loved. And, hey-ho, despite the tears, a couple of hours spent with Ryan Gosling was never a bad thing.

'Blimey, that ending just makes me want to go home and snuggle right up with Pete. But, wouldn't it be awful for someone to just disappear from your life so suddenly?' Bev stopped talking and looked across at Emma. 'Oh balls! Sorry, Em. Films like this must be pretty hard for you, yeah? Like, I know it's a long time ago and all that, but . . .'

'It's all right.' Emma smiled sadly, unable to really voice what she felt inside.

'You must miss that, though, that closeness. Don't you

ever want to go out and find someone? Go on a date? You haven't been out like that in ages. And well, to put it bluntly, have a good shag.' The Prosecco had certainly loosened Bev's tongue. They'd had nearly a bottle each by now. 'Or maybe you have been, and you're keeping it all quiet.' Bev arched her eyebrows.

Emma thought of the hunky man on the beach, but said nothing. That was better kept to herself. Chances were she'd never see him again, and maybe that was for the best. It was probably all illusory. No one had ever come near . . .

'Hah, it's Alan in the village, isn't it?'

Em put her head in her hands. Then they both howled with laughter, until the tears were streaming again. Alan, bless him, had to be over seventy, with teeth stained brown from years of smoking roll-ups, and a tendency to be a bit of a letch, to say the least. He was no doubt lonely, having lost his wife several years before. But he would always stand just a bit too close in the post office queue, touching your shoulder as he asked how you were, and letting his hand linger just a bit too long, and Em was sure that one time he'd actually patted her arse. But it was so surreptitious, and when she looked round he was already two steps away at the newspaper stand, his head deep in the *Northumberland Gazette*.

Emma let out a sigh. Would she end up like that? Lonely, desperate for a fondle, watching Ryan Gosling films or *The Time Traveller's Wife* on repeat?

'Pete's got a mate coming up the weekend after next. Why don't you come out with us?'

'What? A blind date? No way! I remember the last time you tried to fix me up with someone. All he could talk about was bloody computer programming and his gym weights. Didn't mean a thing to me. I couldn't have given a monkey's whether he could lift a bloody ten-kilo weight or a car.'

'Yes, well, he wasn't the most interesting of Pete's friends, I must say. But I've met Nigel before and he's nice.'

'Nigel? Are there still people called Nigel around? You've got to be kidding.'

'Just get yourself out socialising again.'

'I was out. At New Year.'

'And before that?'

Emma couldn't quite remember. 'Look, I don't need you meddling, trying to fix me up with someone.' She could feel herself getting edgy. 'I'm fine. I *like* being on my own. Why do we all have to be in loved-up couples? It's just a myth.'

'There's nothing wrong in trying to be happy. Finding someone to love.'

'I had it. I had all that, okay.' Emma's tone was taut.

'Well, don't you want it again?'

'No, I'm fine. It won't be the same. It couldn't be.'

'So, you're never going to go out with anyone ever again? That's just crazy.'

'No, it's not.'

'It's like saying you don't want to ever eat chocolate again.' Bev dug into the goody bag, pulled out a truffle and popped it in her mouth all in one go. There was a pause, as she ate it, then she carried on. 'One day, it'll sneak up on you and you'll eat a whole bar.' Trust Bev to think of a chocolate analogy. 'And you might just like it!'

'No.'

'What's that for an answer? Come on, Em. What is it, are you afraid or what?'

'Okay, all right!' Her voice was raised now, and she felt her neck flushing with heat. 'Yes, I am bloody afraid . . . afraid no one will ever match up. How can they? And if, in some fantasy universe, they ever did? What the fuck then! What if something happened to *them*? I don't want to go back to that place, Bev. I don't want to *ever* go near those feelings again! So yes, I am bloody afraid . . . You happy now?'

'No. Oh, Em . . . ' She placed her arm around her friend. 'Hey, I'm sorry, hun. So sorry. I didn't realise it was still so raw for you. I know you've told me about Luke, what happened. But seven years, Em. It's *seven* years.'

'I know.'

'But hey, jeez, I didn't know you then. I never saw how much it must have hurt at the time, did I? I see you now, strong and independent and beautiful.' She stroked her friend's red wavy hair. 'And it just seems such a waste. But forgive me, I'm just a silly bloody woman who's had too much Prosecco and hasn't got a clue how hard it must be. How do I know how that might feel seven years on?'

'Yes, you are a silly bloody woman.' The edge of Emma's

lip started to sneak up into the trace of a smile. 'A silly bloody woman in a zebra-print onesie.'

And they slung their arms round each other in a hug.

Two days later, Emma picked up the phone and dialled.

'Okay, so I'll go.'

'Is that you, Em? Um, what are you talking about? Go where?'

'On that date thing that's not a date, that cinema trip or whatever you're planning with Pete's mate in a couple of weeks' time. What did you say his name was?'

'You will? That's great! Well, that's a bit of a turnaround . . . well done you! And he's called Nigel.'

'Ni-gel, how could I have forgotten? Can I back out already?'

'Hah, don't judge by a name. He looks more like a Brent.'

'And what does a Brent look like?'

'Blond, American?' Bev suggested.

'Well, I'm conjuring up Brent from that TV programme, *The Office*. And it's not doing anything for me.'

'Hah, he's fine; not bad-looking, in fact. Easy to chat with.'

'Okay, that'll do. I've said I'll go, so I'll go. But don't expect too much from me. Just friends, on a normal night out. Okay?'

'O-kay. It'll be fun.'

Emma wasn't quite so sure. But even she could see it was about time she got herself out and about a bit more. She couldn't hide behind the chocolate forever.

8

Emma had muddled through January, blowing off the cobwebs on some beach walks with Alfie. But three weeks of daily walks and yet there was never any sign of Mr Kiss. Perhaps he *was* just an illusion. A very warm, sensual figment of her imagination.

She spent some time visiting her family, catching up with her twin nieces and her brother James and his wife Chloe on a Sunday when the shop was closed with it being the winter, and she'd made a trip down to her mum and dad. She had restocked the chocolate shop supplies, but hadn't needed to make too much. January demand was, as per usual, at its annual lowest. Holly came in for the Saturday afternoons although Emma hardly needed her as there was only a handful of customers, but it was nice to have someone to chat with.

Soon it would be February, so the two of them could jazz up the window display ready for Valentine's Day. They could let loose with lots of pink, red love hearts, trails of ribbons, tempting boxes of ganaches and fudge.

And she could hopefully look forward to a rise in income again. Christmas had been good, and she had managed to save most of that money, but there were bills to pay, rent and business rates, supplies to buy in. And the high-quality cocoa she bought from Belgium seemed to be creeping up in price all the time.

Emma was in the kitchen pouring chocolate ganache into love-heart shaped moulds. It was Saturday, so Holly was covering the counter, though Em had heard the door and its bell go only the once in the last hour. The jangle made her look up, and then she heard the voice of old Mrs Clark, one of their regulars, no doubt in for her bag of chocolate brazils, her weekly treat. Emma finished filling the moulds then popped through to the shop to say a quick hello.

By the disappointed look on Holly's face, much as they both got on well with Mrs Clark, the girl had been hoping that the young man who had called at The Chocolate Shop last Friday might call back in – he'd been in during the week, but of course Holly hadn't been there.

'Why, hello, Emma dear. What are you busy making today?' Mrs Clark was shrouded in a heavy woollen coat, a plastic rain cap covering her grey curls.

'Chocolate love hearts for Valentine's Day.'

'Oh yes, that's lovely for the young ones, isn't it?' She nodded towards Holly. Emma had the feeling *she* was being banded with the *old* ones.

'You could do with getting a little chair in here, Emma. Be nice to sit and have a chat and get my breath back a bit. That hill's a bit of a bugger.'

The girls smiled. Mrs Clark used the term 'bugger' freely and easily, as anyone else might use the word 'devil'. It was the only swear word she did use, which made it seem humorous rather than offensive. She was certainly a character, having lived in the village all of her life, and her parents and grandparents before her. She'd often stay for a while in the shop and chat, telling them tales of life in the olden days in the village and the fishing community here. One of Emma's favourite stories was the one about the fisherwomen who used to rock their cradles with their feet, so they could keep their hands free to bait the lines at the same time. It sounded a hard life, though, with poverty and disease rife in the village, but there was always mention of the happier times, too: the dances, celebrations, weddings, christenings. Emma could still recognise that community spirit since moving here to Warkton-by-the-Sea.

'Yes, that might be a thought,' Emma agreed. Some of her elderly customers would be glad of that, the chance to have a sit-down, before heading back down the village hill again.

They watched the old lady slowly pack her chocolate brazils into her large navy blue handbag, which reminded Em of something the queen might have, then set herself away. 'Back home for a nice cup of coffee now. Better wrap myse'n up a bit first, mind.' She tightened the scarf around her neck. 'There's a chill wind out there today. And still a chance of rain. Take care, me dears.'

'Thanks, and you too, Mrs Clark.'

'Bye.'

'Bye, dears.'

And all was quiet once more. Holly gave a little sigh.

'What's up?'

'Do you think he might come back?'

There was no doubt who Holly was mooning over. Funny, those words had been flitting through Emma's head these past few weeks too. Not over the same guy, of course.

'Ah, I expect so. He's been in twice. Seems like he might be local or a regular visitor at least.'

'Or maybe just a holidaymaker on a two-week holiday, and that was it.' Holly looked dejected.

'Maybe. You'll just have to wait and see, Hols.'

'Hmm.'

'Time for a cuppa?'

'Yeah, why not. Thanks.'

Emma went to click the kettle on.

They had their tea sat on stools in the kitchen. They'd soon pop through if they heard the shop door go.

'So, what's the latest with that Tom lad at school?' Em asked.

'Hah, nothing – exactly nothing. It's like I don't exist.'

'Aw, sorry to hear it, Hols. He doesn't know what he's missing.'

'It's all right. It's just we were such good friends when we were little. His mum and mine are still big buddies. We were too. It's like he's changed, totally. It's all football, and flirting with the pretty, sporty girls. It's like I'm just not important or interesting any more.'

'I suppose we all change, life changes,' Emma mused.

'But that does sound a bit mean of him. There's nothing to stop you being friends.'

'I think he might have guessed that I fancied him and it's probably frightened him right off. Oh, Em. I feel such an idiot. So now, I don't feel I can even say hello. I go bright red and get a bit panicky.'

'Oh dear.' Young love, crushes. Why did relationships have to be so bloody complicated? 'It'll all work out somehow in the end, Holly. Just you wait and see.' And as she said the words, she hoped to God that Holly never had to face what she'd had to. She'd learnt the hard way that there weren't always happy-ever-afters. But why spoil the young girl's hopes and dreams?

After their cuppa and chat, next up for Em was making a batch of choc-dipped fudge. She was busy melting butter and sugar together when she heard the jangle of the door again. She hoped it might be Holly's dream man, but the door closed very soon after it opened.

'The post's here.' Holly popped in the back and handed over a few envelopes that Emma placed to one side as she went to fetch cream for her fudge mix from the fridge.

Emma was soon pouring the mixture into a large metal tray to set and cool.

'Mmm, that smells divine!'

'Even better after the chunks get dunked in chocolate.'

'I'd love it if someone brought me home a pack of that.'

'Well, I think we can both think of a certain someone

51

who you'd like to do that – and I'm not talking Tom now,' Emma grinned.

'Hmm. Do you think he's got a girlfriend?'

They both knew exactly who Holly was referring to.

'I don't know. Why don't you ask him the next time he calls in?'

'*Nooo*. I couldn't!'

'Why not?'

'I'd look a right idiot if he has. After all, who's he buying the chocolate for?'

'But, if he hasn't?'

'Then I'd just feel daft and not know what to say next. I'd look too keen, apart from anything else.'

Emma smiled. This girl had another huge crush by the looks of it.

'What about you then, anyway?' Holly was blushing furiously now, and was keen to divert the attention from herself.

Hah, not another one trying to fix her up. She'd had enough of Bev's meddling of late. The foursome with Nigel was looming ominously.

'No one special in your life, then?' Holly pursued.

'Now stop getting cheeky, you. It's none of your business, madam.' Emma was still smiling, but *sooo* not prepared to divulge any information. Not that there was anything at all to divulge.

Twenty minutes later Holly was out in the shop, keeping herself occupied dusting the shelves and the glass counter as it was that quiet, and Emma got around to opening the post. There was the usual junk mail, a bank letter, the quarterly electric bill – ooh, now that was a bit high. Oh well, it was the winter months, she mused. The fourth letter was handwritten on a thick white envelope. Emma opened it, drawing out a sheet of typed A4. It looked very formal. She recognised the name and address of her landlord.

'I am writing to inform you . . . ' Emma stood there stock-still, the letter quivering in her hand.

She was still staring into space when Holly popped back through to put the polish and duster back in the kitchen cupboard.

'Everything okay? You look like you've seen a ghost or something.'

Emma wished it *had* been a ghost. It would be far less trouble than the contents of the letter.

'Ah, no, just a bit of a shock.' She wondered whether to share the news, no point worrying the girl unnecessarily, but oh, she needed someone to talk it over with.

As Emma began to read the words aloud, she felt like her heart was being squeezed. '*I am writing to inform you that as from 1 March 2017 your monthly rent payment for 5 Main Street, Warkton-by-the-Sea, is to increase to the sum of £900.* Nine hundred pounds! That's a further one hundred and fifty pounds a month. I really don't know where I'm going to find that, Holly.'

'Oh no. That's so not fair, Em.'

It might not be fair, but it looked like she had no choice. Either pay it or get out; the landlord was giving her one month's notice. Bollocks! She started reading again, her hand trembling: 'This is due to the desirable nature of the village properties, and the increase in holiday trade.' Basically, her landlord could turn this into a holiday cottage and make a mint, no doubt.

'It's not just my business, it's my home too, Holly.'

'Oh Em, it'll work out somehow. It has to. Warkton just wouldn't be the same without your gorgeous little chocolate shop, or you. It's our little chocolate heaven – all my mates love popping in here. And, you've become a real friend to me. No, The Chocolate Shop can't possibly go – nor you. There has to be a way.'

But the massive implications were starting to sink in. Emma began to feel sick.

For the rest of the afternoon Emma's stomach was churning and her mind was on fast-spin. She could see all the dreams she had had, the business she had grown, her home and her new life here in this lovely village by the sea, all come crashing down. If she couldn't meet the new rent payments, what then?

9

As soon as the shop closed that day, despite it turning dusky outside, Emma headed down for her usual walk past the harbour and towards the dunes to the sea. There was no one else on the beach, just a few terns who would soon be ready to go home to roost. *Home* . . . That thought, that word, made her heart sink even more. Where would home be, if it couldn't be here?

She could try and rent a new cottage locally, she supposed, but without the business, or a job, where would that leave her? And where else could she lease new premises that would work as a chocolate shop, have the kitchen space she'd need and offer accommodation; somewhere where the tourists would flow and she wouldn't have to pay more rent than now? That seemed a challenge too far, and veered towards looking for a miracle.

But she wasn't a quitter, and she wasn't ready to hand in her notice on The Chocolate Shop by the Sea just yet. There *had* to be a way.

She strolled along the sands, Alfie trotting by her side.

She wasn't afraid of the dark, or the beach, or of being on her own – she'd done that for long enough, after all. But she *was* afraid of losing all the things she had built here, and that she knew, by the desperate, sinking feeling in her heart and soul right now, she had grown to love.

She needed someone to talk all this over with. Someone she trusted, who knew her well, but who would also have a business sense, and be able to give sound advice. Her brother, James, was just that person.

'Right, what's up, sis?' James confronted her as they sat in his kitchen.

He knew her so well. She tried to keep her emotions in check in her daily life. In fact, some people might say she came across as slightly cool at times – but that had been a preservation instinct from those toughest of times when she had to try and carry on and keep a brave face. But with James it was different. She was his big sister, and as well as he knew her, she knew him inside out too – his moods, his light, his shade, which exact buttons to press to wind him up within seconds. She'd mastered that at the age of five! And he'd seen her through the very worst of times; held her as she sobbed, provided a sofa, chili con carne – the only meal he could cook back then – bottles of lager and empathy in his shared Newcastle flat when he was starting out as an accountant. He'd helped to bring her back from the brink when she was at rock bottom.

Now he lived in a three-bedroomed house in a hamlet just outside of the market town of Alnwick. Her five-year-old nieces, Lucy and Olivia, had still been up when

Emma had got there, so Emma hadn't felt it was right to start chatting about her troubles straight away. Chloe, James's wife, was upstairs with the girls now, settling them in bed as they had to be up for school in the morning. They'd loved the chocolate cat and dog figures Emma had brought for them. Just a small gift, but the hugs Emma had received in return were mammoth. It was nice that something so simple could make them so happy. She loved living near to them, being close enough to drop in. Would that still be possible in the coming months?

'It's not like you to phone and then want to come across straight away. So . . .?'

'You're right. I need to talk something over with you.' Emma was sitting at their large wooden kitchen table. This room was definitely the heart of the house. James sat opposite her. They were similar in looks, with their red hair and striking green-grey eyes. Emma's hair was a lot curlier, though she styled it to a more manageable wave nowadays. James's was more of a sandy colour, going towards a strawberry-blonde. They'd both used to get teased for their red locks at school but James had just laughed it off; being good at sport, tall, and good-looking, he countered the taunts of 'Ginga' with his own 'Ninja Ginga', and being very good at taikwondo, he used to frighten them off with an air kick.

Emma had been less confident as a younger teenager, soldiering on in the face of the comments. But then, the bullies would pick on you for anything really – being too tall, too short, wearing glasses, being clever, not being clever. Children could be cruel, and teenage peer pressure seemed to bring out the worst in the bullies. Since when did we all have to fit the same mould? Like chocolates, it was the variety that was so lovely.

But suddenly it all changed: at the age of sixteen her hair began drawing lots more attention, *positive* attention, and later, when she met Luke, he told her he absolutely loved it. She was taken aback by that after years of taunts, and in their early, sensual days she remembered him running his hands through her long locks. He used to love it falling over him when they were making love.

'Em? So, what is it you need to talk about?'

'Ah, right, sorry. Yes, me coming here . . . I really needed to chat something over with someone. Someone I trusted.'

James raised his eyebrows, interested and concerned. 'So?'

'Oh, James, the bloody landlord is hiking up the rent on the shop and the cottage, big time. There's no way I'll be able to afford it. I'm only just making ends meet as it is. And I can't just whack all my prices up, I'm pretty sure I'd lose my regular customers if I did. But the thought of having to leave, my business, my home, everything . . . '

'Oh, bloody hell, Em. That's such a tough one. What's the price rise? Do you think there's any room for negotiation?'

'A hundred and fifty pounds *extra* each month. And I doubt he'll negotiate. He's a miserable sod at the best of times. I'm sure he's hoping I'll leave. Nine hundred pounds a month he wants and he's asked for me to give my notice, if that's out of my budget, which he bloody knows it will be.' She started to chew at a hangnail on her index finger. 'I probably do pay a fair price at the moment, and it's not risen for three years, but last time it only rose by fifty pounds per month. He says he could ask for even more with a new tenant, and I reckon he's looking at a holiday cottage option too. Warkton is getting far more popular with the tourists now.'

'But surely that will help your business in the future?'

'Maybe, yes, but even with a slight rise in trade this coming year, I still don't think I can cover costs like that.'

'No.' James rubbed his chin, thinking. He angled his long legs out under the table. 'What about trying to expand the business a bit to source some extra income – going along to local markets, craft fairs, things like that?'

'Well, I suppose I could give it a try. The run-up to Christmas might be good for that, but that's a long way off for now. And then I'd need cover at the shop, or at least to send someone else out to do that for me, so I'd have to pay extra wages. But, it's certainly food for thought. Might be problematic in the summertime, a stall, that is – you couldn't keep the chocolate chilled enough. How do I temperature-control a market stand without having to pay out on a load of equipment?'

'Not sure . . . Hmm, might be tricky. Just thinking out loud. Perhaps that's not one of my better ideas.'

'No, no. It's good brainstorming like this, and you're trying to think practically. I've been wracking my brains since the letter landed, and I've not come up with any magic answers yet.' She very much doubted there was a magic answer.

'Right, right, bear with me.' James tapped his fingers down on the table top. 'This one's a bit better. What about local hotels, restaurants, small shops and delis? Approach them to stock your goods, give them a percentage, and you get to keep the rest. Sale or return might be more attractive at first, but then you should get some regular orders from it.'

'Hmm, yeah. I already do that with The Fisherman's Arms. They have a mini box of two of my truffles as a welcome gift in their B & B rooms.'

'Well then, there you go, just think bigger. What about the country house hotel at Renford, The Swan in Alnwick, the deli in Seahouses, the shop in Bamburgh? There must be several places near Warkton. Take some samples, be brave, and just go and ask. The worst they can say is no.'

'Yes, and there's the hotel in Warkton, just up the hill from the shop. That has to be worth a try.' It was a good starting point. She'd have some late nights crafting choc-olate if some of them took her on, mind, but it would be *so* worth it to keep her shop and her home, and she was never one to be afraid of hard work.

'That's the girls settled finally.' Chloe walked back in, dark air swinging to her shoulders, effortlessly stylish in loungewear that looked like something out of the White Company. She always made Emma feel under-dressed, but she was lovely, had been a real friend over the years. 'Cup of tea?'

Emma was about to say yes, when James cut in, 'I think I'll open a bottle of red, actually. We can brainstorm this together. We're thinking of ways to increase Em's turnover, possible outlets that might sell Emma's chocolate, Chlo. Think this needs a bit of teamwork and a glass of something a bit stronger than tea.'

'Okay.'

'Just a small one for me then, James. I'll be driving back, remember,' Emma said.

'Of course.' He got up to find a bottle of Merlot from the rack, and a corkscrew.

Chloe took the seat beside Emma. 'What's happening then, Em?'

Emma retold the story of the landlord's letter and imminent price hike.

'Oh no, so sorry to hear that, Emma. That must put you in such a difficult position.'

They chatted the situation over further. Emma knew it had been right to come here. It was great to have the support of her family, who were always there for her. No problem seemed quite as bad with them onside. By the time she left at 10.00 p.m., she was armed with an A4 sheet of ideas, a list of companies to approach, a realistic price increase to consider for the shop's goods, and a slightly woozy head from all the thinking. She felt a little more hopeful. It certainly wasn't going to be easy; approaching all these businesses was different to them agreeing to take her goods, and she'd still have to make a decent profit after paying them a cut. And there would be many long nights ahead making the numbers of chocolates required to fulfil any orders as well as keep the shop going.

There was still a long road ahead, but the horizon looked that little bit brighter.

10

It was the night of the non-date date. Emma was filled with a sense of impending doom, but at least it was keeping her mind off the troubles her chocolate shop was facing.

Why exactly had she agreed to this?

It was all Bev's fault, twisting her arm on that girlie night. Now, in the cold light of a late-January day, with a slash of red lipstick, an attempt at mascara, and a cinema ticket reserved for her, she felt she couldn't back out. She looked longingly at the comfy sofa and her TV as she passed by her living room, on the way to the stairs. Even Alfie gave a sad little whimper from his basket.

'Won't be long, Alfie.' Hopefully, not long at all. See the film out, have a quick bite of supper, and then make a quick exit. She'd said she'd take her own car and meet them at the cinema in Berwick-upon-Tweed. Exit strategy firmly in place!

She pulled up her black-and-white Fiat 500 in the car park outside the Maltings Theatre. She usually really enjoyed her evenings here, watching the latest chick flick or thriller with Bev, or sometimes a matinee with her nieces. It had a nice cosy feel. Tonight was going to be different.

They were to meet at the Stage Door Bar within the theatre building.

Well, here goes, Em. Best foot forward and all that. She poked a boot out of the car door, and stepped out. She had chosen a plain black shift dress and a pair of to-the-knee black leather boots. Luckily, she had paired it all with an emerald-green scarf that her mum had bought her for Christmas, or she might have looked as if she was going to a funeral. Oh well, that was a little how she felt.

Right, find some enthusiasm, Em, she rallied herself. It was a night out, after all. It might end up being fabulous fun. This Nigel, who looks like a Brent, might be a bit of a hunk and his conversation could be scintillating. At worst, she'd just keep the chat with this guy polite and friendly and then she could always fall back on her trusted friend, Bev, for a good natter and leave the boys to it. It'd be fine.

Emma collected her ticket at the main desk and treated herself to a share-bag of Maltesers to nibble away at during the film, popping them in her handbag for now. She was to meet the others in the bar which was downstairs, so headed there. She swung open the door on to an old-fashioned room of plush red velvet and an unusual night-and-stars painted ceiling. The theatre bar was cosy and quirky, and she'd enjoyed several glasses of rosé here with Bev over time.

She spotted the three of them ordering, and suddenly felt a little nervous – like she'd fallen back into her insecure teenage years. She smiled across at Bev, and walked over, taking in the outline of the third person. He looked tall, slim – on the side of skinny, actually – as she approached. Blond hair starting to thin on top, a nice smile, phew, and yes, nice grey-blue eyes. Definitely okay at first glance.

'Hey, hello, Emma.' Bev greeted her warmly, giving her a hug. 'Nigel, this is Emma. Emma, Nigel.'

Emma went to shake hands, just as he moved in for a kiss on the cheek, which was fine but slightly out of kilter.

'Nice to meet you, Nigel.'

Pete kissed her then too, and offered to get her a drink.

'Gin and tonic please, Pete. That'd be lovely, thank you.' She'd just have the one, and stick to the plain tonic thereafter. She was driving, after all.

'Busy day?' Bev asked.

'Yes, I'm building up supplies for Valentine's Day now, so I've been busy crafting.'

'Emma is a chocolatier,' Bev announced proudly for the sake of Nigel.

'Great,' he replied.

'Bev makes it sound very grand. I make chocolates and sell them,' Emma explained.

'She has her own business, in Warkton-by-the-Sea. It's gorgeous.' Bev was obviously keen to make her sound fabulous.

Emma smiled. 'It's just a small shop. But I do enjoy it.'

'Good. I have to admit, I don't generally eat chocolate, though. I do a lot of running, marathons, trails – have to keep an eye on my dietary requirements. Stock up on the healthy carbs and proteins, you know.'

'Right. Well, it's good to eat healthy.' She smiled stiffly. And *boring*. So, he doesn't like chocolate. It wasn't the best of starts.

'I suppose you have to do a lot of training?' She tried to make conversation.

'Yes, a lot of it's in the gym at this time of year. Half-hour to an hour running sessions, and I try and do a bit up in the hills at weekends. The odd twenty-miler.'

Twenty miles.

'Do you run at all?' he continued.

That was like asking Emma if she'd ever been to the moon. Emma would have trouble running twenty metres. In fact, she hated running. Cross-country at school was always a disaster.

'Ah, no, not really. I walk a lot, on the beach, with Alfie, my dog,' she explained.

'Ah, I see. Well, no dogs for me, I have a pet allergy.'

Oh my, this was going to be harder than she'd even imagined. Emma gave a sideways glance at Bev, who quickly diverted the conversation with, 'Right, well who's looking forward to the film? I've heard some great reviews of it.'

Pete handed Emma her gin, whilst Nigel sipped his pint of real ale. 'Yes,' Pete added chirpily, 'I think the theme tune is up for a BAFTA.'

'Great.' Emma then took a large slurp of G & T; she had a feeling she was going to need it.

'So, where's home for you?' She persevered with the polite conversation, hoping he wasn't going to say that he'd just moved up to the Warkton area.

'Newcastle way, Gosforth. I moved in to a new flat about six weeks ago. Used to have a country pad, Corbridge way.'

Recent divorcee was clanging like an alarm bell in Emma's mind. Messy divorce? Still in the horrible post-relationship throes? She felt a little sorry for him, if so. He was probably missing his wife and kids. Not wanting to quiz him any further on what might be a difficult subject she just said, 'That's a nice area, Gosforth.' Playing it safe.

'Yes, I'm finding my feet.'

It was a relief when the bell sounded to announce there were just five minutes to the start of the movie. They made their way through to the small theatre and found their seats. Pete filed in first, then Bev. Nigel stood back to allow Emma to sit next to her friend, and then he followed. The seats were fairly close and quite small, traditional pull-down plush red velvet pads, with wooden armrests, and there was the usual shuffling as the audience settled down.

Emma took off her jacket, and then got out her bag of Maltesers at the ready. She opened the pack as quietly as she could, as the intro music of the movie started up, passed them around amongst their group, then carefully wedged the pack between her knees to avoid any spillage.

Ten minutes into the film, she felt a nudge at her knee-cap, and acknowledged Nigel about to dip in to the pack. She hadn't time to lift the pack out, so nodded as if to say help yourself. She felt a slight rummage as he took a couple, smiled at her, then they both carried on watching the film. It was the latest Bond, action-packed as you would expect – there was a high-speed car chase whizzing on noisily at the moment. At least they didn't have to make conversation any more.

Ten minutes or so later, she felt another little dig between her knees. Bloody hell, he was dipping in again. So much for not liking chocolate! This time, as his hand slid out of the pack, it brushed lightly across her knee. *Was that on purpose?* But she couldn't be quite sure. She lifted the pack up a bit to rest on the top of her leg. She felt slightly uneasy – but it was probably her imagination getting the better of her. She settled back to watch the film, taking a few more sweets for herself, enjoying that initial chocolate melt then the malty-sweet crispiness.

Fifteen minutes on and Bev smiled across at her, mouthing, 'Good film.'

She smiled back, yes, at least the film was okay. She needn't be rude about the company; they just didn't have much in common, that was all, but she could just muddle on and see out the evening.

She jumped in her seat as an armed criminal leapt out at Bond from a sidestreet. And then the Maltesers bag started to go again. Nigel was staring straight at the screen whilst rummaging a little more than was strictly necessary, then his hand tracked slowly up her thigh.

Okay, this was no accident. She'd moved the bag on purpose, so no physical contact need be made between them. She darted him a stern look, as if to say: I know what you're up to, matey, and it stops here!

He gave a small, weaselly smile in return, and then popped a Malteser slowly into his mouth. The letch! She might as well have been on a date with Alan Fondle Fingers from the village at this rate!

Emma stiffened, trying to avoid any bodily contact at all, which was hard considering how narrow the seats were, *and* they had shared armrests. She folded the sweet packet down, pushed her knees tightly together and propped her hands on top of both legs protectively. That should stop him. But was she being paranoid?

Bev gave her an odd look as if to say, what are you doing? Whilst Pete was completely oblivious, transfixed as he was on the film. Another fifteen minutes must have passed, and Emma began to relax a little. The sweets were still held fast on top of her knees and were probably melting by now.

Then, just as she was concentrating on the film again, she felt another small tug at the bag, and his hand slid down *beneath* the bag to the inside of her kneecap as he gave her a wink. Oh, for Christ's sake. It certainly wasn't the chocolate he was after, was it? Thank goodness she'd put her thick tights on. He seemed the sort who'd be up and under your knicker elastic in under thirty seconds. Jeez!

'Right,' she fumed, in a strained whisper. 'Take the bloody pack.' She slammed them at him and got up, excusing herself to a middle-aged couple who had to stand up from their seats to let her pass. 'Sorry, sorry. Trip to the ladies needed.' She fumbled out of the row in the near dark. An usher then guided her to the rear of the cinema with a torch.

She hadn't needed the loo, but sat down in a cubicle anyhow, still fuming and scheming her exit plan. Go right now? That seemed a bit rude to Bev and Pete. But could she suffer the rest of the film? Possibly, but there was absolutely *no way* she was going out for a meal with old Fondle Fingers now. He'd be trying to pleasure her with a poppadum or something.

She texted her brother: *Ring me at nine o'clock sharp. Please x* There must only be twenty minutes or so left of the film. They'd be on their way out by then. *Say the dog's been sick and I need to come home straight away. You'd be my hero x*

I hope I'm your hero already ;) bounced back. *Will do. What on earth are you up to?*

Tell you later. Thanks, you're a star. X

Then she texted Bev: *He's a right letch. Soz, but I'm gonna have to dash.*

Emma hung about a bit, washed her hands, checked her lip gloss in the mirror, and made it back to her seat for the final minutes of the film. This was the last time she was going to be persuaded to go on a blind date, possibly any kind of date at all. She didn't care if she ended up as some mad cat or spaniel lady, living on her own.

Bev gave her a quizzical look, her phone being safely

69

on silent mode in her bag for now. She was probably wondering if Emma had a touch of food poisoning or something, the amount of time she'd spent in the loo. Emma sat bolt upright with knees tight, body tense. She couldn't give out any more 'keep off' signals if she tried. It seemed to work, thank heavens. They got to the final credits and she realised she had no idea what had gone on in the film since halfway through. She was just glad to be getting out from there. They stood up and shuffled out along the row, Emma leaving a good space between her and Nigel, allowing Pete to move up next to him as they reached the aisle.

'Great film. Loved the bit where they water-skied up over the speed boat,' Bev commented.

'Yeah.' Emma had no recollection of that part what-soever.

Just as they reached the welcome light and space of the foyer, Emma's phone buzzed into action. Perfect timing. *Thank you, bro.* She'd gladly do some extra baby-sitting for them one night. She held her mobile ready in her palm.

'Hel-lo? Oh, oh *really*?!' She overdramatised her voice, giving Bev then Nigel a concerned look. 'What a shame . . . Okay, no worries, I'll come right away.'

James was laughing down the phone.

'Okay, bye.' She turned off her mobile.

'I'm so sorry,' she said to the three of them. 'I'm going to have to go. The dog's been sick. James, my brother,' she added for Nigel's benefit, 'has been dog sitting for me. Took him for a walk, and now he's seems really poorly. Poor Alfie.'

Bev gave her a curious look. She'd have known Emma never usually got a dog sitter in for an evening at the cinema. Alfie was fine in on his own for several hours.

'Oh, right.' Bev's tone was sceptical and her eyebrows raised.

Emma then saw her friend digging in to her bag for her own phone. The text would soon clarify things.

'Lovely to meet you.' Emma didn't even bother to extend her hand to Nigel who was already moving in towards her, no doubt for a farewell kiss. She ducked away, saying, 'I really have to dash. Catch you soon, Bev. Sorry again. Bye, Pete. Bye, all.'

And she was off like a whippet to the car park and straight back home to the comfort of her little cottage. She was soon sitting stroking her best boy's spaniel head. This was all the company she needed, right now, not some letchy Malteser-man. She wasn't that desperate.

'We're just fine, aren't we, Alfie? Just fine.'

11

It was Friday afternoon, the first week in February, and Holly had called in after being dropped off by the school bus. It was becoming quite a habit on a Friday, even though she wasn't officially working, *and* interestingly so were the visits of a certain blond-haired gentleman, who had a very nice smile.

The door of The Chocolate Shop chimed as it opened. Emma and Holly both looked up.

'Hi,' said Emma. So, he was back.

The young man approached. 'Hi, could I have the medium gift box with half coffee creams and half orange, please?' the young man asked.

'Certainly.' Emma was already positioned behind the counter.

'So, who's the lucky lady, then?' Emma asked with a smile. 'This is becoming quite a regular visit.' She could feel the heat rising from Holly who stood beside her, and was now shooting her boss a warning glance.

'For someone special?' Emma persevered.

'Yeah, you could say that.' The young man flashed his trademark grin.

So, there was a 'she' involved. Emma could almost sense Holly's shoulders sink. Her assistant stayed silent.

'Yes, I've just finished work,' he continued. 'I started at the Seaview Hotel, just up the street, about a month ago. Trainee assistant manager.' He seemed proud of his new position. It was nice to see the young ones getting on.

'Well done. That must be an interesting job.'

'Yeah, I'm just finding my feet. It's going okay so far, though.' He darted a shy glance across at Holly.

Emma hoped Holly might join in the conversation here, but her assistant seemed to have lost the ability to speak. Emma placed the chocolates in their tiny petit four wrappers in a gold box and began tying it with a purple satin ribbon. 'This colour ribbon okay?'

'Yes, that looks great.'

'Well, that's five pounds and twenty pence, please. Is that everything we can help you with today?'

'Yes, that's it, thanks.'

He paid the money, took the gift box, and turned to go. Holly just managed to find her voice at the last, with a shy 'Bye' and he turned to say 'Goodbye' back. Emma was sure there was some frisson in the air. The chocolates would be melting at this rate! After he was safely away down the street, Em announced, 'Well, if he doesn't fancy you, Holly, I'll eat my hat.'

'Nah, don't be daft. He can't do. Who's he buying chocolates for? He said it was a she – the lucky thing.'

She pouted. 'Aw, but he just seems so nice. Why do I always like the ones who are taken or just not interested?' Holly sighed, and then picked up a duster and started flicking away at the shelves, even though she wasn't officially working, obviously needing to keep busy.

Young love, hey? All that angst.

Emma thought back to her own recent dating disaster. There certainly hadn't been any chemistry or frisson with Fondle Fingers the Malteser Man, just the bloody angst. Her thoughts jumped to the man on the beach at Boxing Day, all those weeks ago now. She couldn't quite shake off the memory of him and felt a tug in the pit of her stomach, like she missed him, yet she didn't really even know him. She wondered if he ever thought of her, too.

A figure dressed in a black raincoat was hunched outside the shop window under an umbrella. It had been a drizzly damp afternoon and it seemed to have been dark for hours out there, so Emma was glad that Holly had dropped by – the weather today had kept all bar the hardiest of ramblers at bay. A couple in matching red cagoules had called earlier admitting they'd been hoping for a café, but had settled for a bar of milk chocolate for their coastal walk, and that was the last customers she'd seen until the young man Holly fancied.

Holly went out to the kitchen to make them a cup of tea and the dark-clad figure moved to the doorway. Once his umbrella was let down, Emma had a sinking moment of recognition. It was Mr Neil, her landlord.

He strolled in, dripping rain on to her wooden floor-boards.

'Good afternoon, Emma.' The greeting came out in a flat tone. 'How's business?' He looked around at the empty shop.

'Afternoon.' She took a slow breath. 'Good, thanks.' She smiled. She was never going to tell him otherwise.

'I was just calling to check you have received my letter.'

'Yes.'

'And to remind you that I need your reply by the end of next week, as per its contents. Obviously, you do need to give me a month's notice of your leaving, though I'm sure I could make arrangements if you'd like to vacate earlier.' He gave her a cold smile, pretending to be helpful.

So, he was evidently counting on her leaving the shop. That made Emma even more determined to do everything in her power to raise enough funds to keep it going and make the new rent payments. He couldn't just chuck her out of her home, her business.

Holly wandered through at that point with two cups of steaming tea. She said 'Hello' cheerily to the gentleman in the shop, to be answered with a very cool 'Hello' back. She looked at Emma with raised eyebrows as she passed over her cup, as if to say, who on earth is that misery?

'Oh yes, I'll be sure to answer you within the week, Mr Neil,' Emma replied, giving away nothing about her intentions to stay. But what would happen if she couldn't make these new payments and fell into default? He'd have her out of there soon enough anyhow, and she'd then be disgraced, having brought her business to its knees. Would it be better to leave of her own accord now, look for other premises, start again? But her heart and soul were here in this shop, in this village, with the community that had sheltered her. No, she wasn't going to give up that easily.

'Well then, I look forward to receiving your reply.'

I bet you do, thought Em, *but you might not be so damned complacent when you read it.*

'And the next rent is due this Thursday.'

She was fully aware of that. Thank heavens for the Christmas takings she'd saved, but that was going to take the last of those funds. She'd be at rock bottom then, her bank account empty.

'Yep. That's fine,' she replied.

'Quiet in here, isn't it?' He cast his beady eyes over the shop pointedly, then out to the empty street.

'At the moment, yes.' Crikey, he'd be enough to frighten any customers off anyhow, she mused. 'But it was much busier early on today, before the rain set in.' She pasted on a smile.

'Hmm.' He looked around again, as though he didn't believe it. 'This'd make a lovely living area, open plan right through to the kitchen space.'

He was already planning the renovations to make this into a holiday cottage!

'Maybe. But it does make a lovely shop,' Emma persevered. *Keep calm, don't rise to his bait.*

'Oh yes, it's a fabulous little shop, very popular.' Holly rallied by her side behind the counter.

'Well then, good afternoon, ladies.' With that, he left, dripping water in his wake.

'Yuck!' Holly spat out the word as soon as he'd closed the door. 'He's like a slug.'

Emma had to laugh.

Holly continued, 'What did you say his name was?'

'Mr Neil.'

'More like Eel, all slimy and a right wriggly character. That has to be the landlord, huh? The guy that sent that horrid rent letter. I don't know how you put up with him.'

'A case of having to, Hols. I could never afford to buy this place. Dammit, he is so looking forward to chucking me out.'

'Nooo, that can't happen!'

'I really don't know how I'm going to finance the new rent payments. But I'm going to bloody well try.'

'Go, Em, that's the spirit. You'll find a way. We can't lose The Chocolate Shop by the Sea, or you. How awful would that be? The shop is such a special place. And there's no way I'm going back to the greasy chippie to work.'

Emma let out a sigh. 'Thanks, Holly. I'll just have to make sure I give it my damned best shot then. Time for the masterplan to swing into action.'

'Wow, have you got one?'

'Well, let's just say I have some ideas up my sleeve to get started with.'

'Brilliant.' Holly beamed. 'And me and the whole village will be right there beside you.'

Deep breath . . . just walk in . . . shoulders up . . . smile. The worst they can say is no.

She *so* didn't want them to say no.

Emma was about to try her first sales pitch, and was loitering nervously outside the main entrance to the Seaview Hotel, two hundred metres up from her chocolate shop. She was armed with a bag of goodies, including a selection of mini truffle boxes and some packs of fudge and raspberry white-chocolate hearts. She was pitching that they take her chocolates to trial as a turndown gift for their guests. It could work as a lovely gesture from the hotel, hopefully getting them good reviews and repeat custom, as well as raising awareness of her little shop down the road, where they might come to buy more.

She'd done some research and the hotel had twenty-four guest rooms. She had worked out her costs and was going to ask what she felt was a fair price (reduced from the normal shop retail) at 95p per box of two chocolates, all wrapped and tied with thin ribbon, and the hotel could choose either a white or gold box. Emma had even matched the shade of ribbon to the royal blue of the hotel's logo. Fingers crossed that they'd like the idea.

Maybe she should have phoned or e-mailed before she just turned up like this. But she was here now. All she could do was give it her best shot. Right, enough dilly-dallying around, Em. If they had a security camera on the front door they'd wonder what the hell she was up to, loitering there.

Go girl! You can do this thing.

She pushed open the hotel's swing door and found the reception desk, recognising the girl there as being from the village.

'Hi, Emma.'

'Oh, hi, Laura.' She was the daughter of the lady who ran an art gallery in the village.

'How can I help?'

'Would it be possible to have a word with the manager?' Em asked.

'Ah, sorry, she's not in this morning. I could ask the assistant manager, if you'd like? Is there a problem?'

'No, no problem. Just an idea I've had. Something to put forward. I've come to see if the hotel might be interested in me supplying them with turndown chocolates, actually.'

'Oh yum. Now that *is* a good idea. Give me a second and I'll just try and locate Adam, our assistant manager. Take a seat if you like.'

'Thanks.' As she sat down she realised her heart was racing. This order might just help to save The Chocolate Shop, or at least be a major step in the right direction. She still had to answer Mr Neil's letter, but if she secured some new business she'd have more hope of managing to pay the increased rent.

After a minute or two, who should arrive but the young man who'd been calling in lately. Of course, he'd said he had started working here recently!

'Adam, this is Emma from the gorgeous chocolate shop down the road.' Laura was obviously keen to help.

'Hi, yes, hello, Emma, of course we've already met.' He offered an outstretched hand to shake hers.

'Hello.'

His handshake was warm and friendly, and though he was evidently young he seemed more assured here in the hotel than he had in the shop.

'So, you have an idea for our hotel, I hear. Come on through and we can have a chat about it.'

'Thanks.'

Emma followed him to the hotel's lounge area – all duck-egg blue and cream sofas, some stripy, some plain – where he had organised coffee to be served for them.

'Well, I'm open to new ideas, so what are you thinking?'

'Obviously, I run a local chocolate shop, and I was thinking that a chocolate gift at turndown for your valued guests might prove popular. It could improve things like your hotel reviews on TripAdvisor and the like, and also make that difference between you and your competitors so as to draw repeat bookings and recommendations.'

'Hmm, sounds interesting.' Adam was nodding.

Emma began to relax a little. 'I've brought along a selection of mini boxes filled with two high quality truffles – they aren't too expensive and they would look lovely popped on a bedside table at turndown. These are just suggestions and you could choose what flavours you felt worked best for your clients.' She lifted out all the boxes and the samples of fudge and chocolate hearts. 'With Valentine's Day coming up soon too we could theme the gifts – say raspberry chocolate love hearts with a champagne truffle.'

Adam smiled as he picked up one of the filled boxes in white.

'I have tried to colour theme the ribbon to your logo too,' Emma added chirpily. This wasn't as difficult as she had feared, though actually getting a yes would be the hard bit.

'So, how much are we actually talking price-wise?' Adam asked.

'Well, looking at all my costs. and hoping for an order of at least fifty boxes to start, I could price at ninety-five pence per box.'

He did that hmm, thoughtful noise, giving nothing away.

'It is twenty-five pence cheaper than I sell them for in the shop,' Emma tried.

She took a sip of coffee, trying to divert the tension that was now creeping up inside her.

'I like the idea,' Adam started with a small smile, 'but . . .'

Why was there always a 'but'?

'I'd need to discuss it with our manager, Helen. Especially with the costs involved. But the chocolate boxes do look great and, having sampled your truffles myself, I know just how good they are.' His smile broadened. 'Leave it with me. Do you have a card or anything with the number to call you?'

'Yes.' She dug a business card from her handbag and handed it across. 'Thanks for considering this, and if you or Helen need any more information, or want to talk further just let me know.'

'We'll let you know one way or the other soon.'

'Thank you.' She finished her coffee, then they both stood and shook hands once more.

'Oh, and say hello to your assistant from me – the dark-haired young lady. I didn't catch her name?'

Emma could have sworn Adam's cheeks were reddening.

'Holly.'

'Ah, Holly. Okay. Thanks.'

'I will do. Thanks for your time this morning, and the coffee.'

'You're welcome. I think it's important for local businesses to try and support each other. On that note, would you mind popping a few of our flyers in the shop?' He took a batch from a coffee table in the corner.

'That's no problem at all. Of course.'

With that, she turned to leave. The hotel seemed lovely – comfy, friendly, airy and light. Perfect for a holiday by the sea. She'd gladly put some brochures out for them on her countertop. She waved goodbye to Laura as she passed. Once Em got outside the cool air struck her and she felt a bit wobbly at the knees.

She had tried her best. Now all she could do was wait.

12

What a week it had been! The run-up to Valentine's Day, the landlord's visit, and pitching for the hotel business. It had been all go, go, go, making chocolate hearts – dark choc with mint chips and white chocolate with mini strawberry pieces – assorted truffles, with an extra batch of the Irish Cream and champagne flavours, fudge bags, and her new mini 'hat boxes' made of chocolate and filled with truffles. They were so pretty, and proving popular.

And, *yes*! Adam had phoned her yesterday to say the hotel manager had loved the samples and the idea. They were willing to try an initial fifty boxes, if she could just get them there for Valentine's Day as that would be a perfect time to start. So it had been a very late night indeed.

Emma's hands were sore from tempering all the chocolate she needed (she did have a machine that was a great help, but she had so much to make she was hand-tempering too) and her fingers ached from the intricate work – the piping, filling, mixing – and on top of that her feet were sore. Last night, even though it had been well after midnight when she'd finished the last batch of the day, she'd soaked in a huge bubbly bath for a full hour until the water had gone cold. But she'd been up early at 6.00 a.m. this morning as it was Valentine's Day tomorrow, so she was making more of the chocolate 'hat boxes', as over half of them had already sold. It was hard work, but also lovely seeing everyone come in to choose their special gifts on the lead up to the big day: young lads of about twelve years old up to elderly gents, women, little girls wanting something for Daddy, a flow of customers looking for just the right thing, or sometimes needing a little inspiration. Emma enjoyed suggesting some of the current favourites or a new flavour she was trying out. It was so nice to think her chocolate creations were going to be gifted and hopefully make someone smile – that was one of the best things about being a chocolatier.

Holly had helped her yesterday afternoon, being a Sunday, and was coming in again today straight from the school bus, which was a godsend. It was hard to make the chocolates *and* serve, so if Emma needed to make up any last-minute batches she could. Or, if (fingers crossed) there was a busy run of customers, at least there were two of them to keep the queue down.

This week's sales so far, along with the fabulous hotel order – hopefully the first of many – had thankfully lifted the finances, and she had now saved nearly enough for next month's rent hike – yes! So she was going to write that letter tonight, as soon as the shop closed, and send it off to her landlord first thing tomorrow.

Of course, her supplies were now low, so she'd have to put in another online order for the high quality Belgian chocolate callets she used as the base for all her creations. She could cover her bills for now, but it would still be a juggle, and there was never much left for any luxuries (or indeed some of the necessities) for herself. In fact, she couldn't remember the last time she had bought any new clothes, but it wasn't as though she was off anywhere glamorous. The beach for walks with Alfie and the cottage, kitchen, and shop were her main bases. At work she always wore a black apron (to hide the inevitable chocolate smears), teamed with black trousers and a plain white T-shirt; it didn't really matter what was underneath as long as it was clean.

Five o'clock rolled around so quickly. It had been another hectic day, with a rush over the lunch hour. Emma had managed a bite of Marmite on toast at around 2.30 p.m. for her lunch with a quick cup of coffee. She loved good coffee, and when she had time would grind her own beans. It was one of the few things she spent a little more on – having a really lovely cup of coffee from her cafetière really perked her up, especially on hectic days like this. She had been so glad when Holly arrived about an hour ago.

The door chimed and in dashed the young man from the hotel. He was checking his watch. 'Sorry, are you about to close?'

'Oh, hi, Adam. No, you're fine. We're opening a little later tonight, with it being Valentine's Day tomorrow.' Emma smiled.

She could swear she could feel the heat rise in the room. Holly was blushing furiously beside her.

'How's the hotel order going?' he asked. He looked slightly uncomfortable.

'Oh, you didn't need the mini boxes for the hotel today, did you?' She felt her heart race. She was sure they'd said for Valentine's Day, and had planned to get them finished and delivered first thing in the morning. She felt a little anxious – she couldn't afford to screw this up already.

'Oh no, tomorrow is fine. Helen said for Valentine's Day.'

'So, how can we help today?' Emma asked brightly, feeling relieved, as she shifted slightly out of the counter area. 'Holly, would you mind helping here? I have another batch of dark chocolate hearts to make.'

'Of course . . . so, what would you like? The usual, is it, coffee creams and the orange creams?'

'Aah, yes, please . . . '

Emma couldn't help but listen in as she walked slowly towards the inner door of the shop. He sounded uncertain, as though that wasn't what he was in here for at all. She paused just in the doorway, curious.

Holly got the box out ready, four of each flavour as per usual. Wrapped them up, did the purple gift bow, and then weighed and priced them, which came to the normal five pounds twenty.

'Um . . . ' He sounded a little uncomfortable. 'I'd like something else. Another gift box, one like that, but a bit bigger this time.'

Emma could imagine Holly's shoulders sinking at that point, though she'd be trying her best to disguise it.

'And what would you like in this one, some truffles and ganaches from the counter, maybe?'

'Yes, a selection, please. I'm not sure which – what kind of things would *you* recommend?'

'Well, I love these Baileys truffles, so definitely a couple of those, and Emma has just been making a new passion fruit filling, so you could try that. The raspberry and white choc is very good too, as is the hazelnut praline.'

'Any more favourites?' he prompted.

'Yes, there's the salted caramel, better not miss that. They really are delicious.'

'Two of them as well, in that case.'

She had filled all twelve cases now. 'Done?'

'Yes, that's fine. Thank you.'

'What kind of gift-wrapping?' Holly asked, still managing to sound cheerful.

'I'll let you decide.'

So she went for a bright pink bow and ribbon, which she tied beautifully.

Emma was now spying subtly from the inner doorway. Bless her, Holly was being so helpful, even though she was probably feeling gutted inside. The tension in her assistant's fingers was apparent, however, as she struggled to tie the bow.

'Right, so together that'll be twelve pounds fifty, please.'

She popped the two boxes in one of their crisp white paper bags.

The young man paid, then gave Holly a smile, which she returned wistfully.

'Bye, then,' she said.

'Thanks. Bye.' He turned at the last, with a nod.

After the door to the shop closed, Em heard Holly let out a long, low sigh. As she peered further around the door frame, she saw the young girl's head drop and her hand lift to sweep away a stray tear. 'Life is *sooo* not fair.'

She just had to go and give her assistant a hug.

13

The big day had arrived, Valentine's Day, and Emma was awake before her six o'clock alarm.

Luke would have brought her flowers, no doubt have planned to take her out for supper. They'd only had five Valentine's Days when they were meant to have a whole lifetime of them. It was two months before it happened that they had got engaged. They had been so full of hope. It was their future together that had been taken away: Christmases, wedding anniversaries, a wedding day, their children . . . grandchildren.

It still hit her hard, every now and again. The years didn't seem to dim the pain, they just spread out the time when it jolted through her. She turned on the lamp-light. Being February, it was still dark at this time of the morning, and she looked at Luke's photo there next to her bed.

Right then, time to get up. There was one more batch of salted caramel truffles to make. *Come on, Em, last big push, you can do this thing,* she chivvied herself on as

89

she raised her weary limbs from the comfy mattress.

First, she let Alfie out into the yard and fed him his breakfast in the little kitchen upstairs, grabbing herself a piece of wholemeal toast and butter and a large mug of tea. Her morning wake-up routine.

Down to the main working kitchen at the back of the shop, hands washed, thin hygienic gloves on, stainless-steel board in place on the work surface, chocolate callets ready to melt in a bowl – the dark 70% cocoa today, and the moulds in place. The kitchen window overlooked the back yard of the cottage. It was paved with flagstones with a high stone wall around it. She kept pots of herbs and daffodils that were only just poking a green tip up. In summer, there were colourful geraniums and petunias, but for now the courtyard was still rather bare. In the half light, a little robin sat at the water trough cheering things up, singing away. The early-flowering clematis that scaled the wall to one side would be out soon too; it would soon become a mass of pale pink blossom. Roll on March and the spring! She popped the radio on, listening to the music and chat of Radio 2, Chris Evans and the gang keeping her company until 8.30 a.m. when she took Alfie for a quick walk down to the beach, a brief reward, before the long day ahead.

The fresh sea air with its tang of salt perked her up with the white-crested waves rolling to shore. She found it calming down here, loved the sweeping arc of the bay, the ever-changing light and colours of blues, greys, ochre-blonde sands and the peachy hint of sunrise or sunset, depending on what time of the day or year she was there. Alfie enjoyed his runabout this morning, doing his classic spaniel loop in joyful circles around her as his grand finale.

'Right, let's get back, Alfie. I have one busy day ahead.'

As soon as she got back she completed the hotel order, sealing the bases of the raspberry ganaches with more chocolate. She had a small production line going. Next, she needed to make up the pretty gold boxes ready to fill and hand-tie with blue ribbon. She managed to deliver them all to the hotel before opening the shop at 10.00 a.m., when her 'official' working day started. Phew!

Then it was all go again, with customers waiting at the door for bang-on opening time, and there were telephone orders, and a constant stream of business all day. Her shelves were looking rather depleted by lunchtime as she'd been busy for the last two days as well. But that was all for the good for her finances, if not her feet!

That afternoon, Emma found herself stifling a yawn. It was only 3.30 p.m. – at least two hours to go. Her early start – in fact, a whole week of early starts and late finishes – was catching up on her. A momentary lull in the shop made her realise how shattered she was.

She served a gentleman who looked in his fifties, whom she recognised as being a regular visitor to the village. He said how much his wife loved her chocolates and he'd diverted off the A1 main road especially on his way back from working in Edinburgh for a few days to take her a box back for Valentine's Day. Aw, how sweet.

A few minutes later, the shop door chimed and in

breezed Holly, who'd agreed to help after school again.

'Hi, Em!'

'Afternoon, Holly. It's good to see you, it's been really busy.'

'Ah yes, the big day! Happy Valentine's.'

'Thanks! Have you had any surprises? Cards from secret admirers, or the like?' Em asked her assistant.

'No, sadly not, but there's still time. I can live in hope.' She laughed. 'And you? Any cards?'

'Now come on, Holly, don't be daft.'

'Not even Malteser Man?'

Emma had shared the disastrous-date tale with Holly to cheer her up one day.

'Hah, I think I'd burn a card from him.'

Jeez, just imagine if he actually did call in to surprise her with a Valentine's gift – maybe another grab bag of Maltesers? Hah, what a nightmare!

'I think I'll go and make us a coffee, Holly. I was flagging a bit there. It might keep us going.'

'Good idea. Actually, would it be a pain if I had a hot chocolate? I really fancy that.'

'Of course you can. You deserve it for helping me out so much this week. And I shall put on that swirly cream you like and mini marshmallows.' She remembered there were some left from making the Rocky Road chocolate bars.

'Okay, yes, that'd be fab. Delish.'

Emma was turning to go, when she spotted Holly's head shoot up. The door chimed, and in walked the young man from the hotel.

'Hello,' Holly said rather cautiously from her position behind the counter.

'Hi.'

'I'll just head out back, make our drinks,' Emma said loudly, to give them a little space. She had seen what he was carrying and was smiling to herself, hoping. She couldn't help but hover by the door to listen in, though.

Adam stood at the far side of the counter, looking slightly awkward.

Em could almost sense Holly holding her breath.

'Umm . . . these are for you . . . ' he spoke softly.

'Oh, how lovely!' There was a little quiver in Holly's voice. At just seventeen, she had never been given flowers before.

Emma gave a little air punch in the back hallway. Her instincts had been right all along.

Out in the shop, the young man was handing over a huge bouquet of beautiful pink and white flowers, with roses and carnations and lilies, all tied up with a large pink bow, the exact colour Holly had suggested for the box of custom-picked chocolates the day before.

'Oh, and these, of course.' He passed her the very same box of chocolates, grinning. 'I'm sure you'll like them, seeing as you chose them all yourself.'

Holly seemed lost for words. But the huge grin across her face echoed his. Then her smile dropped a little, and she looked concerned. 'But the other chocolates . . . every week. Who . . .?' She sounded as though she hardly dared ask.

'Oh, right, yes – I get them for my gran.'

'Your *gran*?'

'Yep. I've been staying with her since I got this new job. I couldn't have afforded to rent somewhere on my own – I'm on trainee wages at the moment – and Gran lives just down the road in Seahouses. She's let me have her spare room, so the chocolates are a bit of a thank you.'

'Oh, I see.' All those weeks of thinking he was seeing someone else. Holly could hardly believe it.

Emma was still listening in, and smiling widely at this point, out of sight in the corridor to the kitchen. *Aw, that's so lovely.*

'Thank you *so* much.' Emma could hear the lump that must have formed in Holly's throat.

'And . . . ' he started. There was a brief nervous pause. 'I wondered if you might like to go out with me some-time? I was thinking maybe a coffee or something, perhaps at the hotel? Oh, I'm Adam, by the way.'

Yes, Emma had said. 'I'm Holly.'

Emma couldn't help but peek through the doorway at this point, to see Holly lay the bouquet down carefully on the counter to take the hand Adam was offering in a handshake.

'Actually,' Holly leaned across the bouquet and the countertop, 'I think I need to do this.' And with that she gave him a peck on the cheek, which made the colour soar in his face.

'Thank you for the flowers and the chocolates. And yes, I would love to come for a coffee.'

'Great!' He seemed to relax. 'So, maybe this week?

When's a good time? I get a Wednesday off generally.'

'Oh, I'm at school – Sixth Form,' she quickly added. 'But I get back by quarter to four, so maybe around then.'

'That's fine. Well then, call up at the hotel at a quarter to four next Wednesday and head for the lounge area. We could have some Afternoon Tea. Do you like that?'

'Ooh yes. Sounds lovely . . . Oops, hang on.' There was a moment of panic when she realised she'd still be in her school clothes. 'I'll just need five minutes more.' She darted a look at Emma, who was now hovering at the inner doorway. 'Need to get changed,' Holly mouthed across to her. 'Can I do that here?'

Emma nodded. 'Of course.'

'So about five to four.'

'Yes, next Wednesday,' Adam confirmed.

'That's great.'

'Fab.'

'Brilliant.'

Both were rooted to the spot, grinning, as though neither could quite believe it.

'Better go, then.'

'Yep.'

'See you soon.'

'See you Wednesday.'

'Thanks again for the flowers . . . everything.'

'You're welcome.'

Adam left the shop, with a big grin plastered on his face and a backward glance at Holly.

As soon as he was out of sight, Holly started jumping

up and down. 'Oh my! I have a date.' Bounce, bounce, bounce. 'With Adam.' Bounce, bounce, bounce.

'Blimey, it's like Tigger has taken over your body!' Emma was laughing. 'Watch out or you'll be toppling all the shelves over, and wrecking my chocolates. Hey, honestly though, I think it's wonderful, Holly.' *At last.* 'See, you should listen to your Auntie Emma.'

'His *gran*.' Holly grinned. 'All along it was his gran.'

And they both giggled, just as another customer walked in to the shop. More Valentine dreams to help make come true. It was times like these that made Emma's heart soar. It seemed there really was a special magic about The Chocolate Shop – no wonder it was so very precious to her.

14

It was wet and wild the next morning. Emma had heard the wind rattling around the eaves all night, lifting the roof tiles, with rain spattering noisily against her bedroom window pane.

At least there was no six o'clock alarm, today. Bliss. The room was still dark, and she had no idea of the time, so she switched on the bedside lamp. Eight-fifteen. She'd had a nice lie-in, but a few more minutes wouldn't go amiss. It wasn't the kind of day to be rushing up for anyhow, though she knew she'd have to let Alfie out to the yard soon enough – he'd be crossing his legs other-wise.

She had already decided to close the shop today. Now that Valentine's Day was over, a wet Wednesday in February wasn't going to draw in the crowds, and she could use the next few days to make enough supplies to keep the shop going for now. So, for the first time in a while, she could actually relax, read a book, watch some TV, get the fire on and chill a bit.

She'd have to get out for a walk with Alfie at some point. She hoped it might dry up a little, but maybe a blustery beach walk would do her good. And Alfie wouldn't mind: being a spaniel he positively loved the wet; swimming in the sea, rolling in muddy puddles, walking in the rain – he was still happy.

Emma remembered yesterday, the heart-warming scene in the shop, and thought of Holly and Adam. She hoped their afternoon-tea date would go well. She had a strong feeling that it would – he seemed a nice lad. Aw, the promise and excitement of early love. She was so pleased for them.

She snuggled down under the duvet for a little longer, thinking of first loves, and lost loves, but didn't let herself dwell on it. Somehow, she had to get a grip on the here and now, make the most of her every day. She couldn't waste the life she had.

Later, togged up in rain mac, trousers, wellies, hat, scarf and gloves, she told herself that again. She *really* didn't fancy walking out in this – the rain was relentless. But there was Alfie wagging his tail, and barking now his lead had come out.

'Come on then, boy. Let's do this thing.'

They made their way down the hill to the harbour. She could see the waves bashing up against the harbour walls, sending up an arc of white spray. The boats rocked and rattled, though they were tied safely with sturdy ropes. Hopefully, none of the fishing boats were out today. It wasn't the weather to be out at sea.

No one else was around; they were all sensibly staying

indoors or perhaps planning to make a quick dash later on to gather around the real fire and settle for a cosy supper in The Fisherman's Arms. She hadn't cooked properly in ages, having been so busy making chocolates, and while she might treat herself to a roast chicken dinner at the weekend, she didn't fancy sitting on her own, or making all that effort for one. Maybe she'd invite James and the family over for Sunday; that would be nice. A family beach walk, hopefully in better weather than this, and a Sunday roast when they all got back to hers. Yes, she'd arrange that. She'd phone him when she got back in.

Emma walked down along the road towards the dunes and let Alfie off the lead, then they followed the sandy, spiky grass track and soon reached the beach. The waves were dramatic and stormy, the power of them immense. Emma kept towards the top of the beach, near the dunes, not wanting Alfie to get too close to the sea that was crashing in, though he seemed to sense the danger and was keeping unusually far away from the shoreline. It was fascinating to watch the frothy, rolling seascape and to hear the boom and crash – like turbulent thunder. They strolled along the sands for about fifteen minutes, getting lashed by the rain, then walked back again through the dunes, the strands of marram grass soaking her trouser legs above her wellies.

Another dog owner was now out with his labrador, a middle-aged man she had seen before on the beach, the only other person she'd seen in the past twenty minutes. They nodded to each other stoically, as dog owners out in the rain do, and she headed back up the hill once more. A couple of seagulls were battling the elements above the harbour, struggling to fly. They gave up and perched on a fishing boat mast. It wasn't a day for being out long.

It was a relief to turn the key in her back door, walk into the warmth, and peel off her damp outer clothes. She popped a rack near the radiator in the hallway, hung her coat and trousers on there, and then headed upstairs, where she towel-dried Alfie. She didn't like him shaking off downstairs near the shop; he certainly wouldn't pass the health and hygiene regulations.

Soon they were both settled by the coal fire. She didn't plan on going back out at all today. She might phone her mum and dad for a catch-up chat, and then make that call to James with the invite for the weekend – maybe her parents would like to come along too. Oh yes, and she'd read a book, maybe find a good film on Netflix, perfect. She realised how tired she felt. The build-up to Valentine's Day had been particularly hectic and she was aching. All that stirring, folding, and packing was surprisingly physical, especially on repeat. She'd have arm muscles like Popeye if she wasn't careful!

Later, Em settled down for her rom-com film with Alfie nestled on his blanket on the sofa next to her, all warm and cosy. It was dark by 4.00 p.m. – well, to be fair, with the inky-coloured storm clouds it had stayed virtually dark all day. It seemed extra quiet in her little front room, and once the film credits rolled, she realised she wanted some company, someone to chat to.

She'd ring Bev, see if Pete had come up with any romantic gestures yesterday. Yes, they could have a nice natter.

The dialling tone droned on, with no answer on her friend's mobile.

Em stroked Alfie's head, feeling out of kilter. She finally had the chance to relax, and now didn't know quite what to do with herself. She flicked the TV control back to the Netflix menu. A night in beckoned and a supper of a can of tomato soup for one.

* * *

The man drove down Warkton-by-the-Sea's main street.

So there it was, The Chocolate Shop by the Sea – a cute-looking cottage-style shop. Yes, it suited her. He felt a strange sensation in his gut as he drove past slowly, catching glimpses of chocolates and confectionery, but he couldn't quite make out the figures inside.

Ah, what the hell was he doing? He wasn't even sure what had compelled him to drive up here today. Just a need to get out, get away for a while. He shouldn't really be here at all.

He slowed at the bottom of the hill and pulled the pick-up to a halt beside the harbour, turned off the engine, and looked at the boats bobbing there, the people strolling by.

Sometimes it was just the right thing at the wrong time. This felt so very much like the right thing; he couldn't reason out why, but some instinct had brought him here . . . but no, right now he needed to go back, to sort things out with Siobhan and her family.

He sighed, put the pick-up into reverse, turned around and passed the shop once more. At least she was still here, he mused. Well, she might be. She could have sold the business or anything by now. He could just stop, pull up, see if she was there, say hi. But dammit, it was all too messy just now; there was too much unfinished business. He put his foot on the accelerator, and drove on by.

Emma, relaxed from her well-earned time off the day before, looked up from serving Stan and Hilda, the friendly pensioners who were regulars.

Oh, surely not! Emma did a double-take as she thought she recognised a grey, jeep-style vehicle, passing by.

Could it be?

But it had already driven on by. She hadn't even had a chance to spot the driver. Blimey, Em, she chided herself, how many grey truck things are there around? There must be hundreds of them. For goodness' sake, get a grip, woman.

Sometimes you might meet someone out of the blue, talk and chat for a short while, even share a kiss, but it didn't mean it was anything significant or that you'd ever see them again. They could touch your life for the briefest of times, but it didn't mean they were going to become a part of it. She sighed softly.

'Sorry, Stan, I was off in a world of my own for a moment there. I'll just go fetch your mint creams for you. There's a fresh batch out the back.'

'That's fine, my dear. We're in no hurry, are we, Hilda?'

'No, none at all, pet.'

Emma sorted out their order, had a little chat, and saw them on their way with a smile. What a lovely old couple.

Silly woman, imagining it might be him! Emma was cross with herself, even as she wandered to the window and scanned the road outside just in case. She knew she was just clutching at straws. Sometimes you got the wrong one and the whole damned stack came down around you. And then, sometimes, you could pluck one out – and nothing at all would happen. Surely nothing happening was the safest bet?

15

Wednesday of the week after, Emma spotted the school bus trundling past up the hill.

She knew what was coming next. Two minutes later, in flew Holly, all of a dither.

'Oh my, I've only got like five minutes to get ready.' She'd obviously run up the hill from the harbour-side drop off. 'Right, what do you think?' She started pulling out clothes from her school rucksack.

She displayed a pair of white jeans with a deep-pink blouse and a denim jacket to pop over.

'Nice. I like it.'

'Or . . . ' Holly fished out a to-the-knee dress in navy print with a small red flowery pattern on.

'Ooh yes. The dress. That's really pretty and just right for afternoon tea. What's going on your feet?'

'Ankle boots – I didn't have room to carry anything more. But I do have dark tights, so it doesn't look silly and summery.'

'Okay, that will work well. Pass me the dress and I'll give it a quick iron for you.'

Holly shot her a look. 'Have I got time?'

'Of course. It's been screwed up in that bag all day. It'll only take me five minutes. Go on, pass it over, and you get out of your school clothes and into the tights. I'll have it ready in a flash. We'll just shout out if someone comes into the shop. They can wait a minute or two.'

Emma whizzed upstairs and soon had the dress pressed for Holly. She found Holly in the downstairs kitchen in her underclothes.

'All ready for you, madam.'

'Thanks, Em. It's like having a second mum.'

'You're welcome.'

'Agh, I am *sooo* nervous. I feel so sick, I don't know how I'm going to manage tea and cake.' Holly slipped the dress over her shoulders.

'You'll be fine. The nerves will all settle down once you get there.'

'But what do I say, how do I make conversation?'

'Holly, you never stop talking here. I'm sure you'll be fine.'

'Yeah, but when I get nervous I either clam up and can't speak at all, or else I go into overdrive and jabber out a load of shite.'

Emma had to smile. 'Just breathe and think about what you're going to say first.'

'But what shall I ask him?'

'Well, you could ask about his job there at the hotel. Maybe about his gran?'

'Ah yes, the mystery other woman.'

They both laughed.

'You'll be fine, Hols. He seems a nice lad and I'm sure he'll be as nervous as you are.'

Holly let out a big sigh as she popped on some lipstick. 'I haven't even got time to redo my make-up properly.' She glanced at her watch. 'I need to be there in five minutes.'

'You look lovely, honestly.'

'You sure? Really?'

'Really. You'll make his day. Oh, and I have something for you to take up – Adam rang me earlier.'

'He did?'

'Yep, guess who's just got a repeat order for turndown chocolates?'

'Oh, brilliant.'

'He said they went down really well with the guests last week, and they are going to place a regular order now. So I've a box ready to go – I made them earlier today.'

'That's great news.'

Emma fetched the box from the kitchen side. 'Ready then?' she asked.

'As I ever will be,' came Holly's reply with a nervous grimace. She then popped on her denim jacket. 'Can I leave my rucksack here and get it later?'

'Of course, then you can tell me all about it.'

'Still feel sick.'

'That's only natural. Go on, go smash the first date. Best of luck.'

'Thank you, Emma. Aaghhh, here I go.' Holly slung a little handbag over her shoulder, took up the cardboard box of chocolates, and nearly tripped over the step as she waltzed dramatically out the door. 'Sor-ry.'

Emma smiled, watching her assistant set off, though she feared for the safe carriage of her chocolates what with young love, all that excitement, energy, and angst. Emma doubted she would ever feel that herself again, but it was nice to see Holly full of hopes and dreams.

There was a knock at the back door. It was around six and Emma had closed the shop, but she was still busy in the kitchen, making chocolate bars – her latest flavour sensation being ginger and lime.

'Only me.'

The unmistakeable tones of Holly. She sounded chirpy at least.

'So, how did it go?'

'Pretty good, I think. Hah, except for when I spilt a blob of cream from my scone down my front, that was *sooo* embarrassing.'

'But it went well?'

'Yeah, we chatted okay and the food was delicious – cakes, and little cute sandwiches. We even had a glass of bubbly.'

'Very nice. So, you got your appetite back then?'

'Yep. Oh Em, he's so dreamy. I really like him. I just hope he likes me. I'm not sure how he feels, though, he just seemed a bit too polite.'

'Well, that's no bad thing. And maybe he was a bit nervous too. First date and all that.'

'Maybe. He's *so* not like the boys at school.'

'I imagine he's a little older.'

'Yeah, he said he's twenty.'

'There you go then. A couple of years makes a big difference at that age.' Emma finished pouring melted dark chocolate into the last mould. 'So, the all-important question . . . are you seeing him again?'

'I think so. He's going to call me.'

'Ooh, exciting.'

'I know! OMG, I totally feel worn out now. I've been concentrating *so* hard on not saying anything stupid.'

Emma smiled. 'Well, you can relax now.'

'You're kidding! I'll be on tenterhooks waiting for him to call me, won't I?'

'Ah, yes.'

'Well, I'd better get back and get my homework done, I suppose.'

'Do you need a lift home? I could take you around in the car.'

'Nah, I'll walk.'

'You sure? It's dark out.'

'It's dark when I get off the bus these days, Em. No, I'll be fine. Thanks anyway.' She picked up her rucksack from the bench where she had left it earlier.

'Okay, well, glad that it all seemed to go off well. See you Saturday afternoon, yeah?' It was back to shorter hours for Holly again now the Valentine's rush was over.

'Yep, see you Saturday.'

'Keep me posted. Hope you get your call soon,' Emma grinned.

'Me too.'

16

Adam had called Holly just a couple of days after the afternoon tea, and he and Holly had had a cinema date that seemed to go rather well. The only downside was that Holly had been mooning about the shop with a puppy-dog look on her face for the past fortnight, and was so full of chat about suitable outfits and hairstyles for the next impending supper date. Which was rather cute – but also frustrating when a customer was sometimes left waiting at the counter to be served. Emma had had to remind her assistant to focus on more than one occasion lately, but as the weeks rolled on, thankfully Emma had managed to scrape together enough funds to make the first higher rent payment and Easter had arrived before she knew it.

'So, girls, has the Easter Bunny been yet, do you think? Shall we go and have a look?'

'Yesss, Auntie Emma!' they chorused.

Whilst James had kept the twins busy inside, Emma

had placed a trail of her handmade chocolate eggs wrapped in gorgeous spotted foil around her brother's back garden. Chloe had even strewn a couple of half-chewed carrots and a few torn lettuce leaves for extra effect.

The girls rushed out of the back door, giggling, with Emma on their heels. They spotted the carrots straight away.

'He's been! He's been!' shouted Lucy gleefully, with Olivia alongside her grinning from ear to ear.

The first find was tucked behind a large plant pot on the patio. Emma had grouped the eggs in twos, so both girls picked one up. Then there was a bit more of a hunt in the garden borders, checking under shrubs and the like, and a hydrangea bush was found to be sheltering two more. They split up, and when Olivia found another duo under a short fir tree near the far fence, she called for her sister excitedly.

The last two proved more difficult. There was much foraging in the borders – good job they were in their wellies – and sighing and puffing, until Lucy stopped in the middle of the back lawn with her arms folded.

'Maybe that's it,' she announced.

'Let's just keep trying a little longer,' Emma suggested. She had just managed to surreptitiously move a half-chewed carrot to the base of the old apple tree, where the last pair of eggs were perched, just within sight and reach for a five-year-old, on the lower branches. There was also a note with them.

James and Chloe were standing outside with a cup of

tea, watching the goings on. They gestured to Emma that a tea was ready for her too.

'Don't think we'll be long,' she shouted across to them, with a wink.

Emma wandered nearer the apple tree, seemingly looking around at floor level. Lucy caught her up and soon spotted the carrot lying at the tree's base.

'There, Auntie Emma – but where's the eggs?'

'It might be a clue,' Emma hinted.

Olivia was on the case, looking around her, and then up. The foil glinted in the sunlight from its branch. She reached up on her tiptoes, her fingertips grasping an egg carefully. Lucy barged in, grabbing the last egg and the note.

'Lucy, be patient,' shouted James from the steps.

Lucy unfolded the note, to find a rabbit footprint and a short message.

'Auntie Emma, can you read it, please?'

'Okay. *Dear Lucy and Olivia—*'

'Oohh, he knows our names!'

'*Dear Lucy and Olivia, Please now go to the garden shed where your Easter trail will end.*'

Before Emma had even had the chance to say the word 'end', the girls had bolted off. Lucy managed to lift the latch on the shed, and they dived in.

All Emma could hear was, 'Aww, that's so cute!' And 'I love him!'

Then, the girls were out of the shed door shouting, 'Mummy, Daddy, Auntie Emma, look! Look!' They were clutching large moulded chocolate Easter rabbits, with matching yellow dotty bow ties, which Emma had lovingly crafted earlier in the week. James and Chloe hadn't known about these.

'Oh wow, they are fantastic,' said Chloe.

'Thank you so much to the Easter Bunny,' said James, beaming a smile at his sister.

After a lunch of roast beef, and an Easter egg for the twins for pudding, the girls were tired and sat quietly watching some television. After helping with the washing-up, Emma sat with James at the cleared kitchen table, feeling pretty shattered herself.

The build-up to Easter had been, as per usual, pretty manic – creating Easter eggs of all shapes and sizes, along with chocolate chicks and bunnies, and pretty Easter bonnets moulded from chocolate, upturned and filled with truffles. It was a chance for Emma to be extra crea-tive and she loved that, and the rush and buzz, but it was hard work, resulting in sore feet and sore fingers.

'So, how's it all been going with the shop?' James asked. 'I know that you managed to secure the business at the Seaview Hotel, which is great, but is there anything else on the horizon?'

'Well, the master plan hasn't quite worked out as well as I hoped,' Emma conceded. 'I have been trying my best and approaching other possible new outlets, but they either seem to think that my products are too expensive – which, yes, they would be compared to mass-market chocolate because of the quality ingredients and the hand-crafting involved – or they already have a supplier of some similar confectionery that they are happy with. I seem to have drawn a bit of a blank lately.' She sighed. 'And then Easter has taken up all my time and energies, to be honest.'

'Naturally. But hey, keep going. Chin up, sis. Your chocolates are just amazing. Just look at how thrilled the girls are with those brilliant Easter Bunnies.'

'Thank you.'

'And if you need any help at all, me and Chlo are always here. Even if you need a short-term loan or something.'

'Thanks, but it's not quite come to that yet.' The last thing she wanted to do was to borrow from her brother without knowing how on earth she might pay it back. She would keep trying and thinking of schemes, but at times it all felt like a juggling act – keeping the shop financed, supplied, and stocked with all the gorgeous chocolate creations she needed to make. With the massive rent hike, the end of every month was always tainted with anxiety and angst over finances; she was working all hours as it was, but it never seemed to be quite enough.

17

It was a Saturday afternoon in late May. The Easter boost to finances had now been spent and Emma had managed to pay most of this month's rent payment and was intending to send over the final £100 after this weekend, when she'd have – hopefully – taken it over the till. It would only be a day or so late.

Emma and Holly were both in the shop, Em just putting a tray of Baileys white chocolate truffles into the refrigerated counter, when she spotted the unmistakeably greasy head of Mr Neil (the Eel) lurking outside the shop window. She stayed low, hidden by the glass counter and the rows of chocolate therein, watching his next move.

As he pushed the shop door open, she ducked down to the floor right beside Holly's legs. Her assistant gave her a quick, confused glance but then seemed to realise what was going on.

'The Eel,' Emma managed a low whisper.

Holly's face settled into a pasted-on smile. 'Good afternoon. How can I help you?'

'Can I speak with Emma, please?'

'Oh, I'm sorry, she had to pop out to Alnwick this afternoon.' Holly was cool as a cucumber, though Emma was in fact a quivering wreck at her feet. This was no place for a thirty-something grown woman, but it had been her first instinct, and she just couldn't face him and his snide comments today.

'She had to do some banking,' Holly followed up.

It was a Saturday, were the banks even open? Em mused.

'Interesting . . . ' He let the word linger.

God, he was such a sleazeball.

'Well, when might she be back?'

'Umm, might be an hour or so . . . she did mention a couple of other errands she had to run as well.' Bless her, Holly was keeping it deliberately vague.

'Hmm, I may well call back in later. But,' he added almost to himself, 'I do have another appointment – very inconvenient.'

Well, if he'd said he was calling . . . Em thought from her coiled, extremely uncomfortable position on the floor *. . . she'd have really made sure she was in Alnwick!*

'I'll be phoning. And there may well be a letter to follow. Will you make sure to tell her I called, it's a Mr Neil.'

'Eel, yes,' Holly mouthed as though repeating his name, which nearly made Em chuckle out loud and reveal her hiding place. 'I will do.' Holly held her nerve and gave another helpful smile.

Em held her breath as there seemed to be a second

or two where he lurked beside the counter, then she heard footsteps retreating, and the chime of the door. As the door swung to a close, Holly announced brightly, 'Mr Eel has called.'

Em stayed low, just in case he popped back for a second check, but she had to laugh.

'That was far too close for comfort,' she said to Holly. 'Keep an eye out for a little while, he may well come back.' And with that she crawled on hands and knees towards the back hallway, heading for the safe-zone of the kitchen. 'We'll need some kind of code if he does,' she added.

'Jellied eels?' Holly laughed.

'Yes, jellied eels it is – but won't that sound a bit odd if you just shout it out as he comes in? Like you've got Tourette's or something?'

'I could sing it, like I'm just singing along to the radio.' And with that she launched into 'Oh, je-llied eels' in the tones of 'And so, Sally can wait' from Oasis's 'Don't Look Back in Anger'. Emma poked her head back in to the shop and they laughed together. Emma knew she had to laugh, or else she might just end up choking with tears – the threat to her beloved shop was very real.

'I'm sorry to hear that the shop's having to close, pet.' Old Mrs Clark had just ambled up to the counter and was still slightly out of breath from her walk up the hill. 'It's a bit of a bugger, that.'

'Pardon?' Emma was taken aback.

'Oh yes, heard it from Sheila at the grocer's. She was

116

telling me about all the financial problems you've been having and that you're having to finish.'

It was only two days after Mr Neil's ominous visit. Blimey, the village gossip merchants had been busy.

'Oh, but that's not true, Mrs Clark. I'm not closing at all.' She was keen to put the record straight as quickly as she could.

'Oh, but . . . ' The elderly lady looked confused.

'No, I'm absolutely not closing The Chocolate Shop any time soon.' She felt more determined than ever. Hearing those words coming from an old friend in the village was rather shocking and felt like a knife blade. Imagine if they really were true?

'I'm so, so, sorry, Emma. It's just that as I've heard that from a couple of people in the village now, I believed it.'

'Well, to be totally honest, Mrs C, there was a small issue with a slightly late payment this month, and the landlord has hiked up the rent on me this year. So maybe that's got a little confused in the chatter. But that's all settled and it's fine. I have *no* intention of leaving any time soon.'

'Well, I'm very glad to hear it, Emma. I'd have missed you and your shop so much. I enjoy my weekly stroll up here, despite that bugger of a hill, and your chocolate brazils – they are so much better than any of those supermarket ones.'

'Can I get you some now?'

'Yes, please, pet.'

'I'll put a few extra ones in for free if you can do me a favour and go back and let the villagers and Sheila know there's no truth in the rumours, that I'm not going to be closing at all. The Chocolate Shop by the Sea is doing fine, and is here to stay.'

Well, she mused silently, *for the next few months at least.*

'Of course, I will, pet. I'd hate for there to be any falsehoods going around. I know what the village can be like for gossip. I'm sorry I got caught up in it all and I hope I haven't hurt your feelings, Emma dear.'

'Not at all. In a way, I'm glad you let me know. At least we can put the record straight now.'

'We can indeed. I'm on the case.' The old lady set off determinedly, her chocolate brazils safely stowed in her large handbag.

There was only one place the rumour could have started. Emma hadn't told anyone else, not even Bev; she hadn't spoken with anyone other than James and Chloe about her finances since the initial rent hike, and they certainly wouldn't be in the village gossiping. There was only one person who could have talked – Holly!

18

'Hi there, you okay? Good time to talk, or do you have customers in?' Bev's chirpy tones came down the phone line. It was later the same day that Mrs Clark had been in.

'Yes, it's fine. No one's in now and it's nearly closing time.'

'Em, I've heard the rumours going about that The Chocolate Shop might be closing. Do you want to talk, or come round after work maybe?'

'Oh Bev, it's not true. The shop's not closing at all. Not on my watch.'

'Right! Well, thank heavens for that. So where's it all come from, then?'

'It's all snowballed. To be honest, there's some truth in that I've had a few financial pressures lately, and this month the rent was paid a few days late. Three days, that was all, but that was it, the landlord was on my case. I've never paid late before in all the years I've been here.'

'Well, that doesn't seem very fair.'

Emma sighed. 'He wants me out, I'm sure of it. First hiking up the rent extortionately for this year, and now this. I'm sure he's after selling the place off, or making it into a holiday cottage.'

'Oh, Emma.'

'I just can't relax. It's like this black cloud is permanently over me all the time, with me trying to make ends meet. But even if I do, and I cover the rent, I have a feeling that once this year's contract is over he'll probably serve my notice or hike it up again, anyhow.'

'Oh, hun. I wish you'd told me more about this before.'

'I was just trying to keep going, pay the bills and the rent. Carry on as normal. I didn't want these sorts of rumours getting out.'

'No, I bet. But you know I'd never betray a confidence. And sometimes a problem shared . . . '

'I know. Thank you. I think it was Holly who let it slip after the landlord called to chase the rent. Once the village grapevine got hold of it, well, they had me closing down within the week.'

'Well, it sounds like you might be in need of some time out. It's been such a glorious day, and looks like it's going to stay a nice evening, so I was actually calling to see if you'd like to come round for drinks in the garden here?'

'Tonight?'

'Yes, I'll see if Joanne and Ali can make it too, if you'd like.'

Ali was a friend of Bev's who lived in the next village;

120

she also worked as a receptionist at the doctors' surgery, and was always good company.

Well, it might beat her evening date with Alfie, the television, and pondering her financial woes. She hadn't realised quite how lovely the weather had been as the shop front was shaded – ideal for chocolates, to be fair – with the sun hitting the courtyard at the back of the cottage of an afternoon.

'Pete's been out all day golfing,' Bev added. 'There's some kind of dinner event afterwards too, so I doubt if I'll see him back until past ten o'clock. So drinks with the girls seemed ideal.'

'It sounds lovely. And yes, do ask Jo and Ali, that'd be lovely. What time do you want me around? I'll just have to shut the shop up, take Alfie out for his walk, and give him some tea.'

'About six-thirty, so we can make the most of the sunshine. Bring a cardi or fleece as we'll try and stay outside. Pete brought home one of those chiminea things yesterday. We'll set it up and give it a blast. Beat the Northumberland chill that'll no doubt creep in later on.'

'Great.'

'I was thinking of making up a jug of Pimm's and lemonade, to celebrate the start of summer. Maybe followed by a glass or two of Prosecco.'

'Sounds delightful. Can I bring along anything to help?'

'Now you're asking . . . A scrummy box of your chocolates might be nice. Do you still do those Eton Mess ones? You know, the ones with strawberries, cream, and meringue? I think they'd go lovely with the Pimm's.' Em could hear the cheesy smile in her friend's voice.

'Yep, I do indeed. Made a batch of those yesterday morning, in fact, so I'll bring some of those and a selection of other favourites.' She'd also just made some dark choc ganaches with a hint of lavender, which were surprisingly good. She loved testing out new flavours with seasonal twists and she was now on to the tastes of summer.

'Of course.'

Hmm, Emma mused, a Pimm's truffle might work really well – milk choc with a touch of Pimm's liqueur and tiny freeze-dried strawberry and orange pieces on the top . . . Emma's brain was in creative mode.

Just after the school bus drop-off time Holly popped her head around the shop door. 'Hi, Em.'

'Hel-lo Holly,' Emma's tone couldn't hide her disappointment: she was still so annoyed at the dreadful news of her precious shop closing spreading like wildfire through the village.

'Everything okay?' Holly asked cautiously as she came in. The shop was empty other than the two of them.

'No, not really.'

Holly's eyes widened.

'Word has got out that The Chocolate Shop is about to close. Can't think where that could have come from, can you?'

'Oh! But I only told my friend Freya.'

'And Freya is the daughter of Sheila, who owns the village grocer's. The best place for gossip in the world.'

'Oh . . . ' Holly looked dejected.

'Rumours have now spread and built, Holly. Mine and the shop's reputation are in tatters. And the village is expecting me to close at any time. There are suppliers who'll possibly be hearing about this and I don't want them to think I'm going under. And my orders . . . The new business at the hotel, for instance, has probably got wind already and they'll be expecting me to let them down soon.'

'Emma, I'm so, so, sorry. I never said you were going to close. I was just telling Freya the funny story about you hiding under the counter and I may just have added about Eel Man chasing the rent.' Holly would never have realised what was about to happen next. But so much damage could be done by such rumours. 'How did you find out?'

'Mrs Clark's been in, saying how sorry she was we were closing.'

'Oh, no. Emma, let me put this right. I'll go right away to Freya and her mum and tell them the truth of it, and the village. I can knock on a few doors and put the record straight. I know who the main gossipmongers are. But don't worry, Em, I'm sure they'll all want to support you anyhow. None of them would want to see you or the shop go. You and The Chocolate Shop, you're a part of Warkton now.'

'Thank you.' Emma felt a tear crowd her eye. She blinked it away. She couldn't stay cross with her assistant for long. Holly was young and naïve and hadn't been thinking. 'Just be careful what you speak about in the future, especially when it involves other people's lives,' Emma warned.

'I will. I will. Do-do I have to leave my job?' Holly sounded choked up. She looked tearful.

'Oh Holly, of course not,' Emma replied. 'Just make sure you think before you start chattering on next time.'

'I will. Of course I will. If I'd realised what might happen . . . I never meant to upset you, or spoil the shop's reputation.' A big fat tear spilled down her assistant's cheek.

'Come here, silly.' Em opened her arms wide. They shared a hug.

'Right then,' Holly announced, wiping her eyes with the tissue that Emma had just handed to her. 'I'm off to set things straight. Warkton will soon know The Chocolate Shop by the Sea is here to stay.'

Emma had to smile as Holly marched into action and out of the shop.

Ali was already there at Bev's when Emma arrived. Emma found the pair of them sitting in the patio area, with a jug of Pimm's positioned on the white-painted wrought-iron table and four glasses ready.

'Hi, Em.' Bev stood up and gave her a kiss on the cheek.

'Hello. Hi, Ali, good to see you. Wow – isn't this lovely and what a gorgeous warm evening.'

'Yeah, it seemed a shame not to make something of it. You're just on time, I was about to pour,' said Bev, giving the fruit and ice cubes a final stir.

Bev's house was set at the far side of the village, over-looking country fields. It had been a two-bedroomed cottage, but they had extended it downstairs to make a larger kitchen space and conservatory and an extra room upstairs. Their grown-up son was now at university down in Leeds, so it was mostly just Bev and Pete there now. Emma liked going over to Bev's house; it was always welcoming and a relaxing place to be.

Emma took a seat as Bev handed her a tall glass of Pimm's.

'Cheers.' The three of them raised their glasses with a clink, just as the side-gate swung open and Joanne arrived, bearing a bottle of Prosecco and a huge bag of Kettle chips.

There were more hugs and hellos as the last glass was filled then they all settled back in their seats.

'Sorry to hear about all the gossip going around that the shop is closing,' Ali started. 'Bev's told me there's no truth behind it. What a nightmare. I can't believe what this village can be like at times. We'll be sure to set the record straight, won't we, girls?'

'We will indeed,' said Jo.

Emma was grateful for Bev's discretion and for her other friends' support. 'Thank you. It's just one of those things, I suppose.'

'Hah, do you remember poor Mrs Bell trying to get her husband a surprise new car for his birthday? Well, they had her down for having an affair and everything, with the owner of the garage in Seahouses. There had been a few sightings and comings and goings and that was it. They can put two and two together round here and make six, or even ninety-six, given a few days!'

Emma had to laugh, and she was relieved that the focus had shifted from her problems. The village did have its downsides occasionally, tittle-tattle being one of them, but most of the time it had been a blessing and huge support for her. She began to relax and enjoy the company.

They sat and chatted in the early evening sunshine, looking across the fields to the ruined remains of Dunstanburgh castle. The garden was mostly grass, with some pretty shrub borders, and some colourful pots of petunias beside them on the flagstones of the patio.

The Pimm's jug was getting low. It seemed surprisingly strong, and Emma began to feel quite lightheaded, though she realised she hadn't had a proper supper, just a quick slice of toast before she came out. Thank goodness for the crisps Jo had brought along.

'This Pimm's is gorgeous – what have you put in it?' Em asked. 'I can see the strawberries and the orange. Oh, and I can taste mint . . . '

'And cucumber,' Bev replied. 'Oh, and there's a splash of brandy too.'

Brandy, Em nearly spat out her drink. 'I thought it was Pimm's and lemonade? No wonder it's started going to my head.'

'Yeah, I'm feeling it a bit too,' added Ali.

'Well, when I read the back of bottle it said to add the "spirit" too.'

'Well, the spirit was probably the Pimm's.'

'Oh, I thought it meant another spirit, whatever you fancied, and I thought brandy would go nicely with all the fruity flavours.'

The four of them chuckled.

'Well, it is rather nice,' said Ali.

'Rocket fuel.' Emma pulled a face. 'Oh my.' She might not be able to get up for work tomorrow at this rate.

'Relax, you'll be fine. It was only a dash.' Bev winked across at Joanne.

'I know your dashes,' Emma replied. 'I have vivid memories of that G & T session here a couple of years ago.' In fact, they were not that vivid at all by the next day. But she had to smile, and the Pimm's cocktail did taste rather lovely.

They began to dip in to the box of chocolates Emma had brought.

'Wow, these are delicious, Em. You are so clever.' Joanne said.

'Just scrummy. What's in this one?' Ali asked.

'Salted caramel. Always popular.'

'Mmm, just melts in your mouth.'

'These are my favourites.' Bev spotted the white chocolate of the Eton Mess. 'Bloody lovely.' She popped one in whole, then she couldn't speak for a second or two. She took a sip of Pimm's. 'You know what, why don't you combine the two? Cocktail-flavoured truffles, bet they'd go down well.'

'Well, the alcohol flavours always work well. My boozy truffles, I usually use rum, whisky, and brandy.'

'You could do a mojito,' Jo suggested.

'Or an Irish coffee,' added Ali.

'Now that sounds a great idea. I might have to test out a few flavours. But I'm liking it. You might be on to something, ladies.'

'Sex on the beach!' Bev shouted out.

'Hah, can you imagine if I have "Sex on the Beach" chocolates for sale. The oldies might get offended.'

'Bet the young ones would love it!'

'You never know, some of the older ones might love it too! We're not all out to pasture yet.' Bev was grinning.

'I'm talking cocktails. Right, behave, you lot.' Emma tried to tone the conversation down.

'Do we have to?'

'Nah.' She loved the girlie banter really.

The four of them giggled, and chatted away until the sunset colours of gold, peach, and grey began to fade. The chiminea was doing a sound job of keeping them cosy, and Bev lit a hurricane lantern to give them a glow of light for the table too. Pete found them with an empty chocolate box, an empty jug and nearly at the bottom of a second bottle of Prosecco, all chilled-out and a little merry at 10:30 as dusk was settling around them. He carried out another seat to their table and sat down comfortably alongside them, his arm fondly placed around his wife's shoulders.

Ali's husband, Dan, came to pick her up at eleven, and they offered to give both Emma and Jo a lift home. Jo's bungalow was just down the street and around the corner and a light was still on there – her boyfriend waiting up for her, no doubt. They then dropped Emma off outside her shop. She said her goodbyes and thanked them for the lift. It had been a good night. The car pulled away. Emma had forgotten to put a light on and, heading in the back way, fumbled in the dark for her keys. Her little cottage seemed very quiet; even Alfie didn't raise his usual bark as Em turned the key in the lock. It might just be the effect of the alcohol, or leaving close friends after a special evening, but she suddenly felt a bit odd. There was no one to tell about her evening. There was no one to kiss goodnight . . .

Part Two

19

The days began to shorten; the cool whisper of autumn was now upon them and the first leaves began to fall. Late September, and Emma was still working long hours trying to keep her head and her finances above water. For every step forward seemed to come a slide back. A rise in cocoa prices had hit hard last week, so the chocolate callets she needed to buy from Belgium for her creations had risen in price dramatically. She was concerned that if she put her shop prices up to match, she'd lose trade. It often felt like she was playing a horrible game of financial snakes and ladders.

She'd been up late last night, making up one hundred mini boxes of truffles for the Seaview Hotel and a selection of milk, dark and white gourmet chocolate bars to restock her lovely new client, Lynda, at the Bamburgh deli. It being Saturday, Holly was in the shop today, so was able to cover for her. Em started loading up her car, ready to make her delivery to Bamburgh, a twenty-minute drive away.

'Right, Holly, I'm just away up to Bamburgh. You okay, here?'

'Of course. No worries. I'm in control.'

'Thanks, Hols. I won't be too long.'

'It's fine. I don't think I'm going to be rushed off my feet, somehow.'

'No, maybe not.' They had only seen a handful of people in the last hour; some had drifted past the window looking at the display, but hardly anyone was coming in.

For Holly and Adam, the young man from the hotel, romance was blooming. He still called in for his weekly chocolates for his gran, but also added a box of whatever Holly was fancying that day, which was very sweet. They had been on several dates over the summer and they also liked to borrow Alfie for walks on the beach, which her spaniel was very happy to accommodate. Adam seemed to be a real nice lad, and Emma was so pleased for Holly. It was lovely to see their young relationship developing.

Soon she was out on the open road, driving along country lanes that wound their way along the coastal route, a glimpse of sea here and there, roadside cottages and farms, hedgerows, fields with cattle and sheep grazing. She loved this county of Northumberland; it felt so much like home.

Holly went out the back to get some more packaging supplies and was coming through from the kitchen area, armed with colourful reels of ribbons and cellophane bags, when the shop door clanged, and a rather good-looking, if slightly on-the-old-side-for-*her*, man came in (not that she was looking, anyhow, she was so happy with Adam, but you couldn't help but notice some things). He reminded her of Gerard Butler in the film *P.S. I Love You* – tall, well-built in that muscle-toned kind of way. He had cropped brown hair and a short, stubbly beard.

'Hi.' She smiled.

'Hey.'

'Can I help?'

'Ah, are you the owner of the shop?' She half expected him to have an Irish accent, but no. Just English, with a hint of the local Geordie in fact.

'No, that's Emma. She's not in just now.'

'Oh . . . ' He seemed a little taken aback.

'Can I take a message for her, or anything?'

'Ah, no, that's fine. I was only bobbing in on the off-chance. It's okay. Thanks, anyway.'

He didn't seem interested in looking at the chocolate for sale; perhaps he was with Health and Safety or an Environment Agency or something, Holly mused.

The man turned to leave and she couldn't help but notice the muscled curve of his butt in his jeans. With his smart leather jacket and slightly rugged appearance he certainly didn't seem like a candidate for a Health & Safety inspector at all. Oh well.

Holly got on with making up some gift boxes ready to fill with truffles, and restocked some of the shelves. They'd have to start thinking about their Christmas display soon. Emma liked to have that all set up around

135

the October school half-term time and Holly loved the shop when it was decorated for the festive season – it was just so pretty. Before she worked there she'd loved popping in with her friends and she was *so* glad she'd escaped from the chip shop job. Just think, she'd have been skipping off to see Adam with greasy, fat-smelling hair – now it was all yummy chocolate aromas. They'd arranged to see each other later today, in fact. They were meeting after work, and he was – drum-roll – going back to her house to meet her parents for supper. Things were definitely moving on. In fact, she felt a little nervous for him, hoping that they would all get on really well. She texted him whilst there were no customers: *See you later x Can't wait for you to meet Mum and Dad! x*

Fingers crossed I'll make a good impression! x

You will. It'll be fine. After all, you made a big impression on me! xx ☺

Her dad would no doubt ask loads of questions, wanting to make sure he was a suitable lad, and Mum would be trying to make it all relaxed, and have a nice meal prepared for them for sure. The last she'd heard, her mum was making a roast chicken dinner – a roast chicken inquisition, ha!

Emma got back to The Chocolate Shop about thirty minutes after the handsome visitor had called.

'Agh, the traffic was awful coming back. Got stuck behind a tractor and a queue of vehicles on the coast road. Ten miles an hour. Sorry! So, all been fine here, then? No mad rush?'

'No, just the usual. Actually, that's not quite right, some guy came in, asking to see the owner.'

'Oh, okay. Don't worry, might be some sales person, or possibly a trading standards official or something doing a drop-in check,' Emma mused aloud.

'I don't think so. He didn't look that kind of official council type.' There was a second's silence, before Holly resumed, 'More of a Gerard Butler lookalike. Quite good-looking, really. I don't know why he was here, he wouldn't say.'

It couldn't be, could it . . .? Emma felt her pulse race. She found herself stopped in her tracks in the middle of the shop. 'Oh, umm, how old would you say he was? Hair colour?' She tried to sound casual.

'Not sure, maybe fortyish. Hard to say, he didn't really look old, but then his face was a bit lived-in.'

'Hah, tell me about it. And forty is not in any way old!' Emma laughed. Or maybe it was when you were only seventeen.

'Umm, brown hair, *built*. Stubbly beard. Attractive.'

OMG – it sounded *so* like him. Mr Kiss. The one and only time he turns up at the shop, and she wasn't bloody here!

'Did he say anything about calling back, or leave a number or anything?'

'Nope.'

Bugger.

Holly must have spotted the disappointment in her face. 'I did try.'

'Ah, it's okay.' Emma tried to sound less anxious. It

might have been anyone, after all. She was probably getting worked up over nothing. 'But when was this?'

'About a half-hour ago.'

He might still be here in Warkton. He might have gone to the beach, looked for her there, or just gone for a stroll like last time. Dammit, should she try and look for him, just in case? She could take Alfie out for a quick walk, check out the village and the beach, look in the dune car park for his vehicle? Some kind of jeep thing. She might never see him again otherwise.

She stopped herself. What on earth was the matter with her? It was probably just some customer who sounded a bit like someone she had met once for a few minutes, over nine months ago. What she needed to do was to get on with her work here, not go mooning about after some bloke. She was acting like Holly might, all seventeen-year-old angst. And, surely if he'd liked her enough, he'd have come back sooner than nine bloody months.

Emma headed to the kitchen to take out her misplaced energy on a batch of cappuccino truffles. At least she could always count on her chocolate.

The shop had just closed, Holly had gone home, and it – or more to the point, *he* – was preying on her mind. Curiosity needled at her – could that guy still be in the village? Should she at least try and look? She'd need to walk Alfie now, anyhow. With that, Emma was up the stairs, two at a time, grabbing Alfie's lead – *he* needed no encouragement – and was bounding back down by her side within seconds.

Emma scanned the street, the parked cars. Would she even remember what model of car it was from Boxing Day? She thought the colour had been grey . . .

What if it was him? And he was here, walking down the street or on the beach? She didn't even know what she would do if she did see him. Walk up and say, 'Hi, I'm that girl from nine months ago', or might she just hide in the dunes, take a sneaky look, chicken out and that would be it?

Would she even recognise him? But as she thought about that, already an image was forming in her mind. His face, his eyes, which were warm and intense, the stubbly beard. His smile. Oh, she'd know him.

Off she strolled down the main street, ducking her head into the village stores as she passed, giving a quick wave to Sheila behind the counter there, then on for a quick check of the harbour area. She spotted Beth, from the cottage just along from The Chocolate Shop, who was out with her new baby. Emma said 'hello' and couldn't resist a quick peek in the pram, gently touching a tiny week-old hand. She felt herself melt just a little. All those dreams that were so out of reach. 'She's so adorable, Beth. Just beautiful.'

Should she carry on with her mission, or was she just being silly and clutching at straws? Should she call in to the pub? But there was no vehicle like his in The Fisherman's Arms car park. She felt the beach might be her best bet, and at least Alfie could have a run off the lead there. She strode across to the start of the dunes, heading for the beachside car park where they had kissed all those months ago, thinking all the while: you crazy bloody woman. It might not even be him. And why would he go and walk on the beach to find her – it wasn't as though she was permanently down there.

The beach car park was empty. She wandered down one of the sandy trails that led through the dunes, coming out on to the wide stretch of crescent-shaped bay and scanning it. There was a middle-aged couple out rambling, and a lady walking her terrier. No one tall or well-built. No one that looked anything like Mr Kiss.

What an idiot! Acting like a bloody teenager at thirty-six. She let Alfie have a little play by the shoreline, then had to pick up his dog poo with one of the black scoop bags that were always amassed in her coat pockets. Hah, the guy was bound to turn up now, just as she was shovelling shit. But still nothing, nada. She scanned the beach one last time and felt her stupid little heart sink a little.

It had been worth a try, if only to satisfy her curiosity. But, it wasn't to be – probably wasn't even *him* at all, to be fair. Just some older, not-bad-looking guy.

She looked out across the sea, to the sky, her mind lost in the clouds for a moment. What the hell would Luke think if he could see her like this? What had she been thinking?

'Come on, Alfie. Time to go, boy.'

She'd better get back, back to The Chocolate Shop where she knew what was what and where she was meant to be.

20

The next day, Sunday, the shop door clanged and in marched a sprightly sixty-year-old, her hair set in neat grey curls, with a concerned-looking Adam in tow.

'It's so lovely to meet you at last.' The lady had the bluest eyes with a hint of sparkly mischief about them. She was thrusting her hand across the counter towards Emma.

'This is my gran. I couldn't keep her away,' explained Adam.

'Well, lovely to meet you.' Emma shook her hand warmly.

'It's Shirley, by the way.'

'Emma.'

'Yes, Holly's said so much about you, Emma, and about the shop here. I just had to come and see it for myself. Our Adam invited me across to the hotel for tea and cake this morning. He's doing so well there and I'm so proud of him – assistant manager, you know.'

Adam was grimacing at this point.

'Well, when my grandson said he had to call down for the turndown chocolates, I said why didn't I come along too? I'm so glad I did! Oh, and your chocolates are a real delight. Those coffee and orange creams, they're my favourites. They really do melt in your mouth.'

'Thank you. That's lovely to hear.'

Shirley finally took a breath and took in the shop around her. 'Well, isn't it delightful in here? I don't think I've ever seen such a pretty shop . . . the cottage building, the chocolate displays, everything about it. In fact, I can't believe I've never called in before. Though I'm not often this way to be fair. I live at Seahouses,' she explained, 'keep myself busy over that way, helping with the coffee mornings for the old people. The Golden Oldies' Club, we call it. Actually—'

Adam stepped in, wondering what his gran might be building up to next. 'That's great, Gran, but I'm sure Emma's busy. It was just a quick hello, and I need to collect the chocolates for the hotel and get back soon. I *am* technically working.'

'Ah, yes, of course. He's such a good boy.'

'Gra-an.' He cringed. 'You make me sound like I'm about six.'

'Sorry, Adam. Can't help myself.'

Emma had to smile. Despite the banter, they were obviously fond of each other.

'But, just quickly, Emma.' Shirley was off again. 'I was going to mention that we have a Christmas fete coming up for the old people. It's usually a smashing event and we have all sorts of stalls. A chocolate stall might go down really well for a change. It'd be profitable, for sure. It's always well attended.'

'Certainly food for thought, Shirley. If you could give Holly some more details, I'll definitely consider it.' Any schemes for raising the shop's profits were always welcome. 'But I'd best go and get these chocolates for the hotel now. They're all ready out the back, Adam. I won't be a minute.'

Adam smiled, somewhat relieved. 'Thank you.'

His gran was a one-woman whirlwind, but Emma had warmed to her straight away. She was obviously a doer, a busy bee. Emma identified with that working spirit and talking Christmas events with Shirley started her thinking about her Christmas lines. She'd soon need to source the more unusual ingredients and buy in all the festive wrappings. During a quiet spell that afternoon, she found herself daydreaming about the pretty gift bags and boxes you could order with snowflakes, holly, and all sorts of designs on, as well as ribbons and bows in golds, silvers, reds and green. Emma liked to have a different theme for each Christmas season, so would be looking for inspiration on which colours and styling she'd feature in the window display and throughout the shop. You could really go to town creatively at Christmas. She loved it when the shop looked beautiful and magical – just perfect for that special time of year.

The door went with its usual chiming clang. She looked up, and froze.

Oh. My. Word!

She'd known she'd recognise him if she ever had the

chance to set eyes on him again. Emma felt herself go all hot and flustered. He was still as gorgeous. She hadn't dreamt that up, or over-exaggerated in her mind.

'Hel-lo.' Her voice came out a pitch higher than usual.

'Hi.' His voice was as warm and smooth as tempered chocolate.

'So, you *were* real!' The words spilled out of her mouth and she cringed as she said them.

He gave her a broad smile in response. 'Yup.'

'And yesterday, Holly said that . . . ' Emma was finding it hard to form full sentences.

'Yes, I called in. Unfortunately, when you were out. I just hoped the shop hadn't changed hands since I met you.'

Thank heavens she hadn't had to give up the lease.

'Yes, it's still me here.' She gave a shy smile. 'Can I help with anything? Are you wanting some chocolates?' He might just be here to buy something, after all.

'Well then, what would you recommend?'

'Umm, the salted caramels are really delicious, and the choc-dipped fudge is always popular.'

'I'll try some of each then. Thanks.'

So maybe he was here just for some chocolates. She sorted the confectionary into gift bags, trying to still the trembling in her fingertips. She hoped no other customers would come in just now; she wanted time to have a chat, though she really didn't know what she was going to say. He'd cropped up so many times in her mind these past months. He couldn't just pick up the sweets and walk back out that door, could he?

144

Oh damn. He was paying, putting his wallet away, picking up the gift bag. 'Lovely shop you have here.'

'Thanks . . . Umm . . . ' She had to stall him.

'Ah . . . ' he started. They looked at each other.

She realised she still didn't know his name. 'I'm Emma by the way.' She held out her hand.

'Hello, Emma. Max.'

Max, yes that suited him. *So*, Mr Kiss was called Max. And he took her hand in his warm, steady palm.

'Max Hardy.'

'Nice to meet you . . . *again*, Max.' There, she'd planted the seed, reminding him of their moment together on the beach.

'I was actually wondering what time you close? As in, would you like to go for a drink or something, or a coffee, maybe?' His voice was calm, quietly confident.

Inside her head, she did a huge air punch, and a silent woop!

'Umm, well yes, that would be lovely. I finish at five, but I do have to take Alfie, my dog, out for a quick walk then.'

'Ah yes, Alfie. The spaniel.' He was nodding. 'Cute little guy, brown and white.'

Aw, he remembered.

'Yep, that's the one.'

'Well, I could always come with you for the walk – if you didn't mind, that is.'

'I don't mind at all. What about if we meet at the car park by the beach? Say five fifteen.'

'Great. And then, maybe, we can go for a drink together after that?'

'Maybe, yes.' *Heart performing double somersault flip.*

'See you soon, then.' He turned to go, taking his bag of chocolates.

She watched as he walked away from her to the door. Tall, muscular under those jeans, trendy leather jacket, dark cropped hair.

'Okay, see you later, Max.' She sounded cool, but felt very much like doing the Tigger bounce that Holly had perfected a few months before.

Was this *really* happening, after all those times wondering what had on earth had happened to him, where he had gone? Why had it taken so long for him to come back? Hopefully, she'd soon get the chance to find out.

The metallic-grey jeep was there, parked up by the dunes, looking out to sea.

Emma's heart squeezed upwards and felt like it was lodged somewhere in her throat. She wasn't sure if it was excitement or fear. And for a moment she was side-swiped by thoughts of Luke as a pang of guilt hit hard. What would he be thinking, her fiancé? Would it be breaking his heart to see her get all excited about meeting this guy? Yes, she knew Luke had left her, but in so many ways he still felt so close.

She felt a bit weird. There was still time to bolt. But then there was Max, standing up outside his car, giving her a small wave. She had been waiting for this moment. She felt a little sick. Alfie spotted him too and started pulling eagerly on the lead, propelling her towards him.

146

What if Max was a bit odd, though? She hardly knew him, after all. He might *seem* nice enough, but there could still be that axe in the boot of his car. She suddenly regretted agreeing to meet him on a half-empty beach, *and* she hadn't even told anyone where she was going. Would Alfie protect her? She'd never seen him act fiercely in his life – he'd more likely roll over on his back for a tummy rub or hand her over for half a sausage. Thanks to Alfie they were still hurtling towards Max.

'Hey.' He smiled at her, then knelt down to give Alfie a rub around the ears.

He didn't seem like an axe murderer. Emma smiled back. 'Hi.'

'It's good to see you again.' His eyes were a deep hazel-green, intense in a melt-you kind of way.

And with that look, she knew they were both remembering that moment nine months before in that very same spot.

Down on the beach, the early evening light was beginning to fade from a pale azure to a soft peachy glow and the waves rolled gently in to shore. Alfie was off his lead and happily scampering around.

'So . . . how have you been?' Max asked.

'I'm okay, thanks. You?'

'Great, yeah. So, how's life at the sharp end of the chocolate industry?'

'Pretty good. Keeps me busy and on my toes. Now we're nearly into October, business will start to build for the festive season and the run-up to Christmas is always hectic. I'll be having a permanent production line on the go in my kitchen.'

'Sounds interesting. I'm a bit of a chocolate fan.'

Oh, yes. It gets better all the time.

'Must admit it's more of a Yorkie bar or a Toffee Crisp with our breaktime bait for me, though,' he admitted.

'Hah – you heretic.'

'I'm sure I could be persuaded to try something more refined.' He grinned, with a cheeky sparkle in his eye.

Was there an intentional double entendre there? Emma wasn't quite sure.

They followed the shoreline along the bay, avoiding some small pools of salt water near the rocks left by the outgoing tide. The sands were soft underfoot, the walking easy.

'And what do you do for a living, then?' Emma asked. 'I don't think I ever found out last time?' In fact, she hadn't found out much at all.

'I'm a builder, have a small business of my own. I employ four men, year round, and contract in help on the bigger jobs. We do house renovations, extensions, occasionally a new-build. That kind of work.'

'So, have you always been in the building trade?'

'Well, my parents wanted me to be an accountant, that was my original path. I'd always been good at maths at school, and it seemed a sensible job. But I hated all the paperwork, the equations, pushing figures around on a page, stuck in an office. I couldn't see that being my life. It was never meant for me. So, I flunked out of uni after the first year, much to my parents' disappointment. I didn't want to be pushing a pen. I wanted to push a wheelbarrow, hold a drill, a saw. I was always tinkering with stuff at home, trying out DIY projects. Wonky shelves in my bedroom, that kind of stuff.'

Emma laughed, imagining him wielding hammers and saws as a teenager.

'Anyway, I got myself an apprenticeship with a building firm. Started off lackeying – all the shit jobs to start, basically, then learnt how to lay bricks, plaster, plumb. I worked hard, learnt on the way, until I got made a supervisor, leading the team on site when the owner wasn't around. Then Fred, the guy who owned the company, got ill, had to retire early. I got a loan and bought the business as a going concern. Never looked back. So, that's me.'

'Interesting. So you found your own way.' She liked that – that he knew himself, what he wanted, and had worked hard to achieve it.

'So, where's the company based?' She realised she was hoping it wasn't miles away, maybe down south, and this wasn't some kind of an annual trip.

'Hexham way.'

'Ah, okay.' That was about an hour's drive away.

'I live in a village just outside the town. It's small, friendly, suits me fine. We tend to do a lot of work in that area, as well as in Newcastle and Gateshead, so it's an ideal location.'

'Oh, I love Hexham.' She'd been there on several day trips. Had also been there with Luke for a weekend break. She remembered them walking down by the river, the stunning old abbey, the narrow streets, tea and cake at a gorgeous tea rooms, holding Luke's hand . . . She chewed the inside of her mouth. This was harder than she'd thought it would be – going for a walk with someone else. She looked out to sea for a second or two, concentrating on the flat, dark-grey line of the horizon. The swoop of a gull caught her eye nearer the shore, bringing her back to the here and now.

'Yeah, it's a nice town.' Max broke the silence.

'Yes . . . *So*,' She was edging nearer the question that was burning in her mind, 'how's your year been so far?' *Where the hell have you been these past nine months?* was what she *really* wanted to ask. But she hardly knew this guy. He didn't have to explain himself.

'Fine, pretty busy. We had a new-build project for two properties near the Close House golf club, Heddon way. Right fancy-pants stuff, six bedrooms each. That was fun, though the project manager was never off our backs. Kept me out of mischief.'

So maybe it was just work had kept him occupied. Maybe he just hadn't thought of her much 'til now.

He stopped walking, looked at her seriously. 'I'm sorry . . . that I couldn't come back sooner.'

Emma stopped too. Felt a little surge somewhere near her heart. Didn't know what to say.

'Things happened,' he continued, 'that I didn't expect . . . '

'Are you with someone?' Emma blurted out. She had to know. The way she was starting to feel just seeing him again, tied up in emotional knots already, it had to stop right here if he was in a relationship. She'd been through enough hurt and pain to know better than to go near a man who was already taken. Besides her own self-preservation, she wouldn't want to hurt someone else, some poor woman she'd never met. It was never worth it – life was complicated enough without hurting other people. If so, she'd thank him politely for walking with her, head off home with Alfie, and never see him again.

They stood facing each other, two figures on the expanse of beach. Two lives on the edge of something pivotal.

'No, no. There's no one else – not any more.'

The words were telling. *So, there had been someone.* 'Oh . . . ' So the kiss, that special moment she'd built up in her mind, had he been seeing someone all along?

'It's over now . . . I hadn't forgotten you.' His green eyes held her own. They seemed earnest, trustworthy, but how could you tell?

Me neither, she thought but didn't say. She felt fragile, unsure of what was going on here.

'Right.' She finally spoke. She wanted to know more, but they'd only just met and it didn't seem right to launch into twenty questions. She realised she hardly knew this guy at all: most of it had been created in her own mind.

'Well then, tell me all about life here at Warkton?' He sounded like he wanted the focus off him. 'What's been happening here? It looks pretty sleepy, but I bet there's more to it than meets the eye.' Emma felt that could apply to Max too.

'Well, it's been an interesting year. I've been trying to

source some new business as well as keep the shop going. And with making all the chocolates myself, that takes a lot of time.'

'Yeah, running your own business is never easy, is it? You work all hours, have your staff to look after, and there's a million rules and regulations to comply with. Our industry is a health and safety nightmare, keeping up with all the latest stipulations. Only right, really, but sometimes, honestly – how to climb a ladder training, how to hold a hammer?' He gave a wry grin. 'We've been climbing ladders and hammering nails in for twenty bloody years and now we've got to train for it?'

'Tell me about it. I've got to keep up with all the health and hygiene regs, and all sorts. It's not just making chocolate. I didn't know the half of it when I started.'

'I bet.'

'I do love it, though. Can't imagine doing anything else now. And yes, though the hours are long, it's great knowing the business is mine and I can run it how I want. There's no one to tell me what to do.'

They passed a middle-aged couple out walking their terrier. Said a brief 'hello' as the dogs circled each other, then resumed their stroll.

'What did you do before then? I take it you came to chocolatiering from another career.'

'Yes, I was a teacher. Secondary modern. I used to teach home tech, so cookery basically. That was the link really, baking, trying out recipes with chocolate.'

'Ah, okay.'

'Now teaching, a whole other ball game, that was. I

didn't mind the actual teaching of the kids. But the powers that be kept changing the rules, and the testing and paper trails you needed to record and monitor everything . . . The worst thing was, you'd just get used to one way, and then the whole system would change again. For me, it just felt that teaching had lost its heart, somehow. And then – then life changed for me, personally.' She stopped. It was her turn to hold back, realising she had said too much already.

Max politely left it at that, for which she was grateful, turning the conversation to movies and music.

They reached the far end of the bay where the rock pools started and carpets of lime-green seaweed clung to craggy outcrops, making walking over them slippery and dangerous. Alfie wasn't put off, however, and dived in to one of the deeper pools, then came out to shake himself off vigorously beside them – an arc of spray showering them with salty droplets.

'Thanks, Alfie.' Max shook his head.

'Oops, sorry,' Emma added. They both laughed. 'Think we'll turn around here,' Emma continued. 'It's probably time to be heading back, anyhow.'

The light was fading fast. A hint of dusky peach framed smudgy-grey clouds above a lilting sea. The evening colours were soft and fluid, like a watercolour painting, and already an autumn inkiness was creeping into the horizon. A solitary tern swooped gently above them in the sky. It was calm, peaceful.

Emma felt comfortable walking along beside Max, chatting. She found out he was an only child and his family now lived in the Morpeth area, but he'd been brought up in Newcastle. She mentioned her brother and his family. As they talked, she took a sneaky glance at Max's tall frame, his dark, cropped hair, lightly stubbled chin. He had a presence about him, and a calm inner strength as well as that muscular build that she had to admit was very attractive.

Nearing the car park now, and she felt a little nervous flutter in her stomach. Might he try and kiss her? Would it be as lovely as last time, or feel awkward?

'So, are you still up for coming out for a drink later?'

Should she? It had been really nice chatting and walking. He was easy company, and that way she'd get the chance to get to know him a bit more. But this was such unknown territory. Her very sporadic other dates had fallen flat on their faces since Luke. This felt strangely different, her emotions confused to say the least.

'Okay, yes,' she found herself saying. 'That'd be nice. The Fisherman's Arms in the village is good.'

'Great, I'm staying at a B&B down the road in Beadnell, so I can easily pop back. I'll go and shower and freshen up. Just say a time that suits.'

She had a sudden image of what he might look like all wet and naked in that shower, and felt her cheeks flame. 'Oh . . . ' She checked her watch. 'Let's say eight o'clock at the The Fisherman's Arms. It's just along from the harbour.'

'Yes, I know it,' he replied.

And they were there, back at the dune car park, virtually at the same spot as Boxing Day, and a knot of hopeful anxiety clutched inside her.

He moved to give her a very gentlemanly kiss on the cheek, his aftershave and the slight scratch of stubble provoking a flood of memories. But before it developed to something more she stepped away: she needed time to think about all this, not rush in.

'It's been lovely to see you again,' she managed.

'Yeah,' he replied. 'It's been good to see you too. Would you like a lift back to the shop?'

'No, I don't think I should spoil your nice clean vehicle with a damp, sandy spaniel, but thank you all the same.'

'Okay, well, catch you later, then. The Fisherman's Arms at eight o'clock.'

'Yes. See you.' Her head was in a whirl.

The water felt good pounding her body as she freshened herself up with some zingy mint shower gel. She didn't quite have enough time to wash her hair, as it was thick and wavy and took ages to dry and she only had an hour, which included a quick and easy supper of scrambled eggs on toast. Now her stomach felt a bit queasy. She couldn't quite pin her emotions down as she stepped out of the shower and grabbed a towel. She was kind of excited at the thought of meeting Max again, but then she felt incredibly nervous. Going on a date with this guy seemed too raw – too *wrong*.

Rubbing the towel over her slim body, she had a panicky moment. What if they did get on well? What if there were other dates, what if one day he might actually get to see her naked? Gulp. Instinctively, she pulled the towel tighter around her.

Jeez, her inner voice kicked back, you're thirty-six years old for goodness' sake, and you haven't even been for a date yet, just a bloody beach walk. And, even if anything *might* happen at some point, it's sex, it's normal. It was also something she had abandoned, after a couple of failed attempts, post Luke. So, the last time was what, four years ago?

And the hardest part was it wouldn't be Luke, would it? She felt herself go into a cold sweat, and a tear clouded her eye. How she wished it could be Luke – but it couldn't. It never would again.

Years, it had been years, and it still had the power to hit her like a sledgehammer. That was the way love hurt, when someone left you. But the days still rolled on, the sun rose, the sun set, somehow you managed to smile again, even if your heart was left in tatters.

Emma gave a small sigh and walked across the landing to her bedroom. She looked at Luke's photo in its wooden frame by the bed, remembering how excited she had felt that day when they first met in the school staffroom, how she couldn't stop thinking about him. She sat down on her double bed and popped on her plain white M&S bra and knickers.

Maybe she should just pull out now? Duck out politely from the drink with Max this evening – she could always leave a message with Danny in the bar. Yes, just let the memory of that first kiss and today's walk live on as a pleasant moment in her mind.

Hah, her alter ego kicked in, she was just being silly. It was a drink in a pub after all, not even a proper date. Yes, so Max was hunky, rather gorgeous and he seemed nice and friendly, but hey, there was a long way to go. She might never see him again anyhow after this evening. She pushed her mind to what she was going to wear, choosing jeans with a pretty flowery top. Emma erred towards the boho chic style of clothing for her time off. A spritz of perfume, some moisturiser, quick slash of pale peach lip gloss, and eyeliner and mascara – done. As per usual, her make-up routine was achieved in five minutes' flat.

She brushed her long, wavy red hair. She had to keep it up in a ponytail for work so it was nice to let it loose occasionally. It took a bit of taming, mind you, and when she washed it it needed tons of conditioner, or else the brush battled and generally lost.

She fed Alfie, then let him out into the back yard. After popping him back to his bed in the upstairs kitchen area, she was ready to go. She slung a jacket on, left The Chocolate Shop by the back door, and headed down the hill towards the harbour. By this time her stomach was in full spin mode.

21

She spotted Max getting out of his jeep from a parking space just in front of The Fisherman's Arms.

Her throat felt a little tight. *Here goes.* 'Hi.' She approached tentatively.

He turned and rewarded her with a gorgeous smile.

'Hey. So, you're about to show me where it's all happening in Warkton, then.'

'Oh, yes. If you want a pint of real ale and game of draughts – this is the place to come. We might even stretch to dominoes tonight.' Actually, that was on a Wednesday night.

She wondered if she should have suggested somewhere less rustic. They could have driven into Alnwick or some-where. And, thinking about it, everyone knew everyone in here. There would be no secrets about her meet-up with Max. The whole village would know about it in precisely three minutes' time.

Max held the bar entrance door open for her.

'Thanks.'

A silence descended on the bar as they walked in. There was a nod of acknowledgement to Emma from Dave, the landlord, and then eight pairs of eyes passed over Emma to settle on the imposter behind her.

'Everything okay there, Emma?' It was as though Dave was checking all was legitimate with this guy on her tail, and that she was safe and happy.

'Yes, fine thanks, Dave. You okay?'

'Sure, pet. Right as rain. Well then, what can I get you?' That was the signal for the regulars to start chatting again.

'Ah, a glass of white wine, please. Max?'

'I'll try a real ale. Do you do a pale?'

'There's a nice blonde.' Dave gave a chuckle at that. 'Tyneside Blonde . . . pint of?'

'Yep, I'll give that a try. Thanks.'

They got their drinks, Max insisting on paying, and Emma led them across to a table in the far corner. If they were going to hit the village grapevine soon, she didn't want every last word of their conversation repeated too.

The pub must hardly have changed since the fishermen came in centuries ago, with its low ceiling, dark-wood bar, slate floor, wooden tables and chairs – but at least some of the chairs had comfy seat pads now and a real fire was lit at each end of the room. They had opened out a new area for eating some years ago, which had lovely views out over the bay, and in the summer months there was a beer garden where you could enjoy fish and chips or crab sandwiches whilst you watched the boats bobbing in the harbour.

Old sepia photos on the walls showed the weathered fisherfolk of years gone by. The nets, the cobles, the smoking house for the kippers. There were only a few working boats and fishermen left now.

Max sat down in an old-fashioned spindle-backed wooden chair beside a small round table with a beaten copper top. 'Was it just me, or were everybody's eyes following us then?'

'Hah, yes. They were sussing you out. It's a small village. And they probably haven't seen me with a man in here before.'

'Ah, really? I thought they'd be queueing up.' He grinned.

'Not quite.' She tried to keep her tone light. 'I've kept myself to myself for a while.' That was as much as she intended saying on that particular matter. 'Anyway, by tomorrow the Warkton-by-the-Sea grapevine will be in full swing. And they'll be checking you out while you're here, too. You put a foot wrong and I daren't think what will happen!' She wasn't joking either. It was like having your own personal team of minders, or sometimes snoopers. The community spirit was great here, but at times it could feel a little overwhelming.

'I could be attacked with a draughts board or anything,' Max joked.

'They have a darts team too. So be extra nice to me.' She smiled.

'Oh, crikey.'

They chatted for a while, about the village, her shop, how she got into making chocolate and the courses she went on to train in its craft. She purposely avoided any mention of the main event that had altered her world so dramatically, that had changed the course of her life for good – just kept it vague about wanting a change of career. She moved the conversation on to talk about how things quietened off in October tourist-wise and how that gave her the chance to build up her stocks in advance, ready for the Christmas boom.

Emma felt she'd said enough about herself and wanted to find out some more about Max. 'So, you mentioned you have a building business, yeah? What are you working on at the moment?'

'We're halfway through two new-builds. Need to get them done in time for Christmas. As well as a big extension and renovation to a town house down in Jesmond, in the suburbs of Newcastle-upon-Tyne, for a friend of a friend. And there's a couple of new jobs I need to go and price, ready to start in the New Year.'

'Sounds pretty busy.'

'It is. But I'm not complaining. After the recession in the building trade this is food for the soul. I like being busy. In fact, I need to be getting off soon for an early start tomorrow. So my next drink will have to be a Coke. Can I get you another wine?'

She must have been nervous as she realised that she had nearly gulped the first glass down already.

'Yeah, sure, but let me get them this time.' Emma reached for her purse.

'Okay, thanks, but at least let me go to the bar.'

'Thank you.' She passed him a ten-pound note. Then

161

took a sneaky look at his rear in jeans as he strode to the bar; slightly rounded and firm, very nice. She quickly averted her gaze as she realised one of the locals had clocked her. A middle-aged lady with brassy-blonde hair who waitressed sometimes at the café in the next village was sitting on a stool at the bar. In fact, it was probably Max who the woman was clocking judging from the intent, slightly hungry look on her face as he approached the bar. He did make a fine figure of a man, Emma had to admit.

Was this just a quick trip to a place he liked, to say 'hello' whilst he was here, but then head back to his life, his work? *Would she ever see him again after tonight? And, would that matter?*

Max came back over with the drinks, then settled himself into his chair by the fire, stretching out his long legs. He sat quietly for a while, as if he was thinking about something.

'Emma, when I didn't come back for all those months . . . '

He had her full attention now.

'I wanted to, but I was with someone. That day, I was down there on the beach, just thinking about it all.'

Emma felt a jolt of shock. So, there was someone else involved. She really didn't know this guy, did she?

'We'd had Christmas together,' he continued. 'We were staying in a cottage just outside of Warkton. It was meant to be romantic and special, a chance to chill out and relax, but it turned into a bit of a nightmare. I had to get out that morning, get some air, do some

162

thinking. I knew inside that the relationship was wrong, that we weren't going anywhere. But it seemed pretty cruel to jack it all in just before Christmas, so I went along with it. But the holiday wasn't great, just went to prove how far apart we were. Different values, different goals . . . '

'But, you kissed me – and you were with someone then?' It started to sink in. All the while, her lovely memories of that kiss, and he'd been seeing someone at the time.

'I know. It took me by surprise too that day. Meeting you . . . you were just so different, like a breath of fresh air. Like I'd dreamed you up or something crazy. It just proved, even more so, that I had to finish it. I was all set to tell her. But when I got back to the cottage, I found her in pieces – she'd just had a call from her mum. Her dad had been rushed to hospital. He'd had a stroke.' Max paused.

'Oh no, I'm so sorry.'

'It's okay, he made it through, thank heavens. I was fond of them, her parents. Still am. And so I couldn't do it. How could I tell her then? So I stayed, pretended we were fine, supported her through it.' Max stared at the flickering orange flames of the fire. 'He's a lot better now. A few months in, when her father was recovering back at home, when he was stable and we knew he was going to be okay, then that's when I told her we were over. I couldn't pretend any more. It was still bloody awful doing it, though.'

Emma had never had to break up with anyone, had

never had to hurt someone like that. 'I can imagine that was hard.'

Max did seem a nice bloke, but this was more complicated than she'd realised. Even without her own troubles.

'Would it be all right to take your number?' he asked.

'Um.' She wasn't sure, especially after hearing all this. Wasn't it safer, easier, just ticking away at life on her own, with no added complications, no one else to have to worry about? Did she even have the emotional energy to start this weird dating game again? But a phone number wouldn't hurt, would it? Did she really want him to just walk away?

'Ah, yes, all right.' Emma sounded fairly cool, but as well as the fear that was mounting inside, a small part of her tattered heart was doing an air punch.

'I'd like to keep in touch, if that's okay?'

'Okay.' She read out her mobile number for him to input into his phone. 'It's not always a great signal here in the village, so you can always try the shop line too.' He took that as well.

'Can I take yours?' She didn't want it to work just one way.

'Of course.'

'So, its Max Hardy?'

And so there he was, safely stowed away in her phone. It gave her a little glow of hope.

They chatted some more, enjoyed the glow of the real fire, its cosy warmth. The pub was now a low murmur of conversation, with the odd rumble of laughter. Her friend Danny appeared, collecting glasses.

'Evening, Em.' He gave Max a nod as he took a good look at her companion.

'Oh, hi Danny, I didn't realise you were on tonight. This is Max, by the way.'

The guys shook hands, Danny definitely sussing Max out, before heading back to the bar. Emma had to smile.

Max glanced at his watch. It was gone nine-thirty. 'Sorry, but I'd better be heading off. It's a bit of a drive back to the B&B and I've an early start. I'll walk you back or I can drop you off?'

'Oh, I'll be fine. I'm used to it.'

'Ah, so you spend a lot of time down at the pub then, do you?'

'Hah, no, not really. I mean being out and about in the village. I'm always out walking Alfie.'

'But then you'd have Alfie to protect you.'

'I suppose.'

'I'd like to walk you back.' He seemed politely determined.

'Okay then, of course. Thank you.' She wasn't used to having someone to look out for her. She'd been on her own for a long time.

'I'd better watch out for you anyhow, or I'm pretty certain the guys in here will be on my case.'

'Definitely.'

He finished his glass of Coke and stood up. Emma pulled on her denim jacket, her wine glass now empty too. She waved across to the bar. 'Bye, Dave, Danny, folks.'

'Night, Emma. Night . . . ' Dave gave a polite nod

towards Max. The barflies gave curt nods and glances, no doubt still measuring the stranger up. She'd bet there'd be tongues wagging as soon as they got out of the door, wanting to know about the mystery man in the village.

The air was cool, and the pewter-toned moon was full and rather beautiful as they stepped outside. As they rounded the side of the stone pub building, they could see the harbour and the sea. All dark now, bar a dim orange street light, and the glint of moonlight on the choppy waves of the bay.

Max reached for her hand as they began to climb the hill. It was a surprise, and there was still all the stuff about his girlfriend flitting through her mind, and a mountain of fears and doubts within her, but despite all that she felt a little electric pulse run through her. He looked tenderly across at her in the half-light. Was this going to be the start of something? Did she want that?

It was only a few minutes' walk back to The Chocolate Shop and they were soon outside its bay windows.

'I use the back door after hours,' she said, as he paused by the shop front. 'I need to pop around by the alleyway to the back lane.'

'Okay, I'll see you to there, then.'

'Thanks.'

They were still holding hands. She let go to open the latch of the wooden back gate and they entered the small courtyard area.

She felt in her jacket pocket for her key. Found it. 'Well, that's me.'

Stood face to face, on the stone flags of the little courtyard, with a dusting of stars and the pale-silver glow of the moon above them, Max took a step closer. Emma held her breath. There was a second or two as he looked at her with his gentle green eyes, then he tilted his head ever so slightly. Slowly, she mirrored his movement, her heart finally ruling her head.

Then his lips were on hers, warm and welcoming.

It was every bit as good as the last time, all those months ago, and now even more sensual as they closed the gap between them. She could feel his palms firm against her back.

It felt like a proper, old-fashioned, if slightly hot-and-sexy kiss goodnight. She could almost imagine she was a teenager, and her dad would be shouting out of a bedroom window above them any second that that was enough and it was time to come in.

Hmm, it was a toe-curlingly good kiss.

It finished all too soon.

'Well . . . ' was all she could muster, as he pulled slowly away.

'Night, Emma.'

'Night.' She couldn't manage any more words, as her emotions were in a beautiful tumble.

He turned to go, stopped as he reached the gate. 'I'll ring you.'

'Yes . . . do.' And as he closed the gate behind him, she realised she was missing him a little bit already. She hadn't felt like that in a very long time.

22

'So, who is he then?'

'Who?'

'The hot guy you were spotted with last night? *And*, how come you haven't mentioned a word of this, you dark horse, you?'

'Hi, Bev. Right, well it all happened kind of fast!'

'So, tell all.' Bev sounded animated down the phone. 'In fact, I'm coming around. Put the kettle on, hun.'

'What? I'm in the middle of making salted caramels, and it's only eight-thirty in the morning.' News did travel fast around here and Emma wasn't sure she wanted to talk about it at all. It had been preying on her mind all night. All she could do once she was back on her own was think of Luke. Surely, it was *his* touch, *his* kiss she was really missing, not this other guy's? It was all so damned confusing.

'Well, I'll give you ten minutes to get them sorted, and you'll probably be needing a breakfast break. Knowing you, you've been up since six and haven't eaten a thing yet.'

She had been up early, and no she hadn't eaten. Her mind had been spinning, *and* to top it all there hadn't been a text or anything from Max as yet. The main part of her thoughts was it might be better if that never came, as it would save a lot of complications and stem this feeling of guilt, but the other crazy bit was frantically wanting to check her phone. He'd have got back to the B&B, gone straight to bed no doubt and been up for an early start to get to work, but she couldn't help checking her phone, could she?

There was no saying no when Bev was in this kind of mood. 'Fifteen minutes then – and how do you know he was hot anyway?' That wasn't the kind of word she could picture landlord Dave using.

'My mum's been into the café at Beadnell this morning for a coffee and toasted teacake. The woman behind the counter – Barbara, I think it is – spotted the pair of you last night.'

Ah, the woman at the bar. She'd thought she'd recognised her. No bloody secrets here, then. It was like living with the mafia. Mind you, she should have known better than to have arranged their first meet-up at the village pub. She might as well have strung Max up on a maypole in the centre of the village green, or a mast in the harbour.

'Max. He's called Max. I met him really briefly on the beach last Boxing Day when we were both out walking. Didn't really expect to see him again. Then he just popped up at the shop, on Friday afternoon.'

'And?'

'Not much to tell, really. We went for a drink, that was it.'

'Hah, there's more to this, I know there is.'

'He's nice. I like him. There, does that satisfy you?'

'Not really.'

There was no way Emma was going to mention the kiss. Two kisses, in fact, plus the little one on the cheek, not that she was counting.

'He has my number.'

'Aha!' She heard a clap then a clatter, as though Bev had dropped the phone, then retrieved it. 'That's bloody amazing! The ice maiden has thawed.'

'Ice maiden – is that what you call me?'

'Oops, yeah, did that just slip out? Soz, Em.'

'Thanks.' But, it was a fairly accurate description as far as men were concerned lately. No point thawing for all the silly twats out there. 'Well, then, that's it. I've told you it all now,' Emma continued.

'No, you haven't. I'm still coming over for that coffee. Get your cafetière out. I love that stuff you get from Berwick. With hot milk, please – perfect.'

'Not very demanding, are you?' But Emma was smiling as she spoke.

'I just know what I like.'

'Right, well, I need to get back to my caramel mix, before it spoils.'

'Okay, I'll see you soon.'

'All right, then.'

'I knew you'd see sense. Then you can tell me everything.'

Emma switched off her mobile, shaking her head with a smile. She then gently melted the caramel, adding the

170

sea salt carefully – too much would spoil it, not enough and it wouldn't have the right tang. She tasted a little, on the end of a spoon. Perfect. It would need to cool a touch, then she'd pour it into each chocolate-coated mould.

She put the kettle on, grabbed the cafetière and the freshly ground coffee. As she spooned it in, the smell of it was fabulous, rich and aromatic. Next, she bolted upstairs to change into her work attire of black trousers and white T-shirt, as she was still in her pyjamas and the 10.00 a.m. opening time would soon come around.

'I have fresh croissants.' Bev poked her head around the kitchen door.

'Let yourself in, why don't you?'

'Well, I knew if you were chocolate-creating you wouldn't get to the door, anyhow. And I guessed you'd have let Alfie out into the back yard already, so the door would be open.' Her friend grinned cheekily.

'True. Well, the kettle's just boiled, and I'm ready to take a break. So, thanks.'

Bev perched on a kitchen stool. 'So, how did it go?'

'Fine. He's a nice guy.'

'So, you like him?'

'Yes, I suppose I do. But I still hardly know him.'

'Ah, I think you get a good idea, even on the first date.'

'It wasn't really a date, Bev. He just turned up in the shop and then we had a quick drink in the pub, that's all.'

'Well, it sounded as though you were very cosy there by the fire.'

'Bloody hell! Is nothing private at all in this place?'

'Nope, we're just looking out for you. Don't panic, I don't have a webcam on you or anything.'

'It wouldn't surprise me.'

They both laughed.

'Thank heavens for that.' Em stood by the kettle as it came to a boil, ready to pour into the cafetière.

'So, what next?' Bev took a large bite of croissant.

Em brought the coffee across and a jug of hot milk. She took up the other stool.

'Oh, I don't know, Bev. I'm not even sure if I want a next. It still feels all wrong. Like I'd always be comparing him to Luke. When I kiss someone – it's just not like Luke. I don't know how I get around that.'

'So, you've kissed!' Bev clapped her hands together gleefully. 'So . . . it's not like Luke, but was it good?'

Em stayed quiet. Thinking about it, yes it was. But it felt wrong to admit it. 'It was different,' was all that she was prepared to say.

'Different good, or different sloppy and awful?' Bev needled away.

Emma really didn't want to talk about this any more. She just gave her friend a sharp look.

'Okay, sorry I asked.'

Em found herself smiling but then felt sad too. 'In all honesty, Bev, I just don't know if it's worth all the bloody effort. It's bound to just fizzle out. And then, there's mention of a girlfriend. He says it's all over, but I've heard that line before.'

'Ah.'

'Yeah, exactly. It just seems all too complicated.'

'Life's always complicated.' Bev gave an understanding smile.

They both bit into their croissants.

'Don't I know it,' Em smiled back.

'But he did come back to find you. And he did say that was all over.'

'Well, yeah . . . ' Em's voice trailed.

'Well then. So, do you think he'll ring?'

Emma felt her heart give a little flutter. Now *that* was the million-dollar question.

It wasn't just romantic woes that were on Emma's mind; her struggling finances were at the forefront too. Business was usually a little slower at this time of year, and every quiet week put more pressures on the rent fund. Emma lived a pretty frugal life as it was, not spending much on clothes or shoes, keeping her food bill to a minimum, and she never took a holiday away (though she didn't know where she'd head off to on her own, anyhow) so there weren't many other places to make cutbacks. Even with the hotel and deli new business, unless she could improve her income further, she would soon be struggling, even with the Christmas season coming up.

Oh, and on top of those concerns, she hadn't had a phone call or text from Max yet. Yes, it was still only the day after they'd met up, but he was there in her thoughts, along with the will he/won't he call burning question.

The door clanged. Emma looked up, shaking herself from her financial-no-call-gloom.

'Oh, hi, Holly.' Now that was a lovely sunny smile to cheer up a grey day. 'How are you?'

'Good, thanks. Just off the bus.'

Blimey, was it that time already?

'I was going to call up at the hotel to see Adam before I head home and I thought I'd say hi.'

'Aw, that's nice. Thanks. Time for a cuppa?'

'Yeah, sure. Even better if you can make it a hot chocolate?' Holly gave a grin.

Ooh, yes, that sounded a good idea. It was getting dark and the sky outside was a whirl of autumn leaves. It was now officially the season for hot chocolate with whipped cream and a chocolate flake.

Emma pulled through the two stools from the kitchen and set them up beside the counter; that way she could still keep an eye on the shop.

'So, how's it all going, then?' her assistant asked her five minutes later, as Emma came through, popping two lush-looking hot chocolates in front of them. 'Heard you had a date over the weekend?' Holly continued.

Not another one! The Warkton grapevine certainly spread like wildfire. Even old Mrs Clark had quizzed her earlier over her milk chocolate brazils order, after commenting that it was a bugger of a windy day.

'Six foot two, bit of a hunk, built like Gerard Butler, with the face to match,' Emma responded to Holly, tongue in cheek. May as well spill the beans and get it over with. The whole village was no doubt talking about it.

'Ah, so *that* guy came back then.' Holly looked serious.

Well, he did look a bit like Gerard Butler.

'So, what was he like?'

'Nice . . . we got on well.' Em was playing it fairly cool.

'Woo-hoo. Good for you, Em. It's about time you found a hunky man and a bit of happiness.'

'Thank you, I think. But just because everyone else is loved up doesn't mean I have to be too.'

'No, I know. But you're grinning about it, and that's nice to see. You have a little glow about you.'

Did she?

'Hah. Probably a hot flush,' Emma jibed.

'Mmm. Fab hot chocolate, Em.' Holly resurfaced from the mug with a creamy white moustache.

'Yeah, just right for a chilly autumn day.' Emma took a sip too. Chocolate didn't have to come just in a truffle or a box!

'You know what? I really like this, Em, sitting here, being able to chat and have a cosy drink. Especially this time of year, when it's nearly dark outside already.'

'Yeah, it is kind of nice.'

'There's nowhere like this in the village. Me and my mates, we can't really go to the pub at our age – well, not that I'd let on to my mother.' She smirked. 'And Adam's hotel is nice, but awfully formal and more for the holidaymakers, really. You need to open a little café, Em.' It was half said in jest. 'So I can have a chocolate stop and a natter on my way home. My friends would love it too.'

'And old Mrs Clark,' Emma took up. 'She was moaning about the climb up the hill again this morning and needed a little sit down. I brought her a chair out for a bit, so she could catch her breath. Actually – bloody hell, Hols, that's it! You're a star.'

'I am? And what's *it*?'

'What we need to do – have a little coffee shop so people can have coffee and chocolate by the sea: The Chocolate Shop Café.'

'Brilliant! Can we really do that? Have a coffee shop in here too? That'd be ace.'

'Well, it'd have to be fairly small because we don't have loads of room to spare in here. But yeah, why not? We could put some chairs and tables out in the front space. A couple of stools like this at the counter, maybe – and just there, by the bay windows, we could make those areas into window seats. Ooh, I can just picture it and I can smell rich, warming coffee, hot chocolates, fragrant teas . . . and all things *chocolate*.'

'Brownies.'

'Choc-chip shortbread.'

'Chocolate milkshakes.'

'Chocolate croissants.'

'Yum, sounds lovely.'

'Yes, I can just picture it, all cosy with cushions, snug for the autumn and winter months, when people want to come and shelter and get warm after being out walking on the chilly beach.' Emma was getting excited now.

'Or from a chilly school bus.'

'Absolutely. Yes, I can really see it. Hang on, that's it, I've got it – The Cosy Chocolate Shop Café.'

This could be it, Emma thought, the answer to her

prayers, the extra sprinkle of luck she so badly needed.

'Well then, cheers.' Holly raised her hot chocolate mug and they clinked cups together.

'Cheers, Holly – to the Cosy Chocolate Shop Café.'

23

Emma's mind was spinning in bed that night, but for a change, not about men or money. If she really was going to make the shop into a café as well, how long might it take to add a little seating area, get it furnished, and source the extra kitchen equipment and crockery she might need? Furniture-wise, all she needed to buy (or even better, with finances tight, rummage the odd house clearance or auction room) were two tables, and perhaps six chairs. She could use the two stools from the kitchen to make a counter bar, but she'd need to find a carpenter or builder to make the window seats – hopefully, at a really good rate.

One very lovely builder came to mind, but it was way too early to ask for help like that. And she still needed that particular builder to call her! The thought made her stomach go squishy. It was still only two days since their 'date', and despite her concerns she realised how very much she wanted to hear from him.

Surely, if he liked her, he'd have phoned by now, or

even sent a brief text. Was he doing his disappearing act all over again? She felt like a teenager, all angsty. Damn, she wasn't cut out for all this emotional stuff. She'd been off the dating scene for far too long. Were you still meant to wait for the guy to call you? Did you go ahead and call him? She had his number, after all. Did you send a text? If so, how to phrase it? She didn't want to look desperate or needy, but she didn't want him to disappear into thin air again either.

The next morning, she'd had several tourists in buying fudge and truffles to take home to loved ones, and someone else wanting a gift for the pet sitter. Emma did a 'Thank you' bar in both milk and dark chocolate with white squirly chocolate writing. They were very popular. At different times of year she'd write festive messages on them, and there was a 'Happy Birthday' version too. It'd soon be time to start making some of the 'Merry Christmas' ones, she mused. Then her mind wandered to a 'Text me!' message. Hah – she could send Max a chocolate message, lol – that was if she had known his address.

The day flew and it was soon past five o'clock. She locked the shop's front door, flipped her pretty chalk-painted sign over to closed, and made her way to the kitchen for a quick cup of tea, bite of toast, and then another hour or two of chocolate crafting. It was time to start planning for Christmas, what to make and when, although much of it was instinctive now, with six years under her belt.

This evening she was going to craft some old favourites, the best sellers. Her customers loved the salted caramels, mint-choc discs, whisky, rum and brandy truffles, brazil nuts covered in milk chocolate (Mrs Clark), and her Northumbrian fudge, both the plain and her special recipe made with Alnwick Rum and raisins. She'd concentrate on the fudge, a few chocolate bars and the mints tonight, and then have a truffle-making session tomorrow.

Her tempering machine was already on the go, keeping the chocolate at just the right temperature and consistency – her best investment yet. She had started making everything by hand, initially, tempering the chocolate in a bowl, which was fine and very craftsmanlike, but it gave you a bloody sore arm and wrist! And, with Emma being the sole chocolatier, when the shop grew busier and she needed plentiful regular supplies, it was just not practical. She still did some tempering by hand at her busiest times, and when the mood took her, but her trusty machine was her best friend in the kitchen.

She had just started pouring dark chocolate with mint sugar crystals into the moulds when her phone started buzzing in her pocket. Agh, no. She didn't want to spoil the mix, as it would start solidifying in the bowl, so kept going until the tray was full. By which time, of course, the ringing had ceased. She fumbled quickly in her pocket for her mobile. Missed call – Max! Agh, bloody typical – but yes, her heart gave a little flip, *he'd called.*

Okay, calm down, Em. Put the bowl to soak in the sink, wash your hands, and then call him back, whilst he's still hopefully available.

Deep breath . . . call back . . . go. Ringing tone . . .

'Hi. Is that Emma?'

'Yeah . . . hi.'

'Thanks for calling back.'

His voice had a lovely melted chocolate tone over the phone, with his soft North East accent.

Emma found herself smiling. 'Yes, I'm sorry I missed it. I was right in the middle of chocolate making. Filling the moulds. Crucial point.'

'No worries. So, are you okay?' He sounded slightly nervous.

'Yes . . . ' She found herself at a loss for words, and her heart seemed to be beating double time. She needed to buck up.

'I enjoyed Sunday evening,' he added.

'Me too, thank you,' she forced out.

'Can we do it again sometime?'

Despite the excitement at hearing his voice, all the doubts and fears came flooding back on hearing that question. That would mean taking things further, getting to know Max more, prising open her heart – for what? If she didn't really like him once she got to know him, what a waste of bloody time and energy. And if she did? Somehow, that seemed more confusing and downright scary. Could she really put herself through all that again?

She felt a bit sick.

'Em? Are you still there?' His tone was gentle.

'Yes . . . Sorry, just thinking.'

'Dangerous pastime, that.'

'Don't I know it.' She had to laugh.

Oh bugger, he sounded so bloody nice *and* he'd just made her giggle.

It's only a date, a little voice egged her on. *Find out a bit more about him, and if you don't like him after that, or still have concerns, then that it'll be it: hasta la vista, baby.*

'O-kay.'

'Don't sound so thrilled.'

She could hear the amusement in his tone.

'Sorry. Yes, that would be lovely.' She made herself sound upbeat. The poor chap. Boy, he didn't realise what a heap of troubles he might be taking on here! If he ever found out how much baggage she came with, he'd prob-ably be putting the phone down right away.

'Great. I could come back up this weekend, if that's okay – unless you're busy?'

'Only busy with chocolate. I think I can spare some time.' She sounded way too cool, she knew. Oh yes, she could maybe fit Mr Rather-Gorgeous Hunk into her spare hour on the weekend. 'Yes, I'd like that,' she corrected herself.

'Well, I've got to check a building job on Saturday morning, but then I could come on up. Maybe stay over Saturday night?'

Her heart did a somersault flip and double forward roll. It might even win the Olympics at this rate. '*Sorry*?' Had she heard right? That was extremely presumptuous of him, though her mind was rather warming to the thought, and doing all sorts of naughty things with pictures appearing of his imagined bare torso, which were not off-putting in the least. But blimey! He was a bit full-on; maybe she was right to be cautious.

'Hah, I meant in a B&B, or maybe book a room in that pub we had a drink in.'

'Oh right, yes, yes, of course.' She felt flustered. Now, what would he think of *her*, jumping to conclusions like that?

'Of course, now you're offering . . . ' He let the words dangle, as Emma stood, silently stumped, until he burst out laughing, and the tension between them popped like a bubble.

'Yes, a B&B,' she confirmed hastily. To make things *quite clear* from the start. She was just not that kind of a girl.

They chatted a little more about work and their past couple of days. He said he'd been extremely snowed under which was why he hadn't rung sooner. He then asked after Alfie, who she remembered would actually need his post-supper walk very soon. And then Max drew the conversation to a close. 'So, I'll be up Saturday afternoon, then.'

'Yes, great. I'll have to work until five when the shop closes, though.' She couldn't afford to lose business. 'But I do get Sunday morning off.' She usually used the time to make more chocolates, but she could easily reorganise her weekend, and work later on Friday night.

'Great,' he echoed. 'Maybe we could go for a walk, take Alfie out Sunday morning.'

'Yes, I'd like that.'

'And Saturday evening, have a think on a nice place to go for supper.'

'Okay, will do.'

This was sounding like a proper date. And no Malteser-Man thigh-rubbing date at that. Actually, if it had been Max trying to tease his way in to her Maltesers pack via her inner thigh, from the way she was feeling right now, she might well have let him!

24

She really wasn't sure what to wear on this date – and yes, this really was a proper date, which made it feel far more pressured.

Max had texted several times since he'd contacted her. After having a chat and a bit of a heart-to-heart with Bev, Emma had sent him over a couple of suggestions for suitable supper venues – away from the prying eyes of the village this time – and he'd booked a table at Henry's, one of Bev's recommendations, a bistro in the pretty coastal town of Alnmouth just down the coast. Emma hadn't been sure herself where to suggest as it had been such a long time since she had eaten out, other than a quick snack in The Fisherman's Arms or at Bev's house. Finances hadn't stretched to a slap-up meal-for-one for many years.

So, back to the outfit. She'd already rejected jeans – too casual; the black trousers – too work, and a low-cut top – too obvious. Back to the wardrobe. Dresses: there weren't a huge selection of those, but she gave them a frisk over. Her Little Black Dress? Oh, she'd worn that at a Christmas Ball many years ago with Luke in Durham; they'd gone along with a group of teachers and had had such a lovely night. She sat down on the bed for a few moments, crushing the velvet to her; disappointingly, it only smelt of her, not him.

What on earth was she doing, going out on a date with another man? This just didn't feel right. But Max would be on his way by now. It would be downright rude to cancel at the last minute.

She carefully placed the black cocktail dress back into the wardrobe, then found a green floral print wrap-around that looked promising. Not too smart, not too casual, and a colour she loved – green always contrasted well with the red of her hair. She sat at her dressing-table mirror, the dress now on, and she popped on some red lipstick which looked rather bright compared to her normal gloss. She even ventured so far as eyeshadow.

She could do this thing, she told herself. It was just a meal after all.

Her phone pinged. A text from Bev: *You okay? Chosen your outfit?* x

Em answered: *Yes, the green dress. x*

Yes, I remember that one – gorgeous, good choice! Followed swiftly by another message: *You can do this. It'll all be fine. I'm so proud of you* x

Emma knew her game – she was definitely trying to make sure Em didn't back out at the last.

She was ready; well, as ready as she ever would be,

186

and began checking the road from her upstairs window for any sign of Max. This was all such unknown territory. The odd date she'd had so far (*odd* being the appropriate word) had felt strangely safe. She had kept her distance, realised it was never going to work, and then called it a day. Her technique was to just lie low for a while and not answer their calls – they soon got the idea.

But this . . . *this* felt unnervingly different.

Ooh – there he was. The grey jeep had parked outside and there was Max stepping out, holding what appeared to be a bouquet of flowers. She took a deep breath and headed down the stairs.

Max was hovering at the entrance to the shop, dressed smartly in a navy jacket, white shirt, and dark jeans, looking slightly nervous in a cute kind of way. It was already dark outside, and the street lights glowed as a backdrop.

Max gave her a polite kiss on the cheek as he handed over a beautiful bunch of roses and carnations in shades of pink and white. Their scent was just delightful. She hadn't been given flowers in such a long time. Aw, he'd made a real effort.

'Your carriage awaits, madam.' He gave a mock bow.

'Just give me one second. The flowers, I'll put them in water. Don't want them to wilt, whilst we're out.'

'Of course.'

Emma was as quick as she could be popping them into cool water, and was soon back out, ready to jump into the passenger side of the jeep.

'You look amazing, by the way . . . ' Max grinned across at her.

Emma positively glowed.

The bistro was lovely, set in an old stone house on Alnmouth High Street. They were ushered to a cosy corner with a candlelit table for two. Very nice, very romantic. No wonder Bev had set her up here; Emma would have chosen something far more casual.

They ordered a glass of wine each while they perused the menu – all sorts of delicious options. They talked about how nice it seemed there, and their work that week – safe ground.

Emma chose sea bass for main, served Asian-style with ginger and sweet chilli (she might have room for dessert, that way, not having a starter) while Max plumped for a fillet steak, medium rare. She sipped her wine, a cool, crisp Chablis, as they chatted.

Something had been troubling Emma, and she needed to know before she let herself get carried away with thoughts of this guy. 'Max . . . your girlfriend. How long were you together for?'

He seemed a bit surprised by the turn in conversation. 'Oh, just over four years.'

Wow, so it wasn't some quick fling or anything. No wonder he'd grown fond of her parents.

'Why are you asking? That's all over, you know. I'm not the kind of guy to mess with two women. Not my style at all.' He looked serious. 'And what about you?' He turned the conversation round. 'You seem so cautious.

188

So, come on Emma, what is it with you? Did some guy mistreat you, let you down? It doesn't make us all bad, you know.'

'No, I know.' She tried to smile, but her face felt tight. 'It's not that.' She found she couldn't answer further. This was the wrong time and place to drag out her past. She wanted to just sit, eat, relax, and try and enjoy the here and now. It was her fault for quizzing him first.

His brow wrinkled, but he realised that was as much as she was going to say on that this evening.

'Right, then,' he lifted the mood. 'Are you ready for quick-fire round?'

'What?' Em was confused.

He started firing questions, like they were on a speed date. 'Your age, madam?'

'Ah, thirty-six. Yours?' she fired back.

'Forty.'

Ah, so she had guessed right. He looked damned fine for a forty-year-old, mind.

'Okay, music. Favourite band?' he asked.

'Coldplay.'

'Good choice.'

'Favourite song?' she blasted back, grinning.

'Ooh, "Viva la Vida". Yours?'

'Coldplay tunes? "Clocks", "Fix You", "The Scientist".'

'That's cheating, you're only allowed one.' But he was laughing.

At that point, the meal was served. It looked and smelt amazing. Emma realised that other than going to James's or her mum and dad's her food options had been extremely boring of late.

In between delicious mouthfuls, he asked which was her favourite movie. She settled on *The Time Traveller's Wife*, that was such a special film – she'd loved the book too.

And then, he asked, 'Last meal on earth?'

The silence was tangible, as she felt her eyes fill with tears, and her stomach convulse. She excused herself, found the ladies' toilet and had to just sit quietly on the loo for a while, taking slow, deep breaths.

Her phone pinged with a text, surely it wasn't Max, she hadn't been gone that long. It was Bev. *How's it going? x*

Fine x she texted back. How could she even start to explain?

It wasn't Max's fault – how could he have known? So, she either had to ask to leave now, and get him to drive her home, but that would surely spoil his meal and be the end of it all, before it had even had a chance to start, or she stayed, tried to finish her supper, though her stomach was still quaking, and try and make conversation. She blew her nose, wiped her eyes, reapplied some lipstick, and headed back out.

'Are you okay?' he asked as she reached their table, looking genuinely concerned. 'If you're not well, we can just go.'

'No, sorry about that. I'll be fine.'

Her fish had gone cool but she forked it slowly. Max had already finished his steak dish.

'Now, that was absolutely delicious.' He sat back. 'Good little place you recommended here, Emma. Been here often?'

'Never,' she admitted. 'It was Bev's choice, my friend. I don't get to eat out that much.'

'Ah . . . well, maybe we can change that.' Hinting that there might be more dates, more *them*.

Emma put on her bravest face and rallied, even managing to share a chocolate pudding for dessert, a gorgeously oozing melt-in-the-middle creation. It just had to be done. They had a spoon each and pretty much demolished it within seconds.

'Should have guessed you'd like chocolate. I hardly got a look in there,' Max jested, with a grin.

'Now stop exaggerating, you. Your spoon was dipping in pretty quickly, I can tell you.'

They both realised the double entendre and Em started giggling. It was lovely to be laughing.

He was easy to talk to, not bad at all to look at across the table, he liked chocolate. She felt she ought to give him a chance. His hand slipped over hers on the table top at one point and she felt a little jolt of surprise, then decided to leave her own hand there. It still felt strange, different, the thought of being with someone else, but she decided she should just go with the flow for once in her life. They shared a warm look, a gentle smile. Emma felt strangely vulnerable.

When coffee was served, she took her hand away to hold the cup. It was soon time to leave, and make the twenty-minute journey back. They shared the bill, Emma insisting; she didn't want there to be any expectations at all, and she liked to pay her own way, despite her troubled finances.

They parked up outside The Chocolate Shop, her little haven. She could ask him in for coffee. But they'd already had coffee, and she was feeling way too confused about all this as it was. They were still in his vehicle, so she said a friendly 'thank you', and leaned over to give him a polite kiss on the cheek. He turned his head to meet her lips with his – and ooh!

My, he was such a good kisser, stirring up all kinds of dangerous feelings and sensations that hadn't surfaced for a very long time. It was like he'd rewired her body.

But it was purely physical, she reminded herself. Hah! She could hear Bev's voice in her head now, hilariously: 'It's about bloody time. Just get yourself back in the saddle, girl!' which she ignored. She could get this so wrong by rushing into things and end up getting herself hurt. Why spend all these years keeping herself safe? She felt a little vulnerable already, so where the hell did it go from here? Nowhere in a rush, that was for sure. All this relationship stuff felt rather like an emotional Russian Roulette. She had let herself get carried away enough as it was.

'Goodnight, Max. Thanks for a lovely meal, and a lovely evening.'

'You're so welcome, Emma.' He looked slightly disappointed as she moved to get out of the jeep, but he seemed fine. 'I've had a great time too,' he continued. 'Tomorrow?' he asked. 'Are you still free for a walk in the morning?'

Oh yes, she had already agreed to that. It was only a dog walk, and she'd have to take Alfie out as it was.

'Ah, okay, yes, that'll be nice. Come here for, say, ten?'

'Great, will do. Sweet dreams, Em.'

'You too. Night.' And she felt like someone had shaken her up like a snow globe as she watched him drive off, and head down the hill to his harbourside B&B, wondering where her emotions were going to settle.

25

Emma woke early, all the emotions of last night flooding her brain. So, she and Max were about to go on another beach walk together, stirring up memories of that first meeting on Boxing Day.

She got up and made herself a cup of tea, carrying it through to the small living room where she sat for a while with Alfie. From the cottage window, she could see it was a bright autumn day, just perfect for a wrapped-up, sandy stroll.

'Well, Alfie, what do you think, hey? We'll be meeting Max again soon.' She didn't dare mention the 'walk' word, as the poor dog would think it was imminent. She glanced at her watch; crikey, it was only 7.00 a.m., still three hours until they were due to meet at the beach. She might as well go and do some chocolate-making, or maybe make a tray of fudge. It would keep her busy, help allay the sugar-rush feeling of anticipation that was currently racing through her veins.

* * *

At a quarter to ten she heard a steady knocking on the shop's main door. Em headed through, expecting to see some tourist hovering outside who hadn't spotted the closed sign. But there was Max, looking rather gorgeous, holding a takeaway coffee, and grinning through the glass.

She unlocked the door and let him in. 'Hi.'

'Morning. Sorry I'm early, hope that's okay. But I've just been hanging about after breakfast and thought I may as well wander up and meet you here instead.'

'That's fine. I was up early too. Come through a sec.'

'I enjoyed last night.' He looked serious as he said those words.

'Me too. The meal was lovely . . . Well, I just need to grab my coat and get Alfie's lead, ready for the walk.' She headed towards the stairs, turning to say, 'Grab a stool in the kitchen if you like. I won't be long.'

'Okay.'

She dashed upstairs, took a quick glance in the mirror, popped on some lip gloss, and flicked her fingers through her long hair. She grabbed her coat and scarf (the very same red tartan one that had started this whole thing off), then called for Alfie and took his lead off the coat peg. Alfie needed no encouragement and was leaping down the stairs ahead of her, tail wagging wildly as he reached the back door.

'Max, come through,' she called. 'Alfie's banned from the kitchen and shop, so if you can just hang on with him here, I'll go and quickly lock up out front.'

'Right.' Max smiled as he came into the rear hallway.

'Hey Alfie, good to see you, mate.' He crouched down to pat the spaniel's head whose tail wagged even more.

Emma joined them. 'Ready.'

They set off down the village street, passing the quaint stone cottages that led towards the harbour. Fishing boats rocked on gentle waves within the harbour walls and one or two of the cobles had been pulled up on to the sandy shingle of the small beach. Nets, lobster pots, and colourful floats lay bundled up on the shore.

'It's a gorgeous morning,' Max commented.

'Beautiful. I love these crisp autumn days.'

'Hope you didn't mind me getting to you early?'

'No, no, not at all. I've been up since seven anyway. I usually am. That's when I make most of my chocolates, early morning. I can work away undisturbed. Whereas once the shop is open, I'm limited as to what I can do. I can't really stop in the middle of making something or it'll all be ruined.'

'Wow – you work long hours then.'

'Yep. All part of the job. But I couldn't do it if I didn't enjoy it. And I do, I love it.'

'Don't you ever get tempted to dive in and eat them all?'

'Sometimes,' she laughed. 'But most of the time, just one or two is enough. Probably as well, or I'd be the size of a house. It's nice testing out the new flavours, mind.'

'So, you don't ever get sick of chocolate?'

'No, not yet. And the job's not just the making of it. I love the creative side, designing the displays, making up all the bags and tags, deciding which colour ribbons and bows to use. It can be quite therapeutic.'

'Hmm, each to their own.'

'So, how do you find your job? What's it really like in the building trade?'

'Well, I enjoy it. It's very physical, often quite hard manual work. I still like to keep my hand in, practically, with the tradesmen. And I'm always trying to keep the team motivated, getting in the right building supplies, coordinating contractors – it can be a bit of a juggling act at times, though.'

'Yeah, that's very different from my role.'

'But I do get a real sense of satisfaction when a job's done well and the clients are happy. Seeing my customers' faces when their house or extension is finished is great.'

How would she feel seeing The Chocolate Shop Café all finished, with its window seats made and colourful cushions in place? The new coffee machine on – well, that might take some time, with finances the way they were, but still. Just imagining that, she knew she had to go ahead and make her coffee shop happen soon, and she'd need to act quickly to take advantage of the pre-Christmas run-up.

'Max, I've had an idea for the chocolate shop. Can I run it by you? Get your professional opinion?'

'Of course.'

So, as they passed the harbour and reached the dunes on their way to the beach, they chatted about Emma's plans for The Cosy Chocolate Shop Café.

'Well,' Max responded, 'the only real building-type issue would be creating the window seats, by the sounds of it, and that's more of a joiner's job, so it should be fairly easy to get done. Then, I suppose you'd want to give the shop a repaint and freshen it all up.'

'Yes, a nice fresh shade on the walls to mark the changes. I'm not averse to a spot of decorating. I did my lounge and bathroom myself last year.'

'You're going to be busy, mind, if you're planning to take that on yourself, especially if you're already up at seven every day making the chocolates.'

'I will, won't I? But funds are a bit tight at the moment. Had a pretty challenging rent hike this year,' she admitted, 'so the more I can do myself the better.' That thought was rather scary. She'd be hectic enough as it was with the Christmas run-up; she'd have to get the alterations done as soon as possible, before it got even busier, and she couldn't afford to close the shop for long – a day or two at the most, to get the major work done. But to have a café . . . it would be such a lovely, cosy space for people to come to. And hopefully (after the initial, carefully budgeted expenditure) bring in some much-needed extra income to keep her and The Chocolate Shop afloat.

'I do have a joiner that does some work for me,' Max stated, 'but he's pretty much flat out at the moment. And someone more local to Warkton might be better, save on additional transport costs, as you will have to consider their labour charges and materials. It shouldn't be a particularly long job, though, making the window seats – a day or so, I'd say. I could measure it up for you when we get back if you'd like, just to get an idea of the job.'

'Great, thank you. That will give me a starting point and then I can get a couple of quotes.'

She wasn't quite sure where the money might come from for this, but hopefully it would soon be recouped as extra revenue thereafter. She could possibly ask her mum and dad for a small loan to cover the initial costs, but she'd hate to let them down if it didn't work out. She'd do some more research and then go and visit them to mention her plans. It'd be lovely to catch up with them soon, anyhow.

Max and Emma wound their way down to the sands, the beach opening out before them, metallic-grey and white waves frothing to the shore. Seaweed, shells, and the odd piece of driftwood were strewn in a staggered line, marking the high tide. She let Alfie off the lead and he bounded away joyously as they walked down to the flat, smooth sands nearer the sea.

They reached the shallow stream that made its way down the beach and out to the sea. Emma looked down, realising that, in her rush to get ready, she had left on her deck shoes. She usually put wellies on for her sandy dog walks, damn. The stream was an inch or two deep, and would certainly trash her footwear, as well as leaving her with soggy socks and cold, wet feet.

Max spotted her looking down at her footwear. He had heavy leather work-style boots on that would be fairly waterproof. 'I'll give you a piggy back. Come on.' And with that, he started to crouch down, for her to clamber on his back.

'You sure?' At five foot nine she was fairly tall and wasn't exactly the lightest of women. She'd probably break his back.

'Of course. Hitch a ride.'

She started laughing. She hadn't had a piggy back since mucking about with her brother years ago as a kid. 'O-kay, here goes.' She clambered on, expecting to hear a groan as he realised her weight, but he seemed fine. His back felt very firm and muscular as she clung on. Max reached his arms back around behind him to support her thighs.

'And they're off!' he shouted, as he started hopping across the stream, half-leaping at times to balance a foot on the shallower parts.

Emma couldn't stop giggling, having to grasp even tighter on the mini leaps.

Max gathered momentum as they reached the other side of the stream and kept going in a clumsy jog, veering towards the dunes.

'I'm fine now – put me down! Aagh, we're going to crash,' she shouted.

A toddler stood staring with his parents as the pair of them dashed clumsily by, both laughing hysterically.

'I'm looking for a suitable landing pad,' Max shouted over his shoulder as he kept going, with Emma clinging on like a monkey, but all the while feeling herself sliding lower.

They reached the softer sands at the edge of the dunes, and Max tipped her gently over to place her into a sandy hollow at the start of the marram grass. Unfortunately, he somehow caught his foot on a root and toppled just about on top of her. He steadied himself with his arms at the last to stop a full-on crush. His upper body was then balanced just centimetres above hers, with his lower half in full, warm, and very manly contact.

'Oh,' was all she manged to say. The wind had been knocked out of her sails by the tumble, but more so by the fact that this gorgeous man was now up close and very personal. She was so aware of his body weight on hers, in *just* the right position, his hazel-green eyes fixing her own intensely, their lips mere centimetres apart. And it felt, scarily, just right. She could just go ahead and bury herself in his kiss, and they might just carry this on back at her cottage . . .

Some deep, sensual instinct was flaring within her, but she also had in mind her recent fears, and then she remembered the young family who were most likely watching their antics from halfway up the beach.

'Max – the family.' And she made a gesture back towards the shore.

'Ah, yes. Of course.' And he rolled off her, with a cheeky grin plastered on his face that left her smiling too.

Dammit, she wished she'd gone ahead and kissed him! Last night in the jeep had been almost too polite, had left her wanting so much more. They sat side by side at the base of the dunes. The family had wandered away and were walking with their backs to them, swinging the little boy between them; they wouldn't have even seen.

Emma leaned across, brushed Max's cheek with a

gentle fingertip, and moved in slowly for the kiss that she didn't want to miss. It was tender and passionate, and seemed so very heartfelt for them both. It left her with butterflies in her stomach, a feeling of happiness, yet also vulnerability. It also left her with the sense that life had so much more to give to her. A feeling that was both scary and beautiful.

26

She felt a bit odd watching Max head off back to his B&B after their walk. He'd called in and taken a few measurements for the window-seat dimensions, and then he'd had to get back. She needed to get to work and open up The Chocolate Shop like every other Sunday afternoon, but now she was back in her safe haven, she wasn't sure about all this romance stuff – it left you feeling edgy, nervous about whether you'd ever get to see the guy again. And she was also still feeling a little guilty.

She focussed her excess energy into the shop. Luckily it was a busy afternoon, and in between serving customers she spent her time planning exactly how she might proceed with the café idea. She had a notepad next to her on the countertop, and was jotting things down like: 'Carpenter for window seats', 'Coffee machine/expense?', 'Soft furnishings – seat pads, cushions', 'Colours? Paint the walls'. And her mind went off in a spin. What kind of food would she serve? Would it be chocolate-based only? Brownies, choc-chip shortbread, chocolate cake? How would she make it Christmassy?

The shop door would then go, a family or a couple might come in, and then she'd be serving again. Seeing her customers all wrapped up and coming in from the cold, she knew they would enjoy the chance to sit down with a cup of hot chocolate and slice of cake, as well as buying some goodies to take away. It would be lovely to give this shop, which already was her favourite place in the world, a bit more life and buzz. This café idea could really, really work.

She decided that she'd pop and see her parents tomorrow evening, chat about her plans, and see if they might consider helping with a small loan, which she'd repay as soon as she could, of course. She'd better find out tomorrow how much a carpenter might charge first, and what the likely costs might be to purchase the second-hand furniture. If the chairs and tables she sourced were a bit shabby, she could always give them a spruce up with some chalk paint in a gorgeous heritage-grey shade or something similar.

The afternoon was flying by, with several tourists and locals popping in. Maybe they were just dodging the showers that had set in after lunchtime, but it was all good for trade, and with thoughts of her new café in her mind, Emma was feeling buzzy and happy.

'I'm looking for Max.'

A woman with a sweep of sculpted dark-brown hair, wearing a tailored beige woollen coat and black leather gloves, blasted in just after 4.00 p.m. She looked glamorous, yet her scowl and tone made her seem rather cold.

'Oh? And you are?' Emma started, trying to place her.

The woman gave her an extremely haughty look, apparently shocked to find Emma was daring enough to ask such an impertinent question.

'Siobhan, his girlfriend.'

'Oh.' Emma was taken aback.

She remembered the piggy back, the kiss on the beach just this morning, the feeling that life might just have turned some new corner for her. Em began to feel a little sick. *Had he lied to her? Was he playing them both?*

'Well, have you seen him? I heard mention of Warkton and some chocolate-shop woman.' The words came out sounding as if she'd said 'harlot'.

'Well, yes, I saw him this morning.' There was no point lying, but there was no way Emma was going to mention the cosy dinner for two last night. The woman was fired up enough as it was, angry energy pounding off her in waves. A couple had been browsing in the shop when Siobhan had come in and they looked extremely uncomfortable and had managed to back themselves into a corner.

'Right, I see. I don't know what the hell he's playing at, or *you* come to that, but if you happen to see him again, you can tell him his girlfriend's looking for him.'

'Hang on a minute, I've done nothing wrong here at all.' Emma was very aware that her reputation was at stake, and felt conscious of the poor customers still hovering in the shop having to hear all this. 'But,' she continued calmly, despite her heart going ten to the dozen, 'it certainly sounds as though you and Max have things to sort out. Anyhow, I doubt if I'll be seeing him – as far as I know he's already headed back for work.'

In fact, she doubted she'd be seeing him again at all, after this incident.

'Well, let me just make it clear: he's taken. We go back a long way. So, I'll be on my way.' With that, Siobhan flounced out of the shop.

Em stood behind the counter, feeling shellshocked.

'I'm so sorry about that,' she rallied, apologising to the couple.

'Well, she was a bit of a whirlwind.' The gentleman smiled awkwardly. With that, they picked up a small bag of fudge – the nearest thing to them – paid, and quickly left. It felt like the damned woman had sucked the air out of the place.

Once the shop was empty, Emma felt a tear crowd her eye, dammit.

Bloody hell! What a mess. She might have known something like this would happen. So, she'd gone and dipped her toe into the pool of romance, got swayed by a handsome face and a nice physique and here she was already feeling battered and bruised. See, she knew this romance lark wasn't worth all the bloody bother. Just wait till she told Bev about this one. Maybe it was a lucky escape. Okay, so her heart had had its edges torn, but hey, the centre of it had been ripped out years ago.

The shop was quiet after that, thank heavens, and now it was nearly closing time. Emma still felt a little battered from the day's incidents. She looked around her little shop and let her mind drift back to the start, when she'd first seen this place up for rent seven years ago.

It was a winter's day in the week before Christmas. Of course, it wasn't a chocolate shop then, just a rather rundown cottage that had had its front room converted into a shop.

She was walking her gorgeous new spaniel pup, a gift from her parents, back up from the beach to her car which she'd parked at the top of the village. She'd driven without an end destination that day, just the urge to head north for the coast, and she'd given Alfie his first-ever walk on the beach. She remembered his excitement and confusion at the feel of the sand beneath him, racing in laps then sinking his paws in to it, then dashing for the waves and darting back as the cold water rushed over his feet. Emma was watchful of him, however, careful not to let him go too far into the surf. Being young he'd tired quickly and became a little shivery from the cold water, so she wrapped him in her scarf and carried him back up the beach and through the dunes, setting him down on his feet to walk the last fifty metres or so to the car.

As they were climbing the hill from the harbour, with its Christmas lights aglow and a gorgeously decorated fir tree, past the quaint stone cottages of the main street, she spotted the 'For Rent' sign. The cottage to let was at the end of a row, made of pretty cream-grey stone, but it looked rather sad, as if it needed someone to care for it again. The wood-work around its windows was the worse for wear, all chipped white paint and flakes of rotten wood. She couldn't see into the main shop window, unfortunately, as it was covered from inside with ancient, yellowing newspapers, relating tales of births, deaths, and village fetes from over ten years ago, and any gaps were covered with whitewash. But something about the place made her stop in her tracks. Warkton village was popular with the tourists but still had a sleepy air; it also had the most beautiful harbour and beach. It felt small and welcoming, a place you could relax, start a business, somewhere to rebuild her life. A place for a fresh start.

As soon as she got home she rang the agent's number and asked to arrange a viewing as soon as possible and came back the next day. The cottage was old, and worn, and needed plenty of TLC, but Emma could see its potential; it had a big kitchen downstairs with plenty of work surfaces, the shop space was already shelved out and would be fine with a good clean and a lick of paint. She could picture it there at Christmas, all tinsel and fairy-light festive with colourful bags and boxes of chocolates. She'd already dreamed of making her chocolate crafting a career not just a hobby.

Before she had even left that very first time she had fallen in love with the cottage and its shop. It had stolen a piece of her heart, her Chocolate Shop by the Sea.

So, her heart was a little sore but it was time to step back from her relationship woes and build that wall around it once more. What she needed to do right now was to turn her focus back to saving her beloved chocolate shop, and not only saving it, no: making it the best bloody place to come for chocolate, coffee and cake along the whole Northumberland coast.

27

'Hi, you okay, Em? Can I come up and see you next Sunday?' Max's soft Geordie tones came through on her mobile.

'Max? I'm surprised you're calling.'

'What? Why?' He sounded confused.

'Let's just say I had a little visit from Siobhan. *Your* Siobhan.'

'Oh, but—'

'Look,' Emma cut him off, 'I don't want any ifs and buts and she doesn't understand me – there's obviously some unfinished business there, Max.'

'Hey, on *her* part, not mine.'

'Sorry, Max, but I just can't go there.'

'Em? Come on, give me a chance to explain at least—'

'My mind's made up. It was difficult enough as it was.' Her voice trembled. She needed to protect herself. No more reasons, excuses, tumbled emotions, she'd go back to her straightforward (well, mostly) chocolate shop life. She knew where she stood here. She had her friends, and Alfie, James and her family, she had all the support network she needed. 'I can't do it,' she added decisively. It felt a relief, in fact, to say the words. She'd been so damned churned up the fast few weeks. This would be simpler, so much better.

'But Em—'

Before he could say any more, Emma turned off the call.

Now that relationships were out of the picture, the next challenge seemed to be to find a joiner to do the alteration work for the café. The two local options were too busy, one of Max's contacts gave a quote that was horrendously expensive, and the other was booked up until March next year! In a way, now it was all off between them, she was relieved not to have to deal with someone Max knew anyhow.

Finally, Bev's Pete persuaded a semi-retired carpenter called Ron, a chap in his sixties who lived in the next village and played golf with Pete occasionally, to come and assess the job. As a special favour he agreed to fit the job in on a weekend in two weeks' time – yay! – provided she threw in a half dozen boxes of chocolates for his family and friends. The deal was sealed, and she put a little notice in her shop window that she would be closed on Saturday and Sunday, 21 and 22 October, for renovations.

It was a shame that it would be the start of the school half-term holiday week, but if she had the cushions and seat pads already made and put in a huge effort on the

Sunday night once the joiner had finished, she might just get the walls painted and everything set up for late morning Monday. It would be hard work, but so worth it. That way, at least, she'd have the rest of the half-term to try and make the most of her new coffee shop earnings.

She felt excited and a little scared. Her parents had been more than happy to help her out, but she'd hated asking for their hard-earned savings when she didn't know how soon she'd be able to pay them back. Would it really work out? How did she know how much extra income the shop might take, bearing in mind all the costs involved to set this café idea up? But she would work so hard to make this happen and be a success. It just felt right, something she had to do. She put her fears to the back of her mind. Nothing ventured, nothing gained.

It would work out – it had to, or her little chocolate shop by the sea might not even make it to next year.

Emma kept herself busy, planning what she needed to put into place for when Ron, the carpenter, would arrive. She'd already sourced eight cafetières from a local homeware store that had a sale on (there was no way she could afford a posh coffee machine yet, much as she'd have loved to). She was also going to head over to a local car boot sale that had been advertised for this Saturday morning (she'd leave Holly in charge for an hour or so) and to some of the charity shops in Alnwick to see if she could find some pretty mix-and-match teacups, side plates and teapots.

She'd had a wonderful offer from Chloe, her sister-in-law, who was going to make six cushions in the red-and-cream colour theme that Emma had finally settled on and was planning to make the seat pads for the window seats herself; she'd just need to find some strong red material to cover them. It would really brighten the place up, and look cosy and inviting during the upcoming winter season.

The night after the phone call with Max there was a rapping at her back door. It seemed pretty insistent and was getting louder. She was a little concerned because it was dark out and she wasn't expecting any callers. If someone decided to raid the shop, she was there all on her own; not that they'd get much, there were hardly any takings in the till from today – not that they'd know that.

The rapping continued. She grabbed a broom from the back kitchen, not quite sure how she'd use it, if it came to it.

'Okay, okay,' she shouted.

She unlocked and opened the door a fraction, her broom poised and ready to strike.

'Max?'

'Well, you're not answering my calls, so . . . '

'Ah.' She'd seen missed calls from him and had not replied to his many texts in the past twenty-four hours. It was easy not answering the phone, keeping up her guard. But now he was here, in person, her emotions were once again all over the place.

'Can I come in?'

'Max, I'm not sure—'

'Em?' It was pouring down with rain. His jacket and jeans were soaked and there were droplets coming off his hair, running down his face. He raised his eyebrows cheekily, and she so wanted to smile, but held back.

'Oh, just for a few minutes then.' Dammit, she had caved. *No feeling sorry for him. Stand your ground*, her inner bouncer chipped in authoritatively. She'd keep him standing in the downstairs hallway, that was it.

'Thanks.' He stepped inside.

'So?'

'Yes, so Siobhan, paying you a visit. I'm sorry about that. You probably want to know what's going on.'

'Well, how come she insists she's your girlfriend?' Emma was curious, now he was here.

'She doesn't want to accept it's over between us. I think, because I went back the last time, how I stayed when her father was ill . . . she doesn't believe I mean it this time.' He paused. 'I haven't called her, haven't arranged to see her in weeks. The only times I have seen her is when she's turned up out of the blue at my work or at home. I've tried to be polite, and I've asked after her family, but the message that it really is over doesn't seem to be getting through.'

Emma felt a weird pang of jealousy, thinking of Siobhan turning up, trying to persuade him to take her back, imagining her in his arms. *But that was just some animal instinct.* Inner Bouncer was back.

'Max, even if you two aren't seeing each other any more, I just don't feel this is right for me.'

'But we seemed—'

She cut him short. 'We hardly know each other, Max.'

'But isn't that the idea? You get to know each other. We've got the chance for something special here, Em.'

'It'd never work.' She had to stay strong.

This was exactly how the shitty emotions bowled you over yet again – Luke, Max, hurt, love, fear. She couldn't stand this any more, it was like emotional overload.

'Please, Max, don't push it. This is so hard for me.'

For a second it looked like he might try and put his arms around her. She saw the twitch across his shoulders.

Boy, she could do with those strong arms around her. But it was all futile. There would be no more mixed messages.

'You sure?'

'Yes, I'm sure. Can you please leave?' It took all her resolve to say those words. She knew silent tears were building up. She had that horrid tightening at the back of her throat as she tried to keep them at bay. He could not see her cry.

'Okay . . . well, I had to try.' He gave a gentle, sad smile.

Emma opened the back door for him. He turned to leave, and she couldn't speak. Alfie, who had appeared by her side, gave a little whimper.

'Bye, Em, take care.'

She wanted to say, 'You too.' But she knew she couldn't talk.

He gave a last glance over his shoulder before he closed the courtyard gate. She just stared sadly, gave a slow nod.

That might just be the last she'd ever see of him.

28

Saturday morning rolled around.

'Hi, Em.'

'Hey, Holly. Thanks for coming in a bit earlier to help.'

'That's no problem. It's so exciting about the café. I can't believe it's really happening and that our chat sparked the whole thing off. I can't wait – nor can my friends.'

'I know. It's brilliant, it really is, but there's lots of work to be done first.'

'Yes, and you've got to cram it all into one weekend, so I hear. Adam says if there's anything he can do to help, just ask. I think he has the Sunday off that weekend. Oh, and his gran wants to help too. Apparently, she's a bit of a whizz with the sewing machine.'

'Hmm, that might come in handy. We'll see where we're at. But that's lovely, thank them both from me. Right then, I'd better be getting off to this car boot and there's an auction on at the sale rooms too. I'm on a mission for the furniture and crockery – I'm thinking old-fashioned porcelain cups and saucers, in pretty patterns to mix and match. Give it that vintage look. What do you reckon?'

'Oh yes, perfect.'

'Right, well let's see what I come back with. Thanks so much for covering.'

Four hours later Emma parked her car, which was piled high inside, out front. She had cups, saucers, gorgeous tea plates, cutlery, the cafetières, and twelve glass mugs for hot chocolates. At the auction, she had bid for and won two – mismatched but ideal – large round wooden tables for the window-seat areas, and six wooden chairs. Apparently, they'd come from a pub that had closed down.

'Sounds like you've done brilliantly, Em. Shall I get us a cuppa to celebrate?'

'Oh yes, that's music to my ears. Shall we just bring everything in first?' The bigger furniture was still to collect as the boot of her car was too small to fit it in – she'd have to sort that out later.

The boxes and stacks of crockery took up one corner of the kitchen – a promise of what was to come for The Chocolate Shop. She was so pleased with her purchases, and had kept within her budget.

Just as they were having their cup of tea, Adam arrived with his gran.

'Well, hello, my lovelies,' the sprightly old lady greeted them. 'Exciting times for your chocolate shop, young Emma. Holly's been telling me all about it.'

'Yes, there's still lots to do, but with a bit of hard work it will all come together.'

'Well, you know what they say, pet, "Nothing worth having comes easy".'

'Well, that's very true.'

'They also say "you get by with a little help from your friends" – actually, I think that was the Beatles. That's why I asked young Adam to run me across. I have lots of time on my hands and I'd like to offer my help.'

'Oh, that's so kind of you.'

'I do like to do a bit of sewing, if there's anything like that to be done.'

Emma thought about the seat pads she had intended making herself, but with all the other work going on . . . and, in all honesty, she wasn't the best at sewing. 'There are the seat pads for the window seats to be made. But are you sure?'

'Of course, pet. I wouldn't be here otherwise, would I? So that's settled. I take it you'll be using some foam for the inners, so just get them to me with the material you like and I'll be able to run them off in a day or two. I'll do them with zips so they are easily washable and I'll make a second set of covers. There's bound to be the odd spill and mark.'

Emma hadn't even thought of that.

'That sounds just perfect, Gran. Oh, can I call you Gran? Or do you prefer Shirley?' Emma suddenly remembered her name from before.

'Gran's fine. I'd like that.'

Aw.

'And once you're up and running,' Gran continued, 'I host a little coffee club for the elderly over at Seahouses every Wednesday and Saturday morning – the Golden Oldies – I think I mentioned it last time. We might just bring a minibus across for a change of scenery, and have a little outing to your new café. Make a nice change.'

'That sounds wonderful, and if you come along, the coffee and cake will be on the house, as a thank you for helping with the sewing.'

'Now there's no need for that, Emma. I'll be doing it freely.'

'I know, but I'd really like to.'

'Well in that case, that'd be lovely.'

It was all starting to feel very real to Emma and a bit daunting, but with lovely people like this around her and offers of help coming in, she felt bolstered by the support.

'Next weekend? It's all going to happen *next* weekend. Are you mad? How's it all going to work?' Bev had called in for a coffee mid-week and was perched on a stool in the shop kitchen surrounded by moulds, chocolate callets, melting-middle sponges (Emma was experimenting with her chocolate-inspired baking), facing an animated Emma.

'It's not as bad as it sounds, I'm pretty organised. I'm closing the shop for the Saturday and Sunday when all the work's going to be done. I have a joiner all primed to arrive at eight o'clock sharp, Saturday morning. He'll be making the two new window seats. I already have some fabulous second-hand furniture – I went to a great auction in Alnwick, found just what I needed.' Emma finally paused to take a breath.

'Well, you have been busy.'

Emma nodded, smiling. 'It's going to make such a difference.'

'Yes, I think it will. What colour scheme are you thinking?'

'Red, cream and grey. Nice warm colours for the autumn and winter. A cosy chocolate feel. I even have James's Chloe making me red-and-cream tartan cushions for the window seats.'

'Brilliant. Well, if I can help at all, give me shout. We haven't got any major plans over the weekend. And if you need anything bulkier moving I'm sure Pete will help out too.'

'Thank you. It's all happened so quickly. And yes, some help would be great. I'll need to move out a lot of my chocolates and stock so they don't get spoilt with all the work going on. It's all kind of snowballed, so here we are.' Em took a sip of coffee.

'No more news from Max, then?'

'No – and I'm not expecting any.' Emma's tone was sharp. She had phoned Bev last week, going over the saga of her so-called romantic date followed by the furious girlfriend's visit, and then Max turning up at her door and the end result.

'Oh yes, that two-timing toerag who took you out for a lovely dinner, bought you flowers, said it was all over with his ex. But Emma, you haven't really let him explain fully his side of the story.'

219

'Oh, come on, give me a break, Bev. It's pretty damn obvious. And, even if he has finished it, if she's still hanging around it isn't really over, is it? No, I don't need to be involved in anybody else's dodgy relationships. I'm better off out of there.'

'Hmm,' was all Bev answered.

Why was she taking sides anyhow, she hadn't even met the guy? 'I thought you'd be on my side,' said a disgruntled Emma.

'I am, *always*, and don't you forget it.'

They both knew enough had been said on that particular situation.

'Anyway, whatever you need us to do to help with the changes here, just shout. We're here to help.'

'Thank you.'

29

Friday, it was all hands on deck.

All the chocolate supplies needed to be moved out of the shop after the close of business to be stored safely over the weekend whilst the work was being done.

Emma was carrying a cardboard box of truffles out to Bev's car – her friend was helping with storage over the weekend – when her mobile buzzed in her pocket.

Once the box was safely placed in the boot, she checked the caller ID. Hmm – Ron the joiner's number. Hopefully he was just confirming the start time tomorrow. He had seemed a nice enough guy. Reliable.

On the call back, it was his wife, Maureen, who answered.

'Good evening. Seahouses 315227.'

'Hello, it's Emma, from the chocolate shop.'

'Ah, Emma, hello . . . I'm sorry to have to tell you this, pet, but Ron's gone down with a horrid tummy bug this afternoon. I thought he might get through it, that's why we left off phoning earlier, but he's now got a temperature.

He's had to go to bed and is not well at all. Vomiting and all sorts. There's no way around it, I'm so sorry, but he's going to have to postpone.'

'Ah, I see.' Oh no! Who on earth could she call in at this late hour for joinery work? She'd had enough trouble finding Ron in the first place. Dammit. But it wasn't poor old Ron's fault and Maureen was anxiously still on the line. 'Oh dear . . . not the best news I've had today, but thanks for letting me know. It's just one of those things, I suppose.'

'Ron's terribly sorry to let you down, dear. As soon as he's better, I'll get him to call you and rearrange.'

'Thank you.' But as she was saying it, all she could think was that it would soon be the school half-term holidays, and then the Christmas trade would really start, and she wouldn't be having her café at all. She supposed she could pop the chairs and tables out in the front of the shop, but without moving the counter back and with no lovely new window seats it would all look rather cramped and sad. She'd so wanted to do it right, had been prepared to work hard all weekend alongside Ron, and she'd already planned to have a grand opening for the village community next Friday evening to celebrate. Dammit, she'd already put an article all about it in the village newsletter and invited everyone.

'I'm so sorry, lovey,' Maureen repeated, bringing her back to the here and now.

'It's not your fault. It's okay, we'll manage somehow. But yes, we'll probably have to postpone the coffee shop opening.' Half her customers were expecting her to be closed this weekend so she'd already have lost a lot of trade, and she'd now have to close for yet another weekend too. She rallied and said goodbye to Maureen, trying to sound upbeat and polite. After turning off the call, she let out a long, slow sigh.

She looked around the shop. Most of the chocolates had been emptied from the shelves, some stacked in the fridge in the shop kitchen, the rest ready to go off to Bev and Pete's. She had all the paint ready to make a start once the major joinery work was completed so maybe she should just get on with redecorating anyhow. It would do her good to keep busy.

Bev came back in from the car.

Emma's face must have said it all.

'What's up?' her friend asked straight away.

'The carpenter's ill. He can't do the joinery work. So, no window seats, no counter moves, no extra shelving. No café, basically.'

'Bugger.' Bev pulled a face. She'd wanted this to work out as much as Emma, having seen how much heart and soul her friend had put into the shop over the years, and having found out the devastating reasons behind Emma moving to Warkton over wine and late-night chats. 'I wish Pete was a bit handier, I'd get him on the case. But DIY was never his strong point.'

'What's that? What have I done wrong now?' Pete marched in just as his name was mentioned.

'Nothing, honey. Just that DIY is not your best aptitude, is it?'

'Nope. We've agreed on that point ever since I came

through the bedroom ceiling trying to fix a leaking pipe in the loft.'

'Ah, I see,' Emma smiled. 'And I'd be sure to make a hash of it too. I know my limits. The bench seating area chairs would probably fall apart within the week. No, we need a professional. But I had a real job finding Ron at short notice, and I've tried everyone else locally.'

'Mark Gilbert from Alnwick? He does some joinery work.' Pete tried to help.

'Tried him before I found Ron.'

'Handyman Dave?'

'Yep. He's busy in another job.'

'Carpenter Carl?'

'Away for the weekend. All phoned. All booked up.'

'It's not looking good,' Pete commented.

She could maybe ring her brother, but he'd already given a lot of time and was primed to pick up the tables and chairs for her over this weekend. The window seats might need more of a craftsman too; James was more of a home DIYer. But maybe he'd know of another contact.

'What a bloody shame,' Bev chipped in. 'Shall we take the chocolates back out of the boot? Shall I put the kettle on, hun? Or are you feeling a glass of wine coming on?' she asked kindly.

'You know, Bev, I think I'll just get started with the painting anyhow. I feel like I need to do something. I can freshen up this place at the least. Maybe open up on Sunday again. Get a bit of trade at least.'

'Well, I'll make a cuppa before you start, okay?'

'Okay, that sounds good. I've got a couple of brownies

I made last night in a tin on the side too. I was testing out my chocolate-baking skills ready for the café.' The café that was now not going to happen. She felt gutted.

'Oh yes. Count me in.'

'Me too,' Pete chanted. 'Always partial to a slice of brownie.'

Setbacks happened, it was just one of those things. She had her friends, thank goodness, and her family. She'd have to give James and Chloe a ring now, let them know she wouldn't be needing the cushions just yet. And Adam's gran about the seat pads – and Holly too; she was going to come in late Sunday afternoon with Adam and help set everything up. Oh well, it'd just be herself and her paintbrush for now, then. Emma had a feeling it was going to be a long night.

Her back was aching from perching up the ladder and leaning with a paintbrush in awkward positions. But one wall was finished and she was quite pleased with the colour – a warm honey-cream. She glanced at her now paint-spattered wristwatch. Ten to ten – where did those hours go?

She realised she hadn't eaten anything since the brownie and cup of tea, which must have been over three hours ago. Time for some supper; crackers and cheese came to mind. There was bound to be a bit of Cheddar or some Stilton festering in the fridge upstairs. A blob of pickle, slices of apple, and she'd be sorted. She was just coming down from the ladder when her mobile buzzed to life on the side.

It was Max. What the hell was he ringing for? He had a nerve.

She didn't need any more problems right now. She pressed the red button and stopped the call.

30

It was now Saturday afternoon and Emma was painting the final square of wall four, and her family and friends had rallied with her as best they could. She'd had visits from James to see how she was getting on and if there was anything he could do; Holly stayed for an hour or two to help make her energy-reviving tea and biscuits and to hold her ladder in the awkward, wobbly places. Even Maureen, Ron's wife, appeared with a homemade chocolate cake to apologise for her husband's absence. Emma was initially a little wary of taking food from a sick household, but it looked so damned delicious she and Holly couldn't help but dive in on the next tea break. It was as good as it looked, moist, rich and chocolatey with that perfect melt-in-the-mouth texture. In fact, Emma mused, should the baking prove too much, or for extra busy times, Maureen might just be an excellent contact for cakes for the new café, whenever it finally happened.

It was nearly five o'clock and she was on her own now,

humming away to Radio Two as she finished the last section of wall. Her lower back was aching, as well as her shoulders from reaching up.

Her mobile went again. Max. Ah, good lord, was he going to turn into some sort of stalker now? She ignored it.

There was a toot outside as some vehicle crunched to a halt beside the shop. She glanced up, but it was dark out there. She just needed to get this last square done, and then she couldn't wait to get into a hot, bubbly bath. She'd be up early tomorrow and, with Bev and Pete's help, get all the chocolates back in to the shop and on to the existing shelves again, ready to start business by ten thirty. She didn't want to miss out on any more trade.

Bloody hell, there was someone banging on the shop door now! Didn't they realise it was closed? It was pretty obvious, with her up a ladder painting the walls, bare shelves and nothing left in the shop for sale. She had a little wobble on her ladder, then she started dismounting, disgruntled.

She stood stock-still and stared. *Max?*

'What the heck are you doing here?'

'What a welcome! Hey, I've just driven for over an hour, after a day of plastering walls, no less, as one of my team is ill, to come and help you out.'

'Oh, right . . . But I'm managing fine here by myself. In fact, I've just about finished the painting.' She was a bit stunned that he was actually here.

'It wasn't the painting I'd come to do. Take a look at the roof rack.'

She peered out of the shop window at his jeep parked up outside. There were long sections of wood strapped on the top.

'All my tools are in the back. These, my lovely, are your new window seats.' He pointed to the planks of wood.

'They are? What are you talking about?'

'Well, they will be in about five or six hours' time.'

'Honestly? *You* can make them?'

He laughed. 'I am a master of the building trade, having picked up lots of skills in my time. And Andy, my joiner, stayed an extra half hour to cut them to size for me. I took the initial measurements that day, remember. Kept the notes in my pocket by chance.'

'But how did you even know . . .?' She was struggling to get her head around how and why Max was even here.

'Well, I couldn't leave a damsel in distress, could I? And a launch party without a launch – that's just not on.'

'But I hadn't told you. How could you know Ron had had to let me down? Hang on, how did you even know he was meant to be here this weekend in the first place?' None of this was making sense. And, she was still trying to be angry with him for being a slimy, possibly two-timing toerag.

'Your friend Bev gave me a call.'

'What?' But Bev wouldn't have known his number. She hadn't even met him yet. What on earth was her so-called friend doing meddling in her life like this?

'She was just looking out for you. Found my business number on Google, I think.'

'Ah.' She was going to kill her.

She dropped down her paintbrush and tray and sighed. What was she going to do now, send him away?

Before she had a chance to speak, Max said, 'Right then, no point hanging about, we have work to do.'

Emma found herself silenced. She *so* wanted her shop to get its facelift, but this in no way meant he could just waltz back into her life. There were too many questions unanswered, too many emotions at stake. She'd made her mind up on that.

'You'll have to be my workmate, or this could take all night,' he continued. 'Come on, let's get the stuff unloaded from the jeep first.'

Emma was already tired, but there was no way she was going to stop now. If Max could keep going after an all-day shift, then so could she. This was it! Her Cosy Chocolate Shop Café was really going to happen.

They carried in wooden beams, flat boards of wood, a tool kit, and saws. Max tucked a pencil behind his ear, gave her a wink and set to it. She was limited in what she could help with, but came in handy passing the right tools, nails and hammers as needed.

'Have you eaten?' They'd come to a natural pause when the frame for one of the window areas was complete.

'No, not yet. I came straight on up from the other job. I'm starving.'

'Me too. Hmm, wonder if The Fisherman's Arms will do us a carry out of fish and chips. I'll give them a ring, shall I? Do you fancy that?'

'That would be great. Yeah, go ahead.'

'Got to feed the workers.' She smiled, beginning to feel more relaxed with him. He really had come here to work, and so far there didn't seem to be an ulterior motive.

'Exactly.'

She took up her mobile, punched in the number and began chatting to Dave the landlord. Brilliant – they'd do it. She gave Max a thumbs-up sign as he continued cutting timber to size. She thanked Dave, saying she'd pop down in fifteen minutes to collect. Then she stood watching Max as he drew a level across to the back of the seat area, taking the pencil from his ear, concentrating. Her tummy began rumbling rather loudly at that point which made him look up and laugh.

'Someone's hungry.'

'Yep. I'm not actually sure I had lunch, to be honest.' She'd been too busy painting. Come to think of it, it had been a chocolate cake brunch with Holly.

She left Max sawing more sections of wood, and walked down the hill to the village pub. She had to wait a minute or two for the order to be ready, and chatted to Danny behind the bar.

'Night in?' he asked.

'Yep, it's all go getting The Chocolate Shop turned into a café this weekend.'

'Ah, yes, heard about that. Sounds great. I saw the invite to the opening night on Friday – count me in. Is the work going well?'

'Well, it wasn't going at all until a couple of hours ago – the carpenter got ill. But I got some last-minute help in. Think it's going to end up being a bit of an all-nighter, trying to get the window seats finished.'

'Right. You handy like?'

'Nope, got a builder friend to help, thank goodness. But it's not his usual role, so we're doing our best.'

'Ah, I see. Well, best of luck with it.'

With that, the fish and chips turned up. 'There you go, Emma. Enjoy.' Rob, the chef, handed them over.

'Thanks, I'm absolutely famished.' They smelt delicious even through the foil carton and packaging. She might just have to sneak a chip on the way back up the hill. It had to be done! 'Thanks, Rob. I'm sure they'll be delicious.'

'Cheers, Emma.'

She settled up at the bar, and back at the shop, she and Max sat side by side on the wooden floor eating crispy batter and flaky chunks of cod, with salt and vinegar. She'd found a couple of cans of Diet Coke in the fridge to go with it.

It was, in fact, one of the best meals she'd had in ages.

'Delicious,' Max stated, as he forked up the last of his chips.

'Just right,' Emma agreed.

'Well, let's get back to work again.' Max was keen to crack on. 'This window seat isn't going to make itself. Here goes.'

It was twenty to twelve when they decided to call it a night. Max looked pretty stiff as he stood up and stretched. Emma was feeling achy too. She'd been keeping busy in the kitchen, popping through to see if Max needed help here and there. The physical work of the day was taking its toll, finding muscles she hadn't used in an age. She yawned.

'Right, I suppose I'd better get away.' Max looked at her.

'Oh.' She hadn't even considered where he would stay, but she hadn't imagined him going all the way back home. Of course, coming up last minute he wouldn't have booked a B&B for tonight and it was too late now to contact the pub, or anywhere else for that matter.

'You can't drive all that way back now. And – and won't you need to come back up to finish the job?' She sounded a bit cheeky, she knew, but she hoped he wasn't going to leave the job half-finished. It would be hard to reopen the shop at all, if so.

'Yes, that's what I was going to do, head home. Then come back up early tomorrow morning, try and get this done before I need to be in Gateshead – got to check on a job there in the afternoon. It's the only day the owners are about.'

'Oh, you can't do that. You'll be shattered.' The words came out before she had a chance to think, but she didn't like the idea of him driving back tired after all that work. 'You could stay.' *What was she saying?* Alarm bells were going off in her head as she spoke. 'On the sofa. That'd be fine,' she clarified. There, he couldn't misconstrue that. Yes, he'd helped and she really appreciated that. She'd count him as a friend, one that probably still had a girl-friend in tow, and she needed to keep things totally clear between them and above board.

'Okay. Well, cheers. If you don't mind, that would help and save me a couple of hours' drive. I can start a bit earlier in the morning that way too, as there's still a fair bit to do. I'm not quite as quick as Andy would have been. But needs must.'

'You've been great, that's all I know.' She had to admit that much; his help tonight was just amazing.

'Thanks . . . and the sofa is absolutely fine for me. Em,' he started, just as she was going to clear some empty mugs to the kitchen, 'about Siobhan. It *really* is over, you know. It has been since August, since before I came back to see you.'

'Right . . . but why would she say it wasn't?'

'Wishful thinking, maybe. Hoping I'd come back. I went to see her the other night, though. The day after I'd seen you.'

Strangely, Emma felt her heart sink a little.

'I went to make it absolutely clear. That there's no going back this time. Anyway, I just wanted you to know that.'

'Oh.' Could she really believe him? It was such a messy situation. All those bloody emotions were going crazy inside her again. She hated feeling out of control, confused. Well, this changed nothing.

She went to let Alfie out into the back yard whilst Max tidied some of the tools and equipment ready for the next day. Alfie came back in, delighted to see Max again, sneaking through to the shop where he wasn't normally allowed, curling around Max's legs and thwacking his eager tail against him, having been kept upstairs all the while, out of hammer and harm's way.

They were both pretty shattered, so Emma took Alfie back upstairs and set up a duvet and pillows ready for Max in the lounge. It was quite a big sofa, but ten minutes later she smiled as she passed the open door spotting his legs and feet poking out over the arm end. She noted he'd kept his socks on.

'Goodnight, Max.' She felt a little sad. A part of her would have loved to just walk across and give him a goodnight kiss and a hug. The room was smelling rather lovely of his aftershave with a hint of underlying manly work-sweat. Instead, she just waved from the door. 'Thanks so much for coming up like this, for helping out.' She still couldn't quite believe he'd really turned up and done all this work. But best to stay as distant friends. And meddling Bev was going to get a stern call in the morning.

'You're welcome, Emma.' He looked at her tenderly.

She headed for her own room, feeling confused and yet aware of a little glow she couldn't help but feel inside. She lay down on her double bed, remembering kisses in car parks, Max's smile, then memories with Luke, but despite the jumble of thoughts, she was soon out like a light.

Emma came to in the middle of the night in need of a wee. She got out of bed quietly, aware that Max was there just down the hallway in the front room. It was strange to think of someone else here in her little cottage. Even stranger to think it was a man – and, she still had to admit, a rather gorgeous one at that.

She had a quick pee, wondering whether to flush or

not, not wanting to wake him, yet equally not wanting him to find it lingering embarrassingly in the morning. She went for the not waking him theory, hoping to be the first to hit the bathroom in the morning.

She stepped back into the hallway . . . and felt drawn to go and take a quick peek at the man lying there so near her in her front room, wondering what he would look like whilst he slept. As she approached she could see that the door was left ajar. She could hear his heavy, sleeping breaths. She crept along the hallway in her bare feet and held her breath as she gazed in through the doorway, opening the crack a little wider.

He hadn't closed the curtains, so she could make out his features in the soft orange glow of the street light outside – his tousled hair, defined cheekbone, stubbled jawline, the thick lashes on his closed lids, his lips.

Without realising it, she let out a soft, slow sigh.

Ping, his eyes opened. Eek. She'd been caught acting like a stalker. How embarrassing.

'You okay?' he asked a little warily.

'Yeah, sorry, just woke up.' She didn't mention the need to pee.

'Looking for something?' She could hear the irony in his voice, and saw a half-smile across his lips.

'Maybe.'

'You'll be getting chilly out there. Want to come in?' he lifted the duvet cheekily.

Emma stayed silent. *Could she, should she? Wouldn't she just be heading back into a whole heap of trouble?*

'I'm dressed, if that's what you're worried about. Well,

T-shirt and boxers. Your choice. Just don't stand there all night – it's a bit freaky.'

She laughed. Whoa, she so wanted to feel his strong arms around her. But was that all he was offering? She suddenly felt she was on a pivot, her decision in the next second or two might just change everything – with or without sex being involved.

'Well?' The duvet was still half-lifted.

Emma moved towards the sofa, and saw him shift a little towards the back to make room. She took a slow breath and slid herself in beside him – her back to his front. There wasn't a lot of room, so side by side was the best they could do. His arm slipped around her lower ribs from behind, and felt so very natural there, keeping her close.

'Okay?' His voice was warm and mellow there at her ear.

'Yes.'

'Good.'

And they lay there so very close. And it felt as good as she had imagined it might when she'd lain in her lonely bed many evenings before, trying to push the thoughts of him from her mind. Her breathing began to slow to match his. He held her tenderly, yet making no moves to touch her provocatively; she wasn't quite sure if she was disappointed or not, and then she began to relax, feeling his breath against her hair.

She felt herself drifting off . . .

It was light. Emma felt a bit achy and at an odd angle. There was something heavy across her . . . oh, an arm, not *her* arm; a muscular, slightly hairy arm was wrapped around her.

She opened her eyes, recognised her own living room.

She was there on the sofa with Max. She had a moment of panic, *had they*? Surely she would have remembered something like that. They hadn't even been drinking last night. Her nightshirt was still on and – she tried to concentrate, despite there being a distinct feeling of a 'morning glory' at her lower back (wow, it had been a long time since she had felt that against her; Luke had always been a morning person) – she had a sense that *it* was indeed still safely packed away under boxer shorts.

'Morning,' came a voice behind her ear, with a hint of humour.

'Morning,' she answered, bright as brass. 'I think we have work to do.' She needed to think about the shop, keep her focus on that. And she was up and out from the duvet before he had a chance to consider what he might do with that 'morning glory' after all.

31

By eight-thirty they'd had a quick breakfast of scrambled eggs on toast and Max had now started on the second window seat.

He was hammering away, securing the frame in place, looking slightly stiff as he moved – probably the results of last night's work and sleeping hunched up alongside Em for half the night on a sofa. That thought made her smile.

Emma had a few calls to make to get everything organised for the shop reopening the next day. James, her brother, wouldn't be aware that it was all systems go again, after her telling him of Ron's illness on Friday. She'd be needing a hand to transport the furniture which he'd picked up for her and was storing in his garage, also the new cushions Chloe was making. She'd also need to call Bev and Pete to get the chocolates transported back from their house. Holly was meant to be coming across with Adam this afternoon to help too, so it was all hands on deck again. It was going to be a long couple of days, for sure, but it was exciting, seeing her dreams becoming a reality.

Emma stood watching Max work; she could already imagine the circular pine tables in place by the windows with her mix-and-match wooden chairs. She had decided she would chalk-paint the more battered looking ones, keeping the best two as natural wood. She offered to fetch Max a coffee. He still had a lot of work to do and he had his own business to get back to. She was so very grateful for his help. The café was back on track, with a little – actually, some *huge* – help from her friends and family.

It was wonderful to think that by Friday night they'd be celebrating the opening of The Chocolate Shop Café. A party would be such a lovely way to thank all her friends and family and the local community, not just for their help with this project but for all their support over the past few years. They had made her feel so welcome in the village from the start, taking her under their Warkton-by-the-Sea wing, when they only knew her as the new girl in the village who was setting up a chocolate shop, and when her world was at its very bleakest.

She could picture herself on her launch evening, handing out glasses of Prosecco, with plates of chocolate treats. Hmm, chocolate canapés – she could add a little twist to some of her favourite creations, and have some mini chocolate brownies to give an idea of the baked goods for the café. She knew that time was going to be of the essence this week – there would still be some finishing touches to add to the shop, out of hours. Hopefully, Ron might shake off his bug and be back in action in the week to make the final alterations to the counter area.

There was a loud rap at the shop door. She was surprised to find it was Danny from the pub, with another chap. Perhaps they were coming for a nosy to see how things were going.

Emma unlocked the door and let them in.

'Hi, Em. Meet your new chippie,' Danny announced with a grin.

Chippie? Fish and chips? Their supper had been lovely from the pub last night, maybe they were bringing up some chips for their lunch too, Emma mused.

Max stood up rubbing the small of his back for a second, then came across. 'Cheers, mate. *That* is music to my ears.' And the three men shook hands.

Emma was still wondering quite what was going on, a crease of confusion across her brow.

'Chippie – carpenter – wood chips,' Max turned to her to explain.

'Ah. Oh, wow. You're here to help? Fabulous.'

'This is Nick. An old mate.' Danny introduced him. 'Happened to be staying with me this weekend.'

'Hi, Nick, and thank you so much.' Emma shook his hand. He was tall and lean with smiley eyes and a whiskery-goatee beard; in fact, he looked very much as though he should have a roll-up slanted out of his mouth.

'Used to have my own joinery business,' Nick said, 'but when the recession hit and the work dried up I just couldn't make ends meet. Went to work for a bacon factory, then, believe it or not. Pay was better, and it was a regular income. Been there ever since. But I still miss working with wood. When Danny here mentioned you'd been let down at the last minute, well . . . '

'I have to work this lunch shift at the pub anyhow, so he didn't have a lot on. Saves him lounging around on my sofa all day,' Danny added.

'Yep, I have a few hours to spare, so no worries. Give me a job.'

'Right, I'll make a tea or coffee for us all, whatever you'd rather, and I'll let Max tell you where we're at with the woodwork, Nick.'

The two men had already started chatting and were looking seriously at sections of timber. Danny said he had better go to get ready for his shift.

'Cheers, Danny. Thanks so much for thinking of me and my shop. You're a star.'

'No worries. Couldn't see you struggling when I knew help was at hand. Oh, and Nick's happy to work for a few pints, by the way. We're out this evening, so that will be ideal.' Danny gave a wink.

'Perfect. You sure?' She felt she ought to offer proper payment. She had the money from her parents to pay Ron for the work, after all.

'Absolutely, I'm here of my own free will,' Nick chipped in. 'But a few pints put behind the bar at the Fisherman's for tonight would be brilliant.'

James turned up about an hour later. Little Lucy was with him, beaming and following her dad who was carrying two chairs.

'Hello, Auntie Emma. Oh, who are they?' The little girl stopped, surprised to find other people in the shop.

'That's Max and Nick. They're helping make the seats for the new coffee shop here.'

Lucy studied the two men seriously, then nodded.

Max gave her a grin, and Nick gave a nod.

'Will you do milkshakes too, Auntie Emma? I don't like coffee.'

'Of course, that's actually a brilliant idea, Luce. *Chocolate* milkshakes. And maybe hot chocolates for the winter. What do you think?'

'I think that sounds good. As long as they have marsh-mallows on the top.'

'I think we can manage that.' Emma smiled. 'So, you're helping Daddy today.'

'Yes. Olivia had to stay with Mummy – he couldn't do two of us. They're doing sewing.' She pulled a yuck kind of face at that. 'We had to split up. It's better doing furniture stuff.'

'Are they making my cushions, by any chance?'

'Yep.'

'Well, that will be a big help to me. Of course, this is a big help too. What would I do without you lovely lot, hey?' She looked up at James meaningfully as she spoke. 'Come on then, Luce, you can go choose some chocolates from the back kitchen. I've had to move them all for now, but there's still some in there. Choose something for you and something to take home for Olivia.'

'What about Dad?' called James after them hopefully. 'He's a helper too.'

Emma could hear his deep laugh. He loved her salted caramels. She'd definitely find a pack of those for him too.

'What about the woodworkers? We like chocolate too,' came Max's warm, cheeky tones.

When the girls returned, Lucy clutching her chocolate bounty, James was chatting happily with the two men. Her brother then headed off once more on a second run to fetch the tables.

By 2.00 p.m. the shop was buzzing. Max and Nick were working away on the seating tops. Nick had suggested making them hinged so the inside could be used for storage, a brilliant idea, because Emma's display materials were currently crammed into a cupboard upstairs – you went looking for a favourite jumper and were at risk of attack from Easter bunnies, mini-foil Christmas trees, tinsel, baubles, the works.

Bev and Pete had popped in to see how things were taking shape and stayed to lend a hand. Em felt like she'd been shipped into that TV programme where they transform a whole house in forty-eight hours.

Bev glanced pointedly over at the best-looking of the two men at work. 'So, I take it Max came to help then?'

'Yes – and I need to have words about that,' Em said tersely under her breath. 'You are in *such* big trouble.' Emma then introduced the two men to Bev and Pete.

'Hmm, he is gorgeous,' Bev whispered as they stood back near the hallway door. 'Nothing at all like the guys

I had in to decorate my conservatory,' she continued, joking that she'd have to find some joinery jobs in her own home very soon.

Emma had to laugh. She explained that the other lad was a mate of Danny's at the pub.

Around 11.00 a.m., Holly arrived to see how things were going and stood gazing around the shop in awe, with a cheesy grin on her face, feeling very proud – after all, it was her initial idea that sparked all this off, she reminded them. She said she couldn't wait to try it – she had a group of friends organised, desperately wanting to be one of the first ones in.

Holly then clocked Max. 'I know him, don't I? What's *he* doing here?'

'Oh, he's just helping out, all hands on deck, and all that.' Emma tried to sound bright and breezy.

Holly was obviously thinking about this, then gave her boss a big grin whilst nodding in Max's direction. 'Interesting . . . ' was all her assistant said, but Emma knew she'd be seriously quizzed tomorrow.

After another round of cuppas, served with chocolate digestives, her visitors made to leave. Emma made sure they all knew about the launch night on Friday. A big thank you was in order.

Mid-afternoon, Max and Nick stood up from their work, stretched out their backs, gave each other a nod, and called Emma downstairs to see the finished product. She paused in the shop entrance and grinned with a tear in her eye. It looked amazing; they had even finished the seat-backs with some white-painted wood panelling, which gave it a lovely coastal feel.

'Wow,' was all she could say.

'Right then, I'll be off, if that's everything?' Nick announced. He'd stayed much longer than the shift Danny would have been working, and he had worked so hard, with just a couple of coffee breaks.

'Thank you so much, Nick. And I'll be sure to put some money behind the bar for you and Danny for tonight. And if you're about this Friday, call in for the launch, won't you?'

'Cheers, I'll be back down in Yorkshire then, but thanks for the invite. And hey, you're welcome, I enjoyed it. Turning me hand back to some woodworking. Might have to keep it up as a bit of a hobby, you know. Do the odd job here and there.'

'You should.'

'Cheers, mate. That was *such* a help,' Max said. The two men shook hands.

'All good.' Nick gave a thumbs-up sign. 'That's me off, then.'

'Thanks again,' said Emma appreciatively, as she handed him a box of chocolate-dipped fudge with a twenty-pound note from the till. After all the hard work she couldn't not give him some cash at least, as well as the beer money.

'Ah, cheers.' And he headed jauntily off down the hill.

'I'd better be going too. I've got that other job to check on.' Max turned to face her.

'Yes . . . well, I suppose you had.' She felt a weird pang of disappointment, but of course Max had his

246

own business to run and life to lead. 'Of course, Max. I really don't know how to thank you enough. Can I pay you for the work? For the wood, at least?'

'No, absolutely not. There's no need to pay. I don't want anything.'

'But—'

'It's fine. Honest.'

Aw, he was really lovely. Yes, she still felt a bit confused, but she was sad that he was heading off and she didn't know when, or even if, she was going to see him again. She had to admit he looked pretty damned gorgeous stood there, all ruffled hair, and sawdust on his clothes. He had come up all this way when he was already busy to help her out. She remembered how close they had been last night on the sofa.

'Will you be coming back at all?' *What are you doing, woman?* Inner Bouncer was back again.

'Ah . . . ' He sounded unsure.

It was a long drive, she knew, and he'd worked like a Trojan here. He'd be ready to get back and get on with his life in Hexham, just as she had asked him to do two weeks ago.

'Do you want me to?' he asked.

They held each other's gaze for a second, both wondering what was coming next, where they went from here.

'Yes.' She didn't know how or what or why, but the thought of never seeing this guy again crushed her. She stood looking at Max, who was gazing back at her intently, that one word so meaningful between then.

He smiled. 'Well then, that would be great. Shall I come back tomorrow after work? I could try and get an early finish.'

'Okay, yes, that'd be lovely.'

And the sense of tension in that room notched itself up several volts. Emma felt her cheeks burn and headed off for the kitchen to find something, *anything* to do, whilst Max got on with sweeping up the last shavings of sawdust and emptying them into the dustbin outside, ready to set off.

Once Max had left, Emma had the shop all to herself, and time to think. Was she doing the right thing agreeing to see Max again? Was it just the intimacy of being close last night that had made her cave in? It didn't solve all the other problems, did it? She felt cross with herself.

She needed to get on with some baking for the café's opening; a double batch of brownies and some chocolate cookies. She'd need more than that, but time was short. She could phone Maureen, Ron's wife and maker of *the* most scrummy chocolate cake, see if she could make a couple of her chocolate cakes by tomorrow lunch time. It was worth a try. Then James arrived with the second of the two tables.

'Who were the two blokes, by the way? The ones doing the joinery work?'

'Oh, just a friend and an acquaintance of Danny's.' She kept her answer purposely vague.

'Ah, right, they seemed pretty sound. Great they could help out.'

'Yes, they've been brilliant.'

'Looking good in here, sis. I like the paint colours. Chloe's nearly finished the cushions for you, by the way.'

'Aw, thank you so much, James, and Chloe too. It's going be fabulous,' Emma confirmed, picturing a cosy Christmassy space, perfect to settle down with a slice of chocolate cake and a huge hot chocolate piled with cream and marshmallows. She felt a buzz of happiness. Her dream was about to come true.

'Right, gotta go, sis. I've promised the girls a trip to the park when I get back.'

'Yeah, I'd better go and take Alfie out soon too. He's been cooped up for two days, out of harm's way. He'll be going stir crazy up there. Thanks for everything, bro.' She gave James a gentle punch on the arm, a gesture they'd hung on to from childhood, and then a big hug.

'No worries. It's great to see it all coming together for you. I wish you all the success in the world, Em.'

A tear misted her eye. She so hoped it would all work out for her little chocolate shop by the sea. After everybody's help, she couldn't possibly lose it now.

32

It was the morning of the big opening day. Emma drew the curtains on a pinky-grey dawn that warmed the sky.

This was it! There was still so much to do, and thoughts of the impending evening with Max kept creeping up on her. She needed to take the dog out first, and she knew that the fresh air and a pacy walk on the beach would do both her and Alfie good, so ten minutes later, Emma set off down the road with him. As she reached the dunes, Alfie scampering ahead, she heard a beep on her phone. She took it out of her pocket – a text from Max.

Good luck with your opening day! Looking forward to seeing you xxx

A mix of excitement and fear welled up inside her. Why on earth had she agreed to see him on opening day? There was enough to think of as it was.

Me too x she replied, still feeling cautious about the whole thing.

Another text bounced back. *BTW I have a plan – so don't worry about getting any supper organised. xx*

Okay. Thanks. Xx She was curious, wondering what he had in mind. It would be a busy day, so whatever it was, not having to cook supper was a bonus.

She strolled the sands with Alfie, enjoying the view of the bay, the early morning sun glinting gold on the crests of the waves, the sea-salt scent of the air. There was just a hint of breeze and it was mild for the time of year. Emma felt a strange tingling sensation in her stomach at the thought of seeing Max tonight, and couldn't help but wonder what he had in mind for the evening. And, of course, Luke, her lovely Luke, was there very much in her thoughts too, the what-ifs and what-might-have-beens always there in her heart.

Back in the shop half an hour later, Emma was busy in the kitchen making choc-chip shortbread. She was going to pop the biscuits into a large glass jar on the counter, ready to tempt her café customers, and her brownies were all cut up and ready to go. She had made one batch into mini cubes, as she had decided to give every customer a mini brownie on the side of their tea or coffee. It might well become the Cosy Chocolate Shop Café's 'thing', and make them stand out from any other café in the area. As well as the fact that they were surrounded by chocolate!

She began to feel a little nervous. The Chocolate Shop Café was going to open at 2.00 p.m., only six hours' time. The paint was still drying on the windowsills, the shelves needed restocking – there wasn't a single chocolate in the shop yet – and there were still curls of wood shavings and dust loitering. She turned the radio up loud and set to her task.

Chloe turned up mid-morning, just after Adam had dropped off the red seat pads that had been beautifully sewn by his gran. Emma spotted her sister-in-law half-hidden by a stack of cushions at the shop door and dashed to help her.

'These look amazing, Chloe – they must have taken you ages. Thank you so much.'

As they got the cushions inside the shop, and positioned them in the first window seat, it was obvious how well the colours would go. The cushions were in reds, creams and greys, some plaid. Emma spotted one that was the same deep red as the seat pads with a beautiful appliqué star in a silvery-grey that had obviously been hand-stitched on.

'Wow – I love this one. Did you do all this needlework?'

'Yes, I got a bit carried away. Thought that might look pretty on the centre of each window seat. There's another one the same in the car.'

'Aw, I love them.'

'And . . . ' Chloe began to pull out a long material bunting strip in similar colours to the cushions. As she opened it out, handstitched with a letter on each flag, it read THE COSY CHOCOLATE SHOP. 'Oh, Chloe, this is just beautiful.' Emma felt herself getting a bit choked up. 'It must have taken you *ages*.' She took the bunting in her hands and tried it against the countertop. 'I love it! And look . . .' Next she placed the star-patterned cushion in the centre of the others. 'All set up on the window seat, don't your cushions look just fabulous?'

'Not bad,' Chloe agreed modestly.

'Well, I think we need to be the first to sit and use it, don't you? It's about time I took a breather. How do you fancy a coffee and a brownie?'

A few minutes later they were trying out the new window seat, testing the springiness of the new seat pads beneath them. They chinked their coffee cups together. 'Cheers.'

'Cheers, Chloe, and thank you so much, and James too. You guys have been amazing.'

'Oh, yum.' Chloe had just bitten into a square of brownie. 'These are seriously good. Mmm, and the coffee.'

'Yeah, I've sourced the ground coffee from a chap who's just set up his own business in Berwick. It's great, isn't it, a really rich flavour? He does different blends. This is my favourite, Harry's blend.'

'I'm sure the café will go well for you, Em. It's bound to. What's not to like? Good coffee, chocolates everywhere, tea and cake, and you at the helm.'

'I hope so. I'm feeling a tad nervous right now, to be truthful.'

Only time would tell. Her friends had invested time and energy, her parents had invested much of their savings in this, she'd invested her heart and soul, and her bank account *really* needed this to work out. It wouldn't be long before the landlord would be snooping around again, checking on the work she'd had done, and the next thing she'd know he'd be hiking up the rent yet again, despite the fact she'd paid for all the renovations herself.

'Well, this really is great, so cosy. And look, you can check what's going on in the world outside the window, yet you're here in this little magical world of chocolate too.' Chloe smiled.

Emma looked out at her village. It was now a beautiful crisp autumn morning, the sky a vivid turquoise. She could just see down the hill, past the last of the stone cottages of the main street, where the glint of light was catching on the water of the harbour, boat masts bobbing. It was such a special place.

'I love it, honestly,' Chloe continued. 'I shall be going straight back and telling all my friends about it.'

'Thanks so much.'

They chatted some more about the girls, family life, Alfie. Emma didn't mention Max, it was all too soon and confusing, and she was so busy with the shop she could barely catch her breath this morning as it was.

'Well, I suppose I ought to get going,' Chloe announced. 'And I'm sure you've got lots to do too.'

'I have indeed. But it was nice having a ten-minute breather. I'm expecting the chocolate supplies back with Bev any minute now, ready to fill the shelves with. It's still looking a bit bare in here.' She'd already set out what she could from her kitchen storage, but there were several gaps on the shelves.

'It looks great already. Well then, Emma, very best of luck!'

'Thanks. Oh, and don't forget the launch on Friday, and bring the girls along too. It's from seven o'clock.'

'We'll be there. And yes, I'll let the girls have a late night as a treat. We would never hear the last of it if they knew we'd had a party in a chocolate shop without them.'

'Hah – yes.' Emma gave her sister-in-law a big thank-you hug as she left.

Two hours later, Bev and Emma were sitting outside in the back courtyard at the little table-for-two, grabbing a quick cup of coffee and making the most of the unusually warm October sunshine.

Bev and her husband had turned up half an hour before with a hatchback full of chocolates they'd been storing over the weekend. Pete was now away collecting a second load.

'Anyway,' Emma started, now it was just the two of them, 'what on earth do you think you were doing getting in touch with Max?' Emma was still cross with her friend for interfering.

'Well, *you* weren't going to give him a chance, were you?'

'You had no right.'

'Do you wish I hadn't now?' Bev raised a questioning eyebrow.

Em couldn't answer.

'Look,' Bev tried to explain, 'I could tell you liked him. Yeah, you said about the ex turning up, but you'd already told me it was all over in theory. And then Max came all this way to tell you as much the other evening too.

So, I knew his name, knew he was a builder from Hexham with his own company – Google is a wonderful thing. He sounded really nice and genuine on the phone. I thought he deserved a chance. He wanted to help. He really likes you, Em.'

'Huh! Well, it's still meddling.'

'He is pretty damned gorgeous.'

Emma couldn't help but smile.

Pete arrived back and needed a hand with the last boxes. The chocolates were finally home. Once they were all set out on display, there was less than an hour to go until opening.

'I'll stay if you like. It might end up being busy,' Bev offered. 'I haven't any other plans for today, and I'm sure there's plenty you still need to be doing.'

'Well, Holly is coming in to help soon, and she's bringing in a group of friends to try out the café, but if you don't mind staying, that'd be great. I'm really not sure how busy it might get.' Emma hadn't a clue if there might be an opening day rush. She would just have to wait and see, but an extra pair of hands would be wonderful.

Ten to two, the kettle was filled and ready in the kitchen with some of her mix-and-match cups, as well as teapots, cafetières and milk jugs. Emma had put out two trays – one, a pretty silver-plated one of her mother's, the other with vintage-style roses on, which she'd discovered at the car boot sale. They set sugar bowls out on the tables, with little tongs dangling from the side. The Cosy Chocolate Shop Café was ready.

Holly bowled in. 'Hi, I'm here.' She stopped and looked around her. 'Oh. My. Gosh. This is just lush in here, Emma. I *sooo* love it. Aw, the cushions, the bunting, all the finishing touches . . . ' Her assistant stood open-mouthed, taking it all in.

'Yep, we're all ready to go. We just need some customers.' Emma felt a sense of trepidation.

'Exciting.'

Bev came out from the kitchen just then. 'Hi, Holly. I'm here to help too – all ready for the big rush.'

'Cool.'

Just then, a text pinged in – Max.

Very best of luck. Go The Chocolate Shop Café! X

Emma smiled. Then her mobile rang:

'Hey, I thought it would be nice to speak with you in person, so just ringing to wish you the best of luck, Em. Did you manage to get it all finished in time?' Max.

'Yep, just about. Oh Max, it's all come together so well and really looks great. I am a bit nervous, though. I just hope people turn up.'

'They will. You'll smash it, I'm sure.'

'Thanks.'

'Have a good afternoon. I'm looking forward to seeing you later – I have a bit of a plan.'

'Hmm, what kind of a plan?'

'Now, you'll just have to wait and see, won't you?' he teased.

'Spoilsport. Ah, the suspense is killing me,' she laughed.

'You'll enjoy it, I'm sure.'

What could a girl fit in to four or five hours on a

Monday evening with a rather gorgeous man? One thing rather vividly came to mind – but it was still very early on in their relationship for anything like that.

'It'd better be good.' She pulled herself back from her reverie. Thank heavens he couldn't see her blushing.

'Right. Well, I'll see you later. Good luck.' She heard a shout, another male voice echoing down the line. 'Sorry, I've got to go, the lads need some help here.'

'Right, no worries. See you.'

'Bye, Em.'

Bev had busied herself plumping up the window-seat cushions, ready for their first arrivals. 'Max?' she asked with a big grin, evidently happy with her matchmaking skills.

'Might have been,' Emma answered with a smile, her mind still buzzing. What was he scheming? A meal out somewhere was the most likely, or a cinema trip? Who knew.

'Love is in the air,' Bev started singing.

Holly was grinning. 'Now then, Emma, what has been going on? I knew I recognised that builder bloke the other day.'

'Hah, now is not the time or the place,' she answered cryptically. 'We have work to do, ladies.' And Emma walked to the shop door where she proudly turned her sign to 'open' with a flourish, singing, 'Ta-dah', accompanied by a big cheer from Holly and Bev.

Em poked her head put and looked up and down the street; unfortunately, no one was there.

'We ought to be breaking open a bottle of bubbly or

something,' Bev said to lift the moment. 'I should have thought and brought something along.'

'Friday. We'll wait till Friday and do that at the launch. Remember, we do actually need to work today.'

They took their places behind the counter and waited anxiously. Emma fiddled on, tidying the displays, then read over her new café menu – she'd designed it herself on the computer last night and printed it off on cream-coloured card. To be absolutely honest, there wasn't an awful lot on the menu as yet: pots of tea (breakfast, Earl Grey, green or fruit blends), cafetière of local ground coffee, hot chocolate (with or without cream and marshmallows), milkshakes, brownies, cookies, chocolate cake (yes, the lovely Maureen had come up trumps!) or choc-chip shortbread. She had also put a chocolate truffle selection on the list too. She would extend her range as soon as she could, once she'd seen what might sell best, and she hoped to keep everything homemade, as well as having all her usual chocolate shop creations for sale too.

Earlier, she'd strung some festive stars up in the windows, to tie in with the pattern on the cushions, and they were catching the light beautifully. She hoped they might also catch the tourists' eye. She'd have to plan her full window display in the next couple of days to have it ready for the launch – she hadn't had time this morning – because she was going to go the whole hog and create a full-on Christmas display.

Ten past two, Emma found herself humming and strumming the countertop. Holly was beside her, anxiously checking the door, Bev replumping cushions.

A few people walked by, taking a quick look in, but carried on past. Finally, at 2.25 p.m., came the ambling figure of Mrs Clark, pleased to find the shop back open for her chocolate brazils, no doubt.

'Hello, Mrs Clark. How are you today?' Emma beamed from behind the counter. 'Welcome to the new Chocolate Shop Café. What do you think? You are our very first customer. Would you like to take a seat?' Emma gestured to the new window-seat areas.

'My, this looks fancy.' The old lady had a good look around her.

'And,' Emma continued, 'as you are our very first customer a cup of tea or coffee is on the house.'

'Well, that sounds very generous of you, and I don't mind if I do. That hill up's always a bit of a bugger.'

Holly and Emma gave each other a grin.

Mrs Clark spent some time chatting with them from the comfort of her window seat, enjoying a pot of English Breakfast tea and a mini brownie, which she said was 'delicious' and she bought herself her usual pack of milk chocolate brazils. After half an hour she was thanking 'the girls', saying how absolutely wonderful it was to have the new café area, that she'd see them again soon, and she then set off down the hill again.

Having someone in seemed to start a small flurry of customers, much to Emma's relief. Stan and Hilda came in whilst Mrs Clark was still there, and sat down at the other table for tea and chocolate cake. Then a gentleman who said he was staying in a nearby B&B called in for a couple of bags of fudge to take on his six-mile hike.

Then Adam called with a bunch of red and white carnations for Emma to celebrate the café's opening, in a dash as he was meant to be working, but he wished them all every success, giving Emma a hug and Holly a quick kiss on the cheek before speeding off again.

Danny from the pub dropped by, just to see how it was all looking and how his mate had done, and he couldn't resist picking up a bar of milk chocolate. He nodded his approval at the two window-seat areas, and confirmed that the payment in pints had been greatly appreciated. Emma asked him to spread the word down at The Fisherman's Arms about the new café and gave him a little poster to put up in the pub about her launch night on Friday – all welcome.

Emma had popped out to the kitchen to load the dish-washer, when she heard the door jangle open and the sounds of chatter and laughter. She headed back to help Bev and Holly out, to find four of Holly's schoolfriends there.

'Oh wow! This looks *so* cool.' Jessica, one of Holly's friends, was grinning as she looked around. 'Even better than I could have imagined.'

'Love it,' the girl beside her added. 'It's so pretty. I just want to sit here sipping hot chocolate all day.'

'Surrounded by walls of chocolate no less,' another chipped in.

It was lovely to hear that the young ones liked it. Emma felt a surge of pride.

'So, what can I get you ladies?' Bev was in full swing and obviously enjoying herself behind the counter. 'This is so much more fun than the doctors' surgery,' she added for Em's benefit.

Holly picked up the menu from the counter and passed it to the girls.

'Oh, I'd like the hot chocolate with marshmallows and cream, please,' Jessica said.

'A chocolate milkshake for me.'

'Hot choc with all the trimmings for me, too.'

'Do you do any other flavour milkshakes?'

'I can do banana or strawberry,' Emma offered. (She'd bought some different syrups just in case, but of course chocolate would be the best.)

'Banana then, please.'

It was the first hot chocolates for the café that Emma had had the chance to make and she went to town, filling the clear glass mugs with plenty of swirly cream and mini marshmallows on the top. She even popped in a chocolate-flake stick for good measure. She took these out before they melted too much, pausing by the counter for Bev to add a mini brownie on the side of each. Then she headed back to the kitchen to whizz up, first the chocolate, then the banana milkshakes in her blender, served with a dash of cream and chocolate sauce swirled on top for good measure.

'These look a-maz-ing,' Holly said as she passed them to her friends.

'Better than the milkshake bar in the town,' added her friend, Lily.

It was lovely to see the girls chatting and enjoying themselves.

After the young girls had left, one more couple sat down for coffee and shortbread, which took the time to four thirty. The Chocolate Shop Café was due to close at 5.00 p.m., and after serving one more customer with a box of chocolates, Emma thanked Holly and Bev, gave them both a big hug, and suggested they ought to be getting home.

She was aware of Max's impending arrival and felt a bit anxious. She hadn't actually told Bev about Max coming that evening – she knew her friend would be gloating about it otherwise. Emma just wanted to see how things went without the pressure of everyone knowing. Bev would be quizzing her first thing tomorrow, otherwise. She just wouldn't be able to help herself.

'I've really enjoyed helping out today,' Bev said, as she put on her coat. 'If you ever need any more help, say when Holly's at school.' She didn't want to tread on the young girl's toes. 'I'd love to come in and do a few hours here and there for you. I only work two days at the surgery and Pete's often busy out working or golfing. I really wouldn't mind.'

Hmm – now there was a thought. Emma had realised she might need more staff at some point with the café, but hadn't wanted to commit to taking anyone on until she knew how the takings were going and when the busiest times might be. Holly was still able to help at weekends and the holidays as usual, but having some extra help through the week might prove invaluable, giving Emma some precious time to create her bakes and chocolates.

'I'll have to just see how things go.' Em was cautious about finances at this point, and how she'd cover any extra wages, 'But I'm sure at times I'll need some extra help so that would be fabulous. We'll have a chat about it soon. You do seem a natural.'

Bev gave a wink. 'Always feel at home in a chocolate shop. And it's so much better than people snivelling and coughing over you at the doctors' reception desk, though I'd not leave them in the lurch, of course.'

'Bye, Emma.' Holly moved in to give her boss another hug. 'I'm so happy to see the café up and running. It's just so pretty, too. My friends really loved it. They'll be telling everyone they know about it, for sure.'

'That's great. And thanks to you, and Adam, and his gran. I couldn't have done all this without everyone's help.'

'You are so welcome.'

'See you and Adam on Friday night for the launch, yeah?'

'Oh yes, you try stopping me. But I'm sure I'll be in before then. Those hot chocolates looked delish – I need to come and try one.'

'See you soon, then.'

Holly and Bev were at the door ready to go.

'Bye, ladies. Love you both. Thank you.' Emma felt on a high.

Emma found herself alone in her shop. She didn't lock

the door but turned the sign to closed and took in everything around her. She could hardly believe what they'd managed to achieve in one weekend, with a lot of help from her family and friends, and thanks especially to Max.

Max, she sighed. Who'd have thought how things would have changed there. She'd never thought she'd be seeing him again after last week, and now he was about to turn up. She wouldn't let herself get carried away with it all though, one small step at a time.

And again her thoughts turned to Luke. She was sure he would have felt proud of her today.

Life was so strange sometimes; she often felt like she was on a rollercoaster ride and sometimes all she wanted was to get off, go back to the start, have her chance to marry Luke and live that other life – the one they had never had the chance to try.

33

It was twenty past five when Max pulled up outside. He poked his head around the shop door and smiled broadly. 'Good afternoon, chocolate-maker extraordinaire. Hey, great job in here.' He looked around at the finished Chocolate Shop Café.

Emma felt her stomach lurch in a happy way. 'Hi.'

'So, how did it all go? Were there queues of people? Was it like Black Friday?'

'Not quite,' she smiled. 'But several came in and I think, after the launch night and the press adverts, then more people will get to hear about it.'

'Yes, plenty of publicity. That'll do the trick. Then word of mouth. I can help you with a flier, if you like? Not too bad on the computer, though I say so myself.'

'Excellent. I'll take you up on that.'

'So, are you nearly ready?'

'Yep. Just give me five minutes to get wrapped up here. I'll just cash up the till.' She had a feeling just the few hours' takings that afternoon were pretty good.

266

She then headed for the rear door of the shop that led to her cottage quarters, calling over her shoulder, 'I'll get changed quickly. What kind of clothing do I need?' That might give her a clue as to their activity too; she was still curious.

'Well, warm and cosy. Thick socks. Possibly hat and gloves as well as a coat.' He was following her through.

'Ri-ight.' That didn't sound much like a romantic restaurant meal or a cinema trip. What on earth did he have in mind? After her hectic day, she didn't know if she was quite in the mood for a hike somewhere. 'Really? You're not teasing?' She stopped and turned to look at him.

'Nope.' He had a knowing grin on his face as he followed her through to the stairs. 'Shall I come up or wait here?'

'Come on up. You can sit in the living room while I find my *warm* clothing.' Now she really was intrigued, but it didn't seem like he was going to give her any more clues. 'You're still not going to tell me, are you?'

'Nope.'

Alfie headed out from the living room to greet them, his tail thwacking against their legs.

Emma gave his head a rub.

'Hi, Alfie.' Max rubbed behind his spaniel ears and the dog dropped almost instantaneously to the ground for a tummy tickle. 'Like that, do you, mate?'

'Walking boots, wellies or trainers?' Em asked as she headed through to her bedroom.

'Now you're asking . . . I'd say wellies.' Max's voice carried from the landing.

Why was this starting to fill her with dread? 'Can Alfie come?' It was sounding very like a walk somewhere, though it would soon be dusk.

'Yeah, as long as he behaves himself.'

'Of course. He's very well trained. So, we're outdoors then?'

'Stop angling, woman. You'll find out soon enough.'

'Hate surprises.'

'I can tell!'

She soon came back into the lounge, dressed in jeans, thick socks, and a cosy grey cable-knit jumper, with her tartan scarf on. She'd grab her coat and wellies, and Alfie's lead, from the hall on the way out.

'You look lovely.' Max smiled from the sofa where he and Alfie had made themselves at home. 'It's just how I picture you. Like you were when I first met you that day.'

'Thanks.' *Aw.*

'Very cuddleable in fact. Though I'm not even sure if that's a word.' And he stood up and gave her a quick hug as if to prove the point. 'Yes, very cuddleable.'

It was an extremely gorgeous cuddle, all aftershave scented and big strong arms around her, if rather too brief. 'Right, let's go then. I want to know what I'm in for.'

'Come on, Alfie. We're on.' The dog leapt from the sofa in excitement, and was soon following them down the stairs.

'I've left the jeep just up the road a bit, on a single yellow; not sure how that works of an evening, so I hope it's all right.'

The village streets were quite narrow and the traffic warden eager.

'Yeah, it's normally okay,' Emma answered. 'So, we're not walking straight away?' He was heading from the side alleyway out to his vehicle.

'No.' Again that teasing smile.

They reached the jeep and he opened the hatchback for Alfie to jump on in.

She felt she'd asked enough questions, so got in the passenger side and waited for Max to drive her to wherever it was they were headed. They set off down the main street towards the harbour where Max turned left and went along the coastal lane for 200 metres and made the turn into the beach car park.

'Is this it?' The words were out before Emma had time to stop them sounding disappointed. Some build-up that was. They could have just walked.

'Yes, we're here.' Max's tone was calm, measured.

Alfie gave an impatient whimper from the back; he just wanted out. Any walk was a good thing to him.

Emma tried her best to look enthusiastic.

'I just need to get a few things out of the boot.' Max headed to the rear of the vehicle. Emma joined him, just as Alfie was leaping out, and Max was pulling forward a large wicker basket and a bag with a couple of glass flutes poking out, as well as a soft tartan rug. The corners of her mouth began to creep up.

'Right, let's find a spot somewhere a bit more sheltered in the dunes.'

'A picnic? At the end of October?'

'Yep. Why do you think I told you to wrap up warm?'
He grinned. 'Here, could you take the rug?'

'Of course.' Hmm, well this was a first. 'I'd have put my thermals on if I'd known,' she laughed.

'I'll keep you warm, no worries,' he smiled.

Again, that crazy flutter.

They walked for about ten minutes, Max loaded up with hamper and bags, and found a secluded spot in the front of the dunes area out of the sea breeze, yet still with some of the sea view. There were a few stragglers left on the beach, a man walking his dog, whose terrier bounded across to greet Alfie, and a middle-aged couple wandering the sands hand in hand, who seemed to be heading back towards the village.

'Here okay?'

'Great.'

Max took the tartan rug from her and laid it out on a flattish patch of sand between the spiky marram grass mounds. First things first, he found the two glass flutes and pulled out a very promising-looking bottle with a gold foil seal, then popped the cork on some champagne. Wow!

'Cheers!'

'Cheers, Max! Thank you.'

They clinked glasses and she took that first delicious, bubbly sip that fizzed fragrantly on her tongue. Max sat close beside her and they looked out to sea. It was a dry night, thankfully, and, though cloudy, no sign of rain.

'So, what's in the hamper then?' She realised she was starving, having only had a slice of toast at lunchtime before opening the shop.

'All will be revealed very soon, madam. We have to wait till at least six o'clock or it'll all be over before dusk.'

'You mean we're staying out here in the dark?'

'Of course, that's half the fun of it. But never fear, I have candles.'

'Ah.'

He seemed to have thought of everything.

'I'll let you have a few crisps, if you must.'

'Yes, please.'

He pulled out a bag of salted crisps, which went fabulously with the champagne. Crunch and fizz, just perfect. They watched some terns swooping over the waves, the sea rolling in in a hush of white foam, its rush and pull soothing.

'Been a busy day for you too?' she asked.

'Yeah, pretty much full-on. The Gateshead job is going okay, but then I checked on the other job we've got near Corbridge, a barn conversion, and we were waiting for the kitchen units to come in and half the cupboards are missing. There's always something.'

'And then getting all this ready for this evening . . . '

'Ah, it's just a little something. Good job I have a local deli nearby, that's all I can say.'

'Sounds good to me.'

'So, anyhow, tell me all about your day. The first day of the coffee shop. Did the new window seats hold up?' He smiled.

'Yes, they were well tested, and seemed fine. Very strong and solid, in fact.'

'And there were quite a few people in?'

'Yes, but I don't think everyone knows we have a café now. It'll take a little time. Oh crikey, Max, I hope it works out.'

She felt she could be honest with Max. He had his own business, understood the worries of having to make it work. At least she didn't have a team of workers relying on her like he had. But she'd hate to have to let Holly down if it ever came to it; hopefully the new coffee shop venture would mean more working hours for her lovely assistant rather than less.

'Well, I know how much it means to you and how much hard work has gone in to it. So it deserves every success.' Max topped up her glass. 'Cheers to The Chocolate Shop Café. May it prosper!' He sounded like he was launching a ship or something.

Emma grinned, and put her worries aside for the moment. Yes, they should be celebrating today. 'Cheers!' They clinked glasses once more. It was lovely to be here celebrating with Max. It was lovely to feel happy, as if there was a future . . .

Max opened the picnic hamper. There were pies, prawns, a quiche, some salad, mini tomatoes, olives, grapes and a cheese selection as well as some gorgeous-looking fresh bread. There was enough there to feed a family of eight, never mind just the two of them.

'Blimey, you've gone to town. It looks great.'

He passed her a china plate, no less, and she began helping herself.

'As I said, thank the deli, not me.' He smiled.

'I don't mind at all. I didn't imagine you were busy

baking quiches and pies this morning, whilst popping across to the building site. And I don't think I'd have had the energy to cook tonight.'

'I do make a mean cheese on toast, I'll have you know. You add a dash of Worcester sauce. Delicious.' He did a happy chef gesture with a finger-flick from his lips.

They ate leisurely as the evening sun began to slip away behind them. Being the north-east coast, it set over the inland hills, but the colours of dusk brushed the whole sky. The seaward sky was deepening with shades of pink and coral. As the sun began to disappear, it got a little chillier, and a shiver went through Emma. Max shifted closer to her on the picnic rug, placing an arm around her shoulders. It felt so very natural there. 'Better?'

'Yes, better. Thanks.'

She gave Alfie a crust from the pork pie and he gobbled it down and then sat patiently, his dark brown eyes intent on them, watching and hoping for more gourmet delights to come his way.

Emma mentioned how close she was to her brother and his family, and all about Chloe making the beautiful cushions for her and the special bunting. Max was an only child. He said he got on well with his parents generally, but sounded as though he'd have liked siblings.

'No family of your own?' She put the question out there. Knowing that he was forty, there was every chance that he'd already had a family, that he might have been divorced before Siobhan, though she'd have hoped he might have mentioned it by now.

'No. No children. Of course you know that I had a serious girlfriend for a while. But that was never destined to work out. You? No children?'

It was hard to even think of Luke and the fact that they hadn't had any children together, but maybe it was time to reveal a little of her shattered heart and past. She hesitated, looking out across the darkening sea.

Max waited quietly for the few seconds it took her to form the words.

'No. No children. I was engaged . . . '

'Oh, wow.' Max looked a bit awkward.

She stared into the dusky sky, where the stars were just beginning to come out. She was almost afraid to go there, it was still so raw in her mind, that most awful of days.

'He was called Luke. He got killed, riding his bicycle home from work one day . . . he-he never came home.' And her eyes misted and she couldn't speak any more, the words still having such power to hurt, the memory drawing her back to the ragged edges of that grief.

Max's arm tightened gently around her, and she felt a soft kiss pressed down on the top of her head. 'I'm so sorry, Emma.'

And she really didn't know how she felt. Crying for one man whilst in the arms of another seemed so very strange.

They stayed in their spot in the dunes, keeping close as they watched the darkness creep across the sky. There were strawberries and chocolates – a bar of Dairy Milk, which had made Emma laugh, though she had to admit she did quite enjoy a cube or two. Max had tried and failed to light some tealight candles, as the breeze kept blowing them out. But Emma didn't mind the darkness around them, with the odd star twinkling up above, a crescent moon, and the two of them plus Alfie snuggled up on the picnic rug. But in time it became too chilly to stay for much longer, and a glance at her watch told her it was eight o'clock.

'I suppose we'd better get going soon.'

'Yeah, we might just freeze to death here if we stay much longer. I should have brought a flask of coffee to warm us up.' Max smiled in the half-light. 'But yes, I do need to get back home sharpish. Early start tomorrow.'

She wondered what his home was like – bachelor pad, modern flat, semi, scruffy, neat? She wondered if she would ever get the chance to see it – but why she was even thinking that way? 'Yes, of course.' She pulled herself back from her thoughts. 'Thank you, Max. This evening has been really lovely.' It had been a momentous kind of day, and she felt a bit emotional. She had shared a little of her tattered heart and she really wasn't sure how to deal with what was going on inside her.

'You're very welcome, Emma.'

And they finished the picnic with a strawberry-and-chocolate-flavoured kiss that was so damn tender, it felt almost magical.

After a swift drive back, Emma and Max were once again parked outside The Chocolate Shop.

275

'Would you like to come in for a coffee?' She wasn't sure where this was going, or even if she was quite ready for the next step, but what she did know was that she didn't want this night to end just yet. Going in to her flat on her own seemed suddenly a lonely prospect, even with Alfie at her side.

'I'd have loved to, but I really do have a crazily early start and I think it might be better if I get away now.'

She felt a dart of disappointment. Had she been reading this wrong? Perhaps the knowledge of Luke and her past was scaring him off. But this evening, the winter seaside picnic, was one of the most romantic things anyone had done for her, even considering the many things Luke had done.

And then Luke was there in her head . . . that balmy night when they had made love in the garden of his flat under a canopy of stars, when they thought they had forever and the world was still so sweet.

A tumble of emotions was building within as Max leant across the vehicle and took her in his arms.

'Another time maybe?' he said with a gentle smile, his stubble catching her cheek, gently abrasive, as he moved in to kiss her. His kiss wasn't saying that he was uncertain, or desperate to leave. She felt herself gradually melt into it, as she told her brain to shut up, set aside those thoughts of Luke, and be in the here and now.

As she pulled away, she spoke. 'Thank you for this evening, Max. It was really special. I loved it.'

'You're welcome,' he said, with a smile to make her heart sing.

She got out of the truck, let Alfie out from the back, and the pair of them stood watching from outside the front door of the shop as the vehicle moved off, Max giving them a final wave out of the open window and a toot of the horn. The wave of emotions that hit her was so powerful, she found herself sobbing right there out on the pavement.

'Come on, Alfie,' she sniffed, as he gave a little whimper beside her. 'Time to go home.'

34

'Okay, so what's going on? I've been trying to ring you, to see if you need any help with the coffee shop this week. Couldn't get hold of you at all last night, I tried to ring you at home on the landline and nothing, and your mobile went straight to answerphone.'

'Hi, Bev. I'm allowed to have a social life, aren't I? Isn't that what you've been nagging about for years? I was out. And, anyhow, my mobile doesn't get signal down on the beach.'

'What the heck were you doing down on the beach? It was after dark when I tried . . . Okay, what are you hiding from me?'

'Nothing.'

'Are you okay, Em? Come on, what are you doing taking Alfie down on the beach after dark? If there are things on your mind, you know you can always talk to me.'

'I know, and thank you.'

'You never know who you might meet down there on the beach at night.' Bev was still concerned.

Emma gave a smirk, remembering her romantic picnic. Then replied cheekily, 'What, like a couple of seagulls and a cormorant? This *is* Northumberland.'

'Stop being sarcastic. I can't help worrying about you.'

Emma started giggling then. She might as well put her friend out of her misery and share a little of what was going on in her life. 'I was actually with someone on the beach.'

'You were? It *so* has to be Max.'

'Uhuh.'

'See, for all your complaining, I knew it was right to get in touch with him. And?'

'I like him. We're getting on quite well. He'd made a picnic supper.'

'It's almost winter! Is he mad?'

'Possibly,' Emma smiled. 'But it was really nice . . . Oh, bloody hell, Bev, I'm scared.' Em was only now realising what that strange mix of emotions had been driven by last night.

'He wasn't a bit creepy, was he? A stalker type?'

'Noo, not that – I'm scared that I might like him too much. Scared of what might happen next, scared of what Luke might think.'

'Oh Em, if somehow Luke can see, hear, be around you, would he really want to see you unhappy and on your own?'

'I'm not unhappy. I've just been getting on with things. Focusing on the chocolate shop.' Emma became defensive.

'You've been so busy, yes, but have you really been thinking about yourself? Your needs?'

'I'm fine.'

'Em, maybe it's time for things to change a bit. Maybe this guy is the start of something new.'

'Possibly.'

'Did he stay over?'

'Hah – nosy, or what?'

'Just asking.'

'No.'

'Ah.'

'It's still early days – and I really don't feel ready to take that next step just yet.' Though she knew she was damned close last night.

'Well, make sure you get some condoms, just in case.'

'Be-ev.'

'Better safe than sorry. Forearmed is forewarned and all that.'

'Blimey, you're sounding like my mother.'

But maybe her friend was right. Hah, she could just imagine the gossip if she went into the village stores for a white loaf, Lurpak, a half-dozen eggs – and a packet of condoms. She'd maybe have to take a trip to the larger supermarket in Alnwick.

But how would it feel with someone else after all this time? How would it feel to be with someone other than Luke? Physically, mentally, might it feel like a betrayal? Or just different?

'It's been seven years, Em.' Bev's voice was gentle but firm down the line, as though she'd been reading her thoughts. 'I never met Luke, but he sounds like he was a great guy, not someone who'd selfishly never want you to move on.'

Emma sighed softly. 'I know.'

'Right, so when are we going to meet up?' Bev's tone was cheery. 'Then you can fill me in on all the detail.'

'Hah, perhaps.' There were some details she was definitely going to keep to herself. 'Pop in for a coffee later. I'm just about to open up shop as per usual.'

'Yes, of course. I'm off to work too. So, shall I call by on my way home, say threeish?'

'Great, see you then. You might even get a square of brownie.'

'Yes, well, I hope it all goes really great today for The Chocolate Shop, and I can help for a few hours tomorrow if you need. I enjoyed it yesterday.'

'Brilliant. That might give me the chance to get on with making the chocolate canapés I'm planning for the launch night.'

'Oh my, they sound scrummy. Maybe this coffee shop idea isn't so good after all – my waistline will be expanding by the day.'

'Hah – see you later.'

'Look forward to it. Bye.'

It was Wednesday afternoon, and Bev had come in to help. They'd put the world to rights and had a good natter the day before – well, for all of fifteen minutes until Emma had to serve another customer.

There had been a friendly flow of customers so far

today, both old and new, taking a look, and stopping for a cup of something and a chocolate treat or two. When it became quieter, at around three thirty, Bev said she was happy to mind the shop if Emma needed a chance to get on with things in the kitchen. The two of them had been chatting about ideas for the launch night on Friday, when Emma had invited the local press along, a couple of local councillors, her landlord (she felt she had to and it might keep him sweet), as well as all her friends, family, and the village community, so she needed to make everything look and taste extra special.

Em was in the kitchen deciding which moulds and flavours to use. Some of her harbour-themed chocs might go down well – she had anchor and boat-shaped moulds and puffin shapes for chocolate lollipops to keep the seaside feel, and she'd also make a selection of 'getting-in-the-mood-for-Christmas' goodies including her classic Christmas-pudding truffles, mini white chocolate snowmen, with Santas and reindeers in both dark and milk (Lucy and Olivia would love those). Then she'd have some whisky, brandy, and pink champagne truffles and some melt-in-the-mouth pralines too. That would give a lovely, varied selection and with flutes of bubbly – she could stretch to Prosecco, not quite champagne – it should look rather special.

She made a start on the mini snowmen and the white-choc brandy truffles, pouring white chocolate callets to temper in the machine. She then went upstairs to dig out the Christmas decorations to try for her launch-night window display.

She popped down to check on the shop after fifteen minutes of wrestling with reindeers, tinsel, and baubles, and found Bev happily serving a middle-aged gentleman with a small cafetière of coffee. She'd remembered to put the mini brownie on the side, bless her. Bev made a thumbs-up sign, and Emma headed back to the kitchen to start pouring the white chocolate into the snowmen moulds. She'd already painted a little line of food colouring in each individual mould to make a red scarf for them all.

The afternoon whizzed by as she made the brandy truffle centres ready to cover in white chocolate. It was great getting a step ahead for Friday.

The shop's telephone went. It was carpenter Ron, who'd thankfully made a full recovery and offered to come in that evening after closing to move the refrigerated counter back as originally planned to make some more room in the café area. Excellent news!

They tidied up and were finished by five, Bev saying she'd pop across a bit earlier to help prepare for the launch on Friday.

Emma had just made herself a very welcome cup of tea. She'd been on her feet nearly all day and had just let Alfie out into the yard, so she needed a few minutes to sit on the sofa before it was all go again. Her phone went.

'Hey, been a busy day, Em?' Max.

'Yeah, all go.' She stifled a yawn. 'Sorry, I'm just shattered.'

'Yeah, I bet, you haven't stopped in days.'

'Not really, no.'

'Well, keep smiling, and have a good couple of days.'

It was lovely hearing Max's voice. It seemed to melt away the tensions of the day.

'Looking forward to seeing you on Friday for the launch,' he continued 'And if there's anything I can do, or bring along to help, just shout.'

'Will do. I might actually need a bit of help serving the Prosecco, so you could be my waiter.'

'I can make a very suave waiter, no worries. Anyway, I'm famished, been a hectic day here too. I'd better get away and get myself a takeout. Sweet and sour is calling my name.'

She smiled. 'Sounds like we're both under pressure.'

'Yeah, a bit. There's always something happening in the building trade, to be fair. Joys of running your own business too.'

'Yep. Well, I'm going for some cheese and crackers now, and I'd better take Alfie out for a walk before Ron gets here. He's coming to move the counter back. And then I'm going to have a long soak in the bath. I've still got two chairs left to paint tomorrow.'

'Hmm, that's sounds good.'

'What? Painting? It isn't that exciting.'

'No, the thought of you . . . in a hot bath.'

She felt the heat rise up her neck, as an image of him *and* her in a hot bath flashed up unbidden.

'Yeah, well . . . ' she virtually squeaked.

'It'll all be worth it in the end,' he added in a normal tone. 'See you, Friday.'

'Okay.'

'Have a good week. Miss you.' His final words were

warm and sweet and sounded like they were meant.

'You too,' she answered. 'Max . . . on Friday . . . would you like to stay?'

There was a silent pause down the line, while he registered her words.

'Right . . . great.'

There, it was said now, no chance of backing out or coming up with a million reasons why not. They both knew where this was heading.

Ron turned up soon after the phone call, which helped stop Emma's head spinning. He'd brought his son along to get the job done quicker and Emma had already emptied out the refrigerated counter.

She left them to it, using the time to make some more brownies. They called her back through three-quarters of an hour later and shifting the counter back had really opened out the space.

Lovely Maureen appeared to see how they were getting on, bringing yet another chocolate cake. It looked gorgeous, with thick chocolate frosting. Emma thanked her and asked if she might be interested in a regular baking order, on a paid-for basis, providing at least two chocolate cakes per week. Maureen seemed thrilled her cake was so popular and said she was more than happy to do so. Result!

Ron mentioned he'd had an idea for some shelving for the side wall of the café – somewhere to put small bags of treats to catch the customers' eyeline.

'I have just the thing in mind, lassie. Can you trust me on it?' He had a glint in his eye, as he spoke. He

began measuring up the space. 'I'll make it up in my workshop tomorrow and have it with you ready to pop on the wall tomorrow evening. I'll be in around five-thirty, if that's okay, after you've closed. Save all the hammering and dust annoying your customers.'

'It sounds interesting.' Emma was curious.

Thursday whizzed by; she was hectic manning the shop and café single-handedly, as well as trying to get a step ahead with her chocolate canapé creations for tomorrow's launch. She'd definitely need to take Bev up on her offer of regular help if it carried on being this busy. At least she'd have Holly back on Saturday, but she'd still have to be careful with extra wages for now.

Emma put the shop sign to closed and popped upstairs to collect the Christmas decorations ready to design her window displays. She heard a knocking at the shop door as she came down the stairs with armfuls of decorations. She put them down on a table top and went to open it to find Ron there bearing a large grin and a small upturned boat, or so it seemed. He carried it in and turned it around. The mini hull was painted with blue and white bold stripes. It was the most amazing shelf-rack shaped like a boat, with four shelves inside ready to load with fudge bags, chocolate lollipops and more. Just perfect for a harbour-village chocolate shop, and for her launch.

'Thank you so much, Ron. I love it!' Emma had tears in her eyes as she spoke.

'Well, I felt awful letting you down like that at the weekend, lass. Least I could was make you something a little bit special for your shelves. Anyway, I enjoyed it. And if people like it and ask, let them know I can make more, in different sizes too. See, you're actually doing me a favour having it on display here.'

'Well, all I know is that it will look fabulous with my chocolates and fudge in.'

'Glad to be of service.' He gave a mock bow. 'Nautical but nice,' he added with a cheeky wink.

'Well, let me settle up with you for all the work you did last night as well as this wonderful shelf creation.'

Ron named his price which seemed extremely reason-able. She was very proud to be able to pay him out of her takings for this week and she even had some spare to put towards the bubbly for tomorrow night, though she'd have to delve into her loan to make sure there was plenty for everyone to have at least a glass or two. She wasn't quite sure how many were actually coming. She'd asked several people and put invitations up on the village noticeboard, in the shop, and at The Fisherman's Arms. There was also an article with a photo of her in the new coffee shop area going into the *Gazette* today.

'Now, make sure you and Maureen pop along tomorrow night for the launch.'

'Will do.'

'And your son too; does he have a girlfriend? The more the merrier.' Emma smiled. She just wanted to thank everyone who had helped, and hopefully spread the word about her venue too.

'I'll certainly mention it to him.'

She suddenly wondered how exactly she was going to

fit everyone into the little shop – there could be up to forty people, maybe more. Ah well, if it was dry weather, they could spill out into the back courtyard or the pavement out front. It would all work out somehow.

After Ron had gone, Emma began creating her window display. She loved doing this – marking the seasons with her chocolate themes, hoping it might just catch the eye of a passer-by to draw them in. She set her iPhone to her cheesiest Christmas tracks and soon found herself humming along to George Michael's 'Last Christmas'.

At the base of each window she created a bed of fake snow, then she began hanging wooden-painted stars and silver baubles so they dangled halfway down the windows, along with some of her handmade chocolate stars, which had a dusting of sparkly sugar sprinkles on.

A face appeared on the other side of the glass, which made Emma jump out of her skin. When she focussed, she realised it was Holly, standing there laughing.

Em went to the door. 'Jeez, Holly. You frightened the life out of me. What are you doing here?'

'Well, you said you were going to do the Christmas window displays tonight and I love doing all that stuff, so I thought I'd come along to help!'

'Aw, thanks. Come on in, then.' With that Em turned the music up a notch, and handed Holly some baubles and stars to help dress the other window.

In one window, they set out an old red wooden toy train that had been James's when he was little and filled all the carriages with colourful bags of truffles, fudge, and mini Christmas-pudding chocolates. In the second window, they stood a row of mini Christmas trees alongside a selection of chocolate figures, including a Father Christmas, chocolate reindeer, and snowmen. It was like a festive chocoholic forest.

'Brilliant. I love it,' said Holly as the two of them looked down the back of the window seats, admiring their work.

'Hang on, I'll go outside and check.' Emma stood outside, then motioned for Holly to move a couple of the mini trees, and then gave a grin and a thumbs-up sign.

When she came back in, Em found two red Christmas stockings with appliqué stars on that would look nice pinned to the counter front at each side of Chloe's bunting. All they needed to do now was to string up the white, twinkly fairy lights along the shelving at the back of the counter area and they'd be all set.

'It's beginning to feel a lot like Christmas,' chanted Holly, as Emma switched the pretty white lights on.

Suddenly, Mariah Carey came blasting out from the iPhone, and the pair of them began dancing around the shop together. As they sang 'All I want for Christmas is you' at the tops of their voices, they pointed at all the chocolates, giggling.

'Can't wait for Christmas now,' Holly grinned.

'Me too. Love this time of year.' And she really did, despite the painful memories it sometimes brought back.

'It's going to look great here for the launch night, Em. You have done such an amazing job.'

'Aw, thanks, Hols. And thanks for all your help tonight.'

'Hey, I've had a ball doing it. This isn't like work at all.'

'Right, well I'll get these spare decorations put away.' And she ought to let Alfie out into the back yard. In fact, she might even take him out for a quick stroll down to the harbour and back. The fresh air and a stretch of her legs might do her good.

'I'm going to take Alfie out in a minute, Hols. Shall I walk you back?'

'If you want. Yeah, that'd be nice.'

They soon set off, the girls chatting away, Alfie trotting on his lead by their side. It was only a five-minute stroll to Holly's house on the other side of the village.

'Night, Hols. Thanks again.'

'Night, Em. And I really enjoyed myself tonight. I'll see you tomorrow night for the launch, then.'

'Yes, exciting, hey. I just hope it goes off well.'

'It will do. It'll be brilliant, I'm telling you.'

They shared a hug, and Holly went in to her family.

As she walked back, Emma could hear the buzz of people in The Fisherman's Arms, but she didn't want to join them, just stood leaning on the black metal harbour rail, watching the reflections of light in the calm bob of the water. A half-moon had risen over the sea, casting its silvery light on to the waves outside the harbour. Alfie stood waiting patiently beside her, his tail wagging slowly to and fro. There was a sense of peace here. She was glad she had found this place, had come to think of it as home.

When it had all changed, and her life had been devastated, there was something about this coast, the harbour here, and this particular community, that had captured her heart and helped her heal.

35

Her phone woke her up. She fumbled for it on the bedside table. It was still pitch dark in the room. *Max* lit up on the screen. What on earth was the time?

'Hey.'

'Hi! Is it as early as it feels?'

'Yes, thought you would be up getting ready for your big launch day.'

'Not quite.' She glanced at her watch through foggy eyes. Six thirty and her alarm was set for six forty-five.

'Oops, sorry. I was just heading off for the site. Thought I'd catch up with you before it got hectic there.'

'Okay.' She was still feeling a little woozy.

'Well, you have a good day, and I'll see you this evening.' Neither mentioned about him staying over. 'I'll be coming up as soon as I get finished here, after a quick shower.'

'That's great. I'll see you later.'

'You all organised? Anything I can do or bring?'

'Yeah, I'm pretty much sorted here, thanks. Just bring

yourself and your smile for your waiter job.' She was waking up now, happy that he had thought to call her.

'See you later.' His voice was honey-warm down the phone.

'Yeah, see you later.' And she felt nervous and excited all at once at the prospect of getting to know him even more tonight.

Emma was making another batch of chocolate canapés, afraid she might not have made enough. She had poured melted chocolate into the moulds earlier and was now filling them with golden salted caramel. It was only eight thirty, but she wanted to be sure she was ready for this evening, in case today proved busy in the café.

So much to do, so little time. After dashing about before opening, and making several calls, she was as prepared as she could be for tonight and it was all systems go again because Friday was usually a busier day anyhow.

Some ramblers came in and asked if she did takeaway coffees. For now, she couldn't help, but she assured them that as from next week she would have a supply of cardboard cups for takeouts – another way of making money, hopefully. She could put a little 'Takeouts available' sign in the window.

Adam appeared at lunchtime, grinning cheerily as he came through the door. 'Hey, Emma. It looks great in here.'

'Cheers, Adam. Your gran did a brilliant job on the seat pads for me.'

'I've just popped along from work.'

'Everything fine for the hotel? Have you got enough of our mini chocolate boxes for the turndowns?'

'Yes, that's all fine. They're still really popular . . . It's just . . . I noticed your new window display and it looks really good, but I know Gran's got something that might just make it even better.'

'Interesting. Tell me more.'

'Well, my grandad liked making things – he was really clever like that – and one year he made me a toy sleigh, out of wood. It was really cool. I loved it. Gran kept it at home, so it came out as a special treat every year. Well, the thing is, she still has it. And last night, I spotted your Christmas window display and seeing that wooden train brought it to mind, so I mentioned it to her and she'd like to let you have it for the shop, if you're interested.'

'Well, it sounds lovely.'

'It's got that old-fashioned look.'

'Santa on his sleigh . . . hmm. Does it have room for chocolates in the back?'

'Absolutely. We could even suspend it with some thin wires and have it mid-flight over the forest you've made,' Adam suggested.

'Well, it sounds absolutely perfect. If you're sure your gran doesn't mind.'

'No, she said she'd like to see it used again.'

'Aw, well thank her so much. Actually, take a couple of packs of the coffee and orange creams she loves with you as a thank you. And bring her along this evening too.'

'I'll take the chocolates to her, that'll make her day.

And I'll mention the launch, but she's not always keen on coming out in the dark evenings.'

'Well, if she does fancy it . . . Will you be coming with Holly? How are things going with you two?'

'Yeah, great, thanks, we get on really well. She's getting really excited about Christmas already and I have no idea what to get her. I'm not very good at that kind of thing.'

'Come and see me nearer the time. I'm sure we can come up with some ideas together.'

'Thanks, Em. Right, I'd better head back. I was just picking up some soya milk from the stores – hotel customer with allergies or something. I'll call back in my lunch hour with the sleigh.'

'Brilliant. I can't wait to see it. Sounds fabulous.'

'Cheers.'

'Bye, Adam, and thanks again.' She passed him the bag of chocolate goodies to take away, adding a packet of whisky truffles for himself too.

What to wear? It was ten past six. Emma had set out her chocolate canapés on white china platters ready to pass around and had pretty, red paper napkins with festive snowflakes on that matched the new seating area colours. The cushions had all been plumped and the shelves were full of goodies, including Ron's wonderful boat-shaped stand. The shop was looking so lovely with the fairy lights on behind the counter and soft lighting focussed on the festive window displays.

But Emma had kind of forgotten about herself until

now. She was still in her workwear of black trousers, white T-shirt and black apron. Now then, what should a chocolatier, café-running, chocolate-shop boss look like? She had invited the local press from Alnwick along, as well as her landlord, and couple of village councillors, so she ought to look fairly smart; there might end up being some photographic evidence, which was all good for publicity, but she didn't want to look too stuffy and formal either. Smart casuals, that's what she needed. She had one last check that all was ready in the shop, then headed upstairs to her bedroom where she frisked the wardrobe.

She could get away with keeping on the black trousers if she teamed them with something more colourful. She dismissed a few jumpers and a casual Breton-style top that looked a bit washed out, then she landed on a blouse, navy-blue with a red and green pattern of roses on – that might do. It was a soft chiffon-style material, and would need a strappy vest under it as it was a bit see-through, but yes, it was pretty, and as she put it on she felt comfortable in it. Sorted.

She ran a brush through her long, wavy red hair. Should she put it back? She always wore it in a bun or a high ponytail for work, and when she was full-on chocolatiering she wore a white protective cap to save any red hairs appearing in the mix. She laughed out loud: a hygiene hat, now that would be some sexy look! Hah, perhaps it might turn Max on, she mused. Not that he seemed to need any help in that department. She felt a little frisson of anticipation, thinking that Max would be here with her in less than an hour. And then, later this evening . . . *Right, focus on the task in hand, Emma.* She needed to make sure this launch went off well, to publicise her business and as a lovely thank you to the local community. She dragged her mind back to where it should be.

Bev was the first to arrive at six thirty. Several bottles of Prosecco were chilling in the fridge, and an overflow box of six were outside in the back yard – it was certainly cool enough there to keep them chilled.

Emma hadn't quite planned what would happen when people arrived, other than serving them a glass of fizzy and passing round the chocolate platters. She hoped people would just chat, relax, and mill about a bit. She would have to do a bit of circulating and she supposed she ought to say a few words of thanks at some point and pronounce The Chocolate Shop Café officially open. She didn't really like to think of the attention being on her – she'd keep that bit brief.

'We'd better have a bit of music, don't you think, Bev?'

'Yeah, just some background style, easy listening.'

Emma had a small speaker that linked to her iPhone, choosing a mix of Adele, Keane, John Legend and Coldplay.

The sleigh in the window caught her eye. Adam had come back with the prized wooden toy his grandad had made, as promised. It was now hung in pride of place in the window and she had filled the back of the sleigh with mini bags of fudge and chocolates (ideal stocking fillers), and some small gold boxes tied with festive red ribbon.

She had even found just the right size chocolate Santa figure to pop in the front. Below it, she had rearranged her chocolate reindeer to stand in two rows of four with red ribbon strung from them up to the sleigh, so it looked like they had just landed in the snow. Perfect. It looked magical.

Pete was due to join them soon, but there really wasn't much to do until the guests arrived. First in the door, at five to seven, was Max, bearing a gorgeous smile and a bottle of champagne. He gave Emma a kiss on the cheek, saying, 'Congratulations.'

Bev eyed them curiously, wondering exactly was going on between them. Emma just smiled.

Then several people arrived at once. James and Chloe, with the twins who were delighted to be staying up late drinking lemonade and eating chocolate. Emma's parents, who had driven over from Rothbury, soon followed. Her family had supported her so much, not just with the chocolate shop but with everything since Luke had died. She didn't know how she would have managed without them.

'Hello, darling,' her mum greeted her with a warm hug. 'My, this looks wonderful in here. What a difference.'

A difference that they had kindly funded and Emma was so grateful. 'Yes, I'm so pleased with it,' she said. 'And thank you both so much for your help with it all.'

Her mum clasped her hands together joyfully as she looked about her. 'You are so welcome.'

'Hello, Dad.'

Her father, Geoff, was bringing up the rear as usual

with a bottle of bubbly and some gorgeous flowers. 'Hello, love.'

'Aw, these are so pretty. Thank you. I hadn't even thought of flowers. They will look great on one of my new tables.' She gave him a one-armed hug as the bouquet was handed across. She introduced her parents to Max (as a friend). She saw her mother's eyebrow twitch slightly as she gave her daughter the most subtle of glances; was her mum's intuition kicking in already or was Emma just feeling sensitive? Emma left them chatting to Bev as she went off to find a vase to pop the bouquet of pink and cream roses in.

Lucy and Olivia then spotted their grandparents and ran up to them keeping them busy with their animated chatter.

When Emma came back just a few minutes later with the flowers in a glass vase, Bev was serving Prosecco to Holly and Adam who had just arrived. Maureen and Ron then appeared, closely followed by Danny from the pub with his latest girlfriend, a pretty girl with a mass of wavy blonde hair, who he introduced as Clara.

Soon The Chocolate Shop Café was more than cosy, more like bulging at the seams as Sheila from the village stores arrived, bringing along old Mrs Clark with her. Emma found a space for them to sit down in one of the new window-seat areas and they had to leave the shop door open at this point so some of the guests could spill out on to the street. A few more friends and acquaintances from the village community arrived, as well as a guy from the local newspaper with a huge camera slung round his neck. That sight filled Emma with a touch of dread – she hated being the centre of attention, but she knew she ought to say a few words. After all, that was the whole point of the evening. So, she topped up everyone's glasses, including her own, and took a big gulp from it, before dinging on her glass with a metal spoon.

The room hushed and all eyes fell on Emma. She tried to smile, and took a deep breath. Damn, she wished she'd made a few notes now. She hoped her mind wouldn't go blank on her.

'Hello . . . ' The last few strands of conversations halted. 'Thank you all so much for coming. I really appreciate it . . . ' How to put into words how she felt about this lovely community? 'Well, I hope you like the new Chocolate Shop Café, and I hope you'll become regular visitors and spread the word. But, more than that,' she felt a lump forming in her throat, 'I . . . I just want to thank each and every one of you for all your help, not just with this venture but in welcoming me here to Warkton-by-the-Sea several years ago, when life was quite difficult for me, and for making me feel at home. So many special people have helped me on my journey – Mum, Dad, James and Chloe and the girls, Bev, Pete, Danny, Holly . . . Sorry, I can't name you all . . . and more recent friends,' she looked around and her eyes settled on Max, 'who have helped so much. A great big thank you!'

She raised her glass, because she knew her voice might not hold out much longer as the tears that had misted her eyes were threatening to jam up her throat. 'Cheers.'

'Cheers!'

'To Emma!' Bev shouted out.

'To The Chocolate Shop Café,' Adam rallied.

'To friends and family,' Emma managed, and proceeded to clink her glass with so many people's she was afraid it might break. One little tear escaped her eye and possibly plinked down in to her Prosecco, a happy, thankful tear – she didn't think anyone had spotted it.

Chocolates were passed around – Max and Holly were proving handy – and the platters refilled. Emma stood in the middle of the action, holding a bottle ready to top up glasses, but stopped for a second and just watched – people were chatting in clusters or sat at the new table areas, sipping their drinks in the glow of the fairy lights, with a backdrop of chocolates and Christmas decorations, and Ron's boat-shelf taking pride of place (it had been getting lots of positive comments), the sounds of laughter and conversation. She felt a glow of pride.

Max caught her eye in that moment and gave her the most gorgeous smile. He'd been chatting with her brother James and they looked like they were getting on fine. She smiled back at him, took a slow breath, then began circulating again.

The evening passed in a whirl. Her landlord, the Eel, turned up late and had one quick drink as he cast a greedy eye over the new improvements, no doubt scheming the next rent hike. Then it seemed that, no sooner had people had arrived, than they started to drift away again. In reality, it had been over two hours since the start of the event. Her guests left with lots of thanks and kisses and hugs, until there was only Bev, Pete, and

Max left. Emma suddenly found herself feeling shattered. She stifled a yawn.

'Well, that seemed to go off fabulously,' Bev announced.

'Yes.' Em glanced at her watch. 'Wow, I can't believe it's gone nine.'

'Let's help you get shipshape here.' Bev started clearing the mostly empty platters of chocolate away, swooping two salted caramels into her mouth at once. 'Just tidying up,' she grinned after they had melted enough for her to talk. 'Waste not, want not.'

Emma had to smile, and Max and Pete started on the washing-up.

Emma was busy wiping over the shop surfaces when Bev and Pete came through from the kitchen.

'Right, well that's us done,' Bev stated.

Max came back through too and stood near the counter at that point. 'Well, I'll just help Emma with the last of the tidying,' he said coolly, obviously intending to be the last one there.

'Night then,' Bev said.

Emma felt a little nudge in her ribs as her friend put down the box of flutes she was holding and gave her a goodnight kiss on the cheek, whispering, 'You little minx, you. What *exactly* is going on?'

Emma declined to answer, so Bev added loudly and pointedly, 'Well, I'll be ringing you tomorrow! It's been a great launch. Well done, Em. You should be proud of yourself.'

Emma grinned. 'Woo-hoo to The Chocolate Shop Café! And thanks so much for everything.'

'Always welcome, my lovely friend. Take care.' With that, Bev gave Max a sharp look, as if to say look after her, or else.

'Night guys.'

'Night,' Max answered, as the men shook hands.

'Have a good night,' Bev said as she was half out the door. It was so obvious that she was gossiping with Pete as they passed the window that Emma and Max turned to each other and laughed out loud.

'Well done, Em. It went really well. It looked wonderful in here, and the chocolates were just stunning. I kept hearing loads of positive comments from everyone as I was passing them round.'

'Aw, thanks. I'm happy. Tired but happy.'

There was a tension notching up through the room, as they both knew the time had probably come to take the next step – but who was going to make the first move?

She spotted a few last Prosecco glasses they'd missed on the counter. She picked them up as if to head to the kitchen. *Delaying tactics, you coward,* her mind was heckling her, Bouncer had definitely left her head space. Oh jeez.

Max caught up with her in two steps, brushed the hair from the side of her neck and kissed her there, oh so tenderly, making all sorts of strange things happen to her insides.

She turned to face him, her back now against the counter. He pressed his body against hers as he kissed her once more, deep and sensual with tongues probing, twining. *Oh my . . .*

Sod the washing-up. She placed the glasses back down beside her and cupped the back of his head in her hands, where his hair was short, slightly spiky, firmly holding his face to hers as the kiss continued, intensely. They both knew where this was heading.

Max pulled back gently. His deep green eyes fixed on hers. 'Are you okay? You sure about this?'

'Yes,' her voice squeaked. Bloody hell, why was she so damned nervous? She was a thirty-six-year-old woman, for heaven's sake. It wasn't as though she'd never done this before. 'Ah . . . it's just I haven't had sex in four years,' she blurted out.

'Four *years*?'

'Yep.'

'Well, no wonder you're nervous. And hey, no pressure on me then . . . Better make it worthwhile.' He gave her a gorgeous, cheeky grin, and took her back into a hug.

It might just be all right. Hopefully, much more than all right. In fact, she couldn't think of anyone else she'd rather be about to have sex with, to be honest, and that included Ryan Gosling and Gerard Butler.

Go girl! A new voice took over in her mind. It was feisty and sexy and she hadn't heard it in a very long time.

She took his hand and led him upstairs, heading initially for the living room (she felt slightly anxious about leading him straight off to bed), where she gently told him to sit down.

'You have a thing about sofas, don't you?' he smiled. A smile that was warm through to his eyes – his very sexy eyes.

304

She moved to position herself on his lap, so very close. Took his face in her hands again and began kissing him extremely slowly, yearning growing between them. She felt this huge, rather scary, overwhelming feeling of love for him. Oh my, could this really be love again? He had made her laugh, smile, had wiped her tears, held her hand – he'd even stood in for the carpenter, despite being so busy himself, to make her chocolate shop café come true, dammit – and now this, this last beautiful hurdle.

They were both fully clothed, but couldn't be much closer. She could feel the heat from his jeans, the firmness there beneath her. She was obviously doing something right, even though she was a little out of practice.

She gave a long, slow sigh. 'I think we should take this to the bedroom.'

Alfie, who'd followed them through and was sitting beneath the sofa, raised an eyelid, and then slid his head back down to the floor.

Emma took Max's hand and led the way, excited and slightly anxious all at once.

She was with this gorgeous man in her double room. And there was Luke looking at her from the dressing table. Oh, no, she hadn't thought to move his photo. But that would have seemed wrong too. No, she mustn't think of him now. But how could she not, he was still such a huge part of her life? But she knew if she didn't give herself to Max, she'd never give herself to anyone again. *He's gone, Emma. It's okay*, a voice in her mind spoke out. A silent tear welled in her eye. She blinked quickly, turned to face Max, and buried herself in his kisses.

Max was tender and caring, taking things slowly, yet not too slowly, kissing her shoulders as he slipped her blouse over her head, tracing her body with confident, caring hands. She kissed him back, touched him, tracing the hard, muscular lines of his body so different from Luke's leaner form, his body, so wonderfully new to her.

Then there was nothing but skin on skin, and their slow, rhythmic dance of love. Every nerve ending tingled, delighted, so alive. He plunged deep within her, still kissing her. Oh, my!

And they moved together, until she came in a warm, beautiful pulse around him.

They clung to each other.

'Wow,' Max whispered, still above her.

Then from nowhere tears formed, Emma struggled to keep them back.

'Em, are you okay? Did I hurt you?' Max scanned her tearful face.

She wiped at her eyes with the back of her hand as he gently moved to lie beside her.

'I'm okay,' but she couldn't hide the sniffling from her voice. 'Really, I'm okay. Sorry.'

He held her to him for a few tender moments. She could feel the mass of balled-up emotions within her unravelling.

She needed to try to explain. 'I didn't think that I could ever feel like that again.' It was so beautiful, tender, like he'd reached her soul somehow. It was so much more than sex.

He smiled, relaxed a little, looked at her as she spoke

again. 'And it feels kind of strange too. Disloyal to Luke, you know . . .?'

'Yeah, I get that.'

'I'm sorry . . . Maybe I shouldn't have said anything. It's nothing against you.'

She lay quietly. Her head on his chest, his arms gently around her.

'You know,' he began, 'if I were your Luke I wouldn't want you to be sad or lonely, or not have someone special in your life to care for you. It's been what, seven years, Emma? I think he'll be happy for you, honestly.' He stroked her hair. 'If he thought as much of you as I do, he'd want you to be happy again.'

The words sank in . . . Max must feel so much for her. Were they learning to love each other? She snuggled up close to him. He was still slightly sweaty from their lovemaking, and that felt good. And though her heart was still in two places, yes, put like that, it made sense.

'Thank you.' She spoke against his chest.

'Well, I mean, I'd like you to wait at least *five* years or so, after I'm gone. I'll be haunting you else – if you were to go near another bloke too soon,' he quipped to lighten the mood.

The thought of losing someone else she cared so much for . . . She couldn't begin to imagine being faced with that again, felt a prickle of fear. 'Well, I'm kind of hoping we won't have to go through anything like that . . . '

'Yeah, me too.' And he kissed the top of her head.

36

'Morning, beautiful.'

What a lovely way to be woken up. 'Morning,' she answered.

Emma vaguely remembered coming to in the middle of the night and realising there was a man in her bed; a lovely, gorgeous, Max-shaped man. And then was a little mortified as she remembered how she'd been in a bit of state over Luke.

But Max hadn't taken it too personally by the sound of it. He leaned across and gave her a peck on the cheek, his light beard rather tickly.

'Gotta get up and get going, I'm afraid. I need to be on site at Gateshead by eight thirty. I'm meeting the owner of the property we're working on.'

'Ah, shame.' And she snuggled in a little closer, with her bare breasts nestled against his chest. She *really* did not want Max to leave her bed just yet.

He looked down at what was going on, not able to hide the longing in his eyes as he took in the fullness of her breasts against him. 'Now that's mean,' he smiled, 'when I haven't got time to do anything about it. I really, really do have to go, Em.' He sounded like he was trying to persuade himself, and with a decisive lurch he started getting out of bed.

Emma watched his firm, bare back, the muscles defined there, the neat buttocks below a little paler than the rest of him. Hmm. She lay there smiling to herself, but the bed was starting to feel colder already.

She also had loads to do herself, but she couldn't resist leaping out of bed to follow him. She had missed this physical contact, these feelings so much. She embraced him from behind, her arms tight around his chest, and started kissing the back of his neck. He turned to her, his erection perfectly formed, kissed her mouth provocatively, setting light to every nerve in her body.

'Another time . . . ' He grinned, moving away from her to grab his clothes, then heading for the bathroom. 'I really have to get ready and go.'

'Do you want to come back tonight?' Emma had called Max by mid-afternoon. She'd gone from ice maiden to red-hot lover in the space of a weekend.

'Are you sure?'

'Oh, yes.'

'Well then, I won't keep a lady waiting. Of course. I'll drive up after work.' She could hear the smile in his tone.

'I'll make some supper. But, don't get too excited. It won't be anything too fancy. Anything you don't eat?'

'Not really.'

'Good. See you later then. Better go, there's someone just come in to the shop.'

'See you later, Em.'

After clearing up the final debris from last night, taking a quick shower, and making more choc-chip shortbread as the jar was emptying out, Emma had another hectic day. Whilst Holly served at the counter, Emma was dashing about making up the orders: teas, coffees, hot chocolates (she ran out of spray cream at one point and had to make a dash to the grocer's), and she warmed slices of Maureen's wonderful three-layer cake served with a blob of cream as an option which was proving extremely popular. There were milkshakes to blend, brownies to cut to size for the mini bites – it was all go. In fact, there was someone in constantly from opening to close, which was just fabulous and the till had kept on dinging.

They finally turned the sign over at twenty past five.

'Hey, what a day,' Holly said, as she cleared the last of the cups and saucers. 'It never got this busy even in the chip shop. It's just brill, Em. Everyone loves the coffee shop idea.'

'Yeah, I'm still pinching myself that it's all really happened. Thanks so much for that lightbulb moment, Hols, and for all your help in making it a reality.'

'No worries, Em. I still love working here, even though my feet are done in today.'

'Mine too.' In fact, she felt like she was pretty much aching all over. The physical and mental effort of the past few weeks was catching up on her.

She paid Holly her wages in cash and was able to give her assistant a little bonus. 'Just to say thanks for all the help you've given me over the last couple of weeks too.'

'Aw, Em. You don't have to.'

'No, you've worked hard. You deserve it. Go and get yourself a little treat. Also, Hols, I'm going to need you to do full days on a Saturday for me, right up until Christmas at least, and I know in two weeks' time I've got myself booked to do a Christmas market. Thought I'd give it a try. Do you think you can manage here? I could get Bev to come in and give you a hand, knowing how busy it was today. Yes, that'd be better, wouldn't it?'

'Yeah, the two of us would be good, if you were away. But yes, that's fine. The extra pay will be great for getting Christmas presents. I have no idea what to get Adam yet and I want it to be special.'

Emma smiled to herself. They were both thinking of the other. 'You'll have to have a think on it. There's plenty of time yet.'

'Yeah, I know, but thanks for the extra cash today.' And with that Holly gave her boss a hug as she left.

She'd better think of something to make for supper for her and Max. Salmon, that would be nice; if she could find some fresh fillets in the supermarket down the road, she could pan-fry them in sweet chilli sauce – she had a jar of that in the cupboard. Okay, that was a bit of a cheat, but she didn't have a lot of time to play with here, or a large budget, and she could serve them with some baby potatoes and vegetables. For dessert, she could make a couple of batches of brownies for tomorrow for the shop, and use two of them tonight served with some fresh raspberries – hey presto! Meal sorted. She whizzed to the supermarket – yes, they had salmon in, and raspberries, and she also picked up a bottle of white wine as a treat.

Max arrived soon after seven and they dived into each other's arms. She had missed this so much, this physicality, when you just couldn't wait to be near to someone.

'Good day?' he asked.

'Yeah, pretty busy. I think word is getting around about the Chocolate Café already.'

'Great.'

'You?'

'Yep, all good. Finally made some progress on those kitchen units, so we can crack on again with that job.'

'That's good.'

They chatted, they ate, they enjoyed a glass or two of the wine.

As Emma took the plates across to the sink, Max moved in behind her, wrapping his arms around her waist, burying his head in her neck with a flurry of gentle kisses. She turned to kiss him back, deeply, passionately. They were both keen to get back to where they'd left off rather abruptly this morning.

Then, naked in her double bed, Max was massaging her back with long firm strokes. Boy, was that good. She'd been really achy after a full day on her feet serving in the café, and from the last week's painting, cleaning, cooking, chocolate crafting and more.

She could feel the tension starting to ebb away, her muscles beginning to relax and respond to his touch. Mmm, he was rather good at this. This was going in such a lovely, blissed-out, sensual direction.

She came to. It was getting light. Half-past seven on her wristwatch. What the . . .?

Emma opened her eyes. Max was there beside her, all warm, naked, and manly.

He must have sensed her movement, opened his eyes, saw her looking, smiled. 'Morning, beautiful.'

'Hi, gorgeous.' But she couldn't remember, what had happened before she fell asleep, *had they*? Curiosity got the better of her. 'Uh, last night . . . did we?' She'd been so looking forward to it.

'Nope. I was giving you a massage and you fell asleep on me.' He gave a wry grin.

'Oops.' How embarrassing.

'Snoring and everything. I think you even dribbled at one point.'

'*Noooo*.' How mortifying. 'I was just so shattered, though.' She hid under the covers for a second. The shame. She resurfaced to find him laughing.

'Had you for a second there, didn't I?'

'You swine.' She launched a pillow at him.

'I must admit, though, I really do need to rethink my foreplay technique if that's the end result.'

'Hah, well in that case you might just need to get some more practice in.' She was grinning back at him now. They had time on their side. It was a Sunday. Yes, she had chocolates to make as always, but the shop didn't open till midday on Sundays.

And he did get some more practice in – and it did not send her even remotely to sleep this time. In fact, he woke up every little nerve ending in her body and it was rather bloody amazing.

Max had to leave just after 9.00 a m., as he had to get down to a new building project in Jesmond. He'd missed breakfast, saying it was worth it with a cheeky smile, and mentioned there was a handy little coffee shop near the site which did the most amazing banana milkshakes, so he'd drop by there.

Emma found herself heading downstairs to the shop for the day with a big smile on her face, but already she'd started wondering when she might be seeing him next, and there was a strange sense of fear too. It had been so long since she'd opened up her heart. Yes, the sex was pretty damn amazing, but was she beginning to like this guy too much? Had she just got carried away with it all?

The next evening, she was in Bev's kitchen, a glass of Pinot Grigio to hand.

'Good weekend?' Bev asked.

'Yes.'

'And . . .? Come on, tell me all about the hot hunk. You *have*, haven't you? I knew it! The way he kept looking at you on Friday night – honestly, I'm surprised all those chocolate canapés didn't melt! And then it was so obvious that he wasn't going to leave . . . '

Emma gave a careful smile. She felt it had just snowballed around her, somehow.

'So, what's the problem?'

'I'm not sure. It's just maybe we've both fallen into it too easy, too soon.'

'What are you saying?'

'Well, he seems a nice enough guy and we get on fine. But can it really go anywhere? We're both busy people, with businesses . . . ' She let her voice trail. It was like she was building her own get-out clause, just in case.

'So, let me get this straight, because you both have busy lives you can't have a relationship? Well, that counts out most of the human population, Em.'

'Maybe I'm just a bit wary.'

'Well, that's understandable. Why don't you just take it steady and see how it goes?'

'Maybe.'

Suddenly she was feeling so confused.

37

Despite her emotional wobble, Max stayed over again the following Saturday night. Waking up to find someone was in your bed still felt strange after all these years for Emma, but as they made early morning love, her body felt wanted, and warm, and so very alive.

'Any plans today?' Max asked later, at breakfast, chatting over coffee and toast at her little fold-up table in her upstairs kitchen. 'I imagine the shop's opening as usual this afternoon, but for once I'm not expected on site. It's Sunday and I'm taking some time out. No dramas this week, a full quota of staff. Brilliant.'

Alfie was in his basket beside them, looking up at Emma, hopeful of a crust of toast.

'Well, Bev's coming to cover the shop, actually. Adam's gran is involved with a Christmas Fayre for Age Concern down at the village hall and asked if I'd go across for a couple of hours and hold a stall there. They've got cards and a gift stall coming, and they're organising teas, cakes and coffees. I think there's also a raffle and some kind of auction going on. Sorry, it may not quite be what you were imagining for your day off . . . but you'd be welcome to come along and keep me company.'

'Why not? I've nothing better to do, and at least it means I can spend a bit more time with you. Yeah, we'll go check out the oldies scene, see what we've got to look forward to. It'll be all Zimmer frames and slippers, no doubt.' He grinned.

Emma had been up late that Friday night, making as many chocolates as she could for the upcoming Fayre, and had boxes of chocolates and plenty of Christmas goodies all ready to go. She just needed to take them across in her car, and get set up by 1.00 p.m.

Holly had told her that several care homes in the area were bringing their residents, including the 'Golden Oldies' pensioners group from Seahouses, for tea, cake and company. They'd decided on a Sunday for this event to try and get some more of the local community to attend and hopefully raise a bit more money.

Emma was nearly set up. She had covered a trestle table with a festive holly-patterned tablecloth borrowed from Adam's gran and had set out a couple of wooden table-top stands, made for her by the lovely Ron, to display everything nicely. She also had a mini Christmas tree, with miniature baubles and fairy lights for full festive effect.

After two trips to and fro from Max's jeep, her chocolate stand was ready – looking seriously pretty, with festive gold and red bows and curled ribbon adorning the carefully prepared packs. She had chosen her traditional favourites for this event: whisky and brandy truffles, berry-fruit centres, melt-in-the mouth caramels, mints, and her Christmas pudding truffles made with chopped raisins and a splash of sherry. She had made up gift boxes of chocolates and packs of fudge, both plain and choc-dipped, as well as bags of shortbread.

There was going to be a raffle drawn later, and she had donated a box of chocolate goodies for that. She had also heard some more details on the planned auction, which was to be an auction of favours – things like handyman help, gardening, car-washing, and the like, which would be really helpful for the elderly and a great idea.

Emma was hoping it would prove to be a good event, for both the community and the shop's finances, which were better at the moment, but she still needed to make enough to cover the slow months of January and February, when there was still the rent to pay and other expenses. She had a few flutters in her stomach, hoping it would go well.

After a slow start, several people started drifting in; Emma recognised some local families, and a few people she knew. At 2.00 p.m. a couple of minibuses arrived from the old people's home in the next village. Her chocolates were selling steadily and she was pleased that it had been worth the time and energy in setting it all up. One of the organisers called at her stall, saying they were still looking for 'lots' for the auction and explained a bit more about what they were hoping for. It seemed to be an offer of time and a helping hand for the elderly more than anything, so Max, bless him, said he'd be happy to offer a couple of hours, mentioning that his background was the building trade and that he could turn his hand to most DIY jobs. The organiser seemed most grateful and added his name to the list.

At 3.00 p.m, the auction was announced. There were tables and chairs set out through the centre of the room for people to sit and have their tea and biscuits or cake, and two old ladies that Adam's gran knew had settled at the table closest to Emma and seemed to be eagerly awaiting the auction. Max smiled across and said hello to them.

He was also recruited by the lady serving the teas and coffees to walk around and offer top-ups from a huge metal teapot. Emma smiled, watching him; he quite looked the part, chatting easily to the elderly as he went. Even the ladies beside Emma's stall nodded in approval. She heard one of them saying, 'What a nice young man,' as he left their table.

The other lady responded rather loudly, 'Well, he *is* a fine figure of a man.'

'Hmm, we haven't seen anything like that in here for years, Dorothy.'

Emma watched in amusement as the two ladies scanned the room, taking in the decidedly aged, white-haired, and rather wrinkly assembly of other gentlemen in the hall.

'*Ever.*' There was a mischievous twinkle in Dorothy's eyes now. 'My, I could have two hours of *his* time any day of the week.'

'What's he up for auction for, anyhow?'

'Two hours of his time, like I said.'

'Yes, but what for?'

'Anything you like, I suppose.'

Shirley, Adam's gran, chipped in helpfully as she sat down beside them ready for the auction to start, 'He was thinking DIY, building jobs.'

'That's not what I was thinking, Thelma.' Dorothy winked at her friend.

Emma couldn't help but listen in.

'Hey, what do you think about bidding? We could club together, Dot. We might raise more that way.'

Dorothy gave a wicked grin. 'There's a lot I'd like to raise! Just imagine, Thelma, two whole hours with him indeed. We could have a leg each and share the middle.' She cackled with laughter at that point.

'I could put my winter fuel allowance towards the bid.' Thelma was giggling now. 'He'd certainly warm things up at home, anyhow.'

Emma found herself blushing, surprised by the turn in the old ladies' conversation, but then she began laughing uncontrollably as Max turned up with a confused frown asking what was going on, totally unaware of the chatter.

'If only . . . ' sighed Dorothy, taking a good look at him. 'If I was twenty years younger, well—'

'Twenty? More like forty, don't kid yourself, Dot,' Thelma added with a cheeky grin.

'Now behave, you two,' Adam's gran chided, a smile on her face, as the start of the auction was announced.

There were bids for a delivery of logs, a voucher from the butcher's in the next village, a gardener donating three hours of work, a holiday cottage for a weekend break, a few other lots, and finally Max's two hours of DIY time.

Thelma and Dorothy were whispering frantically as the bidding started. They clubbed together, were outbid for a second by another lady, and then upped their offer and won him for a total of £20, and then dissolved into a fit of hysterics. Emma wondered if she ought to warn him, but Adam's gran had realised that she'd been listening in and said he'd be fine, it was all bark no bite; the ladies were neighbours in the old people's bunga-lows in the next village and were hoping to have an hour each to fix up the odd picture, sand off a door that was sticking, and do a bit of general handyman work – best not to concern him with their capers. Looking at their smiling faces, it had made their day, and probably their week. Max stood up to a small round of applause from the audience and a wink from Adam's gran.

After the raffle, the event was drawn to a close. There were a few last orders from her stall, and it was time to pack up and get back to the shop to see how Bev and Holly had got on.

Thelma and Dorothy came up just before they left, to thank Max and say how very much they looked forward to seeing him again soon. Emma had to duck down at that point, in the pretence of packing up a cardboard box ready to load the car, dissolving into laughter, whilst he made polite conversation with the elderly, sweet-looking pair.

It had certainly been some event.

All too soon Max had to leave. He explained that he'd promised to call on his parents in Morpeth on his way back.

'Thank you so much for helping today. I hope it wasn't too much of a bind. And now you're giving up your time to do even more jobs.'

'It's fine. I enjoyed it. It was nice to cheer people up – I bet some of them are quite lonely back home.'

Emma certainly knew how that could feel.

'Yes, I expect they are,' she agreed.

'I'll catch up with you next week, if that's okay. I've got loads on through the week.'

'Yeah, me too. It's a bit of a hectic time in the shop just now.'

'So, would it be okay to come up next weekend again? Or shall we just leave it for now?'

'Ah, yes, that'd be lovely.'

'Okay, great. I'll ring you.'

And with Max back at Hexham and at work through the week, Emma realised she was missing him *a lot*, missing that physicality, and looked forward to his daily texts so much. It was beginning to churn her up all over again. It felt like a dangerous rollercoaster of emotions that she'd just stepped back on to and the question was: would it all be worth it?

38

'Emma, it's Angela. How are you, darling?' It was Luke's Mum, her voice so warm and familiar.

'Oh, it's so lovely to hear from you. How are you getting on? How's John?'

'He's not so bad. Still doing his cricket duties during the summer, more umpiring than actually playing nowadays. He's finding all the running about a bit much, though he won't admit it, of course.'

Luke's family were big cricket fans. She remembered how they'd all gone to Durham County Cricket matches over at Chester-Le-Street when she and Luke had lived in Durham. They'd even seen England play a 20:20 there once. The fancy dress and atmosphere that day had been incredible and the source of much hilarity. She'd never before seen a Bassett's Allsorts squaring up to Batman and the Flintstones, it was all done in good humour though. It had almost been as much entertainment as the game.

'Anyhow, we're fine, darling. How are you?'

'Extremely busy. I've just opened a café as part of The Chocolate Shop.'

'Oh, how fabulous. You are doing *so* well. Do you like it there and is it working out okay for you still?'

'Yes, it's fine, thank you, Angela. I have my friends and James is nearby with his family. It's a lovely village.'

'Yes, it *is* pretty. I remember coming to visit you there a couple of years ago.'

She wondered now if she should have invited them to the launch, but they lived outside Harrogate in Yorkshire and it would have been over a two-hour journey each way. She had meant to see them more, but gradually they had slipped a little from her life. She was still very fond of them and they tried to meet once a year. She remembered their birthdays and got in touch with them at Christmas. They always phoned her on Luke's birthday too. They shared their loss, protectively.

'And how's the rest of the family? Nathan?' asked Emma. That was Luke's brother.

'He's been off travelling for some time. Australia, at the moment, been getting jobs all over, stays a while somewhere then moves on. He's found it hard to settle since Luke . . . ' Angela let the words drift.

'Yes.'

It had hit him so hard, his older brother dying like that. It had hit them all hard.

'I know it's a little while away yet,' Angela explained the reason behind her call, 'but we've booked a holiday cottage up in your area for a long weekend before

324

Christmas and we wondered if you'd like to join us for lunch one day or something?'

'Yes, that would be really lovely.'

'It's over near Kielder Water. We'll be doing some hiking, that kind of thing. Well, lovely to chat, darling. I'm sure you'll be busy. I'll call again nearer the time to sort out the details. Take care, Emma.'

'Thanks. You take care too. Love to you all.'

Emma felt so much for them, losing their son. How on earth would they feel if they knew she'd been seeing someone else? She'd been on cloud nine these past few days, enjoying the excitement of this passionate new relationship with Max and now it suddenly felt all wrong. Disloyal.

39

It was bloody freezing. Her finger joints were aching with the cold. At least she'd thought to put a thermal vest on and several layers of clothing under her puffy coat, but her legs were chilled through her jeans. She'd have to invest in long johns if she took on any more winter markets, and she hadn't brought gloves other than the thin latex ones she used for hygiene reasons. *Mistake.* She could now hardly move her fingers, so it was really hard to handle the chocolates. She rubbed her hands together in a feeble attempt to bring them back to life, sighing out a puff of white, lukewarm mist.

Emma was at her first-ever Christmas market as a stallholder in the historic town of Alnwick, a twenty-minute drive from Warkton-by-the-Sea. A host of white, tarpaulin-covered stalls were set out on the stone cobbles of the market square, and after spending a half-hour shipping goods to and from her car she felt proud of her very festive-looking Christmas Chocolate Shop, set out carefully with shelves of chocolate reindeer, snowmen,

Santas, boxes and bags galore of fudge, truffles, and chocolate bars, all prettily wrapped in golds and silvers with green, gold and red bows and coloured ribbons. She'd strung up a set of twinkling fairy lights behind her and brought some festive decorations too, including a small tinsel Christmas tree which she had strung with chocolate stars and edible baubles.

Now all she needed was some customers. The market opened at noon and it was now nearly 1.00 p.m. and she had only seen a half a dozen people and sold one bag of fudge. So, as well as freezing her butt and fingers off, she hadn't made any money yet, though as the event wasn't closing until eight, she'd try and stay positive. Right, she was going to head across to the Coffee Cabin place opposite to get herself a hot drink and try and thaw out a bit.

She ordered a cup of coffee from the blonde-haired, rather buxom, fifty-something lady there.

'Bit slow,' Emma commented to the lady who had half-turned to start working the coffee machine.

'Yeah. It'll get going, don't worry. Your first year here?' She must have spotted Emma on her stall, and realised she was a newbie.

'Yep. First market ever, in fact. I have a chocolate shop over at Warkton-by-the-Sea. Thought I'd see how a Christmas market might go.'

'Ah well, this one's always a bit slow to start, then it begins to fill. By evening it's usually bustling, when folk finish work, school, and that. Gets a nice atmosphere after dark with all the Christmas lights and everything. That's why I think people like coming out later.'

'Oh okay. Well, good to know it should perk up.'

'Yes, it will. This is my sixth year.'

'Right. So, it must be worth coming back to, then.'

The woman was busy frothing up some milk to pour in to the rich-smelling coffee. Emma couldn't wait to get her hands round the warm cup.

'Definitely. Your stall looks great by the way, really pretty. Do you make all the chocolates yourself?'

'I do indeed. I usually sell them at my shop, The Chocolate Shop by the Sea.'

'Ah, so that's you. I saw something in the local paper the other day, I think. Have you just opened a café or something?'

'Yes, that's me.'

'Going well?'

'Yeah – pretty good. Early days yet and all that. But it's keeping me busy. Got some help in there today.' Holly was there, with Bev as second in command. They'd assured Emma they'd be fine and she hoped they'd seen a few more people than she had so far today.

The woman handed the coffee over with a smile, and Emma paid.

'I might have to pop across and get something from your stall later. Love a bit of chocolate. Going to be drooling here, looking across at it all day.'

Emma laughed. 'Well, I do have brownies and short-bread as well as the chocolates if anyone is looking for something to go with their coffee.' It didn't look like the Coffee Cabin had food, just drinks, for sale. She'd go back over and put them somewhere more prominent, she mused. They might sell well with having the hot drink stall opposite – fingers crossed.

'I'll mention it to my customers.'

'Thank you.'

As soon as Emma got back to her stall she rearranged her wares, and then headed back over to the Coffee Cabin with a dark chocolate brownie and two choc-chip short-breads for her newfound friend. 'A little taster for you,' she offered.

'Aw, thanks. They look great. And if you fancy another drink later, it'll be on the house.'

'Thanks.'

'You've got a customer,' the woman said cheerily, gesturing towards Emma's pitch.

Em turned to see a woman and child browsing the mini reindeer and snowmen. 'Ooh, fab.' And she whizzed back to take her place behind the counter area.

'Hello, can I help at all?'

'Ooh Mum, look, chocolate Rudolphs! They're so cute! Can I?'

'Yes, okay, and you'd better choose something for Alex too.'

'The snowy snowman.' The little girl was pointing across, excitedly.

The mother picked up both, passed them across to Emma, then carried on browsing, choosing a couple of bags of fudge, and a box of Christmas pud chocolates. 'They look good,' she said.

'Yes, and they will all last until well after Christmas,' Emma reassured.

'Fabulous. Well, in that case we'll choose something for Daddy and Auntie Faye too.'

The little girl chose a big chocolate bar with honeycomb crunch topping for her dad and a box of salted caramels for her aunt.

'Thank you.' Emma bagged up the confectionery carefully. She had brought a stack of strong white paper bags with cord-style handles, and she popped in a pretty new business card that she had designed herself online for the shop and café – might as well spread the word. The order came to over fifteen pounds which cheered Emma.

'It all looks so pretty. Thanks,' the woman commented as she took the bag.

'Can I eat Rudolph now?' the little girl asked her mum hopefully.

'I don't see why not,' she answered, and took it out and unwrapped it for her.

Two happy customers! Despite the bitter cold, Emma felt a little glow inside.

More people began to mill about the market and Emma's parents arrived unexpectedly.

'Oh, how nice of you both to come.'

'How's it going, pet? We couldn't miss your first market, could we now?' Dad beamed across at her.

'Fairly quiet so far, but I've been advised it gets busier later.'

'Oh, I'm sure it will do. And when it does they won't be able to pass this stall by with all its delightful treats.' Dad had always been one of her biggest cheerleaders.

'It really does look wonderful,' her mum commented as she took in the festive display.

It was a lovely surprise, them turning up like this, as they hadn't mentioned their intentions and had travelled half an hour to be here.

'Can we help out at all?' her mum asked.

'Well, if you wouldn't mind looking after the stall, while I take a quick loo break?' The practicalities of being a solo stallholder were beginning to take effect.

'Of course.'

In Emma's absence, her dad proudly commented to any passers-by that his daughter hand-made all the chocolates herself and managed to coax a gentleman into purchasing a box of champagne truffles for his wife's birthday. He seemed very pleased with himself when Em got back. Mum said he was a natural.

They bought a few gifts themselves, to take back to friends in Rothbury, and a reindeer each for the twins, as they were going to call in to visit James on their way back. They headed off with hugs and kisses and good luck wishes. Emma felt so blessed to have such a supportive family.

Coffee Cabin lady was right; once the early dusk began to fall, the market square began to buzz into life and a lovely festive atmosphere filled the area as a touch of frost formed on the cobbles and the white Christmas lights that were strung between stalls began to glow. There was a huge real pine Christmas tree with coloured lights, tinsel, and shiny baubles taking centre stage, just along from her row of stalls, and the smell of mulled wine and spices filled the air, along with the sound of children's eager chatter, and a medley of well-known Christmas carols came from a speaker.

Emma had a busy spell, with several people at the stall at once and lots of purchases made. Chocolate, fudge, and brownies were flying out like hot cakes. On a brief lull, the coffee lady opposite her gave her a big thumbs-up sign and a grin. She smiled back, with her own chilly thumb raised up too.

She heard her mobile phone ring, but had to leave it unanswered, as it was back to action with a gift box to fill for an elderly lady who also wanted several bags of fudge and some dark-chocolate Florentines – a new festive addition to Emma's range. Seeing the selection together, Emma suddenly thought that a small wicker Christmas chocolate hamper might be nice, filled with a pretty selection. A bit late for today, but yes, for the shop in these last few weeks running up to 25 December. Ooh, yes, customers could even select their own items with which to fill it if they wanted – 'build a basket'. Hmm, now there was a thought.

A few more sales later and her stocks were noticeably depleted. She had some extra supplies in cardboard boxes below the trestle table, so she quickly refilled her display and was off again, serving, smiling, chatting. It was going well, and hey presto, with all the activity her hands had come back to life and her body just about thawed out.

In a quieter moment she checked her phone. It was a missed call from Max. Max . . . she'd only spoken to him twice after their last weekend. Physically, things were great between them, but hearing from Luke's mum had really unsettled her, and Em didn't know how it would be when she faced him again, so she had just texted back the last time saying how busy she was and had left off contacting him for the past week. She put the phone back into her pocket. She looked around her at the market in full swing, listened to the animated talk, watched families and couples all wrapped up in hats, scarfs, and winter coats, some holding mugs of hot drinks. Coffee Cabin seemed to be doing well with their mulled wine too, and the gorgeous wafts of spice and cinnamon kept drifting past Emma's stall.

Setting up earlier, Emma had seen a candle stall nearby, another that sold wooden hand-crafted decorations and toys, a jewellery stall, and one that had handmade cushions and soft furnishings. She'd spotted a really cute reindeer cushion on a red background that she might just have to go and buy for her window seat in the shop – now her tin-box till was filling nicely, she could indulge herself. It was going to be used for the business, after all, and would add to the festive feel of the shop, she persuaded herself. In fact, whilst it was quiet for a minute . . . She asked the lady on the stand next to her, who was selling Christmas cards, if she'd mind keeping an eye on her stall just for a minute or two and set off, hoping it hadn't already been sold. There he was, appliquéd on, the cutest Rudolph with his red nose. She picked him up before anyone else had the chance and paid – a lovely memento of her first-ever – and by the looks of her takings, successful – Christmas market.

As she got back to her own stall and thanked the card

lady, a school choir gathered around the Christmas tree and began singing carols, opening with 'Rudolph the Red-nosed Reindeer', which made Emma smile. There was always something special about carols at Christmas, about the magical build-up to the big day, all the excitement and anticipation, especially for the young ones. But she knew, all too well, it wasn't easy for everybody; it was a time when you missed those who couldn't be with you, when you remembered loved ones you had lost. The thought of seeing Luke's parents again soon brought it home all the more too. A happy-sad tear crowded her eye as the choir launched into 'Silent Night'.

The cold was beginning to bite again as the evening air chilled. You could see the singers' breath mist the air. Emma rubbed her hands together and popped them into her coat pockets until she needed to serve again, when a little boy came up with his mum and chose a chocolate Santa. A middle-aged couple bought some rum-and-raisin fudge and a two of her flavoured chocolate bars, in mint and orange. Then it was quieter again; perhaps she'd go and get a hot chocolate from across the way to warm herself up. She took some change and made her way to Coffee Cabin once more.

'Got going a bit, didn't it?'

'Yes, thanks for warning me.'

'You're welcome. What can I get you?'

'A hot chocolate please, with cream if I can.'

'You can indeed. It's quite cosy in the cabin here, with the hot water steamer and coffee machine and all that. I bet you're bloody freezing.'

'You can say that again. I'll be bringing thermal gloves if I ever do this again.'

'I bet.' She mixed up the hot chocolate and sprayed on the whipped cream, then passed it across. 'On the house, like I said.'

'Aw, thanks. It looks amazing.' She went straight in for her first hot and creamy sip – hot chocolate bliss. She glanced across at her stall, still no one there. She was okay for another minute or two.

'My name's Lisa, by the way.'

'Thank you, and nice to meet you, Lisa. I'm Emma.'

'Well, Emma, if you're thinking of ever doing any more markets, I'll let you know which are the best ones to go to, especially for Christmas time. Here.' She handed over a business card. 'Get in touch and I'll be happy to advise.'

'Thanks so much.'

Emma turned to see someone standing beside her pitch. A man, tall, broad-shouldered, in a black Puffa-style jacket and jeans.

'Oops, someone at my stall. Better go. And thanks again, Lisa. I'll be in touch.'

As she neared her stand, Emma paused. The set of that broad back, the short brown hairline – even under his black woollen hat – was extremely familiar. She had kissed the nape of that neck. Max.

He turned, and she stopped in her tracks. Awkward moment ahead.

'Max . . . hi.'

'Hello, stranger.' He looked a little stern. 'So, I've tracked you down at last.'

'How did you know I was here?' He didn't seem the type to be wandering around a Christmas market on his own by chance.

'I went to The Chocolate Shop first. Had a bit of a tour.' He managed a smile then. 'Holly told me you were here.'

She didn't think he'd come to stock up on chocolates, somehow. She took in his face, his dark green eyes, He was looking good, but there was an edge about him, a sense of unease.

'Em, why aren't you returning my calls?'

There had been more than one call she'd not answered, yes. But she'd been so busy, getting ready for the market, getting the shop and café up and running, and the pre-Christmas mayhem was really kicking in. She was building the excuses nicely in her own mind. 'Ah, sorry. It's just been pretty manic.'

'You could have just sent a quick text.'

'Well, yeah, maybe.' She felt herself redden.

A man in smart work clothes with a skinny youth slowed by the stall. The lad picked up a packet of champagne truffles, whilst the chap browsed the display.

'Look. I'll let you crack on just now. This probably isn't the time and place,' Max said. 'When do you finish here?'

'The market is meant to close by eight o'clock.' Emma looked up at the old clock tower of the Town Hall. Ten to six.

'Okay. Are you here on your own?' Max asked.

'Yes.'

'Well, shall I come back and help you start to pack up about a quarter to eight or something?'

'Ah . . . ' She wasn't sure why she felt so awkward, or quite how everything had shifted in the past couple of weeks, but speaking with Luke's mum had left her reeling. 'Umm, okay then, thanks.' She could hardly refuse his help.

'I'll see you later then.' Max made himself scarce.

The lad at the stall was saying to his father, 'I think Mum would like these ones.' He was still holding the truffles.

'Good decision, yes. And we'll put them with some flowers.'

Aw, how sweet. 'Birthday?' Emma mused out loud.

'Indeed,' the man replied.

She put a gift bow on the rectangular box of truffles, and placed it in one of her bags with a business card. She watched the two men as they wandered off, the lad a lanky version of his father. Emma wondered for a second what it must feel like to have a family like that of your own, coming home to you every day – your lover, your child, your flesh and blood. She hoped the woman, whoever she was, appreciated her boys, didn't take them for granted.

Sometimes they never came home . . .

Right, enough of this moroseness, maybe it was thoughts of Christmas stirring things up. You never really got over losing someone, you just learnt to live with it. She thought of Luke every single day even seven years on, and although it got easier, weirdly, every now and again, grief would come back in like a sledgehammer and hit when she least expected it.

By half-past seven the market was beginning to thin out, customers had dwindled, and some of the stalls were already starting to pack away. Emma had sold at least three-quarters of what she had brought, with some items having totally sold out. She had sold far more than she would have done in the shop that day (though she'd still have those takings too, thanks to Bev and Holly), and even with paying for the stall and the fuel to get here and back, she was definitely well in credit. It was worth the sore feet, aching back, and chilled-to-the-bone fingers.

'All okay?' Lisa from the Coffee Cabin leaned out and gave her another thumbs-up.

'Yeah, great,' Emma replied. 'You do all right?'

'Yep, sold right out of the mulled wine. Been a good day. Well, I think that's me pretty much done here now. I'm going to get my vehicle over to hitch this up. Can you keep an eye on the cabin for me?'

'Will do. No problems.'

'Cheers, hen.'

And soon after that, Max reappeared.

'You okay? How's it gone today?'

'It's definitely been worth coming along. Though I am *bloody* freezing.'

He reached out for one of her hands. 'Wow, you feel like ice. Let's get this stuff all packed up and get you somewhere warm.'

40

They were sitting next to the roaring fire in a booth of Sam's Bistro, located in an old stone townhouse not far from the market. Emma was finally starting to thaw out properly. It would have been lovely just to snuggle in a bit closer to Max, to feel his arm warm around her, but there was a polite inch or two between them, and something had shifted since their last weekend, two weeks ago.

Yes, she could have let herself get carried away with it all. He seemed a nice guy and the sex was seriously good. But there had to be more to it than sex. And was it worth all the dating, the getting-to-know-you stage, the shared lives, just for it all to go horribly wrong somewhere further down the line? Better to keep it as friends, and then no one needed to get hurt, she warned herself.

Max had bought her a hot, frothy cappuccino and he had a glass of Coca-Cola set before him on the round wood table.

'So, are you feeling any better? A bit warmer now?'

'Yes, thanks. And thanks for all your help.'

'Are you okay, Em? You just don't seem quite yourself.'

Emma looked around the room awkwardly. 'I'm fine.'

'Well, have you eaten this evening?'

She shook her head gently.

'I haven't had a chance yet either. I could get us some supper here,' Max persevered.

Despite her stomach giving a little rumble of approval – it had been a long time since her midday sandwich – she felt uneasy. 'Ah, sorry Max. I'm just so shattered, all I really want to do is to get myself back and crash out for the night.' She put extra emphasis on the word 'myself'. 'I've got something in the fridge ready to warm up.' Total lie.

'Ah, okay. Fair enough.' He seemed a little disappointed, his brow furrowed. He took a drink of Coke.

Emma sipped her coffee, focussing on the flickering flames of the fire.

Max shifted a little in his seat, his outer thigh touching hers by accident, lighting a little flame of pressure. Might this be the last time they touched each other? Emma felt suddenly sad. It was for the best, she told herself. Focus on her business, keep life simple, straightforward. She shifted her knee an inch back away, creating the void. Took another sip of her coffee.

'How are things with your work?' she asked.

'Pretty good. Hectic. Got a great job on we've promised to have finished by Christmas. Full renovation of a three-storey house down in Jesmond, near a converted church and that great coffee shop that was near the last job.

Lovely property, mind, but been neglected for many years. The new owners want a full makeover and a new extension to the back, right out from roof level. Big master bedroom above and a huge open-plan kitchen and living area below that will open right out on to the garden. It's going to be stunning. But we're still knocking out walls at the moment.' Max paused, aware that he was doing most of the talking.

'Right, lots to do then.'

She felt a little more relaxed. It was safer ground talking about work. They chatted some more until their drinks were nearly emptied.

'Emma,' Max's tone was more serious, 'are you interested in taking this any further? *Us*, I mean?'

So, he thought there was an *us*. 'Ah, well . . . '

'Okay, so you're just trying to let me down gently here. Hey, I get it. It's just, I thought we seemed pretty good together. I'd have liked to get to know each other a bit more.'

Emma really didn't know what to say. It *had* been good. He seemed a nice guy. But . . .

'I really like you, Em,' he tried again.

She just smiled awkwardly. She liked him too, yeah. But if she seemed keen and they got into each other, began to rely on each other, something was bound to go wrong at some point; they'd find out they weren't really suited, and she'd be back at square one. Relationships were like minefields. Better stick to the path she knew. Concentrate on her work, the shop, her friends, her family.

341

'Max, I just feel I need to focus on the shop, the business, right now. Get myself through this busy Christmas period. It's always so manic . . . ' She let her words drift.

'Okay. I get it.' He put his hands up with a sad kind of smile. 'You're just not that into me. Maybe I read the signals wrong. But I thought, you know, well I thought that it was more than sex.'

She didn't answer.

'Hey, come on. I'll see you back to your car, then you can get yourself away.'

Was this it? Was she going to let it end here? Never know him more than this? But it was like there were huge warning signs going off in her head. One step more into this relationship and she'd be in too deep, when it all might go horribly wrong.

'Sorry, Max.' Her voice sounded tired.

'Okay,' he sighed gently. 'Let me just see you safe to your car and then I'll leave you in peace.'

And he was still wanting to make sure she was safe and fine, despite his obvious disappointment.

'Thank you. For everything today and for all your help with the shop too. I'll always remember that.'

They walked side by side back along the cobbled street to where Emma's car was parked. They stopped, stood facing each other for a second. Max then moved towards her, giving her a polite kiss on the cheek, which felt very final.

What the hell are you doing, Em? a voice was clamouring in her mind. Yet another was saying it was the right thing. The best way. They had been good together, but now it was time to let it go. Max turned to walk away. She couldn't watch! She ducked into her car and sat with a weird feeling of relief and regret all mixed up in her heart.

41

'So, let me get this straight,' Bev was on her high horse down the phone line. 'You've just landed a guy that looks like a cross between Gerard Butler and Tom Hardy. He has his own company, can do major DIY jobs, is obviously fit in more ways than one – you can't deny it, I have seen him – *and* he seems a really nice chap. So, you've just gone and told him to take a hike. Are you nuts or what, woman?'

'No. I've thought about it and it's the right thing to do.'

'Who for?'

Emma didn't answer. So Bev started up again. 'Ah, I get it. Was the sex crap?'

Em couldn't help but smile. 'No, it wasn't crap. Actually, it was pretty damned good.' It was indeed more than good, but she wasn't going to admit that to Bev right now.

'So what is the problem?'

'It just wasn't going to go anywhere.'

344

'Well no, not if you didn't give it a chance. Right, that's it, we need wine and we *need* to talk. My place at seven. Pete is out at a local council meeting, organising the village Christmas lights.'

'Okay. I'll wrap up here in the shop, take Alfie out for a walk, and I'll see you later.' She knew there was no point arguing when Bev was in this frame of mind.

Emma was curled on a sofa in Bev's front room with a glass of chilled rosé to hand. It was Monday, two days after the Christmas market, and she'd just put in a full day at The Chocolate Shop single-handedly, as Holly was at school and Bev working at the doctors'. The shop's supplies were seriously depleted too. It was looking more like Old Mother Hubbard's than a thriving chocolate store on the run-up to Christmas so she would have to be up early tomorrow making more confectionery. She still felt pretty shattered, physically, from her long day at the market and her emotions were all over the shop.

She and Bev were working their way down a bag of crisps and had been chatting about the Christmas market and how that had gone, as well as the village Christmas light-up which was due next Thursday evening, 23 November. The local community always set up a big fir tree down on the grassy area by the harbour, with carol singers, mince pies from the local WI and glasses of warm mulled wine provided by The Fisherman's Arms. They had the big countdown to six o'clock when the local mayor would press the switch to light up the swooping strings of white lights hung both sides of Warkton's main street and along the harbour. It was a popular event, and Emma had agreed to do a late-night opening thereafter, with lots of her festive goodies on display, and her new café ready with hot drinks to thaw everyone out. Oh yes, yet more chocolates to craft. It was going to be a whole week of early mornings and late nights, she mused.

Bev took a large sip of her wine.

'Right then, Em. You need to tell me all about the lovely Max, and why on earth you've decided to drop him already.'

Emma *really* didn't feel like going into all this, but she knew she wouldn't get any peace. She just took a sip of wine, and dipped into the bag of crisps.

'So, does Max feel the same way about this? I heard from Holly he'd been looking for you at the shop. Well?' Bev persisted.

'No . . . not really. He wants to see me again, actually.'

'Em!' Her friend sounded exasperated. 'Look, I can see why you ditched Malteser Man, but this guy? Boy, if I wasn't married myself I'd be in there like a shot. So, what is it you don't like about him? Don't you trust him?'

'It's not that.'

'So, what's going on? Are you still missing Luke?'

'Of course I still miss Luke. That doesn't just go away because it's been a few years, or because someone else is on the scene. It's just that I – I'm not sure about things with Max. It doesn't feel right to go any further.' That was about as close to the truth as she could get.

'So, you like the guy, he likes you, and you're saying no – *because*?'

'I'm fine on my own. I know where I stand. I have my own life, the shop, you, Alfie, my mum and dad, James. Why does it always have to be about a man?'

'It doesn't, but if a man's rather gorgeous and interested in you, why not just give it a try? You never know, he might even make you happy.'

'I *am* happy. I'm fine.'

'So you're not even going to give it a chance, Em? You're scared, aren't you? I can see it in your eyes.'

'I am *so* not.' She tried to look fierce.

'I've hit the spot, Em. You're scared of getting hurt again. I can understand that. And, you know what, that means you really like this guy, doesn't it?'

No answer.

'So what are you thinking? You cut him off now, don't take a chance, don't risk getting hurt again?'

'Sounds sensible.'

'Agh!'

'And what about Luke? Our relationship?' Emma shot back. 'I'm meeting up with his parents soon. What the heck will they think if I'm seeing someone else?'

'Emma.' Bev put a gentle hand on her friend's shoulder. 'Luke's never coming back, honey.'

'I know that. I'm not stupid.' Her tone was sharp. She was getting fed up with this.

'Okay, sorry.' Bev softened. 'But I'm sure his parents would understand. I'm sure they wouldn't want you to live a life without a partner to love and love you back.'

There was a second or two of silence. Then Emma started quietly, 'It just seems so very different than how it was with Luke. All those special moments we had, me and Luke, what it was like when we were falling in love. This now, it doesn't feel the same, it's not quite right.'

'It's bound to be different, Em. You're in a different place. You've been through so much. And Max is a different man. It'll take courage to make that leap of faith and try another relationship, when nothing's set in stone, and yeah, it might go wrong, you might get hurt. But deciding to live a life without any relationship, without that kind of special love, holing yourself up here on your own for the next forty years? That's no life at all.'

'It's been fine so far. I just can't go there, Bev. I can't do it.' She felt safe here in her village, in the chocolate shop. Her life as it was now had a steady anchor. 'What if anything happened to Max? What if he got ill? It makes me feel sick just thinking about it. I can't go there again. I couldn't put myself through it.'

'Okay, okay, I understand. But just make sure you are certain, Em. Chances like this don't come often. He won't wait about, you know.' Bev picked up the bottle of rosé. 'Time for another glass, hun?'

The conversation moved on to lighter topics, how much Bev was enjoying working in the chocolate café. She then brought out a tray of local cheese and biscuits with a red onion chutney she'd made, which was absolutely delicious. It was creeping towards eleven o'clock when Pete came back in, having been cajoled into a couple of pints after the village meeting.

'Right, well I'd better be going,' Emma announced.

'Got a few busy days ahead. I'll see you at the shop on Wednesday, Bev.'

'Look forward to it. You take care, Em.'

It was rather lovely having her friend as her new member of staff. Emma just hoped she'd lay off the match-making for now though. It had all been aired, and Emma was sticking by her decision.

42

The village had been buzzing with festive atmosphere all day. Men with a cherry picker were spotted, angled awkwardly, hanging strings of light bulbs between the lamp posts. There were shouts of 'this way a bit', and 'that way a bit', and then a huge fir tree went past on the back of a trailer heading down to the harbour-side.

Emma had made up a big tray of tea in disposable containers and taken them down for the workers at one point with a plate of her choc-chip shortbread. She left the refreshments down by the harbour wall and gave them a shout, spotting Pete up a ladder putting huge silver baubles on the Christmas tree. The tray had only a few crumbs half an hour later when she went back, so that seemed to have gone down well.

She'd agreed to go along later and watch the big village light-up that was going ahead that night. It was usually a lovely event. Every year, the ladies of the WI provided mince pies and the pub gave out mulled wine, with the local mayor arriving for the big moment to flick the switch. There was always that second of tension in case they didn't work, and all would remain dark, but they hadn't had a problem in all the years Emma had been here. Fingers crossed all would go well tonight.

Emma was to open up for late-night shopping thereafter. It made sense with so many people milling about, and it would be a great way to earn some extra income – the shop's finances always staying firmly in her mind. Things had picked up since the opening of the coffee shop, but she had her parents to pay back, as well as keeping up with the rent and other outgoings – Emma knew she was by no means out of the woods yet. She didn't want to miss the lighting-up ceremony herself, so was organised to run back up the hill and open up five minutes after the lights went on. She had added an extra strand of fairy lights to the counter, and The Chocolate Shop was looking all festive and full again. Then, at a quarter to six she turned the sign to 'closed', ran upstairs to pop on a warm jumper and fetch Alfie plus his lead, wrapped herself up in scarf, hat, gloves, coat – she'd learned her lesson at the market! – and walked quickly down the hill to meet up with Bev and Pete.

There was quite a crowd gathered around the fir tree and several people milling about on the little hill that led up towards the pub; there were couples, and families with small children holding tight to their parents' hands. A sense of eager anticipation filled the air as Emma spotted Danny from the pub wandering through the masses balancing a full tray and handing out plastic glasses of mulled wine. She headed his way, quite fancying a glass of something warm and festive. Alfie's tail was wagging happily – he loved a crowd and an event, inevitably getting plenty of affectionate strokes – and he raised his brown nose to the air, smelling the delicious scent of mince pies, hoping a crumb or two might come his way. She thanked Danny, asking how he was as she took a glass of wine.

'I'm great. Seem to be very popular tonight.' He winked. 'Think it's my mulled wine rather than my charm, unfortunately.' And he moved on through the crowd.

Emma then spotted Holly with Adam. 'Hey.'

'Hi, Em. You okay?'

'Yes, fine, been busy at the shop. Only just got away in time.'

'Oh, are you doing the late-night opening too?'

'Sure am.'

'Well, if you need a hand, I'll happily call in afterwards.'

'Thanks, Hols, that would be great.'

'Busy at the hotel, Adam?' Emma asked.

'Yes, we're getting lots of Christmas party bookings in now. Work dos and the like. All go.'

'Well, good luck.'

Emma felt a hand on her shoulder. She turned to see Bev.

'Hey you! Thought you weren't going to make it for a while there.'

'Yeah, me too. Had the café full until nearly six. All good, though. More money in the coffers, so I'll not complain.'

'Absolutely.'

'Hi, Pete.'

Bev's husband joined the group.

'Great effort with the lights today,' Emma said.

'Well, I hope so. Time will tell.' He looked slightly anxious.

The mayor stood up on a small wooden podium, dressed in his velvet-robe finery and heavy gold chains.

'Welcome, everyone, welcome!' The crowd hushed. 'Yes, welcome to the Warkton-by-the-Sea Christmas lights. I am honoured to be the one in charge of the magic button.'

The children in the crowd looked at him in awe.

'Thanks to the WI ladies and The Fisherman's Arms for their excellent hospitality, which I'm sure you've all enjoyed.' The crowd showed their appreciation with a round of applause. 'And we are fundraising this evening for . . . ' He paused, looking a little confused. 'What is it?' he whispered to the lady next to him.

Someone shouted out, 'It's for the Hospice.'

'Oh yes, the North Northumberland Hospice, a fabulous charity. So, if you feel you'd like to contribute there are donation jars about, and there's a raffle being drawn in the pub hereafter, for the same worthy cause. Well then, I think it must be nearly time for the official count down. So, here we go. Five. Four. Three. Two. One!' He went to press the button and there was a second's delay when the crowd held their collective breath, and then *ping*. The most glorious glow of white lights appeared, strung around the harbour walls, and all the way up the street above them. Two of the boats in the harbour had also rigged up lights and lit them at the same time. The Christmas tree was now lit with a variety of coloured globes and a twinkly white star at the top and the whole effect was stunning. The crowd clapped and cheered, and Alfie gave a woof.

It was really lovely. Emma looked around her, from the twinkly festive lights back to the people she was with: Adam, Holly, Bev, Pete, happily chatting as couples. And. for a second, she wondered what it might have been like to have had Max here with her. To have someone to share things with, someone to go back home with. But the moment passed. No point even thinking about that now. She needed to get back up the hill and get The Chocolate Shop open again sharpish, or she'd be missing custom.

'Aw, that was lovely. But I've got to go. They'll be going on home, else, and not calling in to pick up their festive chocolate goodies on their way back up the hill.'

'We'll be up in a mo,' Bev said.

'And I'll come and give you a hand,' confirmed Holly.

'Thanks, folks. See you soon. Come on, Alfie.'

And with that, Emma set off up the road that was now all twinkly and pretty with white lights.

The Chocolate Shop was crazy-busy for the next hour. Thankfully, Holly was soon behind the counter with her, helping out. They could hardly keep up with the hot drinks orders: teas, coffees and a tsunami of hot chocolates. Emma's takeaway cups had proved a godsend tonight too – she was so glad she'd thought to put in an extra order for them. The numbers of customers would never have fitted in the shop, but they were happy to take their drinks away and have them outside. The till kept dinging, and the microwave kept pinging, and they ran out of brownies within half an hour.

Lots of the festive chocolates were sold out too. She could see another week of early starts and late finishes looming. But hey, after the fear of losing her shop altogether this spring, she was not going to complain.

And then, as soon as they all piled in, they all seemed to pile back out. Bev called by and stayed a while to help clear the used mugs, cups and plates back to the kitchen, and loaded the dishwasher, and then she and Holly headed away home after the last customers had left.

Whilst Emma was wiping down the tables, she spotted something outside the window, and stopped. *Oh*, the flurry of customers had been replaced by a flurry of snow. There was something so special about the first snow of winter. She had to go outside to check she was right. And there, flake after flake glistening in the white lights, as though they were being shaken down like glitter from heaven. She stood feeling the soft patter of them on her face, one or two landing on her eyelashes.

She remembered the snow globe her granny had given her as a child. It must still be upstairs somewhere, she'd have to find it. It had an old-fashioned Father Christmas inside, sitting on a tiny wooden rocking chair, and when you shook the globe the glitter fell softly all around him. She used to make wishes to it as a little girl. What would she wish for now?

She knew. To see Luke one more time, to feel his arms around her. But she also knew that if she had that moment, she would never want to let go.

The street was empty, quiet now. 'Miss you,' she said up to the sky, the stars now hidden above the snow clouds. Whoever she met, however lovely they seemed, she knew her heart would always be Luke's.

But, could there ever be room there for someone else too?

43

'It's so lovely to see you, Emma. I'm so glad you could come across.' She was welcomed into Angela's arms.

'Yes, we know how busy you are,' added John, greeting her warmly.

For a second Emma found herself sideswiped; she had forgotten quite how like his mother Luke was. As always, meeting up with them brought back so many memories, so much shared history – and grief.

After a fifty-minute journey through country lanes, she had found the old-fashioned teashop they had recommended a few miles from the Kielder Water reservoir. Holly was looking after The Chocolate Shop for her for a few hours, being a Sunday.

She sat down with them at a pine table by the window which overlooked rolling green hills, dry-stone walls, and herds of grazing sheep, the landscape so typical of rural Northumberland.

'So, how are things, my lovely?' Angela asked.

'Good, thanks. I have now opened a café within the

chocolate shop, so it was all go getting it ready.' Strangely, thoughts of Max and all his help with that filled her mind, which made her feel extremely uncomfortable.

'Oh, that sounds a lovely idea. Is it going well?' Angela continued.

'Yes, it seems to be, and with the usual run-up to Christmas it's pretty full-on.'

'You've put your heart and soul into that shop,' commented John. 'We always say that, don't we, Angela?'

'Indeed. Such a pretty village there too, I remember.'

'Yes, it feels like home. I have some really nice friends,' Emma confirmed. She wanted them to know that she had settled. That life was okay.

'Good.'

They chatted politely over tea and cake, but it seemed harder than usual because Emma still felt caught up in her emotional whirl of the past few weeks.

John excused himself after finishing his tea, saying he needed to check on the dog in the car. They had an ageing golden Labrador, Barney. Luke used to be such buddies with that dog.

'Oh, I'll pop out and see him in a minute, John,' exclaimed Emma. 'Can't miss a cuddle with Barney now, can I?'

'Do you still have Alfie?'

'Oh yes, he's my best friend. He just loves running about on the beach there.'

'I bet. I'll catch you before you go, Emma.' John smiled warmly.

Once the women were alone, Angela asked, 'Have you

met anyone?' Was it a mother's intuition, or did she just know Emma so well she could sense some change in her?

'Ah . . . '

Angela placed a gentle palm over Emma's hand where it rested on the table. 'Emma, don't ever feel that we wouldn't want you to meet someone else. Please, please don't feel that you can't move on. We know how very much you loved Luke.'

'I still do.'

'I know that. Love doesn't die, does it?'

Emma shook her head. She still didn't know quite what to say. After all, the relationship with Max was all over now, anyway. She didn't want to lie, though. 'There was someone . . . briefly. But it hasn't worked out.'

'Ah, I wondered. You seem . . . different. John and I have talked about this a lot and we'd like to think you could find someone one day. Someone to make you happy.' Angela smiled. 'God knows, we've all had far too much sorrow. Emma, please don't feel that you don't have the right to be happy again.'

'Thank you.' Tears were misting the two women's eyes. A mother, a fiancée, who loved the same young man so very much.

They made their fond farewells in the teashop's car park, after Emma had had a big cuddle with Barney, who, from the exuberant wags of his tail, definitely remembered her.

'Thank you so much for coming all this way, Emma.'

'You're so welcome. It's been lovely to see you both again.'

'You'll have to come and stay sometime.'

'Yes, I will do. Thank you. Take care.'

'You too, my lovely.'

'All the best.' John gave her a warm hug.

'And don't forget what I said,' Angela reminded her.

'I won't.' A tear escaped her eye as Emma drove off. Oh, they were such lovely people, they hadn't deserved what life had thrown at them.

44

It had been on her mind all night, this sense that she'd let something go, something so special. She had to find him.

A phone call wouldn't be enough. It couldn't show him how she felt, and if he was as cheesed off with her as he had every right to be, would he even bother to answer?

She had had some long days this week at The Chocolate Shop since meeting up with Luke's parents, and had put the emotions down to feeling tired. But even after a good night's sleep, there it was, this nagging, dragging, lonely feeling. It was Max. She missed him. And, the only thing that was going to put that right was to see him again – to try and explain how she felt. He'd mentioned his building project down at Jesmond, near some church or chapel which had been converted to a house.

She was in the shop on her own today. Being a Monday, Bev was working at the surgery and Holly was at school, but if she put up a sign to say it would be 11.00 a.m.

opening today – surely that wouldn't hurt just this once. It was now nearly eight o'clock. That gave her three hours; it was an hour's drive each way, so there would be a bit of time to see him and talk with him. That's if he still wanted to see her, after her cool dismissal of him after the market. Oh hell. She cringed just thinking about it.

To be honest, she wasn't quite sure how she was going to explain – the emotions were still a little chaotic in her mind. But just the thought of getting in her car and at least trying, that lifted her spirits. Right, that was it. She wrote a Post-it Note and stuck it in the shop window about the later opening, got Alfie, his lead, and some water into the back of her car, and set off. *Let's do this thing, Em.*

It was as she was approaching the outskirts of Newcastle that she realised a three-storey town house near to a converted chapel wasn't that explicit. No address, no street name, and the suburb of Jesmond seemed to be quite big. Yes, she could always ring Max, but what if he was so fed up with her he didn't answer, or worse still answered but then said he didn't want to see her? How could she then just turn up? Better to keep the element of surprise – if she could find the right house, that was.

A church spire caught her eye; right, head in that direction. She knew Max's vehicle and the church seemed to be at the far end of this road, so she'd be looking for some work vans, a skip, scaffolding? Nothing. No dark-grey jeep, either. And the church wasn't converted, there was a board up about services and the like.

Fifteen minutes later she was still circling. Come on, Em, was there anything, any snippet of conversation that might help? He had said something about a coffee shop being nearby, too. Okay, so church/chapel, coffee shop, three-storey house. It was still pretty vague. She took a different turn and found herself on a street with a run of shops – hairdresser, gift shop, little café – but there must be lots of coffee shops in Jesmond, surely. Keep trying, turn left, turn right – she might as well throw a bloody dice, stupid woman. And then, a tall townhouse with scaffolding, several work vehicles parked outside, and a dark-grey jeep. Oh my, this was it!

She found a space to park a little further down the street. Taking a quick look in the rear-view mirror, she added a slick of lip gloss and ran her fingers through her hair to give it a bit more life, took a deep breath, then stepped out. Heading back to the house with the scaffolding, she passed a chap having a cigarette by one of the white vans, possibly one of Max's team. She smiled at him.

Tall metal fencing panels stood across the driveway, one of them ajar. Inside she spotted a chap in a yellow Hi-Vis jacket checking the front of the house and making some notes on a clipboard. Emma was heading for the gap in the fencing, hoping to see Max somewhere. Hi-Vis guy turned. 'Can I help you?' he called across.

'Ah, I'm looking for Max . . . ' What was his surname? 'Yeah, Max Hardy.'

'Okay, and you are?'

'Emma.' She took a step or two forwards.

'Sorry, Emma, but no one's allowed past the gated area without a hard hat: Health and Safety.'

And yes, he was indeed wearing a bright yellow hard hat.

'Oh, can you maybe get me one? Are there any spares hanging about? Or perhaps I could borrow yours just for a few minutes?'

He gave her a look that said, 'You must be kidding me.'

She switched on her most winning smile. 'It's really important that I talk to him.'

He seemed to soften. 'Okay, give me sec and I'll see if I've got a spare in the van.'

He went out to a smart navy van parked beside the house, returning with a hat, which he offered to her. 'I think he's around the back. Be careful, mind, there's trenches and pits round there, as well as heaps of rubble.'

'Anyone would think it's a building site,' Emma quipped, feeling nervous, which didn't go down too well, as the guy's face hardened. 'Right,' she added briskly, as she set off around the side of the house. Her heeled ankle boots were not the best choice for this terrain, but at least she was wearing jeans. It was a big property, rather grand, with a huge garden stretching out behind it. No doubt it would be fabulous when it was all done. As she rounded the corner, there was Max, hard hat on, deep in conversation with one of the workmen. They were discussing something, then looking up at the back of the house, Max pointing. Emma stopped in her tracks. Just then, Max's gaze came down and fell upon her. He didn't smile; he looked taken aback if anything.

Emma then lip-read him saying to his colleague, 'I'm sorry, if you can just give me a minute?'

This was the moment in the movies when they ran into each other's arms, and he'd pick her up and whizz her around, as the backing music swelled into a crescendo.

Emma stood frozen to the spot, feeling a bit sick, as he marched across in heavy work boots.

'What on earth are you doing here?' He sounded abrupt.

'Ah . . . '

But she knew why she was here, and she needed to tell him. 'I missed you.' There was a sense of relief as the words were spoken.

'Look, I'm right in the middle of things here. But if you can just wait for five or ten minutes, I'll take time out for a coffee or something. How does that sound?'

'Okay, I'll go wait in the car. It's just along the street here.'

'I won't be long, honest. I just need to make a couple of calls. There's something I need to sort out.'

'Okay, no problem.' He seemed rather cool with her, which made her heart sink. But, it was no more than she deserved after cutting him down when he had opened his heart to her after the Christmas market that day.

'Suits you, by the way,' he added with his trademark grin. 'The yellow.' He nodded towards the hat, then winked at her.

'Hah.' She'd bet her red curls were springing out wildly

from under the hat in all directions. It was nice to see him smile, and with those words he seemed to soften a little.

'See you in a few minutes, then,' he added.

'Yes, I'll wait.'

She saw Max coming out from the gates at the front of the property and stepped out of her car so he could see where she was parked. She felt so nervous it was crazy, her heart thumping away in her chest. He'd smiled just a while ago, seemed to be okay with her, she reminded herself.

He walked across. 'Sorry to keep you hanging about.'

'It's fine. It's not as though you knew I was coming.'

'No, well it's been a bit of a surprise, I must say. There's a little coffee shop.' He indicated towards the next street. 'We could walk there.'

'Yes, I'd spotted that on the way past. The super-duper banana milkshake place?'

'That's the one – well remembered.'

'It led me to your door.' She smiled.

'Have you been okay?' he asked more seriously.

'Yes, well kind of,' she replied. 'Ah no, to be honest, I've had a tricky few weeks.'

'Me too.' He gave her a look that said so very much.

So, it seemed they had both been hurting, or was that too much to hope? Hah, and she'd thought she was avoiding all that for them. She wanted so much to feel him close, to have his warmth beside her. She took a chance and linked her arm through his as they walked along. He glanced down to where her elbow lay crooked against his, but didn't pull away. Neither spoke. Sometimes words just got in the way.

In the coffee shop, they found a table by the window and ordered cappuccinos from the waitress. Emma realised she hadn't had any breakfast yet, but her stomach was still doing too many somersaults to be able to eat.

'So,' Max started the conversation that they still hadn't had, 'are you going to try to explain? Why you never answered my texts, my calls for weeks and then blew me out at the market that day? Just when it seemed everything was going good between us. I've never known anyone blow so hot and then cold, Em. And now, you turning up like this? I really don't know what the hell to make of it.'

God, she'd made such a mess of things.

'We were getting on well. You were right about that.' She gazed out of the window. How to capture it all in words? But she needed to try for Max's sake. 'I think I was afraid to let you in. Max, my heart has been in a thousand tiny pieces for years, and I've only just begun sticking it back together again . . . I – I couldn't risk it again.' She still hadn't mentioned *his* name, didn't know how it could fit in this conversation.

'You can talk about Luke if you want. I'm okay with that. I know you've had a hard time and I'm prepared to be there for you, but don't shut me out, Em. Be honest with me, tell me more about what happened with Luke?'

The waitress came back over with the cappuccinos, popped them down on the table with some sugar sachets in a white porcelain dish.

'Thanks,' Max said.

Emma nodded in acknowledgement. Her mind was already way back, all those years ago. 'It – it was two days after my birthday, seven years ago. He was going off to work on his bicycle as usual. Luke was a teacher, we both were, that's how we met. He loved cycling, wanted to keep fit and do his bit for the environment. Typical Luke, wanted to save the world, really. But the world didn't save him . . . ' She paused, turning a sugar sachet over and over between her fingertips.

Max stayed quiet, waiting for Emma to carry on.

'It was a lorry at traffic lights. Didn't see him. Turned left straight into him.' Emma stopped speaking for a second, the sugar sachet frozen in her hand. 'The police said he didn't stand a chance. At least it was instant. He wouldn't have known, not other than that first second.' How many times had she imagined that first horrendous second?

'Em, I'm so sorry.' Max's hand settled gently over her own.

'He was only twenty-nine.'

Emma went quiet and stared out of the café window, at the world going by, a mum with a toddler in a buggy, an old lady slowly, determinedly making her way down the street with her walking stick, cars passing, a van, a bicycle.

'It wasn't just Luke they destroyed that day,' Emma took up again, 'though that was bad enough, it was *us*, our whole future. Our wedding was booked for the following spring. My husband, my family – what I thought was going to be my life was wiped out, just like that. That lorry took away everything that was meant to happen.' Her eyes were misted with tears but they hadn't spilled. She wiped her nose with a napkin from the table. Max still held on to her other hand.

'That's a hell of a thing to deal with, Em.'

She nodded sadly.

'So, where do we go from here, hey?'

Emma took a slow breath, looked Max in the eye. 'Up.'

He let her have a few quiet moments, as they both sipped their drinks.

'So how does dinner next Saturday sound?'

'Good.'

'I'll come up to you. There's a really good restaurant in Bamburgh I'd like to take you to.'

'Sounds lovely . . . Oh shit!' Emma stood up in a bit of a panic.

'What? Can't you make it?'

'No, I've forgotten Alfie. He's still in my car.' Her poor dog had gone right out of her head, and oh my, he'd probably be bursting for a wee.

'I'll pay here, you go. I'll catch you up,' Max stated.

A few minutes later, Max was jogging down the road as Emma reached her car and swiftly opened the hatch- back. Alfie seemed fine, waggy-tailed, and none the worse for his neglect. He bounced out of the boot, took a quick pee against a wall, and pulled on his lead to get to Max.

'No harm done?' Max said as he reached them, crouching down to rub the spaniel's head affectionately.

'No, he seems fine, thank heavens. Look, I'd really better get back and open up the shop.'

'Yes, I'll be needed back on site too. Thanks for coming, Em.' He placed a hand on her shoulder and it felt warm and secure. 'And I'll see you Saturday. I'll be there for about seven, if that's okay?'

'Sounds lovely.'

Despite the likelihood of Hi-Vis man reappearing across the road at any moment and a chap working up on the scaffolding at the front of the house, Max moved in for a kiss that promised so much. Alfie whimpered, probably feeling left out, which made them both pull away, laughing.

'See you Saturday.'

45

The next few days at the shop kept her occupied. It was now December and it was beginning to feel a lot like Christmas. The Chocolate Shop Café had a steady stream of customers and her stocking fillers and gift boxes were starting to sell well. She had even sold a couple of her festive wicker hampers, priced at £30, which raised her takings considerably. There was always a lovely atmosphere in the shop at this time of year, even more so now her customers could stay and linger over a creamy hot chocolate or rich cup of coffee. It gave them a chance to chat and relax, and they would often glance over the goods on the shelves as well. The café had most certainly increased sales. The financial pressures had eased, thank heavens, though she was always aware that still the wolf – otherwise known as the Eel – was never too far from the door. But for now, nothing was going to spoil her festive fun – life was looking good.

Bev helped on a Wednesday and Friday, ten until three, which was great, as it gave Emma a chance to get on with crafting the chocolate, as well as them both serving customers when it got extra busy. It was lovely having her friend as company too. During a quiet ten minutes, she told Bev how she had been to visit Max, and admitted that Bev had been right: she had been afraid of a new relationship. She thanked her friend for being so honest.

'Hey, no worries. I just want what's best for you, Em, that's all.'

Just then Mrs Clark trundled past the window and made her way in. The elderly lady had become even more of a regular now; she liked to prop herself in the window seat and watch the world go by with her pot of tea for one and a chocolate-chip shortbread. If the shop was quiet, Emma would go over and chat, and ask how she was keeping. She didn't have much family, having had no children of her own, but there were tales of the village 'back in the day', of fetes and dances, the old fisherfolk. She still bought her chocolate brazils, though she'd begun to complain they weren't doing her dentures any good, a bit too crunchy. 'Tough little buggers, those nuts in 'em.' were her precise words, but, apparently, she just couldn't resist them, and wasn't prepared to give them up any time soon.

Bev went home at three and Emma stayed behind the counter. It was soon school-bus drop-off time and Holly came bounding in.

'Hi, Emma, you okay?'

'Yes, all good. You?'

'Cool, thanks. Actually, I've a bit of a favour to ask.'

Holly pulled a pleading grimace as though it might be a biggie.

'Go on,' Emma said cautiously, 'what is it?'

'Oh Em, Adam's just found out he's got the day off work this Saturday, and he wants to take me to the Christmas markets in Edinburgh. But I know I should be working and it might be busy here and I don't want to leave you in the lurch, but I do *really* want to go.'

'Leave it with me just now.' A Saturday, at this time of year, would be really hard to cover all by herself, but Holly never asked for the day off, and the look on her face told Emma how important it was to her. It sounded so gorgeous and romantic too. Edinburgh at Christmas time – she'd seen pictures of the markets, all beautifully lit up and bustling, with alpine-looking stalls, a Christmas Tree Maze, and a big wheel and all sorts of other exciting things, but she had never been at that time of the year herself. 'Let me make a couple of calls and I'll see if I can get some help in. I'll get back to you as soon as I can.'

'Aw, thanks, Emma. If you can it would be *so* amazing. I'll work extra another day, or cover a shift for you.'

'Thanks, I might need that favour some time.'

So, Saturday was going to be an extra busy day. A full-on chocolate shop, no Holly, hopefully someone else to help, though, and then her meal to look forward to with Max. She'd give Bev a ring right away.

Bev could only do couple of hours on the Saturday morning as she had promised to take Pete's mum into Newcastle to do her Christmas shopping. His mother didn't drive any further than the local market town these days, being nervous in city traffic. Bev couldn't let her mother-in-law down, and Emma wouldn't want her to. Oh well, two hours in the morning would help, so she took Bev up on her offer, and she'd just multitask herself for the rest of the day. No point disappointing Holly.

She could tell Holly was literally bouncing as she heard the good news when Emma phoned her later.

'Oooh, thank you so much. Love you, Em. Can't wait to tell Adam. Yay!'

It felt good to make someone's day.

It was a bit of a mad rush to get ready and changed that Saturday by seven for her dinner date with Max. The restaurant sounded fairly swish, so she'd opted for a red wraparound dress which she usually wore in the summer, but teamed it with tights and black leather knee-length boots for a winter look. She felt comfy in it, and it clung in just the right places. She flicked a brush through the curls of her hair, which she had left loose, falling past her shoulders, and checked in the dressing-table mirror to see if she had remembered to put any lipstick on. Grabbing a small black-velvet clutch bag, she popped in her purse and the red lipstick she'd just used and spritzed herself with some perfume. She felt a bit nervous: this was the first date since she had gone to see Max down in Jesmond and she hoped all her doubts and fears hadn't spoilt things for them.

She heard an engine pull to a halt outside. She got up off the stool and checked out of the bedroom window.

There he was, parked up in the jeep. She saw him get out of the vehicle, smart in dark chinos and a pale-blue shirt. He was also holding the most gorgeous bouquet of flowers, wrapped in tissue and cellophane, most definitely not from a supermarket. She saw his broad shoulders rise slowly as he took a deep breath before he knocked on the chocolate shop door. She felt his nerves too. It felt a bit like a new start for them both; they didn't want to mess things up this time.

She settled Alfie in his bed in the kitchen, grabbed her smartest beige winter coat, and headed swiftly down the stairs, not wanting to keep him waiting.

'Wow, you look gorgeous,' he said, beaming, offering the bouquet at the same time as leaning in to kiss her.

He smelt divine, even better than the flowers. 'Thank you so much, they are just beautiful.' The blooms were white, cream, and a delicate soft pink with roses, carnations and some others she didn't know the names of, with sprigs of green foliage that set them off perfectly.

'Your carriage awaits.' And he motioned to the jeep with a smile, bringing them both back down to earth in a lovely way. This was all rather fabulous, but they could be themselves too.

It was a twenty-minute drive north to the coastal village of Bamburgh. They passed through a couple of country villages, along winding lanes with farmland each side of the road, though it was too dark to make out much en route. Arriving in Bamburgh they passed the impressive stone castle lit up and set on the rocks above the dunes which marked the start of the village.

Lights were strung along the main street, highlighting cottages, a hotel, and small shops. In the centre of the village was a green with an area of grass and established trees, which had been lit with white lights. As they parked, she spotted a family of wooden reindeer, made of twined willow and fairy lights and all different sizes, in the middle. It looked like some mini magical forest.

'Oh, wow, isn't that just so pretty?' she commented to Max.

'Cute, isn't it?'

It was cold as they stepped out of the vehicle, one of those crisp winter nights that would bring frost. She snuggled into her coat and took Max's hand as they walked to the Saltwater Bistro. Max held open the door for her in a gentlemanly fashion, which was rather nice.

There was a central hall which had a large pine Christmas tree decorated with big silver and blue baubles and silver tinsel. It looked fabulous and festive in a coastal kind of way, which fitted perfectly with the restaurant, which was themed with sea and sky colours of blues, greys, and creams. A waiter came across and took Emma's coat and led them to their table for two, asking what they would like to drink.

'Oh, I'd like a gin and tonic, please,' Emma said. That seemed a lovely drink to start with, and a treat.

'Coke for me, please, pint.' Max added, 'Driving,' for Emma's benefit. 'Though I will stretch to a nice glass of wine with the meal. We'll order that later though, thanks.'

It felt nice here, not too stuffy; the lights were muted and candle votives glowed on the table; you could relax and chat. The waiter delivered their drinks and then passed them menus, typed stylishly on thick cream card. They were left to peruse and muse, whilst Emma sipped her chilled, bubbly glass of fragrant G&T. She had never read so many gorgeous-sounding things in one place.

'It's a great place, isn't it?' Max said.

'Have you been here much before?'

'Just a couple of times. The food is always good.'

'I'm sure it will be.' She wondered then who he'd been there with. Siobhan, maybe, and weirdly felt a twinge of jealousy. But the past needed to stay exactly where it was tonight. Tonight was a night for moving forwards.

Emma ordered a scallop starter and turbot with a hollandaise sauce for main, Max, a crab cocktail, followed by seafood 'Frito Misto' – 'fried in delicate breadcrumbs'. They were served homemade breads whilst they sat chatting, and Max asked for two glasses of Chablis, checking that Emma liked that. 'If it's a dry white, that'll be fine,' she said, smiling. She'd possibly had some at her parents' before, but expensive wines were not something she could indulge in lately.

They chatted about work, the busy build-up to the festive season in The Chocolate Shop, their plans for Christmas. Emma realised she hadn't actually got that far yet, but perhaps she ought to invite James and his family and her parents and cook a roast turkey dinner for them; after all, they had helped her so much this year. Yes, that'd be nice. In fact, having two days off in a row for Christmas and Boxing Day would be absolute bliss.

Max said he was likely to be staying at his parents'

house over Christmas; they lived in Morpeth, about forty minutes away from Warkton, and as he was an only child, they'd no doubt be looking forward to spoiling him. His mum was a good cook, so he said he'd be well fed and looked after. It sounded like he was on the meals-for-one syndrome too – something quick and easy after work.

'So, what do you cook, then?' Emma was curious. 'Or is it all ready meals and takeaways?'

'Hey, cheeky. I can cook! It's just not that inspiring after a full day on site sometimes. But I can make a mean curry, from scratch I'm talking. I make a passable roast chicken. And pasta, yeah, bolognese, carbonara – I can manage those. Otherwise quite a few jars come in handy. Or yes, I confess, the takeaway down the road.'

'It's okay. I like cooking, but after a whole day making and serving chocolates, sometimes it's just cheese and biscuits for me, or something easy on toast. So tonight is a real treat.'

The starters were served, and Emma was soon tucking into the most exquisite scallops thermidor, with flavours of cream and cheese, and the most juicy scallops.

'Well, this is certainly a step up from beans on toast. Delicious.'

Max's crab was served in a large v-shaped cocktail glass, with a crab claw and a huge shell-on prawn hung decoratively over the side of the glass that looked amazing.

The food was fabulous. Emma's turbot was served with crisp-cooked asparagus and yummy herb-buttered new potatoes and Max's plate was piled with a selection of seafood all in a light crispy-coating of breadcrumbs. Emma tried a piece of calamari, which she'd never had before because she'd feared it might be rubbery from its thick, elastic-looking appearance, but it wasn't; it was more like a delicate white-meat ring. Oh, it was good to try new things, new places, new experiences.

'I've never been anywhere as nice as this,' she admitted.

'Well, you deserve to. Just relax and enjoy it. And tonight is my treat, okay?'

'I will, and thank you.' And with that she dipped another forkful of her thick white flaky turbot into the superb hollandaise sauce, wondering if she might yet have room to try a dessert. She didn't want this experience to end just yet.

'So, how did you first discover The Chocolate Shop?'

She paused and took a sip of her wine. 'After Luke died, I used to come up to the coast just to get away from the house, go someplace else that wasn't too near the home that no longer felt like home, and walk Alfie. We'd go for miles. And then one day I headed further than normal and found Warkton. I was walking up the street, heading back from beach, when I saw that the little cottage with its shop was up for rent. I was already making chocolates as a hobby for all my friends – just focussing on crafting something helped me get by – and everybody seemed to love the end result. I saw the cottage and I remember that feeling of possibility, like it was something I had to do, as I wrote the number down. I got in touch with the agent, went and saw the property the next day, got myself booked on a formal chocolatier course. I had some savings, which I used to buy the equipment I needed to set up the shop, and the rest, as they say, is history.'

'Good for you.'

They clinked glasses.

She realised then that her life in the past six years had focussed on work, work, work. It had kept her days structured, kept her busy, and she'd felt safe in its day-to-day confines, but this evening was just lovely, spending a little time out away from the shop, however much she loved her job. And her world was suddenly full of maybes, of new possibilities, all stacked up for her. She still wasn't sure if she was scared or excited, but she knew she had to give it a try.

46

It was Friday evening, just before closing, when a call came from Adam.

'Emma, we've had a bit of a nightmare here at the hotel. I really need your help.'

'Okay, what's happened?'

'A mouse, or probably a whole family of bloody mice by the looks of it, got into the storeroom and had a right go at all the mini chocolate boxes for the turn-downs. The little bastards – excuse my language, but they've made a right mess – nibbled through the boxes, pooped everywhere. We've had to throw the lot out – over a hundred boxes in all. That was our stocks to take us right up to Christmas. Rentokil are here right now, or we'll be having Environmental Health on our case next.'

'Oh, how awful, the little devils.' Mice *loved* chocolate – she'd had an incident in The Chocolate Shop soon after she had bought it, when they munched their way through two very expensive packets of the chocolate callets. She had been extremely careful with storage and keeping traps down ever since.

Damn, Emma had been looking forward to a few hours' chill out with Max, who was probably heading up from work right now. It had been one hell of a week and her wrists were aching from crafting chocolates every day as it was. She could feel a very late night coming on, and was racking her brains, wondering if she had enough supplies to make an extra two hundred or so chocolates out of the blue.

'Okay. Leave it with me, Adam. I'll do my best. I can get you, say, the first fifty boxes for now and some more in a few days' time, because I'll probably need to buy in extra supplies, and being the weekend . . . ' She let the words drift.

'Yeah, I understand. But anything you can do to help will be appreciated.'

'Do you have enough for this weekend's turndowns?'

'Doubt it. We really can't use *any* of them. There are droppings everywhere, even if they don't appear to have been eaten.'

'Ah, okay. Well, I have some chocolates in the shop that I can box up for you. Will a dozen or so boxes do for now?'

'Yeah, that'd be brilliant. Don't want to disappoint the guests. They love your chocolates – it's become part of the stay, now.'

'I'll get those organised right away. If you can pop down to the shop in say, fifteen minutes, I'll have them made up and ready. Then I'll have to start making all the others.'

'Emma, you're a star. Thank you so much.'

So much for a quiet night in.

Ten o'clock, and she and Max had a little production line going. Truffle centres ready to dip in the melted chocolate was the next stage and Max had even learnt how to make the little alcohol-infused balls evenly sized, by rolling them in the palms of his hands. It was delicate work for big builder's hands, and it made Emma smile watching him. One day, there he was sawing wood and making window seats, the next truffles; where would it end? Hopefully in bed, she mused, though that seemed a distant prospect at this point. She stifled a yawn.

The dark chocolate was tempered now; time to dip the whisky infused truffles carefully in with metal tongs. They had to work quickly, whilst it was at the right temperature, yet still ensure all sides of the truffle were evenly coated, so it was quite an art and the truffles might not have been quite as neat as usual, but the fifty they made looked pretty good. Emma left them to cool on the metal board on the side and cleared the other equipment to the dishwasher.

Earlier on they'd had a snatched supper of cold chicken and salad. She'd cooked the chicken, but hadn't had time to do the full roast dinner she'd intended.

'Sorry, Max, this wasn't the kind of evening I meant for you to have. I think we've done enough for now. Thanks so much for your help. Let's call it a day.'

'I didn't know making chocolate was so physically demanding.'

'Hey, tell me about it. I could do with a hot bath.'

'Me too.' He had that cheeky look on his face again.

Well, that idea was almost better than going to bed. She filled the tub, pouring in some scented bubbles. It wasn't the biggest of bath tubs, but she managed to sit between Max's sturdy legs and squashed herself in. The water slopped out over the side a little, the bubbles popping and crushing around them. This was rather lovely. She lay back resting her head on his chest, and Max began to smooth the soapy bubbles over her breasts, washing her very sensuously, until a sigh escaped her lips. His hand then slid down temptingly between her thighs and she could feel him ready behind her; if she just shifted a little here . . . and there – oh yes! And she was gliding down on to him, the water warm around them. It was difficult to move much at all, but she could rock just enough. She felt his hands tighten round her waist, gripping as he could hold back no more, beautiful, hard thrusts within her. And then, a little later, she turned to face forward to kiss him, resting her forehead against his, and closed her eyes, to just hold the moment.

Max had another early start, told Em not to get up, to catch up on her sleep. He said he'd come back again on Sunday evening and see her around six. She vaguely remembered him kissing her forehead, then a short while later heard the noise of his jeep engine start and move away. She rolled back under the duvet for another hour.

When she got into the kitchen to check on last night's truffles an hour or so later, they seemed to have been moved. Strange. She put the kitchen light on; they appeared to form letters, words in fact. Was she still in bed dreaming? She squinted. No, they'd definitely been rearranged. She focussed her sleepy eyes, read 'I Love You' made from whisky truffles. There was a handwritten note beside them saying 'Don't worry, I used the hygiene gloves!' Max obviously not wanting to ruin all their hard work last night.

How sweet was that? Aw. She was left with a soppy grin on her face and took a photo on her iPhone to keep, as she'd soon have to box them for the hotel. Oh Max. Thank heavens she hadn't let him slip through her fingers. He was sexy, and he was kind and loving too. She couldn't wait to see him again on Sunday. But until then there was more work to do. Adam's hotel order was yet to be completed.

Saturday afternoon and Max had usually called her by now, or at least texted, especially when they'd just spent a night together. It was like they couldn't stop thinking about each other. She wanted to thank him for the chocolate 'I Love You' message, so tried his mobile a couple of times. It seemed like it was dead, the battery down or something. Oh well, he must just be busy at work. She'd speak to him soon. Her happy loved-up bubble couldn't be burst that easily.

47

'Hello, is that Emma? Max says you are a friend.'

It was late on the same Saturday afternoon.

The voice was of a middle-aged, well-spoken woman. It sounded far too formal, and for some reason the hairs on the back of Emma's neck rose and she felt a cold prickle run through her.

'Yes, this is Emma speaking. Is everything all right?' She noticed her hands had started to tremble holding the mobile phone.

'Well, he's had a bit of an accident at the building site.' The woman paused, seemingly gathering herself. 'He's serious but stable in hospital in Newcastle. They have to do some CT scans before we know more. He asked me to call you, to let you know.'

Oh dear God, no. 'What's happened?'

'He fell off the scaffolding early this morning; one of his colleagues found him in a bit of mess, maybe an hour or so later. We're not quite sure. The doctors say he's broken his collarbone and cracked some ribs, but they need to check his brain . . . ' The phone line went quiet for a few seconds, then Emma thought she heard a stifled sob, followed by a slow breath. 'They think he hit his head, though thank the lord he did have his hard hat on.'

Thank heavens for the yellow helmets.

'Oh . . . ' Em's throat was starting to thicken with the knot of threatening tears. Dread filled her soul. *Please, dear God, not again.* 'Can I see him?'

'I think it's best the doctors do what they need to today, and it's close family only at this stage. Sorry . . . I'm his mother, by the way, Christine. Shall I speak with you tomorrow, Emma? Maybe you can pop down another day, when we know more.'

'Of course. And thank you for letting me know.'

'You're welcome, dear.'

'Can you tell him I'm thinking of him, and to get well soon.' Emma just about held it together, to say goodbye.

'Yes. I'll keep in touch.'

As soon as she clicked the phone off, Emma crumpled in a heap on her living-room floor, the tears flowing uncontrollably.

A night of worrying and praying for him followed, hoping against hope that history was not about to repeat itself. All she really wanted to do was to drive straight down there, though she wasn't even sure which infirmary he was in, and find him in that hospital bed and hold him tight in her arms. But she had to sit there and wait. She had called Bev in the late evening as she had to talk to someone, and her friend knew more than most about the background to all this.

'Shall I come round, Em? Do you want some company?'

'No, I'm all over the place. Can't settle to anything, even though I've loads to do. Just talk to me a minute. I'll go off to bed soon. I should really try and get some sleep.'

So they'd chatted about all sorts of inane things. It was too hard to go too near the truth. What might be happening in that hospital an hour away? They couldn't change anything, they just had to wait for news, which Emma didn't expect at least until morning when the CT scan had been done.

'He'll be okay, Em. I'm sure he'll be okay,' Bev tried to reassure. 'I'll call again in the morning. And if you need anything, even if it's in the middle of the night, just shout.'

'Thank you.'

Emma had saved Christine's phone number, but felt she ought to give his family their space for that evening. After all, they hadn't even heard of her until today. She was still holding her phone in her hand after speaking to Bev. She looked at the photo of Max's message written in chocolates and a tear dropped down on to her wrist.

She had a broken, dream-filled sleep, waking, with sharp snatches of memories of Luke's death gripping her every now and then, then she'd sleep restlessly once more. She had to be ready to start work again in the morning. There was still so much to do. But at least it would keep her occupied. It was only one week until Christmas.

It was twenty to eleven in the morning, when her mobile rang: Christine. Emma froze, almost too scared to answer it.

'Excuse me for just one second,' she said to a gentleman who was browsing in the shop. 'I really need to take this call.'

'No problem.' He carried on looking at the boat-shelf selection.

Emma walked towards the inner hall doorway and pressed 'green'.

'Christine? How is he?' She hardly dared breathe.

'They did the scan first thing this morning, and it's clear.'

'Oh, that's brilliant!' She didn't care if the guy in the shop saw her tears of relief.

'They're just keeping him in for observation through the day. He dislocated his shoulder yesterday and that was put back in, and the broken collarbone is in a support sling. It doesn't need surgery, though he'll need physio later.'

'Oh, poor Max! But it could have been so much worse.'

'He's been lucky.'

'Yes. Thanks so much for letting me know. Can I come down and see him?'

'We're not sure quite when he'll be released from hospital, it may well be later this afternoon. Shall I let you know? You could call at the house this evening – we'll be having him with us to convalesce for a while. Make sure I can keep an eye on him so he's not doing too much with that arm. I know what he's like.' She spoke the words fondly.

Emma had to smile. 'Yes. Well, I'll come down straight after work, if you're sure that's okay.'

'That should be fine. I'll confirm later, when they've discharged him from the ward.'

'Thanks again, Christine, for letting me know. Send him my love. Oh, I'm so glad he's going to be all right.'

'We are very relieved too. I'll be in touch soon, Emma. Bye.'

'Bye.' Emma clicked off the call.

'Oh, sorry.' She realised the chap was still standing there, with a bar of chocolate orange and another of mint crisp, ready to pay.

'No worries.' He was smiling.

'He's going to be all right,' she couldn't help but blurt out, still tearful. She didn't even know this guy, but he was bound to have heard most of the call.

'Well, that's good news.' He was still holding the chocolate bars.

'Oh, that's four pounds ninety-eight, please.' And she popped them into a bag.

He passed over a five-pound note. 'Thanks, and you have a happy Christmas.'

'You too. Merry Christmas.'

Just the customer saying that made her feel all emotional. She needed to go get a tissue or she'd be blubbing all over the chocolates at this rate.

Emma found the address Christine had given her in a tree-lined avenue in Morpeth. It was a large red-brick townhouse. She pulled up outside and found herself feeling a little nervous. As well as seeing Max all bashed up, she'd be meeting his parents for the first time too.

She rang the doorbell and stood waiting anxiously, desperate to just run in and find Max and *gently* give him the hugest of hugs.

A tall, elegant-looking lady came to the door. She was very slim, with coiffed short grey hair, wearing smart navy trousers, a white blouse and a blue-patterned scarf at her neck. Her eyes were a kind blue-grey but they looked tired.

'Hello, you must be Emma. Lovely to meet you.' She extended a hand in greeting. 'Come on in.'

It all seemed quite formal.

'I'm sure you'd like to see Max. I'll show you through . . . we've set him a bed up in the dining room. Saves the stairs,' she explained. 'He seems quite sore with his ribs.'

'Hey.' Max tried to prop himself up on the pillows, with a grimace. They had set out a sofa-bed for him to rest in. Emma noticed the large green-black bruise he had on one cheek.

'Hi there. What have you been getting up to?'

'Doing acrobatics off the scaffolding. Forgot the safety net.' He tried to smile.

'I'll go make some tea,' said Christine, politely leaving them on their own.

Ah, dammit, the tears were starting again.

'Hey, come here. I'm okay, Em.'

Max knew exactly why this was so hard for her. He reached out his good arm and she found shelter in his clumsy half-hug. He winced again.

'Sorry.' She moved back a little, afraid of hurting him.

'It's all right, don't you go anywhere. Just here is fine.'

And he motioned for her to snuggle up on the good side of his battered chest.

It felt so good, to feel him right there beneath her head, feel the warmth of his skin through his T-shirt, hear his heart beating loudly in his chest.

'Max . . ' She didn't raise her head, just spoke the words loud and clear. 'In answer to your chocolate message: I love you too.'

A while later, Christine brought in tea and biscuits on a tray and asked Emma about her chocolate shop and the village. Emma shifted from the bed, feeling a little awkward being that close to him with his mum right there – not that Christine batted an eyelid when she came back in. Emma pulled up a dining chair next to the bed. Max's dad, Trevor, also popped his head in the room at that point to say a friendly hello. He had no doubt been warned to give them a bit of space. He seemed a nice man, a thinner version of Max without the stubbly beard.

Emma stayed for over two hours in the end, sharing a tender kiss with Max as she said goodbye, and promising she'd call back again tomorrow after work, even though it was a forty-minute drive after a long working day. But it would be harder not to see him. It was difficult enough leaving him there as it was, now they had found each other again. As she walked out of the room she was already missing that contact, that closeness, but she knew he'd be well looked after by his family.

48

'Emma, you've got to help me. They are scheming to take me to Uncle George's for Christmas Day,' Max was whispering down the phone line. It was four days later. 'It was already arranged before the accident. A *family* Christmas Day and they hadn't told me. Honestly, he's batty as a hoot, his wife can hardly cook, and they have three cats who hate me. The claws will be out. Can you come and rescue me?'

'Are you able to come here?'

'Yes, I'm feeling sore but I'm way better. And I'd love to be with you.'

'Well, I have James and the family for dinner, but yes, no problem, you could come along too. That'd be fine.'

'The only thing is, I'm trapped here. I can't drive yet and Mum won't let me stay home on my own, absolutely won't hear of it on Christmas Day. Is there any chance you could come and fetch me? I'm sorry, I know that'd be a pain as you'll still be flat out at the shop.'

'Oh, after work tomorrow, Christmas Eve, I could

come down and get you then. You'd better clear it with your mother first, though. I don't want to be in the middle of any family dramas when I get there.'

'Will do, but she'll be fine if I'm with company and being fed. She just didn't want me left alone. Honestly, she's great, my mum, don't get me wrong, but I feel like I've reverted to being eight years old this week. She even cut up my dinner for me yesterday. She did just about hold off spoon-feeding me, however.'

Emma chuckled. 'She's only trying to look after you, I'm sure. I bet you're sitting there all grumpy like Victor Meldrew. Okay, I'll come and save you. But clear it with the family first. Call me back to confirm, and I'll try to get there around six.'

Christmas Eve arrived at last. Holly was helping, and Bev was due in later. At eleven o'clock it was pretty hectic already, lots of last-minute gifts and stocking fillers being bought, and people looking stressed-out calling for pep-up coffees on their way back from the supermarket, or visiting family. Then there were the lucky ones who were already off and relaxing for their Christmas break in their cottages and B&Bs by the sea, with the workers still going strong, like a little army of ants keeping all the cogs going, the chocolate supplied, the teapots filled.

Emma was tired, but she did love this time of the year. Yes, it was busy, had been for weeks, but it was also special. She had her Christmas lights on, carols and festive pop music playing, and was sporting her old faithful reindeer jumper, which made its outing every year, with red bauble earrings. Bev was about to turn up shortly in her elf costume, apparently (they'd decided a Christmas outfit was a must) and Holly was here as Father Christmas in a red-felt suit, with a white beard and all – though she was having problems as the beard kept dunking in the hot chocolates! Oh yes, less than twenty-four hours to the big day itself, and they were in full Christmas mode.

In one way, Emma couldn't wait for the door to close, for the final customers to be gone and allow her just to kick off her shoes, chill out, and make the most of three days' holiday. She had decided to take the day after Boxing Day off too – everyone would have had so many chocolates over Christmas no one would be wanting more that soon. And it was time she took a little bit of time out for herself.

Mind you, she would be driving down to Morpeth straight after work today, to collect Max, so not quite kicking off her shoes. But then, she was really looking forward to having him here with her and the family too.

They served a group of six sitting around one of the window-seat tables, and then Holly's mobile went off. Emma nodded to let her know it was okay to take the call, and her assistant went out to the kitchen to speak more privately.

Holly came back looking a little upset.

'Everything all right?' Emma asked.

'Not really. Adam's gran is quite poorly with the flu, bless her. We were going there tomorrow for dinner. She wanted to cook for us, as we really wanted our first

Christmas together and my mum and dad are away down south visiting my brother. Adam's mum died when he was young, that's why he's extra close to his gran, and his dad's got to work. He's a chef and someone has to cook all those Christmas dinners, so we don't really have anywhere to go.'

Two more wouldn't hurt, Emma mused; she had a turkey that was big enough to feed a family of twelve, and she could soon prep some extra vegetables. 'Why don't you both come here? It's fine. I've got James and the family over, and Max now too. He's on the mend.'

'Aw, I'm so glad about Max! That's such good news, Em.'

'So two more will be fine. Oh, and make sure you take a turkey dinner away for Adam's gran too. You can call and visit her, see how she's doing. I wouldn't like to think of her on her own all day for Christmas. What do you reckon?'

'I think that would be amazing.' She gave Em a big hug. 'I'll ring Adam straight away. Are you really sure?'

'Absolutely, the more the merrier.' It'd be a busy day cooking, but hey, she'd have plenty of helpers and wasn't that just what Christmas was all about?

49

'Merry Christmas!' Max was sitting beside her; he'd managed to prop himself up against the pillows and had a big cheesy grin on his face.

'Merry Christmas, Max.' She smiled, and moved carefully across, remembering his injuries, to plant a kiss on his cheek.

So, it was real, not some Christmas wish she'd been running in her mind. He was really here, his arm in a sling, and apart from the broken collarbone and cracked and bruised ribs, he was okay, though no doubt sore.

Last night had been interesting. She had offered to sleep on the sofa to give him the chance to get some uninterrupted rest, but he insisted she stay with him, that he'd be fine. But she was frightened she might roll over or starfish and bang into him in the middle of the night, so kept herself tight to her side of the bed.

It was Christmas Day. She had a turkey to cook, presents still to wrap for James and his family – she would have done them last night, but then she'd had her last-minute trip down to Morpeth – and they'd be arriving all too soon. Holly, Adam, James, Chloe, the twins, all to feed and entertain. She had invited her parents too, but they had already made plans to have lunch with close friends. They were going to call in and see her late afternoon on Boxing Day. But hey, it would all come together, there was no mad rush. For now, what she really wanted was to just cherish a few quiet moments with this gorgeous man beside her.

'Surprise!' Max bellowed above her head.

Or maybe not so quiet, then.

'Now, I can't quite reach it,' he continued, 'but there's something wrapped up for you under my side of the bed. Do you mind getting it out for me?'

Emma sat up and got out of bed. She was just about to lean under the bed, when she realised she was totally starkers and thought better of it – that particular position might not look very elegant, so she slipped on her satin dressing gown.

'Spoilsport.' He grinned from his nest of pillows.

As she got down on her hands and knees she saw a gold-foil, gift-wrapped box, which looked profession-ally done with a lovely silver-and-gold trimmed bow. She took it back into bed with her. Max watched her carefully as she began to unwrap it. She wasn't a rip-and-go kind of girl; always liked to savour gifts. Inside she found a black velvet box and carefully opened it to reveal a beautiful silver necklace with a delicate heart pendant.

'Oh, I love it! Thank you so much.' She touched the

heart and smiled at him. During these past few weeks, it felt very much like he had given her back a piece of her heart. She gave him a quick kiss on the lips, then placed it round her neck straight away, popping her long hair over her shoulder to reach and fasten the clasp more easily.

'Phew, glad you like it. I thought the heart was just right – hopefully. It's white gold, by the way.'

'Thank you. Now I feel like my gift to you will be a bit of a letdown.'

'Never. Just being here for Christmas with you is pretty damn good, to be fair.'

Emma had wrapped Max's gift up a few days ago and placed it in the cabinet of her bedside table.

He opened it to find a bottle of Armani aftershave and a new scarf to keep him cosy out on the building sites. It seemed appropriate, seeing as it was a scarf that had brought them together in the first place.

He fumbled one-handedly with the wrapper and box, then gave himself a spritz of the aftershave. 'Hmm, yes I've had this one before. I really like it.'

Emma inhaled. Ooh yes, it smelt even better on him than in the shop in fact.

'And a scarf – that's great. I can wrap up and think of you.' He smiled warmly as though he was genuinely pleased.

It was a nice Barbour one, in a checked blue pattern on grey. She had wanted to get him something nice, but she hadn't had tons of money to spare. She'd also popped in a box of whisky truffles, his favourites.

'Not too boring, I hope.'

'Just perfect, thank you.' And he leaned in to kiss her.

An hour later they were in the downstairs kitchen. Max offered to help with the mass of vegetables lined up ready to prepare: potatoes, Brussel sprouts, carrots and parsnips. Emma looked at him, and then his arm in its sling, with a wry smile.

'Thanks, but maybe you could set the table for me? That'd be great.'

'Aah . . . ' Max twigged. 'Yep, of course.'

'I'm going to set the table up out in The Chocolate Shop, at the big round table and new window seat made by an ever-so-lovely builder chap I know.' She grinned. 'With a couple of extra chairs, we'll be able to fit the eight around.'

'Yeah, that sounds ideal. And yes, I know that guy – he's sound. I'm sure he'd make someone a great catch.' He winked at her.

'Right, I just need to get out my Christmas tablecloth and the cutlery's all in that drawer.' She pointed.

The tablecloth was one her mum had given her. They always used to have it on the family table every Christmas when she and James were children. It was so pretty, a cream linen with silver and gold stars hand-stitched on in a delicate glittery thread. Mum had wanted a change one year, back when Emma was a student, and had gone out and got herself a new Cath Kidston holly-patterned one and Emma asked if she could have the old one. She'd used it every year since and it had become a part of her

Christmas. Funny how things meant so much, especially at this time of year. Traditions, memories . . . she and Luke had had their first Christmas dinner together, using this very tablecloth. Her heart clenched a little.

She had sent a card to Luke's parents and his younger brother Nathan, with a Christmas gift of her handmade chocolates and a bottle of Prosecco. It would be a difficult day for them too because there was always the feeling that someone was missing . . .

Time to think about today, Em, she reminded herself, as she watched Max trying his best to gather knives and forks together with one hand. It was going to be a slow process setting the table, but she knew he wanted to do something practical to help. Whilst Max toed and froed with the cutlery, she set to the task of peeling her mountain of vegetables.

The turkey was already in the oven, and Adam's gran had sent over her homemade stuffing and pigs-in-blankets, bless her, as she was no longer able to cook and didn't want them to go to waste.

Max's mother had also sent them away with a heap of food last night 'to keep them going': a whole cooked gammon joint, cheeses, a box of crackers, chutneys, grapes and mince pies. She had smiled knowingly at Emma, saying she knew how much he ate. So there would be plenty for a late supper – if they could fit anything else in, that was. At least there would be no need to cook tomorrow. Emma set the huge pan of potatoes to parboil and headed to the shop front to see how Max was getting on.

For dessert, Emma had already made a large chocolate-orange Christmas pudding instead of the traditional fruit version, knowing that James's girls would prefer this – who wouldn't, it was made of chocolate! It was created with rich, dark Belgian chocolate sponge and then had a molten-middle, choc-orange centre. It had been going down a treat with the customers as a festive special in the café these past two weeks, served with a blob of thick cream. She had made an extra one yesterday, to keep back especially.

James and Chloe were bringing a smoked salmon starter with them, and some wine and champagne, so it really was an all-hands-on-deck festive event.

Max had a bottle of champagne chilled and ready to open as the first guests arrived.

Holly and Adam were first, followed soon after by James and the family. The Chocolate Shop looked extra magical with the table all set up for Christmas dinner. There were Christmas crackers and star-decorated napkins set out now too, and the chocolate favours that Emma had specially chosen for all her guests, two each, wrapped in holly-patterned cellophane bags with a twist of gold ribbon. The girls had a chocolate reindeer and a snowman, James two whisky truffles, Chloe a Baileys white-choc truffle and a champagne in milk, Holly a salted caramel and raspberry cream, Adam a mini rum-and-raisin choc bar and Max a whisky and brandy.

Max struggled a little, but managed determinedly to

uncork the champagne and they all had a glass, with the girls having a flute of lemonade, and they all toasted 'Merry Christmas!'. Gifts were exchanged, with thanks and hugs, and excited chatter. Alfie had been allowed to join them as a one-off down in the chocolate shop, and was sporting a smart red-tartan patterned dog neckerchief and having great fun attacking a rather noisy turkey-shaped squeaky toy that the twins had wrapped up for him. It was keeping him happy anyhow.

The day was just brilliant – busy, noisy, with gifts and love and laughter.

Adam and Holly had headed off with hugs and kisses and big thanks to deliver Adam's gran's dinner, saying they'd call back later. Emma's family decided to go for a stroll down on the beach to blow away the cobwebs and try to make a dent in the turkey dinner, so they took Alfie and went out. Max was happy to stay behind. Emma thought he was probably still in some pain, and that he didn't want to hold them up on their beach walk.

Down on the sands, the girls ran about with Alfie, their giggles filling the air, the gulls swooping and the sea rolling in, in a vibrant froth of winter waves. Chloe and James walked along holding hands, evidently happy in their world, and that was lovely to see.

There was a mini-crisis as Lucy got a bit too near to the water's edge and a big wave came in, filling her wellington boots. There were tears until Chloe whisked her up, pulled off the boots one at a time, and tipped out the cold salty water. 'All done.'

James caught up with Emma and they walked together slowly. 'Max seems a nice chap,' he prompted.

'Yeah,' Emma said smiling, not wanting to say too much.

'Things going okay?' Her little brother checking she was all right, protective, and at the same time, hoping for good things for her.

'I think so . . . it's early days yet, though.' She was just finding her relationship feet again, and wasn't sure she wanted to chat about it quite at this point.

'Well, I hope he makes you happy, Em. He seems a good sort.'

'Yeah, I think he is.'

He put an arm around her shoulders and gave her a brotherly hug.

The girls whizzed back, wanting hugs too, and were soon swept up in a line of adult, child, adult, child in a row, with Auntie Em in the middle. They made a swinging action with their arms which the twins delighted in, giggling as they swooped to and fro, shouting 'More. More!' until all their arms were aching.

Within a further five minutes, though, grey clouds started gathering above, and a damp, hazy drizzle surrounded them. Oh well, it had been nice to get outside, but it was now past four and would be dark soon, so they were ready to head back for some essential chill-time, Emma especially. A family movie, something Christmassy, would be on the telly – no doubt something they'd watched before, with them all piled on the sofa, or the floor in her lounge. She might even manage a mince pie with a glass of Baileys, or perhaps a good old cup of tea.

This was what Christmas was all about: family, friends, loved ones. Life was special and so precious, and sitting there a little while later, back at her cottage on a cushion on the floor, with her family, Max, and Holly and Adam, she was full of gratitude for what she had, despite the pain of the past.

James and his family left soon after seven, as the girls had nodded off by the end of the film. Lucy had taken a shine to Max and had nestled next to him on the sofa, on his good side, and chattered herself to sleep beside him, questioning him all about the blue bandage thing, and if they had had to cut his arm off, and did it hurt. It had been a long day for them: apparently, the girls had been awake at five, full of excitement and energy, desperate to see if Father Christmas had been. Of course, he had.

Her brother and his family left with hugs and kisses and thank yous and invites for Emma and Max to go and visit them soon. James shook hands with Max firmly and Em noted her brother also giving him an approving pat on his good shoulder.

Holly and Adam left soon afterwards. Gran had been most thankful for the Christmas dinner and the visit from them earlier, and they were pleased to report that she was starting to feel a little better.

So, Max and Emma had a cosy night in. Alfie managed to sneak up on the sofa after polishing off a delicious bowl of turkey and trimmings, and lodged himself between them – well, it was Christmas after all. Emma felt really tired, but in a happy, contented way. In fact, it had been the best Christmas she had had in years.

Bedtime, and after helping Max remove his clothes, they snuggled together under the double duvet in her room. She wasn't quite so afraid of banging into his injured shoulder now. In fact, it was amazing how you could adapt sexual techniques to compensate for a broken collarbone, and though she was tired, she wasn't *that* tired. There was just one point where she wasn't sure if the groan above her was of pleasure or pain, so she quickly popped her head up over the duvet to check.

'Huh, what the hell are you stopping for?' came a frustrated cry.

'Okay, okay, just checking I haven't hurt you.'

'*That* was pleasure not pain,' he grinned, with such a yearning please-don't-stop-now look in his eyes.

'Sorry, sorry,' Emma muttered, and went back to finish what she had started.

After making love, very carefully, she lay beside him, aware of the amazing feelings growing within her that she hadn't felt in such a long time. She curled up against his good side, relishing the feel of his skin against hers; his warmth, his body so close, and they were soon fast asleep.

50

Boxing Day, and she wasn't alone this year. Emma woke up with a gorgeous, very much alive – though a little bashed-up – man in her bed. A man who had helped her bring The Chocolate Shop back to life, and was making a damned good effort at fixing her shattered heart.

'Morning, beautiful.' He looked across at her from the other pillow.

'Morning, bashed-up gorgeous.'

And despite his battered ribs and shoulder, she managed to snuggle a little closer to him.

Christmas Day had been just wonderful in a busy, beautiful way with her family and friends, and her parents were due later on, but for now today was their day. There was no need to rush, or to be anywhere in particular, and Emma was intent on savouring their time together.

Late morning, they drove down to the beach to get some fresh air and give Alfie a bit of exercise. Emma pulled up in the car park in the dunes, and slowly, due to Max's injuries, they walked down the track to the sands. He was struggling a bit, so said he'd sit on a rock for a while and watch as Emma took Alfie for a short stroll to the shoreline, where the waves frothed in. The sound of the sea, its rush and pull, was relaxing, rhythmic. Alfie was having a ball with a stick she was throwing into the waves for him, which he fetched back to her countless times, full of bouncy spaniel energy.

Emma looked out across the sea and thought of Luke, and how arbitrary life could be, how harsh; and yet it could also be beautiful. She turned to see Max, who waved at her from his rock seat. This patient, kind, sexy man who she had a feeling might be about to play a part in her future.

She headed back towards him, Alfie at her heels.

'Okay?'

'Absolutely,' he answered. 'Just been enjoying the view.' He smiled. 'Fancy seeing you here again,' he quipped. 'Haven't I met you here before?'

'Possibly.' She grinned. And that fateful day with the scarf, exactly one year ago, came to mind for them both.

Thank heavens it had been a wild, windy day this time last year, or they might never have stopped to say hello. Who knew where life would take you next?

Max stood up with a wince. 'Ribs.' He gestured.

They walked back to the car steadily, hand in hand, then stood at the top of the rise, more or less in the exact same place where they had kissed last Boxing Day. Emma leaned across, being extra careful not to bang into his damaged shoulder, and placed a gentle kiss on his lips. He pulled her closer with his good arm, and the kiss grew deeper, full of tenderness, passion, yearning and hope.

When they finally pulled away, Emma smiled.

There might just be some room in her tattered heart after all.

Acknowledgements

In the making of this book I had to research and of course taste a lot of chocolate! Thanks to the wonderful Louise Frederique, chocolatière-pâtissière at her fabulous chocolate shop and café, Cabosse, in Warkworth. Also to the lovely June Carruthers who not only welcomed me into her home, but also showed me how to make truffles and chocolates by hand, as well as craft the most amazing things – the filled chocolate hat-box idea is all hers.

Bev Stephenson, thanks for a great phone chat talking out the highs and lows of chocolate-making and answering my many questions.

Thanks as always to my family: Richard, Amie and Harry as well as their partners, Toby and Rowan. This book was written amidst wedding plans, hen dos and all sorts, so between all the festivities I had to hibernate at times. Much love and happiness to the newlyweds!

Mum and Dad for all their support over the years, a big thank you, and also to the wider family. My sister Debbie, very best of luck, you are so near to achieving your dream – keep going. Cheers to all my friends – the fun, laughter and Prosecco moments have fuelled me along.

Ongoing thanks also to my friends at the Romantic Novelists' Association for their support and advice over the years.

To my wonderful home county of Northumberland for inspiring me yet again. Warkton-by-the-Sea is a mix of Warkworth village and Craster with a few tweaks of my own thrown in to make the perfect setting for this book, capturing the beauty of the Northumberland coast.

Thanks to my wonderful editor Charlotte Brabbin for her help in shaping this book to something more special and to all the team at HarperImpulse and HarperCollins. My lovely agent Hannah Ferguson and to all at Hardman & Swainson, thank you.

Last, but never least, my readers and the book blogging community, huge thanks for reading my books, posting reviews and for taking the time to contact me with your lovely comments. I would never have enjoyed the success I have without your support. It took me over ten years to first get published, and I am still pinching myself whenever I see my books online or in a shop.

Well then, I hope you have been curled up with something chocolatey whilst reading this book. And if you are yet to dive in, relax and enjoy – happy reading!

All best wishes,
Caroline x

The chocolate magic doesn't end here!

*Turn the page to discover
Emma's favourite festive recipes*

Festive Chocolate-Orange Truffles

(Makes approx. 36)

<u>Ingredients:</u>
250g of good quality (at least 70%) dark chocolate
125ml fresh orange juice (or home squeezed even better)
150g caster sugar
Zest of 1 orange
150g dark chocolate to decorate

<u>Method:</u>
1. Finely chop the dark chocolate and place in a bowl.
2. In a saucepan, bring the orange juice, sugar and zest to a simmer, and stir until the sugar is dissolved.
3. Pour onto the chocolate and stir until melted.
4. Chill until firm in a fridge (around 4 hours).
5. Scoop out a teaspoon of mixture and roll into a ball between the palms of your hands, place on a tray lined with greaseproof paper; repeat.
6. Melt the decorating chocolate gently in a bowl over hot water. Using a fork or cocktail sticks, dip the

truffle balls into the melted chocolate to coat. It needs to be smooth but not too runny to coat the truffle centres properly; just allow to cool a little more if it seems to slide off.

7. Transfer to greaseproof paper to set.

Emma's Boozy Truffles

(Makes approx. 36)

Ingredients:
125ml double cream
250g of good quality (at least 70%) dark chocolate, finely chopped
2 tablespoons whisky, Irish Cream, brandy or rum
To decorate, 150g dark, milk or white chocolate

Method:
1. Bring the cream just to the boil in a small pan. Remove from heat and stir in the chocolate until melted and the mix is thick and smooth.
2. Stir in your chosen liqueur. Pour into a bowl and chill until firm (in a fridge for around 4 hours).
3. Scoop out a teaspoon of mixture and roll into a ball between your palms, and place on to a tray lined with greaseproof paper; repeat.
4. Melt the decorating chocolate gently in a bowl over hot water. (White chocolate goes well with the Baileys Irish Cream, dark with whisky, but choose your own preferences.) Using a fork or cocktail sticks, dip the truffle balls into the melted chocolate

to coat. If it slides off the truffle centre just allow to
cool and thicken a little more first.
5. Transfer to greaseproof paper to set.

As these boozy truffles are made with cream, store in a
fridge and eat within one week.

*I hope you enjoy these truffles! Ideal to share with friends
and family, or as gifts.*
Merry Christmas!

Discover more baking adventures in Caroline Roberts'
heart-warming 'Cosy Teashop' series

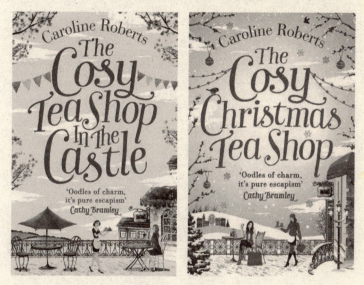

'Oodles of charm, it's pure escapism'
Cathy Bramley

Both available to buy now!

And don't miss this beautiful page-turner from
Caroline Roberts

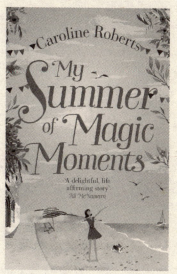

'A delightful, life-affirming story'
Ali McNamara
Also available to buy now